A
Jewish Girl
in Paris

A German and US national, Melanie Levensohn studied literature and international relations in France and Chile. She earned her master's degree from Sciences Po in Paris. Later she became a spokesperson for the World Health Organization in Geneva, Switzerland, reporting from countries in crisis around the world. From 2006 to 2013 Melanie worked as a communications expert at the World Bank in Washington, D.C., managing corporate external relations for the Caribbean region. When she got married, she joined her husband in the Napa Valley, California, where they created an award-winning estate wine over ten years. In 2021, they moved back to Geneva.

Praise for *A Jewish Girl in Paris*

'In this vivid, affecting novel of intertwined destinies and the enduring power of love against the bleakest odds, Melanie Levensohn weaves a tale saturated with historical accuracy, yet surprisingly intimate. *A Jewish Girl in Paris* delivers romance and intrigue to spare, but the novel's real power lies in its portrayal of how deeply and sometimes mysteriously we can find ourselves connected to the past, and to each other' – Paula McLain, *New York Times* bestselling author of *The Paris Wife* and *When the Stars Go Dark*

'A beautiful and hard-hitting story' – Kate Furnivall, author of *Sunday Times* bestselling novel *The Betrayal*

'Inspired in part by her own fascinating family story, author Melanie Levensohn has crafted an emotional tale of two women . . . desperately searching for answers . . . *A Jewish Girl in Paris* is a deeply researched, emotional rollercoaster ride of love, fate and second chances' – Kristin Harmel, *New York Times* bestselling author of *The Book of Lost Names*

'An elegantly drawn tale . . . [with] a pacy narrative, relatable heroines and an eye for historical detail about life in occupied France' – *The Jewish Chronicle*, London

'*A Jewish Girl in Paris* crafts a warm and intimate tale full of historical accuracy. Furnished with passion and intrigue, this historical romance is a powerful novel about forbidden love' – Hive

'I was hooked from the very beginning because it is like a family history detective story . . . *A Jewish Girl in Paris* pays great attention to the accuracy of historic details and the depiction of the 1940s feels extremely authentic. The novel would appeal to anyone who is interested in the Second World War, and the plight of Jews who lived in France at this time' – *Who Do You Think You Are?* magazine

MELANIE LEVENSOHN

A Jewish Girl in Paris

Adapted from a translation
by Jamie Lee Searle

PAN BOOKS

First published 2022 by Macmillan

This paperback edition first published 2023 by Pan Books
an imprint of Pan Macmillan
The Smithson, 6 Briset Street, London EC1M 5NR
EU representative: Macmillan Publishers Ireland Ltd, 1st Floor,
The Liffey Trust Centre, 117–126 Sheriff Street Upper,
Dublin 1, D01 YC43
Associated companies throughout the world
www.panmacmillan.com

ISBN 978-1-5290-7576-2

3 5 7 9 8 6 4 2

A CIP catalogue record for this book is available from the British Library.

Typeset by Palimpsest Book Production Ltd, Falkirk, Stirlingshire
Printed and bound by CPI Group (UK) Ltd, Croydon, CR0 4YY

Visit *www.panmacmillan.com* to read more about all our books
and to buy them. You will also find features, author interviews and
news of any author events, and you can sign up for e-newsletters
so that you're always first to hear about our new releases.

For Pascal – my love, my life and my home.

*And in memory of Melanie Levensohn,
my namesake, who was deported to
Auschwitz in 1943, at age nineteen.*

Author's Note

Love and extraordinary coincidences not only changed the lives of the protagonists in this novel, but also my own.

When I married my husband Pascal in 2013 and took his last name 'Levensohn', I became the namesake of his first cousin once removed. Melanie Levensohn lived in France as a student in the early 1940s and was deported to Auschwitz in December 1943. No one knows for sure if she survived the concentration camp or not.

My husband found out about this part of his family history in 2005, at the bat-mitzvah celebration of his oldest daughter Amanda, when his cousin Jacobina Löwensohn revealed the existence of her half-sister Melanie. Her father had told Jacobina about his first marriage and daughter Melanie only on his deathbed in 1984 and made her promise to search for Melanie. Jacobina spent over ten years trying to find the half-sister she never knew. She contacted Holocaust organizations, experts and researchers around the world. All traces ended at Auschwitz.

Jacobina kept the letters and historical documents she compiled during those years in a binder labelled *Melanie Levensohn* and gave it to Pascal. Finding the binder in his office, I immediately immersed myself in her tragic fate.

The remarkable coincidence that, exactly seventy years after Melanie became a victim of the atrocities of Nazi Germany, another Melanie Levensohn – from Germany – joined the family, and the fact that I studied in France, just like my namesake, caused an emotional upheaval in our family.

Melanie's fate and our identical name captivated me completely. I felt an urgent need to create a special memorial for her. That's what inspired me to write this novel. Yet, it isn't a biography. Although the book is based on real facts and lives, my characters are all fictitious.

When I was pregnant, my personal coincidences and emotional connection with Melanie reached a peak with the due date of our daughter, Aurelia, being on Melanie Levensohn's birthday.

Whether it is fate or destiny that inspired me to write this novel, I hope that the readers of *A Jewish Girl in Paris* will share some of the intense emotions I experienced when crafting the twists and turns of this story.

Melanie Levensohn

Melanie Levensohn, probably 1942
Photo credit: private family archive

1

Jacobina

Montréal, 1982

'Blood . . .' wheezed the old man, breathing heavily through his mouth. 'Blood . . .'

His voice cut the silence like scissors through paper. The first word in two days. Jacobina, who was curled up on the narrow armchair next to the bed, sat up with a start and looked at her father. His eyes were half open, tiny flakes of skin peeled from his lips.

She had been sitting there in the overheated room for hours, watching him sleep. He lay motionless, the corners of his mouth turned downwards, the slight rise and fall of his chest the only sign that he was alive. A few times, Jacobina herself had dozed off.

Every fifteen minutes, the silence was broken by the muffled chiming of a church tower, a regular reminder that some more time had passed. Jacobina would then glance at her watch, to see which quarter of an hour had just been rung out. Was it half past three already? Or only half past two?

A nurse came in four times a day. In the mornings, the

calm blonde woman appeared to take his temperature and blood pressure. She handled the instruments deftly and confidently, placing the cuff gently around the patient's arm. Jacobina heard the rubber ball being pumped up, and a short while later, the hiss of the air being released. The sister made a note and disappeared.

In the afternoons, the red-haired nurse with the squeaky rubber soles came. 'You should go home now,' she said each time, in her broad Québec French, as she changed the drip or emptied the urine bag. 'He's exhausted.' But Jacobina only ever shook her head, the nurse's coarse accent ringing in her ears.

She did go eventually and spent the nights in a small hotel. The accommodation wasn't particularly well maintained, but it was cheap, and right next to the hospital. Brown curtains, a saggy mattress. Jacobina heard the church tower every quarter of an hour there, too. Her head felt dazed. Images of her father whirled before her eyes, the lovable man from her childhood contorting into the emaciated one in the hospital bed. So far, sleep had been impossible.

'Blood,' repeated the old man, a little louder now, with a slight whistle on the 'd'. Then his voice failed him. He pressed his lips together and tried to swallow, something that was clearly a great struggle for him.

Jacobina stared at him. Would he be pleased to see her?

'Father?' she asked softly. 'Can you hear me?' A hollow sensation spread through her stomach – a mixture of relief and uncertainty. Should she sit on his bed, take his hand and try to hasten his awakening? No, she thought. It was better to give him a little time. He would need a moment to get his bearings.

With halting movements her father pulled his arm out from beneath the blanket and wiped it across his eyes. He didn't seem to notice Jacobina. He fixed his gaze on the wall opposite his bed and studied the picture, which was hung a bit low, and had probably been put there to give the hospital room a little colour. Even in the half-darkness, the Eiffel Tower was clearly discernible. A cheap reproduction of some Impressionist painting, Jacobina had presumed when she first entered the room. But not one of those typical Monet motifs that were always printed on wall calendars. She had never seen this picture before. In her long hours of waiting, she had studied it in detail. Not because she particularly liked it – she didn't – but because it was the only thing in this room that didn't make her think of death. Death and the expectations she would need to fulfil when it came – *if* it came.

Would she be able to cry? Would she be able to feel the grief you're expected to experience when your father dies? That permanent ache that claims a space in your heart when you finally comprehend that the loss is final? Or maybe she wouldn't feel much at all. She had already lost her father more than two decades ago. Back when she was barely twenty-one, when she left Canada for New York. He had never forgiven her.

Her mother's death had been hard. After her talkativeness, it had taken Jacobina years to finally accept her definitive silence. She missed everything about her. The short, almost daily phone calls that always came at the wrong moment. Insignificant chatter.

'Jackie, sweetheart, how're you?'

'Mom, I'm at the office. I can't speak for long.'

'I only wanted to see if everything's okay.'

Mother's unsolicited parcels, containing dark chocolate and bagels from the Saint Viateur bakery. Her letters, with the scrawling handwriting that Jacobina could recognize even from a distance. Winter was going on too long, her mother wrote, her health wasn't good. Jacobina had almost never answered them. Every year at Passover, her mother sent more *matzah* bread than Jacobina could ever have eaten. There were more kosher shops in New York than in Montréal, but her mother refused to listen. Back then, this attentiveness had irritated Jacobina. Now, years later, she still missed it. Longed for the many phone calls. If only she had been more caring, she often thought; it was the least she could have done. She had realized too late that her mother had been her only home. Sometimes, even the magic of nostalgia fails to cover the pain of regret. The 'what ifs', the 'what could have beens'. All the words left unspoken.

But her father. That was a different matter.

Jacobina's gaze returned to his hospital bed. She wouldn't miss his coldness. And yet she had still come to say goodbye to him. He had been through enough in his life; he shouldn't have to die alone as well. The only child's sense of duty.

Suddenly he coughed so violently that his head thrust forward in short jabs. Then he tried to speak again. 'Blood,' he spluttered, pausing briefly and then straining to continue: '. . . is thicker . . . than water.' Groaning, he closed his eyes, as though uttering this sentence had taken the very last of his strength.

Jacobina flinched slightly. How often he had preached

that in the past. It had always been his explanation for everything: for war and peace, for loyalty and betrayal.

Was he speaking to her? Or was he delirious? 'A neighbour found him lying unconscious on the floor,' the doctor had said when he'd called and asked her to come as soon as possible. That raised a lot of questions. 'We need to watch him,' the doctor had added.

Since arriving in Montréal, Jacobina hadn't been able to extract much more information. The doctor was busy and had only taken a few minutes for her. It was good she was there, he had said. A brief squeeze of the hand. Her father was weak, it was just a matter of time.

Father had never spoken to her about the state of his health. Sure, his mobility had rapidly decreased in recent years, and he had suffered from insomnia for a long while. Normal signs of ageing. 'Getting old is awful,' he used to say. 'All your bones hurt.' But where more precise details were concerned, whether he was contending with high blood pressure or diabetes, whether cancer was rampaging through his body or why he swallowed those little white pills, on this Jacobina had no idea. And it hadn't interested her, either.

A cleaning lady had mopped the floor over an hour ago, but the acrid smell of disinfectant still hung in the air. Jacobina stared out of the window that couldn't be opened. Life outside seemed far away. Unreal.

Even though it was only four o'clock in the afternoon, the street lamps were already on. It was snowing again. The snowflakes made their way towards the ground in slanted lines. These damn Canadian winters. How Jacobina had always hated them. The unending darkness, the red, frozen hands. She had hated almost everything here. Why had her father never understood that?

But was it really the darkness of winter that smothered her, or was another darkness forming, something only she could see?

Jacobina stretched her fingers towards the switch to turn on the bedside lamp. But then she changed her mind and withdrew her hand. Her father loved dusk, she remembered with a sudden tinge of indulgence. The twilight, ushering in the evening and allowing everything to gradually calm down. At home he had often sat there in the half-darkness, content to let the peace swell over him as if it was a salve for some invisible pain.

She left on only the small wall lamp which the nurse had turned on that morning. Her father's right cheek took on a dull gleam in its light.

He cleared his throat and opened his eyes again. Jacobina picked up a glass from the table, filled it with water from the jug the blonde nurse had brought that morning, and held it out towards him silently. But he didn't react and again just stared, spellbound, at the silhouette of the Eiffel Tower. His face looked even more sunken now than in daylight. There were broad, black lines like fissures across his forehead, and the little hair he still had clung in strands to his head. My God, how old he looked! He *was* old. Eighty-two. Even though she had been staring at him for two days almost without pause, the gaunt figure with the grey cheeks seemed like a stranger to Jacobina. Nothing reminded her of the cheerful, slightly chubby Papa Lica who had held her tightly in his arms when she was a little girl and spun her through the air. Who had pressed his rough cheek against hers and whispered amusing things in her ear. His voice, his laugh, the scent of his aftershave – everything about him had exuded warmth and security. She was eight back then, and the world big and bright.

'Wild Lica', that's what everyone had called him. Yes, he had been wild and loud. He had demanded a lot of life, respected nothing and nobody. Apart from the holy rules of the Sabbath, when Mother devoutly lit the candles, while he poured himself a generous measure of wine and blessed his family. Jacobina liked thinking back to the Friday evenings of her childhood. The house tidied, money and other worries postponed, the aroma of *challah* – the braided white bread that her mother took from the oven and sprinkled with salt – drifting through the rooms. When her mother was still alive and Lica not yet the crotchety cynic he became after her death. How long ago it all was!

Jacobina had tried in vain to suppress the other, less pleasant memories. The many arguments. The accusations. The silence. The silence would stay with her. His death wouldn't change a thing.

'Paris,' said Lica, breaking the stillness as unexpectedly as he had a few minutes ago. His voice sounded raw but steady. He no longer had to clear his throat. 'Judith . . . my child.' He took a deep breath and fell silent again.

Who was he talking about? Was he hallucinating? 'Father, it's me. Jacobina.'

'Paris,' he repeated softly, almost melancholically, without averting his gaze from the Eiffel Tower.

'Father. How are you feeling?'

He didn't answer.

Jacobina leaned forwards and touched his hand. Why wouldn't he look at her? Surely he must see her there!

A wistful expression lay on his face. He slowly turned his head to Jacobina and looked at her. Through her. He was somewhere else entirely. 'How could I do that to you, Judith?' He wiped the back of his hand over his mouth.

Jacobina stared at him. 'What are you talking about?'

At that moment, the door opened. The ceiling light went on and filled the room with a bright neon glare. Jacobina blinked.

The red-haired nurse with the squeaky rubber shoes walked in and positioned herself at the foot of the bed. '*Bonsoir*, Monsieur Grunberg. Did you have a good rest?' she asked in a loud voice, giving him a wink. Then she turned to Jacobina. 'How long has your father been awake?'

Before Jacobina could answer, he spoke instead. 'Water.'

'Five minutes, perhaps,' murmured Jacobina, standing up. She was just about to raise the glass to his lips, but Lica grasped it with his trembling hand and pushed her arm aside.

Typical, thought Jacobina.

He clasped the glass in both hands and took small, greedy sips.

The nurse walked around the bed, busied herself with the drip settings and pulled the curtains shut. Lica sank back down onto the pillow, loosening his grip. The half-full glass rolled across the blanket and fell to the floor, where it shattered.

'Do be careful, madame,' said the sister, as she grasped Lica's slack arm and felt his pulse.

Jacobina leaned over to gather up the shards. Her legs ached from sitting still for so long.

8

'Forty-four,' said the redhead. 'Quite low.' She laid Lica's arm back down on the blanket and made a note of the number. 'Make sure he eats something,' she ordered. She pressed the call button for the nurses' office and said, 'Dinner for room fifty-four.' Then she left.

Jacobina pulled a few paper towels from the box on Lica's bedside table, using them to clean up the last splinters from the floor. *Don't make trouble*, she had promised herself, *no waspish remarks*. It wasn't worth arguing with the nurse.

A young orderly came in and brought a tray with food and a pot of tea, placing it on Lica's nightstand. He smiled shyly and wished Jacobina a good night. She glanced at the plate: a piece of bread topped with a square slice of cheese, and alongside it, a few dried-out pickles.

'Garbage,' snorted Lica, once they were alone again.

Jacobina smiled. That was the Lica from her youth – his loudness a deliberate slap in the face, the 'I-don't-care-what-people-think', full-of-life man she had adored then. Maybe he was still there, behind the gruff exterior that had grown up over his years of loneliness. Perhaps the doctor's fears had been too hasty. She brushed a strand of hair from her face, turned off the ceiling light and pulled her chair closer to the bed. 'Would you like some tea?'

'I need to talk to you,' he said, without looking at her. His voice was quiet, but sounded very resolute now.

Jacobina looked at him in surprise. So he *did* know she was here.

'Life is complicated, Jackie,' he murmured, using the shortened version of her name he had called her when she was little. 'We only have each other now.'

If he'd had this insight ten years ago, she thought, as the bell tolls rang their incessant reminder, it would have spared her a lot of pain. Anger was building up inside her. Now that he was suffering, he wanted to make everything good again with a few empty words. *We only have each other now.* The words echoed inside her head, just like those godforsaken bells. It wasn't that simple. And it was too late. Far too late. Jacobina tried to breathe calmly and let her gaze wander around the room. *No bitter comments*, she reminded herself. She couldn't lose her composure.

'How should I put it?' Lica continued, brushing his hand across the water stain on the blanket. 'I . . . I did some things wrong.'

Some things! Jacobina felt like laughing bitterly. *Everything!* But she pulled herself together and stayed silent. She remembered the terrible fight they'd had on her last visit. When she'd sworn to never come back again. They had always argued, every time they saw each other. Intensely and angrily. As soon as the coffee and superficial chatter of the first hour was behind them, he launched into recriminations. About her life; the fact that she hadn't completed her studies; that she contented herself with a job as a 'key basher', as he put it, even though she had brains. That she had exchanged Canada for the USA.

'You should have stayed with Louis,' he would then say, over dinner at the kitchen table. Heated-up stew from a can. The only thing he liked to eat. 'He would have made something of himself. Then you'd have a good life now.'

Louis, her teenage boyfriend. She had never really loved him and didn't feel the absence of either him or the boring life she might have led with him. 'I *do* have a good life.'

'In that shoebox of yours?' One of his spiteful references to her tiny apartment in Manhattan. 'Don't make me laugh.'

It was pointless. What did he know about her? About her giddiness upon first coming to New York? The lightness that warmed her soul when she looked down from her apartment on the fifty-seventh floor? Her happiness and feeling of fulfilment because she was living her dream? Nothing. How could he? Her mother's death had driven a wedge between them. And now, the distance felt too great to overcome with bedside small talk.

Jacobina couldn't remember the last time they'd had a peaceful conversation with one another. In the first few years after her mother had died, that's when it had begun. He had spoken with her less frequently, rarely answered the phone, and retreated more and more. He no longer greeted the neighbours and sat in front of the television all day. Jacobina had never stopped worrying about her father, and went to visit him for long weekends. Agonizing days. He kept the window shutters closed all day. Barely touched his food. Always wore the same grey cord trousers. No longer shaved. The house smelled musty; the garden lay neglected. And when he did speak, it was only to reproach her. His tone of voice! This darkness! Jacobina began to hate her childhood home, a place that had once held so much love.

But this heavy sense of duty gnawed away at her, something she couldn't free herself from. And so she forced herself every six months to take the Greyhound bus and travel the hundreds of miles over the border to Montréal, in order to see her isolated father. She stayed one night, two at most. She couldn't cope with any longer.

'He shouldn't be living alone,' Iris, a neighbour and her late mother's best friend, had said. She used to check in on Lica from time to time, and then telephone Jacobina with a report. 'Try to understand him.' But Jacobina hadn't been able to, or wanted to.

On her last visit, he had been especially harsh. So harsh that, afterwards, she hadn't contacted him for a year. 'Someday you'll get your comeuppance!' he had yelled after her as she stormed angrily out of his house. 'You'll find yourself sitting there sick and old in your apartment, and you'll regret your life.' That was a few years ago now. Since then, she hadn't visited him, she had just called now and then. Why was he so angry? And why with her? she often asked herself. She hadn't done anything to him. Sure, she had disappointed him. She hadn't brought a husband home or put grandchildren in his arms. But she was still his daughter, even if she had followed her own star.

And now he wanted to beg forgiveness for all the bitterness and rejection he'd hurled at her? An apology for everything? Would she be able to accept that? Jacobina crossed her legs, bobbing her right foot up and down.

Lica was staring at the Eiffel Tower again. 'Paris . . .' he said, 'that's where everything began.'

Jacobina looked up in surprise. She wanted to ask him what this was about. But then she decided to stay silent and wait. Perhaps he would tell her soon enough.

'Claire,' he whispered, 'beautiful Claire . . . I loved her.' He sighed and wiped his eyes. 'Then the baby. It came too soon. Such a tiny thing.'

'Who are you talking about?'

'The midwife thought she wouldn't make it.' He paused

and swallowed. 'But Judith . . . she survived.' Then he turned to Jacobina and looked her straight in the eyes for the first time. 'Your half-sister.'

Jacobina looked at him in confusion. He was hallucinating. The medication. She would have to call the doctor.

Lica frowned. His gaze wandered back to the Eiffel Tower. 'Claire and I got divorced,' he said hoarsely. 'I went back to Romania but I promised to write to Judith. To visit her. Send money. After that, I met your mother.'

Jacobina's breath caught in her throat. She felt a sudden flush of heat rushing through her body. Was it the warmth of the room that was suffocating her, or his words?

'Then came Hitler, and later the war.' Lica paused. 'The foolish Romanians joined the Nazis. They wanted to wipe us out. First, they came for Uncle Philip, then me.' For a while, he didn't say a word. As though he needed to summon all his strength to utter the last part of his confession. 'I . . . I lost contact with Judith. I never saw her again.'

Jacobina's stomach cramped, pain squeezed her head. Her gaze followed the black marks that the rollers of the beds had left on the floor. In the corner next to the window, small balls of dust had formed. Hadn't the floor just been cleaned? Or had she simply imagined all of that, just like her belief that she knew her father? The church bell sounded again, hammering in Jacobina's ears. This man lay there before her, old and deathly pale, and was spending his last hours thinking about a woman he had once loved and a child he had kept a secret for decades. Life was one big lie.

'Why have you never told me before?' whispered

Jacobina. Small pearls of sweat had formed on her brow. She wiped them away with her index finger.

'The curls,' he murmured, 'golden-brown curls . . . just like Claire.'

A *half-sister*. All these years, he had lived *with* this truth and she *without* it. He had shirked his responsibility as a father twice. Neither made the effort to find his first daughter, nor told the other one about the existence of her half-sister. What a coward! Jacobina wanted to tell him that. Now. To scream it out. Scream out the pain. But she only swallowed. Her tongue felt heavy and dry.

As a child, whenever she had asked Lica about his life, he had only ever motioned dismissively with his hand and said, 'Oh, the war . . . it destroyed us.'

She had known about his deportation to a labour camp. That he'd been lucky he hadn't landed in one of the extermination camps in Poland, but had stayed in Romania. Yet, he never wanted to talk about it, and always brought the conversation to an abrupt end. She didn't know any of the details. All she knew was that, at some point, he had escaped and then immediately left the country and Europe with her mother and her. Jacobina had never pushed him into talking; she hadn't liked the dark expressions that settled on her parents' faces when they uttered the word *war*, strained and full of horror. The war had no meaning for her. Europe was far away. It was long ago. She had been a toddler back then, and couldn't remember any of it. In her passport, Bucharest was noted as her place of birth. That was all she needed to know.

'Soon it'll be over for me,' mumbled Lica. 'I don't want to carry on.'

'You should have told me.' Jacobina struggled to speak.

Lica turned towards her. His eyes were watery and had lost all colour. 'I couldn't,' he said. 'I was too ashamed, Jackie.'

Jacobina bit down on her lip. His honesty came as a surprise.

'The last time I saw Judith was in Paris,' he continued. 'She was thirteen. Or perhaps fourteen already . . . Long before the occupation. It was springtime.' He looked back at the picture.

Jacobina followed his gaze and noticed for the first time that the picture was at a slight angle. Lica made a few awkward movements with his arms, trying to pull the pillow out from under his back. He soon gave up and looked towards her. She stood up, grateful for the silent request for help, grateful to be able to do something that didn't require speaking. She helped him to sit upright, pulled out the pillow, smoothed it out and placed it behind his head. As she touched his bony shoulders, she shuddered. There was hardly anything left of him.

'We were sitting on the Champ de Mars. Admiring the Eiffel Tower. It was just like in this picture. Almost pink in the morning light. And proud, like its people.'

Jacobina raised her eyebrows.

The door opened and the young orderly who had brought the evening meal came in to remove the tray. The cheese-topped bread lay pale and untouched on the plate.

'Do you perhaps have some soup or hot broth?' asked Jacobina. Not out of concern that her father hadn't eaten anything, just to say something. Something that wasn't connected to what she had just heard. Something normal, something everyday.

The orderly, his face filled with freckles, looked at her through small, round glasses and shook his head. *François* was written on the name badge attached to his apron. 'I'm sorry, madame. For special requests you have to fill out a slip and give it to the sister in the mornings.'

Jacobina nodded absent-mindedly as she watched the orderly pick up the tray.

'Would you like a sleeping pill, monsieur?' he asked.

'He only just woke up,' hissed Jacobina before Lica could answer. 'You can't offer him a sleeping pill now!'

'Oh, I'm so sorry,' said the man hastily, taking a step backwards. The cutlery slipped around on the tray, clinking. 'The pill is for another patient.' He smiled meekly. 'Long day today.'

Jacobina didn't answer.

'Life is long,' Lica exclaimed. 'Far too long.' He gave the orderly a grim stare.

'Would you mind leaving us now?' Jacobina asked. Then she added 'François', in the hope that he would react more quickly if he heard his name.

The orderly hurried out and shut the door with a loud bang.

'Turn off the light, Jackie,' said Lica. 'It's blinding me.'

Jacobina flicked off the switch for the wall lamp and sat back down in the armchair. Then she loosened the laces on her boots and stretched her legs out in front of her. In the darkness, she could only just make out the contours of the bed. She saw the black outline of Lica's head. He breathed raspingly.

Jacobina listened to the steps out in the corridor. Muffled voices. A brief laugh.

'Jackie . . .' Lica began after a while, 'your mother was my life. After her death, everything fell apart.'

Jacobina's eyes filled with tears. What about *her*? Didn't she have a place in his heart?

'The memories caught up with me,' he continued, 'everything came flooding back. Judith's curls. Paris. And then Romania. The camp. We lived like rats, sitting in our own shit eating trash. We had lice. Typhoid. Without your mother by my side, I started to relive it all, day and night. It was unbearable. But I couldn't talk about it.'

Jacobina bunched her hands into fists. 'You had me.'

And then Lica said something completely unexpected. 'I was scared of you, Jackie. You were so independent. You never listened to me, you weren't afraid of anything. Just like I used to be.' He paused briefly. Jacobina heard him rub his hand over his face. 'Your heart was in the right place. I felt so small and old when you were around. What would have been the point of moaning to you about the war?'

Jacobina's throat felt sewn shut. Her father's words slid into the dark air of the hospital room like a confession and a balm. But what had gone unsaid between them for so many years felt too wide a chasm to cross.

'I hated myself,' he went on. 'And I took it out on you.' His voice sounded strained. 'I didn't know how to do anything else. I never was able to talk about emotions. Especially not with you.' He fidgeted around in the bed, groaning. The mattress springs squeaked; a pillow fell to the floor. 'Your mother organized our escape from Romania. She was so strong.' Jacobina thought she could hear a gentle smile in his voice. 'She made my life full again.'

Jacobina reached for the pillow in the darkness and laid it back on the bed.

'I was able to carry on for years. Acting as if everything was good.' His breath made a wheezing sound. 'But nothing was good. I was pretending to all of us.'

Jacobina's eyes drowned in tears. She desperately wanted to feel like she had when she was a little girl, when Lica and her mother had each other, when everything was right. But she swallowed the urge to weep, afraid that her father would hear her. Even now her pride prevailed, almost impenetrable over the years of hardness between them.

'There's no forgetting,' he muttered, 'and no escape.' He coughed loudly, choked and spluttered for breath. Then he gradually settled. 'Forgive me, Jackie,' Lica whispered into the darkness.

Forgive me. The words she had waited so long to hear.

Jacobina could no longer hold it all back. The stored-up emotions were too strong, and they burst out of her. Her upper body shook. She leaned forwards, pressed her hand over her mouth and tried in vain to push down the tears.

'Come here, my child.'

She gave a hiccoughing sob, reached for Lica's hand and grasped it. His fingers were stiff and cold. Like the fingers of a corpse. For a long while, she wept without restraint, her face buried in the blanket. All those lost years, all those bad feelings.

'You have to find Judith,' said Lica. His voice sounded pleading. 'Promise me!'

Jacobina calmed down at once. Had she heard right? She released his hand and raised her head.

'I want you to . . .' his voice failed him. He swallowed

and inhaled loudly through his mouth. 'I want you to finish what I've spent my entire life putting off.'

Jacobina, dumbfounded, could only stare into the dark.

'Please,' wheezed Lica. His hand searched the blanket for hers.

She stretched out her arm again. Lica gripped her fingers and squeezed them. The most intimate sign of affection from a broken man. A man who had pushed down his pain for years, suffocating it with fear, shame and self-control. Whose wounds were too deep to ever heal.

At first, Jacobina felt sorry for him, but then an over-whelming tenderness enveloped her – an unfamiliar feeling. She had a sudden urge to stroke his head. But how to cross over to this new place of affection after living so long in a world of anger? Her reticence won, as it so often did.

'Promise me,' he repeated in a scratchy voice, struggling for air.

'I promise,' Jacobina uttered. What else could she have said?

Acknowledging her pledge, he squeezed her hand once more.

Outside in the corridor, the industrious hustle and bustle fell silent. Jacobina listened to the stillness.

'Can you open the curtain?' asked Lica. 'I'd like to see the snow.'

She got up and pulled the curtains aside. Clouds of snowflakes were swirling in the amber glow of the street lamps, reminding her that she didn't have the proper attire for this weather. Her departure had been so rushed that she'd left her gloves at home and grabbed the wrong jacket. She was glad the hotel was just a few steps away.

'I'm going to sleep a bit more now,' her father said. His voice sounded light and confident, almost like he used to speak to her when she was a child. Had his confession so thoroughly unburdened him?

'You should leave now, Jackie.'

'I'll stay here till you're asleep.'

'No, it's fine. I'll watch the snow. It's calming.'

With great effort, he turned onto his side to have a better view out of the window. Jacobina looked hesitantly at the stiff silhouette of his back. But he didn't say another word.

If he really wanted to be alone, she should go, she thought, and reached for her jacket. 'Okay then. I'll leave and come back tomorrow morning.' Jacobina wound her scarf around her neck. 'And I'll bring you something nice for breakfast.' Her stomach growled at the thought. She hadn't realized how hungry she was.

'Goodnight, Father,' she murmured, stepping out of the room and closing the door with a gentle touch. On her way to the lift, she stopped at the nurses' station where a young woman with long braided hair was sitting and distributing tablets into little plastic cups. Next to her stood a large mug of coffee and an open packet of biscuits. Jacobina knocked briefly on the half-open door and greeted the sister. 'I'm leaving now. You know where you can reach me?'

'Which patient?' asked the nurse in a slightly confused tone, taking a sip of coffee. *I love Canada* was written in large lettering on her mug. Jacobina hadn't seen the woman before.

'Room fifty-four. Lica Grunberg.'

Without setting down the cup, the sister looked at the pinboard above the desk. 'You're staying in the Auberge. That's fine,' she murmured, taking another sip.

'Please call me immediately if anything happens,' said Jacobina, reassured to see that the sisters were well organized. 'I'll come back right away.'

The sister nodded and turned back towards the pills.

Perhaps she shouldn't go yet after all, Jacobina suddenly thought to herself, turning around and retracing her steps. The red-haired nurse stepped out of one of the rooms. As she saw Jacobina, she mumbled something and pointed a finger at her watch.

Jacobina didn't care that visiting time was over and walked past the nurse with her chin held high. In front of Lica's door, she paused and looked around her. She felt as though she were being watched. But the nurse had already disappeared.

Jacobina placed a hand on the door handle and hesitated. He wanted to sleep, he had said. Tomorrow there would be plenty of time to talk. She would bring him fresh croissants and coffee, the coffee with lots of milk, just how he used to love drinking it. For the first time since Mother's death, they would have breakfast together without arguing because he'd no longer fear her, and she'd no longer hold him in contempt. She would ask him about Judith, and perhaps tell him a little about herself too. They would rest together in the peaceful light of his confession. No more darkness. A new beginning, so close to the end. She let go of the door handle, turned and went over to the lift.

*

Jacobina flipped on the light. The hotel room was freezing; someone must have turned off the heating. In the depths of winter! The cold made the room even more unwelcoming than it already was. The maid had spread the brown blanket across the bed and placed two pillows with embroidered flowers at the head. Jacobina's pyjamas lay on the nightstand, carefully folded. A water pipe was hissing somewhere.

Jacobina went over to the radiator and turned the dial up high. Then she opened the curtain, switched the light off again and sat down by the window. She kept her coat on. Her stomach was growling again, but she didn't feel like going back out and eating alone somewhere. Not today.

She rummaged around in her handbag and pulled out an already-opened bar of chocolate. She hurriedly ripped off the paper and bit into it. The sugary mass made her stomach cramp, but the hunger abated a little.

She watched the dancing snowflakes, just like Lica was doing now too. If he hadn't already fallen asleep. The street was empty. Now and again, a gust of wind whirled the snow in wide arcs through the air. At that moment, Jacobina felt very close to her father.

On the other side of the corridor, she heard a door opening. She settled deeper into the armchair and listened to the hum of the heating.

Lica had never made snowmen with her, she remembered. He hadn't read fairy tales to her, nor had he helped her with her homework. Her mother had been responsible for these things. Lica's influence and involvement had been on another level. He had read to her from the Torah, told her about the exodus of the Jews from Israel, and taken her to the synagogue with him. He hadn't followed the rules of his religion with absolute precision: he loved seafood and, for him, kosher wine was nothing but sweetened dishwater. But he had placed great value on conveying to his daughter a sense of belonging, far away from their Romanian homeland, a feeling that had nothing to do with the geographical distribution of the world. As a child, that hadn't meant anything to her. It was all she knew. What child ever realizes the value of such deep gifts? Father had given her their history, their story, their identity. And though she never pressed into her religious education with more curiosity, years later in New York, when she was on her own, it became the cornerstone of her life. Something that provided her with strength and community and connected her to the happy family she'd once had.

The room was gradually warming up. Jacobina peeled off her jacket and closed her eyes, the heat lulling her into a state of comfort. Images filled her mind. She saw her pale father before her again. Unshaven, sitting on a kitchen chair, his hands covering his eyes. A mug of cold tea in front of him. 'Pull down the shutters,' she heard him order her sullenly, 'the light makes me sick.'

Years before. In spring. He was laughing and lifting her onto the small seat that he had screwed onto the middle bar of his bicycle. She, proudly enthroned between him and the handlebar, her breakfast roll still in one hand. 'Be careful!' her mother called after them as he rode with her to school.

A knock on the door woke her up with a start. Where was she? How long had she been here? Another knock, louder this time. 'Madame? Are you there?'

Jacobina stood up, stumbled over her handbag in the darkness and reached out her hand towards the wall. Where, for God's sake, was the light switch? 'I'm coming,' she called.

But the woman outside hadn't heard her and knocked a third time. 'It's urgent.' Her voice sounded agitated. 'Are you there?'

Jacobina opened the door.

The receptionist stood before her, completely out of breath. Presumably she had run up the stairs. 'Please come down,' she spluttered. 'There's a phone call for you.'

There wasn't a telephone in her room that the call could have been forwarded to. *The hospital*, flashed through Jacobina's mind. Leaving the door ajar, she hurried down the stairs, over the faded carpet with the Oriental pattern. He wanted to speak to her. He wasn't able to sleep.

But as she grabbed the receiver and held it to her ear, she knew that they were about to tell her something completely different. She could feel her heart pumping in her temples. A searing pain ripped through her chest. It had come. The moment she had been preparing for for days, years – it had come. The moment she had believed wouldn't change anything.

'Madame Grunberg?'

'Yes,' Jacobina whispered into the mouthpiece, holding the phone with both hands.

'This is Sister Louise.' She paused. 'I'm sorry to tell you your father has passed.'

Jacobina said nothing.

'It must have happened shortly after you left,' the sister explained. 'I'm so sorry.'

We only have each other now, Jacobina could hear Lica saying.

She stared out the window into the dark, a storm of emotions swirling inside her. The church bells rang out, their noise mingling with the quiet snowfall. How many different stages of the day they had marked. A lifetime of bitterness broken by a revelation, a confession that ushered in that long-forgotten feeling of grace and affection. She'd had it for only the briefest of moments, and now he was gone.

Was it enough to wash away the pain that was so ingrained in her? Years of resentment, neglect, the secret of her half-sister. Could she forgive him for unloading the weight of his guilt onto her shoulders so he could die in peace? Could she forgive him for leaving her with such an enormous promise she didn't know she had the strength to fulfil? Could she forgive him for leaving *her*?

Only later, back in her room, was Jacobina able to cry for her father.

2

Judith

Paris, September 1940

I was standing on one of the middle rungs of the rickety library ladder when I discovered the note. It was written on unusually thick, sky-blue paper, folded multiple times and hidden within Marcel Proust's *In the Shadow of Young Girls in Flower*. Éditions Gallimard, 1919. 492 pages. The volume was well thumbed, the spine crooked; students constantly requested it. As part of my literature studies at the Sorbonne, I myself had battled my way through Proust's labyrinth-like sentences and eccentric metaphors last year. Words like heavy perfume that I could breathe and almost feel but not hold on to.

My first thought upon seeing the slip of paper was that someone had forgotten their notes. I laid on the shelf the other books which I'd been clasping under my arm and pulled out the blue note. *To Judith* was written at the top, in small, neat letters. I stared at my name, puzzled.

A light gust of wind swept through the room, slamming shut the half-opened window. Startled, I almost lost my balance. I gripped on to the ladder, climbed down hastily and unfolded the paper.

The flowing movements of your delicate, pale hands that never rest, was written in black ink. *Your slender figure, your effortless gait. Whenever you enter the room, you light it up. C.*

My heart beat faster. I'd never received a message like this before. Who on earth was C? I turned the note over; perhaps the sender's name was written on the back. But there was nothing.

Was this the beginning of something exciting and different, luring me into some sort of *liaison dangereuse*, so masterfully described by Choderlos de Laclos? Or could the letter be a door to the romantic journey I'd always yearned for but had only lived in the books by Flaubert, George Sand and Balzac?

Romance – what an audacious, forbidden idea. I folded the paper with a resolute gesture. Life was too unsettled and risky right now. These days, sometimes even the sunrise felt like a threat to me.

Around three months before, the French had capitulated and the Germans now occupied half of our country. A 'ceasefire' was how Marshal Pétain had named this humiliation of the French people. Since then, the Germans had settled into our luxury hotels, and our city had become alien to me. Signs shot up everywhere around us, bearing long German words which no French person could pronounce. A swastika banner fluttered on the Eiffel Tower, and we had to put our clocks forward an hour in line with Berlin time.

Someone called my name and I looked up. Monsieur

Hubert, the head librarian, came towards me, running his hand through his sparse hair. 'Have you already entered the new acquisitions into the card index?' he asked. Behind his small, round glasses, his eyes twinkled good-naturedly.

At least one person was acting as though life were continuing as normal. It had, admittedly, normalized a little since the 14th of June, the day when the first German soldiers had reached the Porte de la Villette, at the outskirts of Paris. Many of the Parisians who, in fear of the German threat, had fled to the south in early summer had now returned. Cinemas had resumed their programming and cafes and restaurants reopened. The city seemed to be pulsing with life again. But things were not as they appeared. For weeks now, a ghostly uncertainty had been hanging over Paris.

'Yes, of course, monsieur. I did it yesterday,' I answered absent-mindedly, still staring at the paper in my hand.

'Then you can go home now, mademoiselle,' he said. 'It's getting late.' He sighed softly as his gaze swept over the bookshelves. 'There's a long queue at Georges again. Supplies are getting scarce. Get yourself there quickly before everything's gone.'

Dear, sweet Monsieur Hubert. I smiled at him. He was always thinking of others. He reminded me of my father, or rather the image of my father that I had composed from the few cherished puzzle pieces of my memory. Thanking him, I said goodbye, tucked the mysterious blue note into my skirt pocket and left the library.

As I stepped out onto the Place de la Sorbonne, I was greeted by a warm September day. The boughs of the grand beech trees that lined the square swayed lethargically in the afternoon breeze. The cafe on the corner advertised, as always, its *plat du jour*, and the latest editions of *Paris Soir*, *Le Temps* and *Le Figaro* were set out at the newspaper kiosk. But something was different. Even though the academic year had only just begun, the university square, usually so lively, was oppressively quiet. A few students stood together in small groups, their heads close together. They didn't dare watch the passing German soldiers who were strolling across the square in their crisply ironed uniforms, laughing and smoking. They were handsome, the German occupiers. Tall, with close-cropped hair and powerful legs. They radiated an ominous strength and a repulsive virility. I looked away quickly. I didn't want to risk making eye contact.

Blinking in the sunlight, I made my way towards Georges, the grocer in the Rue des Écoles. Even from a distance, I could see the seemingly endless queue which had formed in front of his store. There had to be well over fifty people in it! Yesterday it had only been half that. By the time I'd finally reach the front, there would be nothing left.

But I joined it regardless; there was no point trying my luck somewhere else. The hunt for food defined our day-to-day life in Germanized Paris. We had to queue up for every loaf of bread. Yesterday I got hold of three eggs and some real coffee. Milk had long since run out. Georges had said there might be some new deliveries next week.

A woman wearing a black dress was standing in front of me. A boy in shorts clung to her, and in her arms she held a screaming baby, swaddled in a shawl. She was talking to him in soothing tones. But the baby didn't stop crying. The knees of the boy next to her were grazed, and in his hand he held an empty shopping basket. When I looked at him, he buried his face in the folds of his mother's skirt.

I turned around and saw that at least another twenty people had joined the queue behind me. And there, between an elderly lady with a hat and a young man in a dark suit, I spotted my friend Alice. As children, Alice and I had been inseparable. Now that we were both busy with our university studies, we saw each other less often. Since the arrival of the Germans, we hadn't got together at all.

I waved at her with a bright smile, excited about the surprise encounter. She briefly looked at me, and the faint trace of a smile appeared on her lips. Then she turned her head away and stared ahead.

'Alice,' I called.

'Shhh,' someone hissed behind me. The sound brought me back to our new reality. Life under occupation was different. Strange. No one was laughing any more. No one asked any questions. People were silent, but with tense expressions on their faces, a mixture of nervousness and fear.

I tucked my chin and looked at the ground. Shortly afterwards two German soldiers walked by.

A few minutes later, I pulled the sky-blue note back out and read it. Such beautiful, expressive handwriting. Even though the message was very short, it seemed well thought out. As if C had watched me from his seat for a long time until he had found the right words for me and every one of my movements.

I studied my hands. Were they really delicate? And was my gait as effortless as he thought? I looked down at my feet, which were encased in worn-out leather shoes. I resolved that on my next shift I would find the lending card for the Proust volume and look up who had borrowed the book today. I was curious.

After waiting for almost an hour, I finally stepped into the shop. I was lucky. Against all my expectations, not everything had been sold, and I got a few slices of cheese and four apples. Mother would be happy that I wasn't coming home empty-handed.

When I stepped out of the shop, I looked for Alice again. But she had left.

3

Béatrice

Washington, D.C., 2006

Click clack, click clack. She could recognize his hasty, almost stumbling gait even from afar; would have been able to identify it amongst thousands of footsteps. The quick, furious thud of his leather soles against the linoleum floor. Béatrice's throat tightened. She knew what was coming. In a moment Michael would storm into her office, without knocking, his eyes squinting, his chubby face slightly flushed. He'd slam her press release onto the table and present his edited version. Her headline would have been chopped up, the introduction buried somewhere on the second page, and entire paragraphs would have vanished. Just to flex his muscle, he'd demand she fix it all on some impossible deadline.

She hadn't yet finished her thought by the time he flung the door open. His frame rose before her as far as his small, stocky figure would allow. In his hand was a sheet of paper. Her text.

Béatrice's eyelids twitched, her breathing quickened.

The stench of cold tobacco streamed towards her. How

on earth he found the time to escape his tight meeting schedule every other hour for a smoke outside, she had no idea. Sometimes she saw him standing in front of the main entrance when she came back from her lunch break. She always hurried past, greeting him with just a nod.

Michael looked at her, his expression dark, and dropped the piece of paper on her desk. 'Do I really have to explain how to write a press release?' he snorted, as expected.

'What's wrong with it?' she asked, trying her best to keep her voice firm and professional. 'I wrote it just as we discussed. And the project manager liked it.'

Béatrice did not play the games everyone else did when it came to confrontations with Michael – pleasing him to get ahead. But their resulting tensions were exhausting. Toxic. His mere presence in her life triggered a nauseating combination of dread and repugnance she'd never experienced before. Nonetheless, she was committed to standing her ground. She had promised herself when she first started working for Michael that she wouldn't let his arrogance or barrages of criticism cripple her. Her candour only fed the feud.

'The project manager is an economist,' he grunted. 'Those guys know nothing about media relations.'

Béatrice reached for the paper and looked at her words. Unrecognizable. Red handwritten comments everywhere – above, between the lines and in the margins. Sentences were crossed out or underlined, with arrows running through the page to indicate a new, Michael-approved flow.

'I can't read what you wrote at the top here,' she said as she raised her head, trying to look at Michael's face. But he had moved so close that she could only see his tie, the ugly brown one.

'You can't read it? That's all you have to say?' he barked. 'Start working on those stilted quotes from the president. He'd never talk like that.'

'He used those exact words in a speech last week,' Béatrice objected.

'This is poorly written. End of story,' Michael insisted.

Her heart dropped at the blunt insult. *Keep your cool*, Béatrice cautioned herself. Whatever she'd say, he'd find a condescending way to brush it off.

The number of times she had talked this through with her therapist! 'Don't let yourself get worked up by that man. Count to ten or use one of the breathing exercises we've been practising. That'll help,' he had suggested.

It didn't. As soon as her Texan boss entered the room, all her good intentions and strategies evaporated into thin air, and she barely managed to transform her aversion into diplomatic distance. But there was also a deep-rooted insecurity that overwhelmed her at times, especially during his assaults of criticism. A feeling she had been trying to overcome in vain.

Life hadn't been easy. When Béatrice was growing up in Paris, her mother had struggled to make ends meet as a nurse – there was never enough. That didn't deter her mother from doing all she could, working day and night and through most weekends. And without the aid of a husband. Béatrice's father had abandoned the family for another woman when Béatrice was still very young. She used to think, if only she'd been a better child, smarter, stronger, perhaps he wouldn't have left. If only she'd been enough. But she wasn't, and she would never understand why.

This mindset weighed heavily on her and became part of her personality. She trusted few but still craved affection, a dynamic she found difficult to reconcile. Yet, Béatrice refused to give in to this deep-seated angst. Instead, she let it fuel a burning desire to escape her condition, ultimately forging her path to success. She earned scholarships, graduated with distinction, and soon afterwards, landed a position in the French Ministry of the Interior. But it wasn't until she was forty-one, when the World Bank hired her and she moved to the political epicentre of the world, that she'd felt she'd really made it.

No, she wouldn't let Michael take away that hard-earned feeling of achievement and pride, regardless of what he said. And yet – Béatrice couldn't shake off the distress his very appearance provoked in her.

Michael moved his hand up to his tie and straightened it. 'I want numbers, Béatrice. Success numbers. How many times do I have to tell you?' At the word *success*, his eyes flashed angrily. 'I read in the report that, thanks to the bank project, thirty thousand more kids are now going to school in Haiti. That's a major accomplishment. And you don't even mention it in here. It should be in the headline.'

'But Michael,' Béatrice countered, 'our experts didn't agree over that number and requested additional information from the Ministry of Education. Until then—'

'Our economists never agree on anything,' he interrupted her. 'And we can't wait that long. The release has to go out tomorrow morning.' Two deep creases formed between his eyebrows. 'The bank pumped a hundred million dollars into the education sector in Haiti. People need to know how well their tax dollars were spent.' His voice grew louder.

He reached into his trouser pocket and pulled out a roll of breath mints. 'Main title: thirty thousand more children in Haiti now going to school. Subheading: World Bank commits one hundred million dollars to support quality education.' He tore the wrapper off the roll and a few mints dropped into his hand. 'You get a good photo with a few schoolkids for the website and done. PR 101. That's what you're paid for.' Michael popped the mints into his mouth and ground them noisily between his teeth.

Béatrice sighed but knew better than to continue to challenge him. Things would only escalate further, and she just wanted him gone.

'Before I forget,' he added, still chewing. 'I don't see our keywords anywhere: sustainability. Growth. Prosperity. Equal opportunity. That's what we're working for. That's what the bank stands for. So get those in there too.'

The chemistry between them had never been right. Sure, he had employed her, so she must have convinced him in her interviews. But before even a year had passed, she had made the fatal mistake of correcting him in front of the entire team. Hearing him claim that the bank's loan commitments to Africa were higher than those to Latin America, she simply hadn't been able to keep quiet, and had quoted from the annual report, which stated the exact opposite. Since then, barely a day had passed when he didn't try to get her back for showing him up.

But there had to be more to the story, she often speculated. Maybe he just didn't like her personality. Or, could it be that he actually feared her? Maybe he was afraid that she, an attractive mid-career professional with glowing references, would take over his job one day?

Michael stepped away from the desk and went over to the door. Then he turned around again. 'I want the new version on my desk in three hours, tops. Make an effort, Béa, otherwise we'll have to have a serious talk about your future here.' He slammed the door behind him with a bang.

Béatrice was sure that the rest of the team along the corridor had heard the entire exchange. Later, her colleagues wouldn't say a single word about it. Brief glances, a knowing silence. But nothing more than that. They rarely dared criticize Michael behind his back, because somehow, he always found out. And then exacted his revenge. Not immediately. Not upfront. But in his own way. He would pass over certain employees when the time came for salary increases or promotions, withhold his approval on holiday requests, refuse to authorize business class for long-duty travel overseas. Béatrice had always believed that his secretary betrayed them to Michael. Veronica, the blonde Brazilian with ample curves and shiny pink fingernails. She loved to gossip. But Béatrice was no longer sure, because the previous week Michael had also given Veronica a lecture in front of the entire team.

There was a knock, and Veronica popped her head through the door. 'The team meeting's about to start.'

Béatrice nodded silently, looked at the scribbles in front of her and closed her eyes with a sigh. Three hours. She would never get through it.

*

Conference room I-8001 had an unreal feeling to it. White neon light illuminated the windowless room night and day. The tables were arranged in a horseshoe formation, and there was a small microphone located at every seat. On the wall hung an oversized screen, for the regional offices to be connected via video conference. One of the many feel-good World Bank marketing posters was pinned up next to the door, depicting a group of slender children of Asian heritage. They were laughing, revealing gaps in their teeth. Beneath them, in large letters, it read: Our dream is a world free of poverty. The World Bank Group.

The bank was one of the largest funders of global development projects. Every year, it provided up to thirty billion dollars in loans, credits and grants to developing countries. It supported poor countries in their reconstruction efforts after earthquakes and civil wars; battled corruption and climate change. It helped develop education and health systems, built bridges and dams, and boosted economic growth in countries that people had stopped believing in.

Back home in Paris, Béatrice enjoyed telling her friends how special it was to work for 'the bank', as staffers affectionately called it. She was proud of being part of an organization that had dedicated itself to the noble goal of battling poverty. Working here was more than just a job for Béatrice; it was her chance to make the world a little bit better.

But as is often the case, reality and high ideals don't always match. Just one year after joining this gigantic organization Béatrice grew increasingly disillusioned. Everything took for ever, progress moved like an iceberg. She felt compelled to make a difference, but her job kept her out of touch with the lives of those she wanted to help the most. When she realized that the humanitarian goals of the bank and the reality of her job there had little in common, she decided to get involved in a different way: by supporting local charities with generous donations. Washington, D.C. had one of the highest poverty rates in the country. It was visible everywhere, even right in front of the fancy World Bank building where homeless people gathered every day, asking employees for some spare change.

Writing cheques to relief organizations in the District wasn't much more hands-on either. However, knowing that some of the homeless Béatrice saw on her way to work every day would receive a hot meal made her feel a bit better.

Despite her professional disappointment, quitting her job was not an option. She couldn't – and wouldn't – return to France having blown her big chance. The bank's moral shortcomings were undeniable. But Béatrice had grown accustomed to the perks. Regardless of her shattered altruistic dreams, she enjoyed a tax-free salary, excellent benefits, global travel and, best of all, she was able to help her mother. Besides, she was hopeful that once she could crawl out from under Michael's shadow, things would change in her favour.

*

On most other days, conference room I-8001 hosted important political discussions. Debt crises in Argentina, water privatization in Bolivia, change of government in Brazil, trade between Latin America and China. This was where things were speculated, evaluated and decided.

Today the media relations team of the Latin America department was meeting here to go through the most important events of the week: the vice president's visits and speeches, announcements of new development projects, and the publication of international economic prognoses.

Before the meeting even started, Béatrice was already shivering. The AC was on high, in March! So American. She buttoned up her blazer and pulled a woollen scarf from her handbag. There were many things she loved about the United States. Americans were open-minded and easy-going. They smiled a lot and felt comfortable calling strangers by their first name. But she would never adjust to the arctic interior of their conference rooms, supermarkets and homes.

Michael sat at the head of the table, his reading glasses pushed down low on his nose, an open folder and a can of Coke Zero in front of him. His arms were spread out across the table like wings. 'Let's begin with the VP's visit to Peru next week,' he declared. 'First meeting with the new finance minister. On the agenda: priorities for the next three years. Ricardo will join and organize the press conference.'

Handsome Ricardo. Always well dressed, always well prepared. The women at the office had all lusted after him. Until the day they found out there was a man in his life.

Hearing his name, Ricardo sat up straight and brushed his hand through his black, smoothly gelled hair. 'Everything under control, boss,' he said loudly and clearly, with visible anticipation for what he was about to announce. 'Here's the plan. Lunch with minister and closest advisers immediately after arrival. Followed by a press conference in the ministry. In the afternoon, visit to a village which is part of the bank's rural electrification project. Photo with VP, minister and mayor. Interview on location with *El Comercio*. Journey back and dinner at the Belmond Miraflores Hotel.'

Michael grunted a contented, 'Excellent, Ric,' and made a note in his folder. 'Marcela? How far are we with the launch event for the *Doing Business* report?'

The meeting droned on. Béatrice listened but her mind drifted to her looming deadline. She would have to call Martine, the task team leader for the Haiti project, and discuss the number of school pupils. During their last conversation, Martine had emphasized the fact that there wasn't yet any reliable data on the number of students going to school, and she referred to a footnote in some document. But Michael wanted a number that 'screamed success'. He wanted the thirty thousand in the headline. What was she supposed to do now?

She would have to come up with another number. A number that was validated by the experts *and* of interest to the press. She needed to go through the statistics in the appendix once more. Look for figures on new school books and teachers employed. There had to be something else. Béatrice's thoughts began to somersault.

Next, she needed to alert Alexander, the director of the Haiti programme, that a redacted press release would be coming his way. He had to sign it off before it was sent to the journalists. Alexander was based in Port-au-Prince, an hour ahead. The team there started work at seven in the morning and left the office around four in the after-noon. Everybody was expected to get home before dark. Security level I. This was a new regulation, introduced after Alexander's driver had been shot at two weeks previously.

Béatrice looked at her watch. She would call as soon as this meeting was over.

Then she still needed to contact the translation department and request that the press release be translated into French as a rush job, first thing tomorrow. That would mean being invoiced an extra fee. And that meant another unpleasant discussion with Michael about rising costs and budget cuts.

Her stomach was knotting up. Would she get it all done? In France, she had managed career challenges effortlessly, embracing fierce academic competition, and later the rigid demands of her superiors at the ministry. But here, under Michael, she felt stuck.

Béatrice took a deep breath, a single thought calming her: once she got her promotion she would leave Michael's team for good. Her job interview two weeks ago in the president's office had gone smoothly. Cecil, the hiring director, had wanted to bring her on to his communications team for a while now. He clearly knew she was a perfect match – she had seen it in his smile. She would get the offer any day.

'Béa! Hel-lo. Anybody home?'

Michael's growl tore her from her thoughts. Everyone was looking at her. Béatrice felt her face getting hot; it probably looked bright red.

'How about an update on Haiti?' Michael took a sip from his Coke and looked at her expectantly.

She had to stay factual. Like Ricardo. Trying her best to seem relaxed, she leaned back and tugged at her scarf. 'I'm going to speak to Martine after this and then rework the press release,' she said.

'For heaven's sake. You know very well that Martine has been on a plane since this morning,' he snarled, slamming the can down so abruptly that some of the brown liquid sloshed out of the opening.

Béatrice cringed. No, she hadn't known that. Why not? Had Martine mentioned it? But if she had, she wouldn't have forgotten. Or would she? Her hands cramped up.

Veronica stood up and wiped the spilled liquid away with a serviette and a smile. Her fingernails gleamed.

'*Obrigado*,' said Michael, thanking her in his American chewing gum accent. It was the only word he knew in Portuguese, even though he claimed to be fluent. Veronica smiled and went back to her seat. Placating an angry cowboy was something she was now well versed in.

'You'll have to sort it out with Alexander himself.' Michael turned his voice back to Béatrice, his tone icy again. 'Right away!'

Béatrice grabbed her things and left the conference room. As soon as she closed the door, she let out a sigh of relief. Over. At least for a short while. But before she went back to work, she needed some fresh air to clear her head. Should she take that risk? Béatrice hesitated. Of course she should, she quickly reassured herself. If Michael could have his smoke breaks, she could take a few minutes outside as well. She would be back in her office before the team meeting was over and get everything done. No one would be any the wiser.

4

Judith

Paris, September 1940

I pulled the cart behind me through the reading room, piling it high with the books that were lying around, returning them to where they belonged.

A library can't function without perfect order. Many students didn't care about that and treated carelessly the books we entrusted them with. They bent the corners of the pages, wrote silly things inside them and, for the most part, simply left them on the desks after they were done, or put them back on the wrong shelf. The never-ending reordering, tidying and shelving wasn't always fun, but I didn't mind. I loved the industrious silence of the reading room, the students' whispers, the rustling of paper. It filled me with awe and faith. The solid shelves, as tall as a building, offered me shelter and comfort. Now more than ever, in these troubled times, being here made me feel safe.

The books kept my dreams. They were my light, my freedom, a sacred space no one could ever take away from me. Father had taken the innocence of my childhood, Mother the lightness of my spirit. And now, the Germans had taken my country. But the books I read would always remain mine and warm my heart when life was cold.

Every day, they inspired and enlightened hundreds of students; tormented and informed them. I sometimes wondered how many questions these books had answered over the course of time, and how many new questions they had prompted?

But I wanted more than the silence of a library and longed, one day, to have my own bookstore so I could share my infinite joy for literature with others. I aspired to become like the famous Adrienne Monnier, France's first female bookseller. How I admired her! When Paris was still free, I visited her shop in the Rue de l'Odéon as often as I could and leafed through new releases. My store would be like hers – a well of beautiful words, unforgettable characters and stories. I would introduce new writers and host readings. People from all over Paris would come to my shop. Though that dream felt almost too distant now.

I turned the book cart around to roll it back into the stacks. On the top of the pile, on the English–French dictionary, I spotted a blue piece of paper. *For Judith.* The same handwriting, the same thick paper.

My heart jumped. I looked around. The room was almost empty, there was nobody nearby. How had the note found its way onto the cart? I unfolded the piece of paper with trembling hands and read: *You look so serious and sad. I can only imagine how beautiful you must be when you smile. C.*

Embarrassed, I lowered my gaze, my brown curls falling across my face and hiding my burning cheeks. Out of the corner of my eye, I stole a glance at Monsieur Hubert. He stood at his desk, speaking quietly with two female students. A tall young man whom I had seen here on numerous occasions was limping slowly past them towards the exit. Further behind, a woman pulled one of the thirty-five volumes of Diderot's Encyclopedia off the shelf. I instinctively hoped she would put the tome back in the right place; I would check later to make sure she had.

I tucked the note into my skirt pocket and got back to work. Immediately after finding the first message, I had closely studied the lending card of the Proust volume, but hadn't found a single name on it that started with a C.

Slowly pushing the cart down the narrow aisle into the stacks, I caught myself smiling, flattered by the words on the blue note. At this moment, did I look how he had imagined? Quickly feeling ashamed of my self-involved thoughts, I pulled myself together and became serious again. I worked in silence all afternoon, accompanied by the sound of the rustling blue note in my pocket. It gave me confidence and pride as I walked through the aisles.

*

After work, I set off to Georges, walking along the queue of silent, sad faces and positioning myself at the end of it.

Perhaps the queue was shorter in the mornings. Tomorrow, when I didn't have to work, I would try to come early.

For a short while now we'd had to use food coupons, torn from a perforated book. After waiting for an hour and a quarter I procured, for me and my mother, half a kilo of pasta, 200 grams of real sugar, a bag of saccharine and 350 grams of chicory coffee. That would have to be enough for a while.

On my way back to the 4th arrondissement, I walked past a fur shop. Mother used to help out there on the weekends to earn a little extra money. In the display window hung a large, yellow sign with the inscription *Jewish Business*. My insides cramped. I thought of the terrible reports from the German Reich, where the Nazis were setting synagogues ablaze and destroying Jewish shops. Where Jews were being disenfranchised, dispossessed and persecuted. Good God, was it starting here too?

Our day-to-day life had already changed so much; I felt more and more isolated. Just as my relationship with Alice had faded, I rarely saw my other girlfriends any more either, and when I did it was brief and restrained. We never mentioned a word about our foreign occupiers. No one complained about the Germans or criticized them in any way. We were all afraid of saying something unguarded and being overheard. It was the same in the library. Before, I had often chatted with the other employees, sharing coffee breaks. But lately everyone just got on with their work in silence. We greeted one another briefly, and said goodbye, but nothing more. Even the relationships with our neighbours had changed. For as long as I could remember, Madame Berthollet from the fifth floor had dropped by every week, to bring me a piece of cake or to ask Mother whether she needed anything from the market. Now she scurried past our door without knocking.

Ever since the swastika flags had unfurled over our city, the French had become distrustful. We moved cautiously through our days and thought long and hard about who to trust.

When I finally opened the door to our small apartment in the Rue du Temple, I saw my mother's brown briefcase lying on the floor. Folders, pens and papers had slipped out and were lying scattered, as if they had fallen from a schoolchild's overturned satchel. Normally she arrived home several hours after me. Something bad must have happened. I felt a sudden rush of anxiety.

'You're back already?' I called out.

Mother didn't answer.

She was a teacher at a small primary school in the 3rd arrondissement. It lacked pretty much everything: space to play, textbooks and, above all, staff. My mother worked long hours, standing in for absent secretaries and teachers, preparing lessons, and even helping to keep the old building in reasonable condition.

Despite these challenges, she loved it. The school was her sanctuary, just as the library was mine. As soon as she stepped onto the premises in the morning, she became immersed in the children and their problems, forgetting her own worries. But I became an afterthought too, even after she'd come home for the day. It was better that way. Better for her.

Everything had changed for us when Father divorced my mother years ago and left. Once my mother had reverted to her maiden name, Goldemberg, she became a different person. The carefree woman who used to laugh with abandon and bake sweet cakes for my dessert vanished, and her beautiful thick hair turned white. One day, without a flicker of emotion, she cut off the ice-grey braids with large scissors. For a long time afterwards, I couldn't banish from my mind the image of the two plaits lying before me on the floor. On that day she discarded her femininity once and for all. Since then, she kept her hair short, only ever wore trousers, and never looked another man in the eyes again.

The failed marriage aged her prematurely, turning her into a haggard figure with hollow cheeks and thin lips. She had never forgiven Father. I had, albeit not immediately, and with a heavy heart.

Once, when he came to visit me, he had explained that he'd never been happy in Paris. He had really tried, he said, without looking at me as he spoke, but he'd always been a stranger here. Someone who was merely tolerated. Mother hadn't wanted to move to Romania with him. So, eventually, he had gone alone.

That was the last time I saw him. We were sitting stiffly next to one another on a bench, staring at the Eiffel Tower, like two people who barely knew one another. I understood what he meant. I was Judith Goldemberg now, and he had already become a stranger to me, too.

*

I went into the kitchen. Mother was sitting motionless on a stool, her hands clasped around a mug of steaming tea. 'We have to go to the police,' she said tonelessly. 'We have to register.' She sipped at her tea.

'Why?' I asked, proudly setting the pasta, sugar and coffee substitute down on the table. Mother paid no attention to my goods.

'Because we're Jews,' she replied and stood up to put

the cup in the sink. 'I went to the synagogue this afternoon; they were handing out flyers. All Jews have to register with the police by the twentieth of October.' She turned around to face me. Her eyes glistened slightly, as if she were about to cry. 'They hate us. The entire world has turned against us. I'm so scared.'

'And what if we don't go?' I asked, sitting down.

She raised an eyebrow. 'Don't be naive, Judith! Of course we have to go. And as quickly as possible – before Yom Kippur. God protect us.'

She went into her room. A short while later I heard her pull the curtains, then the sound of sobbing. I sighed. Had it come to this again? Was she going to crawl back into her bed and stay there for days?

My mother's depression came in powerful and regular waves. Often, she was fine for months. During those times she would wake up early, brew strong coffee and work as many hours at her school as she could. But when the dark side had her in its grip, Mother was at the mercy of her inner demons. She would darken our apartment and stop the large wall clock in the living room, because the ticking disturbed her. For long days, a sombre silence fell over our small life of two.

The cycle started when I was thirteen, after Father had returned to his Romanian home town, and it only grew worse when he got married again. Before he left, Father had confronted her with an impossible choice. Either move to Romania with him, become a foreigner and perhaps experience the same loneliness he had felt in Paris. Or stay in France and raise me by herself. The thought of moving was too much for her. But so was his absence. She remained trapped between sadnesses, and it left nothing of the mother I had known and adored, the mother I had grown up with. A gloomy stillness divided us during those interminable weeks she stayed in shadow. It was hard not to react to her bouts of emotional extremes. Hard not to want more from her.

Father's departure had taken away my youth all at once. His physical absence, and Mother's emotional one, was a grief I carried silently – unseen and unheard by anyone but myself. I wouldn't show my sadness like my mother did, because she and I had switched roles. *I* looked after *her* now, doing what I could to keep her alive when she fell into darkness. I cooked soup she didn't eat, skipped my classes through fear that she might hurt herself in my absence, and lied through my teeth so that she kept her job. I told the headmaster of her school tales of scarlet fever, whooping cough or smallpox, and reassured our neighbours that everything was okay. After two, sometimes even three weeks, Mother would leave her bed of her own accord, set the hands of the wall clock back into motion and return to work. We lived as though nothing had happened – that is, until she was overcome by the next wave.

Not again, not now, I thought when I heard her sobs. The term had only just begun. It was hard enough to deal with her when I only had to study and do my work at the library. But since the occupation, I spent hours every day standing in line for the scant supply of groceries. I didn't have time to take care of her now as well.

The sobbing gradually became quieter, then she was silent. I sighed in relief, leaned back and closed my eyes.

5

Béatrice

Washington, D.C., 2006

With a large paper cup of coffee in one hand and a piece
of cake in the other, Béatrice sat down on a bench in
Murrow Park, which, in spite of its name, was nothing
more than a traffic island on the corner of 19th and H
Streets with some greenery.

Murrow Park was neither beautiful nor well maintained
and was popular with the homeless. They often sat there
on stained blankets, with plastic bags alongside them into
which they had stuffed their few belongings.

From her bench, Béatrice had a good view of the main
entrance to the immense World Bank building whose
twelve floors towered up into the sky. Sipping her coffee,
she watched the people walk in and out. An Asian delegation in dark suits, a group of African diplomats in
colourful kaftans and two Indian women wearing traditional saris.

At the other corner of the park, an African-American
man in blue shorts stood playing the trumpet. Béatrice
knew him. She always dropped a dollar or two into his

open trumpet case in the morning before entering the bank.

The cake in her hand had got moist and sticky. In truth, she didn't really feel like eating anything, much less something that sweet. She shouldn't have bought it. Standing up, she threw it into the nearest bin.

'Hopefully no one saw that,' said a stern voice behind her. Béatrice whipped around and looked at a woman in jogging bottoms and a baggy orange sweatshirt with *Sunset Aid* written on it. The woman was a bit older than her, perhaps around fifty, and wore black glasses. Her short auburn hair gleamed in the sunlight like copper.

'Throwing away a nice big piece of cake like that in front of all the poor people around here, that's a bold move. They've been queueing up for an hour already,' commented the woman, gesturing towards 19th Street and lighting herself a cigarette. Béatrice turned around, spotting for the first time a large group of people gathered around a bus. Plates of soup were being handed out of its windows. Each time a plate appeared, more hands immediately shot upwards to receive it.

'Oh,' she said, flustered and embarrassed, 'I . . . I didn't even notice. I'm really sorry.'

'Do you work there?' The woman nodded towards the bank building, taking a drag of her cigarette and coming a few steps closer.

'Yes,' said Béatrice. In the presence of this person it felt like a confession.

'So you're one of those who rake in a huge salary and don't pay any taxes,' the woman declared.

Béatrice tried to ignore the dismissive comment. To

her, right now, the bank only represented a tight deadline. Stress. She had to get back to work. Make her phone calls.

By now the woman was standing next to her. 'You're quite a bunch! Sitting there in your chrome and glass tower spouting drivel all day long about battling poverty. But you do nothing about the drama going on right at your door.' She blew some smoke into the air.

Béatrice knew the woman was right. But in her expensive coat she felt increasingly uncomfortable in front of this stranger. 'I'm sorry,' she repeated, turning away and walking down the street.

The woman followed her, still talking. 'You saunter around the slums of Africa, posing in your Armani suits, but none of you actually want to get your hands dirty.'

Béatrice searched for some conciliatory words. 'I agree, it's not perfect, but we're doing what we can.'

'You guys are so out of touch,' the woman ranted.

Béatrice saw no point in arguing and explaining the functions and roles of the World Bank. Especially not to someone whose mind was already made up about it. Besides, she had no time for this right now. As she was about to cross the street, she felt a hand on her arm.

'Wait a second,' the woman pleaded. 'I'm sorry. I didn't mean it personally. I'm just completely wiped out. We started at four a.m. today.'

Béatrice freed herself from the woman's grip and stepped aside. 'No worries, I'm stressed, too.'

A bus and a few cars were approaching, so she had to wait before she could walk over to the bank.

'We could really use your help,' the woman continued.

Her voice now sounded softer, almost friendly. 'There are a lot of people in need here.'

Béatrice briefly glanced at the woman and noticed two tulip tattoos on her neck, just beneath the ear. 'Maybe another time,' she said, turning her head towards the street. 'I have to get back to the office now.'

'Just a minute,' the woman insisted, 'please!' She flicked the smouldering cigarette on the street. 'I'd like to show you what's going on here while you sit up there in front of your charts.'

Any other day Béatrice would have stayed and listened, even offered help, but her deadline loomed as tall and dark as the bank building in front of her.

'You know, anyone can fall on hard times,' said the woman, glancing over at the bus. 'And then things go downhill quickly.'

The words and the sad tone of her voice sent a shudder down Béatrice's spine. An image of her mother flashed through her mind, delicate and exhausted, warming up a meagre supper over the stove after a double shift at the hospital. The woman, sensing that her words had moved something in Béatrice, stepped towards her.

'I'm Lena,' she introduced herself, before pushing up the sleeves of her sweatshirt and stretching out her hand. Slightly hesitant, but at the same time somewhat curious, Béatrice shook it.

Lena told Béatrice about the organization she had founded, Sunset Aid. She emphasized that donations were their lifeblood and how the work that needed to be done only increased.

'Sunset Aid?' Béatrice exclaimed in surprise, as she

remembered the charity's colourful flyer in her mailbox one day and the cheques she sent them regularly to support this worthy cause. 'You take care of the elderly,' she said, 'I've been one of your donors for some time now. So nice to meet you in person.'

'Oh, thank you.' Lena smiled and lit another cigarette. 'Pleased to hear that.' She took a long, deep drag and let the smoke stream out of her nose. 'Yes, we predominantly work with seniors. And sometimes we help with the soup kitchens too. The buses here, they're converted school buses.'

Béatrice listened, trying to resist the urge to look at her watch. 'Impressive,' she said earnestly. 'You really do change people's lives.' Though part of her wanted to hear more of what Lena had to say, her thoughts were pulled back to her press release. To Michael storming into her office. 'Unfortunately, I have to go now.'

'Got it,' Lena replied and swiftly tucked her business card into Béatrice's coat pocket. 'Why don't you come and see me tomorrow after work? We urgently need more volunteers.' A sudden warmth appeared in her eyes. 'Maybe I can talk you into that?'

Béatrice sensed that this could be an opportunity to finally contribute something that really mattered. Writing cheques was not enough. She could do more. Much more.

'Sounds great,' she said with a keen nod.

'See you tomorrow, then.' Lena waved goodbye and strolled back to the bus. Soon she had disappeared into the throng of people crowing around it.

*

It was late. A twelve-hour day, almost every minute of it under Michael's merciless control. 'You don't have any kids you have to pick up from school,' Michael had remarked dryly when he caught her sneaking a furtive glance at the time. 'So you'll stay here until you've finished your work.'

He hadn't let Béatrice leave until the press release had reached a standard he considered acceptable, and until she had telephoned Alexander in Port-au-Prince, interrupting his business dinner. Just like Michael, Alexander, too, had emphasized that the thirty thousand needed to be in the headline as a wonderful opportunity to showcase the bank's excellent results in Haiti.

Béatrice walked along P Street in a daze. Dark clouds that resembled exotic mushrooms had piled up in the sky. Soon it would start to rain. The cherry trees had already put forth a few buds. White and tender, they stood out against the sombre sky.

Her new shoes were rubbing, the laptop in her shoulder bag seemed to be getting heavier and heavier, and she had accidentally left her umbrella at the office. Béatrice was never armed for the sudden downpours in Washington. She wasn't armed in general for life in the American capital. The tropical summers with hurricane-like thunderstorms that regularly triggered blackouts. The cold, snowy winters that paralysed the traffic for days. The ubiquitous, dark *Starbucks* cafes that served huge portions of coffee in paper cups. The rattling air conditioning units which were everywhere and always set to freezing cold. The exaggerated craze for exercise which hounded the population into the gyms at five o'clock in the morning.

Béatrice missed the centralized slowness of France. The long summer holidays that began on the same day for the entire country. The fashion-conscious Parisiennes in high heels who navigated their way through the city as if they were walking on stilts. The street cafes where people sat for hours at small, round tables, drinking bitter espresso and complaining about the unfriendly waiters. And sometimes she even missed her country's strike culture, the large demonstrations on the Parisian boulevards which brought traffic to a standstill and plunged the city into organized chaos.

She thought wistfully of her homeland. Even though she'd been living in Washington for almost two years now, Béatrice hadn't been able to make close friends here. Her extensive travel schedule, late nights at the office and sheer exhaustion from it all made anything that wasn't casual a luxury she could hardly afford. Sure, she had friendly colleagues whom she sometimes went to the cinema with, or out for dinner. But throughout her time here, no deep or intimate relationships had come into being. They talked about their jobs, criticized the management and debated which airline offered the best service. After an evening of expat small talk, it often took weeks to get together again, as someone was always travelling for the bank.

But still: she had wanted this job at any price. She had dreamed of it for years and fought for it. She was proud of being here. And she was proud of being here as a Frenchwoman as she quickly came to realize that the French language and culture were considered *très sophistiquées* in the United States. Her accent enchanted the Americans, her carefully chosen clothes garnered admiring glances. Complete strangers would stop her in the street: 'I love your shoes,' they'd say, or 'Where did you buy that gorgeous dress?'

Americans really seemed to believe that life in France was better, that everyone there was beautiful and slim, despite eating buttery croissants on repeat and ordering champagne with lunch. People in the US seemed to be convinced that no French person worked more than thirty-five hours a week, that French children in restaurants ate with knives and forks, and that Paris was the most romantic city in the world. Béatrice wanted to leave their beautiful images untainted.

The gathering clouds had grown pitch-black. There was no way she would make it to her apartment in R Street without getting drenched. She peered down the street, but at this time the Georgetown bus only went every quarter of an hour.

Her stomach growled and she realized how hungry she was. She hadn't eaten anything since lunch. Her favourite restaurant, the Trattoria del Sorriso, was nearby. The thought of a plate of spaghetti gave Béatrice a sudden burst of energy, and she quickened her steps to the next corner. From there she could already see the warmly lit windows of the restaurant. By the time the first drops of rain began to plop onto the asphalt, she was sitting at a small table draped in a red and white checked cloth. At the neighbouring table sat a couple, engaged in lively conversation.

Lucío, the owner, waved at her with a big smile from behind the counter. A few moments later, he came over with a carafe of red wine and poured her a glass. Exactly what she urgently needed. Béatrice started to unwind. Slowly, the grim memories of her workday faded away.

Lucío was Mexican, but always greeted her with a singing '*Buona sera, signorina*', trying to imitate the melodious voice of the Italians. After all, it was a trattoria and not a taquería, as he had once quipped.

'Hard day?' Lucío asked.

'Pretty much,' she sighed.

'Okay, *bella mia*, I'll tell the chef to make something special for you,' he said with a twinkle in his eyes and trotted back to the counter. By the time he returned with bread and olive oil, she had already emptied her glass.

Béatrice took out her Blackberry and saw with relief that no new messages had arrived from Michael since she left the office. She refilled her glass and leaned back in her chair. After a few more sips, she felt pleasantly buoyant. Soon a scrumptious plate of steaming pasta under a glowing green pesto sauce appeared. With gusto, Béatrice plunged her fork into the food. When the first bite touched her tongue, a deep sense of well-being flooded through her body. The pasta reminded her of a similar dish, one she used to eat in Paris at a charming little eatery in the Rue du Cherche-Midi. She could almost taste home in that spaghetti. The wine hit her with a rush of nostalgia and pleasure. And that was home, really: comforting, satisfying and beautiful.

Her telephone rang, the shrill tone startling her. She looked at the display, her nerves jangling, then relaxed again. Joaquín. She hadn't spoken to him today yet. Putting down her fork, she reached for the phone.

'Honey, finally!' he cooed, then launched right into talking about his work at the *Washington Post* – editorial meetings, a difficult interview and tomorrow's headlines. It was good to hear his voice. But she knew him all too well. This tone was usually a sign that he was about to deliver some less pleasant news. And then her general frustration settled back in.

The couple at the next table were holding hands while sharing a dessert. The man whispered something into the woman's ear that made her giggle. How happy they looked. How loving. Joaquín and she would never be like this couple again. Ever since his big promotion from business reporter to editor he was under an incredible pressure. Along with his new responsibilities, he was expected to take on key feature articles which demanded much time and care.

Béatrice longed for the early days of their relationship, when spontaneity and shared passion for their work drew them close together.

How quickly the simplicity of it all disappears. She missed being able to call Joaquín for a quick bite. Although it was spur of the moment, it would have been nice, even romantic, to share this meal together, watching all that rain coming down. But now, in Joaquín's life, there simply was no more room for anything that hadn't been planned at least a week in advance. Appointments. His office. An important article. Heavy traffic. And mostly Laura.

'How was your day?' he asked gently.

Béatrice skilfully wound some spaghetti around her fork, tiredly mumbled, 'You don't wanna know,' and pushed the pasta into her mouth.

'Let me guess. Michael?'

'Yup.' She wanted to spare him the details. Over the past few months, she had spent entire evenings explaining her problems with Michael to Joaquín. And the food tasted like heaven. All she wanted now was to eat and listen.

Joaquín didn't inquire any further, instead changing the subject. 'So, I'd like to speak with you about the weekend.'

He paused briefly and a slight feeling of uneasiness flared up inside Béatrice.

'Unfortunately, we're going to have to delay our trip. I need to finish the Ben Bernanke interview for the Monday edition. It'll be the lead story.'

Postpone again? Her pulse quickened. She chewed hastily, then put down the fork.

'I'm sorry, Béa,' he added quietly.

Outside, the rain was coming down heavily. From her seat, Béatrice could see the raindrops splashing on the green metal chairs in front of the restaurant. A few pedestrians ran across the street.

'And you can't do that beforehand?' she asked eventually.

'Well. There's also this birthday party on Saturday that Laura really wants to go to.'

So *that* was it. She should have known. Laura always mattered most. Béatrice loved that Joaquín cared so deeply for his daughter. His wife had passed away when Laura was just a toddler. He was all the girl had. His devotion spoke to Béatrice, an endearing quality that had drawn her to him right away. Her own father had never shown the slightest interest in her, and she had suffered deeply from his absence and lack of attention. *If only she'd been enough.* So it was refreshing, uplifting even, to see a father dote on his daughter.

And yet, at the same time, it was infuriating. It hurt her that Joaquín never thought twice about casting aside his plans with her if it interfered with Laura's in the slightest way. Sometimes Béatrice felt as if she had to compete for his affection, and that was wearing on her in more ways than one.

'I see,' she finally replied. She wanted to sound indifferent, but she was barely able to conceal her disappointment. Béatrice took a large gulp of wine and gestured to Lucío to bring another carafe. She shouldn't really drink any more, she immediately thought, but when she saw that Lucío was already opening a new bottle, she stopped worrying about it and ate another forkful of spaghetti.

'Don't get me wrong,' Joaquín tried to explain, 'I'd have loved to go to the country with you . . . But I've barely seen Laura all week.'

'I understand,' Béatrice muttered and washed down the pasta with another generous swig of wine.

'We could all go to the cinema together on Sunday,' he suggested.

The cinema. With his daughter. Béatrice stared down at her half-full plate in irritation. Their long-planned weekend in a romantic bed and breakfast in Virginia was being traded for a cinema visit with a teenager and a bag of popcorn. The thought of the getaway had been a light in the tunnel for her. A relaxing reward after such a taxing week. Dating a single dad was really hard sometimes. She poured herself a bit more wine. Perhaps that's why her mother had remained single. Because a child and a job didn't leave much room for a relationship.

'Well, and the Bernanke story will be major,' Joaquín

went on. 'His first month in office as the new chair of the Federal Reserve. Every sentence has to be perfect.'

There was always a reason. Béatrice's memory was filled with countless examples of Joaquín's plan changes, excuses and apologies. And yes, of course she had empathy for him and his responsibilities. It wasn't easy. But her empathy had its limits.

And on those occasions, like now, when it was late and the wine had loosened her tongue, she found herself struggling to hold back her frustration and anger. Béatrice exhaled loudly. She felt ready to pour her chagrin over Joaquín like a jug of water. Ready to end the day with a bad argument.

But she managed to pull herself together. It was futile. Accusations and criticism wouldn't get her anywhere, and all she'd end up with was a sleepless night. She never slept well after confrontations. Conflicts quickened fear in her – the fear he'd end their relationship and push her back into the black hole of loneliness she had been in before she'd met him. And if they had got into it, the aftermath would be the same as always. Radio silence for a few days. Eventually, she would send him an email and apologize. He'd reply, ask her to forgive him. He would pick her up from the office on Friday, overworked and late, as usual, and they wouldn't even talk about it. And on Sunday, they would go to the cinema with Laura.

'The cinema,' Béatrice slowly replied. 'Why not?' Being alone all weekend was worse than giving in. After that, she barely heard another word Joaquín said, just the sound of the rain pattering against the window.

*

At nine o'clock the next morning Béatrice was sitting at her desk. Her head hurt, and her contact lenses were itchy. That second serving of wine at Lucío's last night clearly had been too much, and the six hours of sleep that followed too little. Watching the silent traffic flow along the street deep below her office, Béatrice's mind circled back to her career options.

Around three months ago, at the beginning of January, she had barely been able to keep a perspective on things. The mood in the office had been as dark and icy as the wintry streets of the nation's capital. Another long year with two difficult men lay before her – one that she was trying to love, and one she was trying not to hate.

But just a short while later, her patience had been rewarded when a manager's position in Cecil's team was advertised. All the requirements and qualifications described her. The job specification had clearly been written for her; she could feel it. Cecil had kept his word, and soon everything would be different and better.

Then came his recent call and their one-to-one meeting. She ran through it again in her mind. She had worn a well-cut suit, her hair was pulled up into a neat bun. The coffee had been so hot she'd burned her tongue.

'You did well in the interview,' Cecil had reassured her, giving a conspiratorial smile. 'Extremely well.'

His praise made her blush. 'And do you think anyone will raise an objection?' she asked.

He thought for a moment, then shook his head, his short grey curls bobbing back and forth. 'Don't worry,' he said with a broad grin. 'It's as good as in the bag.'

Any lingering doubts extinguished, Béatrice smiled,

overjoyed. Cecil swallowed, his Adam's apple protruding, then whispered, 'I'll announce our decision anytime soon.' He drank his espresso down in one gulp. 'Trust me.'

Trust me. Ever since, these two words had been wrapped protectively around Béatrice like a soft coat, and she wore them through the cold days. The days which, from that moment on, she was counting.

Climbing the professional ladder in a multilateral organization like the World Bank had to be approached strategically, otherwise you could easily remain at the same desk until retirement. Making your way through a strictly hierarchical and, simultaneously, highly political bureaucracy, against competitors from a hundred and ninety-four member states, was like a cleverly thought-out chess game. You constantly had to anticipate your competitors' moves. Find allies on the executive floors who had a say in influential personnel committees. Work tirelessly to make yourself indispensable to your superiors until they rewarded you with a promotion. Regularly lunch with colleagues who occupied advantageous positions. Keep your eyes and ears open. Always prepare for meetings and make meaningful interventions.

World Bankers who wanted to make something of themselves in this bloated organization were shrewd, slightly arrogant, and spent at least a third of their working time planning their next move on the international board of career chess.

Béatrice was not a good chess player. Often direct and unable to let Michael's provocations go. And instead of tactically sitting in the canteen to network with her colleagues at lunchtime, she preferred to walk around the block, alone. It was her escape. Time to decompress.

With Cecil things were different. She never had to put on an act with him. She was convinced that, from the very beginning, he had recognized her true potential. Her ability to think strategically about the bank's audiences and messages, her proactive mindset and attention to detail. Hadn't he told her at the annual meetings in Cairo last year how much he appreciated her outreach to international reporters, resulting in excellent press coverage for the bank, and how keen he was to have her on his team as communications advisor? His plan was to put her in charge of increasing the president's visibility in the media, with a special focus on Europe where she still had excellent relationships with journalists.

Béatrice admired Cecil. He was experienced and sly, using the change in leadership to manoeuvre himself further towards the top. And now he was running the presidential office. A chess player *par excellence*. And he wanted *her* to work for him. They would make an excellent team; of that she was certain.

Béatrice yawned, twisting a strand of hair between her fingers, and continued editing the French translation of the Haiti press release that had just come in. There was no way a native speaker had prepared this. Her irritation flared as she entered her many corrections. Fabrice Perie from the news agency *Agence France Presse* wouldn't be unjustified in complaining to Michael if he read this. 'You have no respect for the French language,' he used to grumble when he received sloppily translated press material. And to think they'd had to pay extra for work like this!

Trust me. Cecil's words soothed her once more. She had been waiting many months for her opportunity to work with him. In the interim, she had made sure he wouldn't forget about her. Sometimes she'd write him a quick email, sometimes she'd call him. Whenever she ran into him in the lobby, she commended him on how smooth communication with the office of the president had become since he was running it.

'And I can't wait to have you on my team,' he'd say, returning the compliment in that casual, friendly tone that made him so likeable. 'Things move slowly, but they move. Just be patient.'

Béatrice knew this only too well. Job postings, hirings, internal reforms, project approvals. Fifteen thousand employees. The large wheel of bureaucracy turned slowly. But Cecil was different from all the others. Sophisticated, almost cunning, yet still honest and straightforward.

She read through the edited text one last time. The most obvious linguistic errors had been fixed and the title no longer sounded like 'Frenglish'. There wasn't time for anything more. Now the central press office could officially release the document to journalists around the world. Free education for thirty thousand more students, read the headline. $100 million World Bank project improved public school system in Haiti, it said underneath. As far as Béatrice was concerned, getting to the thirty thousand required rounding up, wishful thinking and general speculation. But Michael and Alexander had insisted on that number of pupils being in the title. She clicked 'Send'. Done.

Relieved, Béatrice leaned back in her chair, relaxed her shoulders and daydreamed again about her new job – a fresh start, a good match, and freedom from Michael.

*

The door opened. Béatrice spun around in her chair. Veronica peered in. 'Are you sleeping or what? I just tried calling you. I've got the *Post* on the line. Can I put them through?'

Béatrice hadn't heard the phone ring. 'Of course.' Veronica's head vanished again.

Béatrice stretched her arms and looked at her watch. Why was the *Washington Post* always so quick off the mark? The press release had only just gone out.

Her thoughts turned to Joaquín and his tiny, paperwork-and-book-stuffed office at the *Post*, which he had practically lived in for the past twenty years. She had met him there, over a year ago, when she'd been invited along to an interview with Michael and two directors. They were to talk about the future of development aid, and Béatrice had spent days composing an arc of questions and answers to prepare the two of them for all the potential journalistic tricks and traps.

The door to Joaquín's office had been ajar, and Michael was the first to enter, pushing his bulky frame through the door. Joaquín stood in the middle of the room. His jeans were stonewashed, the sleeves of his dark-blue shirt rolled up. He wasn't a great deal taller than Béatrice. Laughter lines shimmered around his eyes, and his thick, uncombed hair looked in urgent need of a trim. Béatrice guessed he was around fifty. When she later learned that he was already approaching sixty, she was shocked. She was about to turn forty-two back then and the age difference scared her. Eighteen years was a lot of time. The loose folds on his neck and his laughter lines were endearing now. But how would she feel about them in a few years?

Joaquín came from a humble background, just like she did. His parents had fled from Mexico into the USA when he was a kid, undocumented and penniless. They could barely read or write and never learned proper English. His mother cleaned houses for many years while his father stocked shelves in a supermarket at night. Joaquín was raised as an American and thought of himself as one. He liked wearing shorts and trainers and his Spanish had a strong American accent. But he was proud of his Mexican roots and the fact that he was the first in his family who went to college. He never forgot the sacrifices his parents had made to pay for his education.

In one hand, Joaquín was holding a mug from which the string of a teabag dangled out; in the other, a kettle.

'Tea, anybody?' he asked his visitors by way of greeting, putting the kettle down on his desk.

During the interview, Joaquín barely took any notice of Michael. His vivacious, friendly eyes flicked back and forth between the directors and, with increasing frequency, to Béatrice. They rested on her, investigated her. As he smiled at her, his laughter lines stretched across his cheeks like a peacock's feathers.

It was as though all his interview questions had a double meaning which only she could understand.

'Do you believe that the World Bank's decision-making processes are influenced too heavily by the USA?' meant: 'I want to get to know you.' 'Will newly industrialized countries still receive loans from the World Bank in the future?' meant: 'When can we see one another again?'

Béatrice had discreetly returned his smile, then evaded his gaze and looked at the two directors as they waved their arms around and talked about the benefits of conditional cash transfers. But a few minutes later, when she dared to glance back in Joaquín's direction, his eyes immediately went to her.

He called her that very same evening. She didn't feel any butterflies when he asked her out on a date. But he was intelligent, well educated and his sparkling eyes exuded an almost fatherly warmth that gave her a sense of home she never had.

*

Béatrice answered the phone on the first ring. 'Béatrice Duvier speaking.'

'Daniel Lustiger here,' replied a sonorous voice. 'I have a few questions about the Haiti story.' The voice was so deep that the receiver vibrated in her hand. 'You know, this thing about the thirty thousand school pupils – how was that number calculated?'

Béatrice pulled out her pen. Her head was pounding. She hadn't fully understood Alexander's long-winded explanations the previous evening. It had been late and the phone connection poor. Michael's words snapped into her mind: *Never give a rushed answer. Do your research first, then call back.*

But then she remembered one of Alexander's comments, and immediately repeated it: 'The information is from our office in Port-au-Prince in collaboration with the Education Ministry.'

'Excellent,' mumbled Lustiger. 'And – did somebody verify this?'

Béatrice answered in the affirmative, without giving it

much thought, and wondered what he was getting at. She reached into her handbag and groped around for a packet of aspirin. It had to be there somewhere. She'd thrown it in just a few hours ago as she was leaving her apartment.

Meanwhile Daniel Lustiger was talking, in deep bass tones, about the article he was currently working on, something about responsibility and accountability.

Her fingers touched the spiked teeth of her comb. Where were the damn pills?

Lustiger, she thought to herself, massaging her throbbing temples. *Lustiger*. The name sounded familiar. Wasn't that the columnist her colleagues in the press department feared, even hated? The one who always painted a negative picture of the bank to convince his readers that international development aid was a waste of taxpayers' money?

Now she remembered him clearly. About half a year ago, he had written a nasty article about how the bank supported corrupt governments. It had caused a major crisis within the management team. Lustiger was not like other honest, hardworking reporters Béatrice knew at the *Washington Post*. He was a manipulator. A hitman.

An inner alarm bell went off. He could turn her words around and use them against her. This call could threaten her career. Maybe even end it. Everything she'd worked so hard to attain – gone, just like that. The alarm bell roared louder through her head. High time to end this conversation, call Alexander, and clarify the facts.

But Béatrice did none of that. An odd numbness overwhelmed her and her mind went blank. Panic choked her. What was happening to her? She had never experienced anything like this before. Instead of advocating for the bank, which she was perfectly capable of doing, she just sat in her chair, rooted to the spot, with the receiver gripped firmly in her hand. Her mind a void.

Every heartbeat sent hammering blows to her hungover head. Staring vacantly at the bony rounds of her knees which protruded from beneath her silk tights, she noticed a tiny run on the right knee. *Hopefully they will hold a little longer*, was all she could think.

Lustiger cleared his throat. The line crackled loudly. Then he went on the offensive: 'Well, we have different figures here. From an NGO. They show that the World Bank included in the calculations school pupils who haven't seen a classroom in years.'

His words prompted a sharp, stabbing pain in Béatrice's belly.

'This means the actual number must be *far* lower than thirty thousand.' He paused briefly, then repeated the word 'far', drawing it out.

She anxiously drummed her fingers on the desk and glanced at the press release which lay before her, freshly printed. *Thirty thousand children*, it said, in large letters, but nowhere was there any indication of how Michael and Alexander had calculated this number.

'Now, I'm asking you,' Lustiger continued triumphantly, 'how could something like this happen? This is about millions of dollars and clearly falsified statistics.'

'We rely upon the information from our economists, not on some random NGO,' was the response that shot out of her. Not a perfect answer, but nor was it incorrect, thought Béatrice in the second of silence that followed her words.

'Uh-huh,' he murmured. She pressed the receiver closer

to her ear and heard Lustiger's fingers bashing against the keyboard. Her head was about to explode. His typing reverberated in her ears like hundreds of tiny hammers beating against her brain. All of a sudden, the fog cleared. He was typing far more words than she had given him, and whatever breaking news he was making up could cause a disaster – for the bank and for *her*.

Béatrice sat up straight. 'You should speak to the director of our office in Haiti,' she suggested. 'I will set up a call immediately.'

'No, no, your statement is sufficient,' he assured her. 'Exactly what I needed.' He asked how her surname was spelled. And what her accent was. She spelled it out; Lustiger typed. Then he muttered a 'Thank you' and hung up.

Later, when Béatrice thought back to this fateful conversation, all she could remember was how the receiver vibrated with the deep bass of Lustiger's voice. And the tortuous throbbing in her head.

6

Judith

Paris, October 1940

Autumn was brief but intense, with bright sunshine and glowing foliage. In contrast to our heavy hearts, the air was filled with warmth and life. Every day we felt the Germans taking more and more control of our beautiful city, but no man could deny autumn its glory.

Wednesday afternoon. My heart pounding, I reached for the sky-blue note that lay before me on the card index box, and unfolded it. *'For he who loves, is absence not the most certain, effective, vivid, indestructible and true presence?'* writes Proust. *I missed you yesterday, Judith.*

I read the note again and again. *I missed you yesterday, Judith.* As I studied the Proust quote, my chest tightened. *For he who loves . . .* Every word resonated in me like the aftershocks of an earthquake. How could these words, written by a stranger, have such an impact on me? And how had the letter even got here?

I glanced around the room. But once again today, I couldn't spot anyone looking at me in a suspicious way;

nor anyone hurrying swiftly away from the card index boxes. He must have been here yesterday, waiting to see me. But I hadn't come in yesterday; I had taken the afternoon off to go with Mother to the police. She'd been really afraid about registering. Scowling *gendarmes* in uniform had always made her afraid. But it hadn't been as bad as we'd feared. We just had to give our names and address. The policeman also asked for the name of my grandparents – I didn't understand why. Then he stamped the word *juive*, bold and red, into our identity cards, and we were allowed to leave again.

On the way home, my mother had alternated between cursing, sobbing and laughing. I was worried about her. 'It's only a stamp,' I kept saying, trying to reassure her. 'Besides, we're *French* Jews and *French* citizens.' Though I wasn't ashamed of my heritage – quite the contrary, I was proud to be a Jew – I shared her despair about the occupation and its anti-Jewish propaganda. The fear was always there, deep in the pit of my stomach. I did my best to ignore it.

I forcefully pushed the open card index box, and it disappeared into its compartment with a loud bang. Startled, I looked around expecting angry glances, but no one seemed to pay the noise any attention.

Monsieur Hubert waved me over to his desk. I went across at once.

'Mademoiselle Levy can't come in today,' he said. 'I think she has a similar appointment to yours yesterday.'

I nodded understandingly.

'Could you please help distribute the books?' he asked with a smile.

'Of course,' I replied, turning around and picking up a pile. From the topmost book I pulled out the small, hand-written slip that showed who had requested it, and which seat in the reading room I had to deliver it to. I made my way swiftly through the room, along the penultimate row of tables, and handed the volume to a student with black horn-rimmed glasses. She grabbed it from my hands as though she were dying of thirst and the book were a glass of water, opened it and immediately immersed herself in reading.

I checked the card in the next book and searched for the corresponding desk. For a good half hour, I worked on like that until I found myself before the desk of the tall, thin student who was familiar to me because of his limp. A few days before, I had seen him hobble over to the index catalogue, one leg dragging heavily behind him. Shortly before he reached the catalogue, it had looked as if he were about to fall. But then he stretched out his arms and regained his balance. So tall and yet so helpless. I felt sorry for him and wondered how he had been injured.

Stepping up to his desk, I handed him the book he had ordered. The *Code Napoléon* was lying in front of him. Presumably he was studying law. Now, seeing him up close for the first time, I noticed his warm, brown eyes; his thick hair; his long hands. He had to be a few years older than me. In his dark wool blazer, which was surely made to measure, he looked almost too elegant to be a student.

Then my gaze fell on his notes, and my heart lurched. Sky-blue paper. His table was blanketed in it; blue pieces of paper everywhere. Inscribed with small, black hand-writing. I froze.

Immediately reacting to the change in my posture, he leaned forwards and whispered, 'Could we go outside for a moment and talk?'

'I'm working,' I said abruptly.

He smiled, tore a sheet of blue paper from his pad and scribbled something on it. Then he pressed the note into my hand and closed his fingers around mine for a moment. His skin felt warm and dry.

I quickly pulled my hand away and walked on. Only after a quarter of an hour had passed did I dare read the note, hiding myself away between two shelves on the other side of the room, where I was out of his line of sight. *Six o'clock. Cafe de la Joie, Rue des Carmes.* The same thick paper, the same handwriting. Yes, it was him.

Rue des Carmes was nearby, right behind the Collège de France. I immediately began to have doubts. What would be the point of going? I didn't have the time, much less the desire, to sit around in cafes with a stranger. After my shift was over, I had to queue up for bread with my coupon, look after Mother and prepare for my lecture. Just thinking about it all clouded my spirit. My shoulders were tightening. I crumpled up the piece of paper, tossed it into a waste basket and tried to concentrate on the pile of books I had to shelve.

*

At six o'clock on the dot, I left the library and set off homewards along Rue des Écoles. But instead of veering off to the left, towards the Seine, I turned right, drawn by some secret force, into Rue des Carmes. Somehow, I couldn't resist the magic that emanated from those blue notes. They sparked an excitement in me I'd never felt before. Why not take a little risk and experience more than the daily ration of stale bread? My heart craved such adventure, but my mind, always timid, retreated from the idea. I slowed down. But then I spotted his tall figure in the dark blazer further up the narrow little street. He was sitting outside, at one of the round tables, looking at me. In front of him was a bottle of wine chilling in a metal cooler, two glasses alongside it. An entire bottle!

It was too late to go back. He watched me as I crossed the street. My eyelids began to flutter, and I stared shyly at the ground as I walked towards him. Just as I was about to sit, he stood up, grasped my hand and leaned forward to greet me with a kiss on the cheek. But I ducked away, stammered '*Bonjour*', and sat down shakily. My heart leaped into my throat.

'My name is Christian,' he introduced himself, taking the wine bottle out of the cooler and pouring me a glass. 'Thank you for coming.' He smiled at me.

I gave a brief nod, unsure how to answer. Perhaps 'You're welcome'? Or 'My pleasure'? It all sounded so odd and out of place. Christian pulled a packet of Gauloises out of his trouser pocket and proffered it towards me. Feeling the rough smoke fill my lungs would have been comforting, but I was too shy to take one and declined.

He lit his cigarette and crossed his legs. 'I owe you an apology, Judith,' he said, inhaling the smoke and immediately blowing it out again. 'I'm sorry if I made a nuisance of myself.'

'It's fine,' I murmured, smoothing down my skirt.

'I . . . I'd like to explain . . .' He clearly wasn't the type for mundane small talk; he didn't ask the usual questions, like where I lived, or what I was studying. But perhaps he already knew all of that. After all, he knew my name.

His hand, shaking slightly, moved to his mouth once again as he took another drag on his Gauloise. Was the author of the provocative, eloquent notes with so many confident adjectives as nervous and uncertain as I was? The trembling of his hand endeared him to me, making him approachable. Evidently, beneath the made-to-measure blazer beat a heart just as shy as mine. He was unlike any other student I had met before at the Sorbonne.

My inner turmoil subsided and I became calmer. I finally dared take a proper look at him. He was dressed like a cross between a young intellectual and a son from an affluent home. Dark blond hair, in a side parting. A few long strands fell across his right eye. He brushed them away and fixed me with a steadfast gaze. We sat there like that for a long while. I studied his high forehead, his long eyelashes. I didn't quite understand what was happening to me, but I knew something powerful had ignited between us. My whole body – not just my mind – was floating, swept away by Christian's presence, lifted above the table by his eyes and the soft breeze that ruffled through the street.

He lowered his gaze and pointed to his right leg. 'Polio. I was five when I got sick. Ever since then, this leg has been half lame.' He stubbed out his cigarette. 'The only silver lining is that I didn't get called up. I would have made a bad soldier.'

'I'm sorry,' I said.

'The illness changed me,' he continued. With the tip of

his index finger, he pushed his wine glass around on the table. 'It turned me into an outsider.' He picked up the glass and took a sip. 'I could never do what the other boys did. Play football, get into fights, climb trees . . .' He stared thoughtfully into the distance.

'Everything that mattered took place inside my head. And in the books I read. The children in my class only came to see me because their mothers forced them to. So I spent most of the time sitting alone at home in our big library, the only place where no one could make fun of me.' He brushed the hair off his forehead once again. 'I feel safe in libraries . . . where it doesn't matter how fast you can run, or how far you can throw a ball. I come to the big reading room almost every day, devouring everything I can get my hands on. Stendhal, Balzac, Zola . . .' He looked at me and grinned. Small dimples formed on his cheeks. 'And Proust, of course.'

For the first time since I'd sat down, I smiled.

'And then, one day, you appeared, Judith.' His expression turned serious again. 'I immediately sensed that something connected us. That you carry a sadness inside you, like I do.'

His words shook and stunned me. How had he been able to so clearly read the pain of my youth in my closed expression? My head turned hot; pressure built behind my eyes. I quickly took a sip from my glass.

'Given that I can't impress you with an athletic physique, I had to try with words. And Proust seemed a worthy messenger for what I wanted to say.'

'It . . . it was a beautiful note,' I whispered, biting my lower lip. 'Why Proust?'

He looked at me attentively. 'Because he unsettles and captivates. Because he's the greatest. No one can describe the depth of human emotion like he can.'

I shook my head indecisively. 'Hmm . . . I think I prefer Balzac,' I said. 'The adventures and intrigues he writes about have such eloquence and power.' I spoke quickly, softly; happy to not have to talk about myself.

Christian nodded. 'Certainly. But if someone, like me, can't walk properly and spends weeks on end within the same four walls as a child, he sees a lot of things differently.' He propped his elbow on the table and rested his head in his hand. 'My life was always very slow and quiet. That made me sensitive to the small details that other people don't usually notice. Perhaps that's why I appreciate Proust's descriptions so much.'

'How do you know my name?' I asked, unable to restrain my curiosity any longer.

He chuckled. 'Monsieur Hubert likes to chat. And he likes you.'

We fell silent for a while, and I listened to the sounds of the city. A few chirping birds, a car from far away. The streets had become so still and empty since the swastika had been hoisted over the Tricolour.

'Would you come to the theatre with me?' asked Christian.

'The theatre?' I repeated, astonished by his request. For weeks now, every minute of my day-to-day life had been filled with working at the library, queueing up for groceries, collecting coupons and studying. And now here I was, sitting in the middle of occupied Paris, in front of a bottle of wine, being invited to the theatre.

'It's not all that absurd,' he said with a laugh, as if he had read my mind. 'The theatre season is open, like every year. My parents have subscription tickets, but often can't attend. How about next Tuesday? I think Michel Francini is playing in the Théâtre de l'Étoile.'

'But . . .' I paused.

Christian laid his hand on my arm reassuringly. 'We should enjoy life while we still can.'

Now he sounded precocious, and I couldn't help but roll my eyes.

'Yes, the Germans have marched in,' he went on, undeterred, 'and now they're bombing London. But in the theatre, they're just part of the audience, like everyone else.' He leaned over to his bag and pulled out a newspaper. 'Here, look, today's edition of *Le Figaro*. And what's this on the very first page? "The Frenchwoman of tomorrow won't have to dispense with elegance. She'll wear artificial silk." *Voilà*, life goes on.' He gave me a contented wink.

Precocious, but endearing.

A church bell rang nearby. Was it already seven o'clock? Mother would be worried. The spell broken, I sprang out of my chair. 'I have to go. My mother's waiting.'

'Until Tuesday, Judith. Eight o'clock at the theatre.'

7

Béatrice

Washington, D.C., 2006

A mild spring breeze wafted towards Béatrice as she stepped out onto the street. She breathed in the fresh air. Her headache had finally disappeared, thanks to finding the aspirin, and her tiredness had subsided too. The sky was cloudless and infused with tones of dark orange and blue. Helicopters hovered over the White House before descending, clattering loudly. Michael was on his way to a TV interview, and Béatrice had used this opportunity to leave the office a little earlier than usual to see Lena at Sunset Aid.

She pulled out the business card Lena had tucked into her coat and looked at the address. Her office was on Q Street. That was nearby, right behind Dupont Circle. As Béatrice walked down 19th Street passing K Street and L Street, her thoughts returned to their encounter yesterday in Murrow Park. 'We urgently need volunteers,' Lena had said.

Instead of writing just another cheque, Béatrice could get directly involved with this noble cause, serving those who needed care and affection. Wasn't that what she wanted?

But as she approached Dupont Circle, doubts overcame her, and she slowed down. Did she really have the emotional and physical strength to help others after a long day at the office? Listening to their stories about ailments and absorbing their misery?

Her inner voice grew louder. Whispers from her childhood bubbled up. She heard the strained voice of her overworked mother, and it struck at her heart. Yes, this was her opportunity to offer some consolation to people in need. She had to give it a try. She was good at public relations outreach in her job, and wasn't this just another kind of outreach? Visiting lonesome seniors, making a small but meaningful difference in their lives with her presence. Definitely a much better use of her time than sitting alone at home, waiting for a call from Joaquín.

Béatrice had made her decision. Feeling determined again, she crossed Dupont Circle, walked past Kramer's Bookstore, where she normally liked to rummage around for travel guides, and turned into Q Street.

*

Lena's office was located in a two-storey, pink-painted building. Above the door hung a sign with *Sunset Aid* in bold lettering, accompanied by a black half-circle with three vertically protruding beams, presumably intended to depict a setting sun. A handwritten sign was tacked to the wall of the building: *Volunteers Wanted*.

Béatrice climbed the small flight of steps to the entrance and rang the bell.

'It's open,' called a rusty-sounding female voice from inside, which Béatrice immediately recognized as Lena's. Only then did she notice that the door was ajar. She stepped into a chaotic office. It was sparsely furnished and smelled of stale coffee and chlorine. Alongside a desk, which was piled high with index boxes, rolls of toilet paper and open files, stood a tatty, artificial leather sofa, yellowed filling bulging out of its seats.

Lena was standing in the centre of the room, a pen in her hand and a flipchart in front of her, upon which she had scribbled some names. She was surrounded by water bottles, crates of food cans and sacks of clothing. Lena was wearing the same jogging bottoms she'd had on the previous day, and a dark T-shirt; her orange sweatshirt hung over a revolving chair. The tulip tattoo flashed out from beneath her ear.

'Great, you made it,' Lena greeted her. She took an index box from the desk and pressed it into Béatrice's hand. 'Here, you can start right away. Take your pick.'

Béatrice looked at the box in astonishment, then back at Lena. 'I thought we'd talk about it first,' she began, looking around the crowded room. 'I mean, I might have time for a few evenings a month—'

'Excellent decision,' Lena interrupted her, grinning broadly. Then her expression turned serious. 'I'm afraid we have to talk another time. Right now, I need to revise our schedule,' she said, pointing towards the flipchart. 'Two of our volunteers just called in sick. It's a complete disaster.'

She took the box back from Béatrice, pulled out a card and held it towards her. 'Ms Jacobina Grunberg. How about her? She really needs a hot meal this evening.'

'You mean right now?' asked Béatrice, startled, looking at her watch. 'But . . .' There was no way she wanted to do this so unprepared.

But Lena simply wouldn't take no for an answer. 'Oh, come on. It's not far from here. I can't manage on my own.'

Before Béatrice was able to think of a plausible excuse as to why she couldn't start immediately, Lena had already explained the quickest route to Jacobina Grunberg's apartment.

'Grunberg's an old Canadian woman, from Québec, I think, but she was born in Romania,' she said, pulling a few cans from one of the crates and packing them in a paper bag. 'She's single and doesn't have any children or other relatives to look after her. Lives off social security and whatever we bring her. It's really sad, the poor woman.' Lena added a packet of porridge to the cans and handed Béatrice the bag. Then she gave her a critical look. 'I don't think you should turn up there in your designer outfit.' She picked up her Sunset Aid sweatshirt from the chair and tossed it to Béatrice. 'Better put that on and leave your jacket here. You can pick it up tomorrow.'

*

Twenty minutes later, clad in Lena's oversized sweatshirt, Béatrice was standing in front of a run-down residential building on the corner of 15th and U Street. Just ten years before, the U Street area had been a haven for drug dealers. But then the city had built numerous apartment buildings in the neighbourhood and opened a metro station. Slowly, the area had evolved into a lively multi-cultural quarter with interesting second-hand shops and ethnic restaurants, which Béatrice and Joaquín liked to visit from time to time.

In front of the entrance to the grey, concrete building where Jacobina Grunberg lived lay a stack of bound-together marketing brochures. The sound of children's squeals pushed its way out of an open window. An African-American man in shorts and trainers sat, smoking a cigarette, on a partially capsized wall. He wore large head-phones and was nodding his head up and down to his music. There were no nameplates; the doorbells were arranged by number. Béatrice pressed the bell for apart-ment 1350B and waited. When she heard a loud buzzing tone a few seconds later, she leaned against the door and walked inside. The entrance hall stank of mouldy water and fried food. Broken glass bottles and cigarette butts lay around on the floor; the plaster was peeling from the walls. The gentrification of the neighbourhood had presumably stopped at the entrance to this building. Béatrice waved her hand in front of her face to fan away the stench. Why did Lena have to send her straight to the very worst loca-tion? She wanted to leave, but reluctantly stepped into the lift instead. She was committed now. And though she felt outside of her comfort zone, she wanted to see this through. No excuses.

Arriving at the top, she knocked on Ms Grunberg's door. A deep, raspy voice rang out. 'Who's there?'

'Sunset Aid,' replied Béatrice. The words felt like sticky sweets in her mouth. On the right-hand side of the door frame, she noticed a small horizontal metal plate, engraved with Hebrew characters. It had been nailed on at a slight angle.

The door opened, just a crack at first, then completely. When a tiny lady with dark, button-like eyes and grey hair came into view, Béatrice felt startled. The woman's hair looked unwashed and stood up at wild angles from her head. Jacobina Grunberg was shaking slightly, leaning against a walking stick. With a nod of her head, she gestured for Béatrice to follow her.

'About time too,' she muttered as she shuffled back into her living room. 'I was worried you wouldn't come at all.' She wore a tattered terrycloth bath robe, blue floral pyjama bottoms peeping out below the hem. Her feet were clad in thick tennis socks.

Béatrice followed her into the dark flat. She squinted but could only make out hazy outlines. The shutters were down, the cracks around the sides letting in just a few narrow strips of daylight. A muted television cast flickering shadows on the wall, and a radiator clanked noisily some-where nearby. The flat was permeated by the pungent smell of air freshener.

'Hello, Ms Grunberg, where's the light switch?' she asked, putting down her bag.

'I don't want any light,' grumbled the old lady, sitting down on the sofa with a groan.

Once Béatrice's eyes had adjusted to the semi-darkness, she followed the woman and sat down next to her. As her body felt the embrace of worn upholstery, her palms touched fluffy polyester fabric. Béatrice looked around the living room. It was small and not very tidy. In front of the sofa stood a round glass table covered with bric-a-brac. Crumpled newspapers and a blanket were lying on the floor, flanked by a rickety folding wooden armchair. The bare walls hosted only an uneven pattern of nails, their intended picture frames forgotten in a pile against the wall.

'I brought you some tomato soup,' Béatrice said, making an effort to sound cheerful.

'Soup,' cried Ms Grunberg, letting out a clanging laugh. 'Geriatric slop. Am I toothless, or what?'

'It's just what they gave me to bring,' Béatrice replied coolly.

'Goddamn canned soup,' ranted the woman, letting her walking stick drop to the floor. 'I need some proper food.'

Béatrice had pictured her involvement with Sunset Aid as a nice chat with Washington seniors, but not this! What had she got herself in to?

Ms Grunberg coughed. 'I can't stand any more of that soup and gruel,' she rasped.

'Then order something from a delivery service,' Béatrice suggested. 'Chinese. Thai. A burger and fries. Whatever you fancy.' She felt the strong urge to open a window.

'Delivery service. Ha! You haven't been working for Sunset long,' the woman retorted, pulling her hand through her curls. 'If I could afford something like that, there's no way I'd be begging from you lot.' She leaned forwards, her breath rattling, and reached for her stick. 'Before . . . everything was different.'

Béatrice immediately regretted her thoughtless comment and fell silent. What could she do to calm this poor lady down?

Lucío! Everyone loved his cooking. She pulled her

mobile out of her trouser pocket and dialled his number. As she waited for the ringing tone, she turned around to the woman and asked, 'Do you like Italian? My treat.'

Jacobina Grunberg didn't answer. But in the flickering glow from the television, Béatrice saw a smile flit across her face.

'*Ciao*, Lucío, I'd like to place an order,' said Béatrice sweetly, as soon as she heard the familiar *buona sera*. She ordered her favourite dishes: tomato bruschetta, creamy mushroom pappardelle, penne with Lucío's famous pesto sauce and a double tiramisu. It all sounded so appetizing. She remembered that deep sense of well-being – even home! – every time she tasted Lucío's pasta after a difficult day at the office. She felt Ms Grunberg needed that too. Who didn't? Béatrice decided to stay and have dinner with the grumpy lady, trusting in the magic and comfort of spaghetti. If she asked Lucío to send along a bottle of wine, maybe even Jacobina Grunberg would lighten up.

'It'll take a little while,' said Béatrice once she had hung up. 'I'm going to open the shutters. This place really needs an airing.' She stood up and went over towards one of the small windows.

'Please don't touch anything!' the woman pleaded. 'I like it like this.'

Béatrice paused indecisively. Then she sat down again. She'd have to take a gentler approach. 'Tell me something about yourself,' she asked encouragingly. 'How long have you been living here in D.C.?'

Ms Grunberg stared at the silent TV screen. 'For too long,' she muttered. 'My friends are all gone. No more evenings playing bridge, no more chats at the coffee shop. I'm the only one left.'

Her loneliness hung in the air as heavily as the smell of air freshener. Maybe Béatrice was the first person she had talked to all day. The mere thought made Béatrice shudder.

'Where did your friends go?' she asked.

Jacobina Grunberg sighed. 'Two of them are older than me and moved to retirement homes in different states. I wouldn't be able to live there. No privacy, only crap to eat. The third one, Nathalie, was lucky, though. Moved in with her daughter and grandchildren.'

'Don't you have family?' Béatrice wanted to know, settling deeper into the sofa. How wise of Lena to insist she should look after Ms Grunberg right away. She really needed some company.

'My friends were my family,' the old lady mumbled, without averting her gaze from the TV. On the screen was a female figure skater in a pink sequined costume, spinning around on the ice.

Béatrice decided to change the subject. Maybe that would take the woman out of her gloomy mood. 'I'm from France,' she said, 'Paris.'

Ms Grunberg jutted her neck forwards and stared at Béatrice, her eyes now wide open. 'Paris?' she gasped.

Béatrice nodded, surprised by the strong reaction. 'Yes. My mother still lives there. It's not easy to feel at home, here in the US,' Béatrice continued. Ms Grunberg leaned back on the sofa but didn't say a word. Her hands were shaking.

'Are you alright?' asked Béatrice with concern.

'My father,' the old lady whispered, 'my father.' Then her voice drifted off. Béatrice didn't feel comfortable probing further.

The two women sat alongside one another in silence, listening to the clanging of the radiator and watching the figure skating. After a while Ms Grunberg's breathing became even and calm. She had fallen asleep.

*

Finally the doorbell rang, and Béatrice hurried to answer it. She exchanged a few words with the delivery man, and took in the wine and numerous plastic bags. Soon the apartment was filled with the enticing aroma of Lucío's cuisine. When Béatrice returned, she saw that Jacobina was yawning and rubbing her eyes. The doorbell must have woken her.

'Where can I find plates?' asked Béatrice, reaching into the bags and placing warm, white boxes of differing sizes on the glass table.

'Over there,' murmured Ms Grunberg, nodding her head towards the corner of the kitchenette. Then she stretched out her legs and studied the boxes, frowning.

The kitchenette was located next to a narrow door which led into the bathroom. In the sink lay dirty plates and coffee cups. The electric stove top hadn't been cleaned in a while either. Nearby stood a small refrigerator, adorned with the remains of pulled-off stickers, emitting hissing sounds.

Béatrice reached into the sink and began to wash up the plates.

As Jacobina Grunberg chewed her first mouthful, she

closed her eyes in pleasure. 'Oh my, that's good,' she exclaimed, her cheeks flushed. Before long, she was a different person. The deep lines on her forehead smoothed out, and her button-like eyes twinkled happily. Her right arm was no longer trembling.

Béatrice drank a sip of wine from a coffee cup with bright blue polka dots and watched the old lady piling pasta onto her plate. She devoured her supper with desperation, seemingly unaccustomed to such plenty.

'I'm Jacobina, by the way,' Ms Grunberg introduced herself between two bites.

Béatrice smiled. Jacobina's whole manner had changed now that she'd been well fed. The fact that Béatrice had been able to assuage this woman's day-to-day suffering, even just for a short while, filled her with a contentment she hadn't felt in ages.

'And I'm Béatrice,' she said.

'Sorry for the chaos here. I slipped and fell in the bathroom last week,' Jacobina explained. 'Since then my back hurts like hell and I can't move around much. Can't even wash my hair without pain.'

'I'm sorry,' Béatrice said, thinking already about when she could return to help Jacobina with some chores.

Jacobina washed down the last few forkfuls of tiramisu with half a cup of wine, gave a blissful sigh and sank back down into the sofa cushions.

'You're heaven sent, Béatrice,' she said, making a few smacking sounds with her mouth. 'The other volunteers Sunset sends usually just drop off a bag of cans and scarper.' She wiped one of Lucío's grey paper serviettes across her mouth. 'No one has time. No one's interested.'

She looked at the empty boxes on the glass table and asked imploringly, 'You'll come back soon, won't you, Béatrice?'

*

'Can't we eat some *proper* food?' The tall, gangling girl stared in disgust at the plates of tomato salad, roasted vegetables and brown rice which Béatrice had just placed on the table in front of her. Laura raised her narrowly plucked eyebrows, brushed her long, smooth hair out of her face and scanned the kitchen for better alternatives.

Friday evening. Instead of sipping cocktails in a bar in downtown D.C., like she and Joaquín used to do at the very beginning of their relationship, Béatrice was cooking dinner in his old-fashioned kitchen. She missed their Friday night flings, the light-heartedness that transported them when they got away from their duties and responsibilities – even if it was just for a couple of hours.

At the same time, Béatrice also enjoyed the sense of family – a feeling she had never had before – when the three of them gathered around the delicious smells of a freshly prepared meal, asking about Laura's week at school and listening to her stories. At one point she even felt as if she and Laura were connecting. Those early days together were happier times, times filled more with family than dissonance.

Béatrice dried her hands on her apron. Laura's desire for 'proper food' made her think about Jacobina Grunberg, who had spoken the same words with similar intensity a few days before. She smiled at the thought of her new acquaintance. She sensed a strange kinship with Ms Grunberg she couldn't yet account for.

'So what do you consider to be "proper food", Laura?' she asked, although she knew the answer already.

'Well, pizza, for example,' said Laura as expected. 'Or a burger. Just something normal.' She slipped her flip-flops off her feet, put her legs up on a kitchen chair and studied her toenails, which were painted with black polish.

Béatrice was about to respond with an equally smartarse comment but refrained. She wanted to try, if only to save the memory of the relationship she and Laura once had – before puberty hit and turned the cute little girl into a typical teenager. Béatrice wondered, had *she* ever been like this? Impossible. She hadn't had the luxury.

She opened the freezer compartment and studied the piled-up packets of ready meals. Today had been demanding enough: full of deadlines and unnecessarily long meetings. As always, Joaquín had picked her up late from the office and spent the entire car journey on the phone with his editorial team. They had made their way through the evening traffic at a snail's pace. Down K Street, over the Potomac and then, after a seemingly endless stop-and-go on George Washington Memorial Parkway, up to the final destination of McLean, Virginia. The unassuming house on the corner.

Why on earth had she offered to cook a warm meal? Laura certainly needed something homemade, at least once a week. And Joaquín was a lousy cook. Béatrice didn't mind. She wanted to make things a little easier for him. But she should have known better – Laura would never approve of her dinner menu, and this made her sad and frustrated.

Béatrice reached into the frozen meal stack and pulled

out a packet at random. Macaroni with bolognese sauce. She waved the rectangular aluminium carton in the air. 'How about this?'

Laura's mouth curved into a smile. 'Cool.'

From somewhere nearby came the sound of a cat miaowing – Laura's latest in a series of annoying ringtones. She straightened up and pulled her phone out of her trouser pocket. Every time she moved, the countless metal bracelets around her wrist clinked against one another. She immersed herself in her text message conversation – probably with Sarah, her BFF. At the weekend, the two girls texted one another non-stop. And the ringtone changed as often as the colour of Laura's nail polish, spanning the spectrum of animal sounds to a door being slammed, or the opening notes of a hit song.

Béatrice shoved the macaroni in the microwave, shut the door and sat down at the table. This could be her 'every day', she thought as she listened to the oven hum. Joaquín often mentioned how much he dreamed of waking up next to her during the week, too. At times, when Béatrice was sitting alone in her apartment in Georgetown in the evening, the only sounds the thudding footsteps of the neighbours on the floor above, she toyed with the thought of giving it a go. On a trial basis, at least. She wouldn't give up her independence just like that. But a single Friday evening in McLean cast an inescapable doubt on those thoughts. Could she do this day after day?

Béatrice pulled the warmed-up pasta carton out of the microwave, tore the lid off and placed it in front of Laura.

Joaquín entered the kitchen, closely followed by Rudi, his stubby-legged fox terrier. 'Hello, cuties, are you having fun?' he cried cheerfully. Rudi dashed under the table and snuffled around the floor.

Joaquín put a bottle of wine down with a flourish and kissed Béatrice on the forehead. 'What's for dinner?'

An answer seemed superfluous, because Joaquín was already happily inspecting the serving bowls and mumbling a contented 'Mmm'.

Laura paid no attention to her father. Without looking up, she tapped away industriously on her phone, all the while spooning the heated-up macaroni out of the carton. For a moment, all that could be heard was the jingling of her bracelets and the sound of the dog lapping up something he had found on the floor.

Joaquín didn't seem bothered that neither of them was enlivened by his good mood. He plucked a few tomatoes from the salad bowl with his fingers, then uncorked the bottle and poured two glasses. One he filled to the brim, then pushed it towards Béatrice; into the other he poured just a sip, which he drank at once.

'Béa,' he cooed, stroking her hair. Béatrice knew what he was about to say. 'I'm afraid I need to work a little longer. But I should be done within two hours. You two enjoy, okay?' He gave her another kiss and left the kitchen. Rudi trotted out behind him, panting.

Béatrice sat motionless at the table, listening to Joaquín's steps on the creaky wooden stairs. Almost as soon as he'd closed the door to his study, Laura dropped her spoon, went into the living room without a word and turned on the TV.

Béatrice stared at the nearly untouched meal, then her eyes wandered over to the dirty pots on the counter and welled up with tears. Why had she tried so hard?

Maybe it was the recent stress built up from her work, or the sea change in her relationship with Joaquín, or the disintegration of her relationship with Laura – or all of it at once, avalanching upon her in a dirty-kitchen moment of loneliness. Whatever it was, it coursed through her. Seized by the sudden burst of emotion, she jumped out of her chair and ran up the stairs.

The dog, hearing her coming, began to yap loudly. Béatrice flung open the door. For days, she had suppressed her disappointment and frustration. But now she could no longer hold them back.

'Why the hell am I here?' she said loudly, as soon as she entered the room. 'You don't even make the time to have dinner with me. And I . . .' – she put her arms on her hips in a defiant gesture – 'idiot that I am, I went to the effort of cooking a nice meal!'

Joaquín looked up from his laptop and sighed. He seemed distracted.

Rudi, curled up by his feet, had stopped barking and instead let out a soft whimper, as if he was trying to apologize for the rude behaviour of his master.

'I've had it up to here, Joaquín.' Her head felt hot. 'You treat me like a maid.'

Joaquín took off his reading glasses and ran his fingers across his eyebrows. 'Honey, I'm sorry. You're completely right. How thoughtless of me.' He stood up and wrapped his arms around her. Béatrice stiffened.

'Calm down, baby. I'm really sorry. You have no idea what's going on at my office these days,' Joaquín continued. 'It's killing me.'

Béatrice wanted to say that she was tired of it all. The

99

never-ending demands of his job, Laura's attitude, and the long weekends at his house in the suburbs. She wanted to call a taxi and leave. But then she remembered the stark silence that was awaiting her at home. The unheated bedroom, the empty fridge. She thought of the many weekends she had spent in stifling solitude, on her couch, reading French novels. With Joaquín and Laura at least she had the trappings of a family, even though it wasn't perfect. Béatrice closed her eyes and took a deep breath.

Joaquín held her tightly and stroked her back. His body exuded a pleasant warmth and the subtle scent of the aftershave Béatrice had given him for Christmas last year. How she had missed being close to him. She didn't want to be alone now. He was trying his best. She had to be more understanding, show more empathy. Hesitantly, she put her arms around him.

They stood there in silence, holding one another. Joaquín ran his hand over her hair comfortingly.

'Tomorrow we'll do something fun together, okay?' he purred. 'Just you and I.'

She pulled away brusquely from the embrace. 'You and I?' she repeated, anger flaring up at those words. 'That's rich. There's always something else more important.'

He touched her face and kissed her. 'We'll change that. I promise.' He looked deep into her eyes. 'I miss you and I want to be more with you. But my day-to-day life is brutal. I hate that it doesn't leave much of me for you.' He kissed her once more, then turned around, opened his desk drawer and took out a small box. 'Here, I was planning to give you this later. But you should have it now.'

Béatrice pulled the ribbon off and opened it. On a velvet

cushion lay a silver chain with a teardrop-shaped pendant.

'Remember, we saw it a few weeks ago in a window on Connecticut Avenue.' Joaquín picked up the necklace and fastened it around her neck. 'You loved it.' He looked at her expectantly.

Even though she was touched that he clearly *did* think about her after all, Béatrice struggled to feel any real delight over the present. But she didn't want to spoil the romantic moment and his attempt to make up for his behaviour. Most of all, she didn't want him to stop holding her. She swallowed her disappointment and smiled.

'Let's go downstairs and have some wine,' he suggested.

She nodded.

He took her hand and led her to the stairs.

*

When Béatrice woke up the next morning, the other side of the bed was empty. She sleepily propped herself up and brushed her hair out of her face. Warm morning light streamed in through the half-drawn curtains. She glanced at the clock that hung alongside the door, the one with the old-fashioned face and the unrelenting tick that sometimes woke her up at night. It was just after seven.

Joaquín's pyjamas were stuffed onto the white armchair by the bed, together with a pile of books he was planning to read over the next few weeks. *The World is Flat* by Friedman, the new Rory Stewart about Afghanistan and *The White Man's Burden* by William Easterly, which Joaquín had bought for her because it was about development aid.

Every Friday, there were new books on the chair, the

dresser and sometimes even in the bathroom. Béatrice had no idea how he found the time to devour these veritable mountains of literature, especially when he seemed to have no time for her. 'I read when you're sleeping,' he had once told her with a laugh.

On their first date, he had asked her what kind of books she liked to read. 'A lot of fiction and mostly in French,' she had replied.

'Aha.' He nodded absently. Béatrice could sense he wasn't interested in contemporary French literature. After a moment of silence, she'd asked him what *he* was currently reading.

'Ron Chernow's fascinating biography of Alexander Hamilton, the first US Treasury Secretary,' he explained, getting animated. A monologue of several minutes' duration had followed. Since then, he liked to buy her American non-fiction books he considered 'must reads'. It was a bit pretentious, but she knew in his heart he didn't mean it that way. Though she would never have his political knowledge, and sometimes felt her shortcomings in conversations with him, she admired him for his journalistic curiosity and desire to learn. If anything, it inspired her to read more.

Béatrice yawned. The faint aroma of coffee drifted towards her nose. She looked around and spotted a large mug of coffee on the round nightstand. Next to it lay an opened envelope with a note scribbled on the back.

Honey, I had to dash into work. Small emergency. Really sorry. See you later. Love you, J.

Letting out a loud sigh, Béatrice grabbed the cup, took a sip and pulled a face. The coffee was almost completely cold; he must have put it there a while ago. Putting the cup back down, she reached for the Easterly book and flicked through it sullenly. Then she tossed it back onto the chair, sank down onto the pillow and thought about what to do with the day that was supposed to have been about just the two of them.

A short bark echoed up from downstairs. Béatrice heard Laura stomping up the stairs and scolding the dog. A few seconds later, without knocking, she opened the bedroom door. Rudi padded into the room, his tongue lolling out of his mouth, and began to jump up at the bed.

'Can you drive me to Sarah's, please?' asked Laura, keeping her gaze fixed on Rudi, who stubbornly persisted in trying to climb up onto the bed, despite his legs being far too short. Laura was wearing hot pants, a summery tank top, and blue eye shadow. In her hand she held a huge plastic beaker, filled to the brim with a pinkish liquid and ice cubes. She sat down on the bed, reached for Rudi's collar and dragged him away from the edge. The dog whined and immediately started jumping back up again.

'Shouldn't you do your homework first?' asked Béatrice. Stepping into the role of stepmother was generally not something she was fond of, especially not when Joaquín was absent and left the pedagogical details to her.

It didn't happen very often, but when it did, she struggled not to sound too strict and at the same time not too easy-going.

'I did it ages ago,' Laura replied, sucking at the straw. 'So will you drive me or not?'

'It's a quarter past seven,' Béatrice replied after another glance at the clock. 'Far too early to turn up on people's doorsteps.'

'Says who?'

'Says I,' answered Béatrice, a little more loudly and firmly than she had intended. She stood up, pulling Joaquín's bathrobe over her bare shoulders.

'Daddy said it's okay,' replied Laura cockily.

'Well, I think it's too early.'

'Come on,' the girl objected, rolling her eyes, 'Laura is my BFF. I can go there any time of the day.'

Béatrice couldn't even wake up in peace. But the longer she thought about it, the more she came to the conclusion that it was much smarter to get Laura out of the house than be exposed to her adolescent moods for a few more hours. And who knew how long Joaquín would leave her waiting here! A 'small emergency' at his office could take half a day.

'All right then,' Béatrice said, 'I'll take you.'

And so, before it had even struck half past seven, Béatrice, without having showered or eaten breakfast, found herself in Joaquín's second car driving through a desolate McLean, taking a triumphant Laura to her friend's house.

*

The man with the headphones was sitting on the wall again, just like three days before. This time he was holding a can of beer. Seeing Béatrice, he gave a loud whistle. She ignored him.

She hadn't expected to find herself back at Jacobina's so soon. But Jacobina's imploring question as to whether she'd be back soon had moved Béatrice. There had been so much genuine despair in the woman's eyes, so much hope in her question, that Béatrice had been unable to forget her.

After she'd dropped Laura off, Béatrice hadn't driven back to Joaquín's empty house, but directly to Washington and then U Street. En route, she'd gone shopping, fetching coffee, pastries, washing-up sponges and a scouring agent.

'Who's there?' came the tone from the intercom.

'It's me, Béatrice'.

'*You?*'

Then Béatrice heard the hum of the door buzzer. A few minutes later, she stood in front of Jacobina's apartment door and rang again. The old woman pulled the door open just a crack, like last time, then completely. She was smaller than Béatrice remembered and looked exhausted. There were dark shadows beneath her eyes, and her hair hung down in curly strands. Jacobina wasn't wearing slippers, and had on the same floral pyjamas as last time.

'Good morning,' Béatrice greeted her.

'Morning,' Jacobina mumbled, visibly surprised.

'Did I wake you?'

'No . . .' Jacobina waved Béatrice in, wiping her eyes with the sleeve of her pyjama top. 'I rarely sleep.'

'I brought breakfast.' Béatrice waved one of the bags. As soon as she stepped into the darkened apartment, the penetrating smell of air freshener reached her nose. 'That man down by the entrance, does he live here?' asked Béatrice as she closed the door behind her.

'Which man?' Jacobina trotted over to her sofa and dropped down into it, wheezing.

'The guy with the headphones.' Béatrice pulled off her jacket. There wasn't a coat hook, so she threw it over the armchair.

'No idea,' murmured Jacobina. She picked up a tissue

and kneaded it in her hands. 'A lot of guys hang out down there.'

Béatrice flipped on the light. 'Tell me, what do those Hebrew symbols by your door mean?'

Jacobina squinted as the light came on, but didn't protest. 'That's a *mezuzah*,' she said, smoothing out the tissue then scrunching it back together. 'A Jewish tradition. It's supposed to protect my home.' Her voice became quieter. 'It belonged to my father.'

Béatrice headed for the kitchenette and began to wash the crockery. 'Where did your family come from?'

The old woman didn't answer.

On the windowsill was a small coffee maker, furred with limescale. Béatrice pulled out the pot and filled it with water. 'Coffee?'

Jacobina nodded. 'What a lovely idea. Why are you here so early? Don't you have anything better to do at the weekend?' Her eyes followed every one of Béatrice's movements.

'It wasn't planned. But my boyfriend had to go out early this morning, so I thought I'd check in on you.' Béatrice pulled the cleaning products from the shopping bags and began to scrub the sink and stove. 'He's always so busy,' she continued, scratching away a thin crust of burned-on food.

'I appreciate it. My back hurts so much, I can barely bend over,' Jacobina said, fiddling with one of the buttons on her pyjama top.

Béatrice looked at her. 'Maybe I should take you to the emergency room?'

'Nah.' Jacobina waved her off. 'Too much of a hassle. It'll pass.'

Béatrice brewed some coffee, handed Jacobina a mug and put a plate with fresh pastries on the glass table in front of them. Then she sat down on the other side of the sofa. Jacobina immediately reached for a Danish. 'Why are you so curious?' she asked.

'I'd like to help you.'

'That's what they all say in the beginning.' Jacobina's mouth tightened into a hard line. 'They come once, maybe twice. Then I become a burden.'

'I will try my best,' Béatrice replied cheerfully. She didn't want to make a promise she might not be able to keep, but she didn't want to let Jacobina down either. 'Let me start by cleaning up a bit more.'

Without waiting for a reaction, she picked up the newspapers and the blanket from the floor. Then she dusted the television, raised the shutters and cleaned the narrow linoleum floor which ran alongside the kitchenette. When she opened the door of the small wall cupboard to clear the newly bought kitchen towels away, a pile of unopened letters and marketing flyers tumbled out and landed on the floor.

'There's a bunch of letters up here,' Béatrice called. 'Don't you want to open them?'

'I stopped reading my mail a long time ago,' Jacobina grunted. 'It's only bills I can't pay.'

'But there could be something important in here,' Béatrice persisted. Picking up the mail from the floor, she noticed several envelopes from AT&T that looked like bills indeed, including follow-ups reminding Jacobina to pay.

Béatrice held one of them up. 'I think you should pay at least this one. Otherwise they'll shut down your phone line.'

Jacobina made a dismissive gesture with her hand. 'My phone's been shut down for weeks now. It's okay. I don't need it.'

'And what do you do in an emergency?' Béatrice asked.

Jacobina shrugged her shoulders. 'If it's really urgent, I go to the convenience store down the street. They've got a phone I can use.'

Poor lady, Béatrice thought, throwing the junk mail in the bin and laying the other letters, in a neat pile, back in the cupboard. The AT&T bills, however, she slid into her handbag. She'd pay them tonight. Jacobina had to have a functioning phone line.

In the bathroom, Béatrice discovered an ancient washing machine with a top-loading drum, the type that whisks the washing around in lukewarm water with a kind of electric stirrer. To Béatrice's surprise, it still worked. As she turned the dials, the drum set in motion, thudding and juddering.

Jacobina watched Béatrice work her way through the apartment with her cleaning cloth, and continued to slurp at her coffee.

'I was born in Romania,' she said, all of a sudden. 'I could barely walk when they deported my father because he was a Jew.'

She reached for another Danish. 'But Lica was a brave man. He escaped the camp . . . And then we fled to Montréal.'

Béatrice, who had been wiping down the windowsills, paused and turned around. 'So, if you grew up in Québec, do you speak French? Would you rather we speak that?'

Jacobina shook her head. 'I haven't spoken French since I left Canada and moved to New York. That was nearly half a century ago.' She rubbed her swollen feet together.

Béatrice put down the cloth and sat down next to her, looking at the old woman attentively. 'What did you do in New York?' She was pleased at Jacobina's chattiness. She seemed to enjoy her company.

'First, I did some shift work, waitressing and things like that. Then I temped in various offices. Until eventually I got a proper contract as a secretary in a law firm.'

'Did you like it?'

'I loved it. I wasn't paid much, but without a diploma I didn't have a choice. My father stopped supporting me. He was hopping mad when I quit my studies and went to live in the Big Apple. Studying just wasn't for me.' She laughed hoarsely.

'And why did you move to Washington?'

'An affiliate of the law firm I was working for needed an experienced assistant, and I applied for the position. After all those years I was happy to leave New York. The noise, the traffic. And everything was so expensive.' She took another sip of her coffee. 'I had good years here, too. Met a fantastic group of women who turned into very close friends. Samantha, Daisy – and my dear Nathalie, of course. They were like sisters to me. We did everything together, went out to parties, restaurants, concerts. Supported each other when one got sick or had problems in her relationship or marriage. Great gals.' Her face darkened. 'But now they're all gone.'

'I'm sorry,' Béatrice said.

In the bathroom, the washing machine was clanking so loudly that Béatrice feared it might bounce its way out of the door. Jacobina didn't seem bothered by the racket.

'Losing Nathalie last year was the hardest,' she remembered, flicking a few crumbs from her pyjama bottoms. 'That's when I realized I was totally on my own.'

'And you never got married yourself?' Béatrice wanted to know.

'Sure, I did,' Jacobina replied with a grin. 'But it only lasted a year. Can't tell you how happy I was when I got my maiden name back. I always liked my independence. But now . . . it's suffocating me.'

'I'll come see you more often.' Béatrice laid her hand gently on Jacobina's arm. For a few minutes, they just sat there. Then Jacobina lifted her head and gazed around the apartment. 'Well, I must say, everything's really tidy here now.'

*

'You look so beautiful,' Joaquín breathed in Béatrice's ear when he returned home in the late afternoon.

Béatrice was standing in front of the mirror, applying lip liner around the contours of her mouth.

Joaquín had put his hands around her hips from behind and was smiling at her reflection. 'Am I allowed to kiss this seductive mouth?' he joked, turning her around and pressing his lips against her dark red ones.

Béatrice freed herself and put the lid back on the lip liner. 'Not now, we have to go.'

'I'm suffering from acute love withdrawal,' he whispered, pulling her towards him again. His embrace was a little firmer now.

'Well, that's not my fault,' Béatrice commented matter-of-factly, turning her face to the mirror to check her make-up one last time. 'You were gone all day.'

'Against my will,' grumbled Joaquín, playing with a strand of her hair. 'I was thinking about you the whole time. Did you have a nice day with Laura?'

'She asked me to drop her off at Sarah's. And then I visited someone I know,' answered Béatrice. As soon as they had a quiet moment together, she would tell Joaquín about Jacobina.

He glanced at her lipstick, which lay at the edge of the sink. 'Dior, of course,' he said, with a sarcastic smile. 'Only the best.'

'Just let me enjoy my things.'

'Don't you think the ones at CVS are just as good?' he insisted. 'And they only cost ten bucks.'

Béatrice dropped the lipstick into her bag with a sigh. His exaggerated comment reminded her of her mother, who had reacted similarly when Béatrice was a young girl. The memory of her constricted, frugal upbringing was one that she didn't like to look back on. 'We can't afford that,' her mother had constantly admonished her, and this sentence still echoed in Béatrice's ears. It had shaped her life with long-lasting impact. She would make a better go of things, she had sworn to herself. And she had. She was independent and didn't have to deny herself anything. If she spent fifty dollars on a lipstick, she did it with the delight of a defiant child. Because now she *could* afford it.

'Are you guys ready?' Laura called impatiently from downstairs. 'Sarah's party has already started.'

It was shortly before seven p.m., and Laura had been pushing them to leave for over half an hour now, so that she could finally get to the birthday party for which Joaquín had postponed his long-planned weekend away with Béatrice.

Laura had squeezed herself into a clinging mini-dress and made herself up with heavy black eyeliner. Béatrice had thought there was no way Joaquín would let his daughter leave the house looking like that. But when he eventually came home from the office towards six, he only called out, 'New dress, sweetheart?' to Laura, and didn't seem to have any objection to her make-up.

'I can't wait to drop her off and finally have you all to myself,' he whispered to Béatrice, giving her a kiss on the cheek. Then he turned around and called out, 'Coming!' from the open bathroom door.

*

The small front garden was enclosed by a fence. A path led the visitors between spherical box trees and rose bushes to the veranda, which was decorated with countless fairy lights.

'Christmas is over,' Béatrice commented.

'Shh,' hissed Laura, shooting her a reprimanding glance.

As soon as the three of them approached the entrance, they heard a dog barking from inside. Mrs Parker, Sarah's mother, opened the door even before Laura had rung the bell. Loud laughter and a rhythmic pounding bass pushed its way outside.

'Laura!' cried the woman with a beaming smile, pulling the girl into an embrace with a warmth that seemed genuine. 'So lovely to see you. The others are already downstairs in the basement.'

Béatrice looked on in astonishment as Laura, who didn't

usually let anyone close to her, returned the hug. This girl was a closed book. Béatrice immediately felt inferior to the unfamiliar woman.

As soon as Laura had disappeared inside the house, Mrs Parker turned to Joaquín with the same warmth she had just shown Laura. 'Hi, Joaquín. Wow, it's been a while,' she said, her blue eyes sparkling as she greeted him with a kiss on the cheek.

Béatrice stood there, staring enviously at Mrs Parker's toned, muscular upper arms. The woman was in her mid-thirties at most and moved with the authority of a fitness trainer in front of a camera.

'You didn't come to our last parents' meeting. What are you up to these days?' Mrs Parker chatted on, throwing Béatrice a quick 'Hi', and showcasing her flexed arms with sweeping gestures.

Joaquín patiently answered her insistent questioning as Béatrice studied the colourful flower pots by the front door. Eventually, he stepped aside and introduced the two women.

'Your girlfriend, aha . . . I'm Anne,' said Mrs Parker, giving Béatrice a brief smile. Then she turned back to Joaquín. 'Now that you're here, I'm sure you have time for a glass of wine, don't you?'

Béatrice was about to shake her head and say something about their table reservation, for they were already late, but Joaquín spoke before she could. 'We certainly wouldn't say no!'

Anne beamed.

Béatrice gave Joaquín a gentle nudge with her elbow.

'Just five minutes,' he whispered with a wink.

They went into the house. There was something old-fashioned about the furnishings, which didn't match the first impression Béatrice had of Anne. Lace curtains, thick rugs and cumbersome armchairs topped with floral cushions. Ceramic ducks and carved wooden figures stood on side tables.

'What do you think of the new maths teacher, Joaquín?' asked Anne as she poured wine into three glasses. 'I think she's way too strict,' she added.

Béatrice was no longer listening. With the glass in her hand, she wandered around the living room, lost in thought, studying the numerous photos which hung from the walls in ornate frames. Anne with Sarah on the beach, Anne with Sarah in the garden, Sarah playing sports, Anne with a man – her husband? The wine tasted like cherry juice with alcohol, but Béatrice politely forced it down.

Every few minutes, she was dragged back to reality by Anne's throaty laugh. The floor beneath her vibrated from the loud music in the basement. Voices rang out from the kitchen, footsteps echoed on the stairs, a door was slammed shut.

Five minutes turned into twenty-five. Anne's warm nature, which Béatrice had envied her for not long before, now seemed feigned and excessive.

Every now and then, Béatrice tried to catch Joaquín's gaze, to remind him they needed to make a move. But in vain. He was deep in conversation, sitting next to Anne on the couch, and didn't even protest when she topped up his glass.

'Joaquín,' Béatrice interjected once she was no longer able to hold herself back, startled by how shrill her voice sounded.

Anne paused mid-sentence and stared over towards Béatrice in surprise, as though she had completely forgotten that there was anyone else in the room.

'We have to go, we're late,' urged Béatrice.

'Already?' trilled Anne, looking at Joaquín. 'I was hoping that you . . . I mean, the two of you, would stay for dinner.'

Béatrice looked at Joaquín pleadingly. This time he understood. He got up reluctantly, expressed his regret at not being able to stay, thanked Anne for the wine and apologized for their sudden departure. After a verbose goodbye, in which Joaquín had to promise Anne that they would catch up again soon, and for dinner, Béatrice and Joaquín were finally back in the car.

'My God, what a pushy woman,' groaned Béatrice as soon as she had closed the door behind her.

'Are you jealous or something?'

His tone was so smug. Clearly, he was flattered by the idea.

'Me? Not in the slightest.' Béatrice put on her seat belt. The metal tongue clicked into the holder. 'She pretty much ignored me, and so did you, come to that.'

'Oh, don't take all the small talk so seriously. She's the mother of Laura's best friend. Laura is always hanging out there and has dinner with them a lot, too. So it's not like I can be abrupt with her.' He started the engine.

'Sure,' muttered Béatrice, tossing her handbag onto the back seat. 'You always have an explanation for everything. I wanted to spend time with you this weekend but now I don't know why I even bothered to come here.' The disappointment she had suppressed the entire day was seething inside her. But there was something else too. And Joaquín had immediately sensed it. Yes, she was jealous of this toned, young woman. And, in particular, of what connected her and Joaquín: they were parents and part of a world Béatrice had no access to. A world that was all about school reports, picky eaters and sports camps, about responsibility and care. As soon as any parents struck up a conversation, they always had things to talk about, and it made Béatrice feel like an outsider. She hated the sympathetic looks when she was asked whether she had children too and said no. Was someone who didn't have any somehow of lesser value? It wasn't that she hadn't wanted any; the right moment or the right man just hadn't come.

'Let's have a nice dinner, shall we?' Joaquín put his hand on her leg.

Béatrice pushed it away. 'That's all you have to say?' One more conciliatory word and Béatrice knew she would explode.

But Joaquín's next words were far from conciliatory. 'If you took a little more interest in our current economic situation, then you'd know we're on the brink of a recession. And that's why I had to go into the office today, to rewrite my entire article and talk to Ben Bernanke about the hike in interest rates.'

Béatrice was reminded of the words of Monique, her friend from university and one of the few people back in Paris with whom she still stayed in touch: 'The things you love about this man are the very things you hate about him.' At the time, Béatrice had laughed. But now she understood what Monique had meant. Embarrassed, she pressed herself deeper into the seat and stared out of the window.

Joaquín fell silent too. They drove through the dark

streets. A few minutes later, they reached the small Tex-Mex restaurant with the blinking *Open* sign in the window: their usual port of call when they didn't want to eat at home. Béatrice wasn't a fan of tortillas with refried beans, but Joaquín believed people ate to be fed, not to be seen. And you could do that in a budget-friendly restaurant too.

Without exchanging a word, they sat down at one of the small tables next to the bar. Béatrice was about to grab the menu and choose a strong cocktail when Joaquín took her hand. He looked tired and old.

'I know things aren't so great between us at the moment,' he began, 'and that it's mostly my fault . . .'

A waiter approached and put two glasses of iced water and a basket of corn chips in front of them.

Joaquín let go of her hand and reached into the basket. 'But the thing is, I have a job that I can never leave by six, and a daughter who needs me,' he continued.

A flush crept up Béatrice's face. All of a sudden, her outburst and accusations seemed childish. She took a sip of water. It tasted of chlorine and was so cold it made her head pound. 'I'm sorry,' she said quietly.

'It's okay.' He took a drink too and, at last, smiled again. 'We'll work it out.'

8

Judith

Paris, October 1940

'I don't have a thing to wear! Nothing at all!' I called through my bedroom door, in the hope Mother would notice my bad mood, and fell back onto my bed. I couldn't remember the last time I'd been to the theatre. Over the past years, we barely had had a spare franc for nice things, like going to exhibitions, concerts or the theatre. I sat back up and took another look at the threadbare clothes hanging in my wardrobe. Patched skirts, far too long and too wide; old-fashioned blouses that had once been my mother's; shoes with worn-down heels. Christian, in his smart blazer, would be ashamed to be seen with me. I was nineteen years old and didn't possess one single beautiful piece of clothing. Feeling helpless, I covered my face with my hands and began to sob.

Then I felt my mother put her arm around my shoulders. 'Come now, my little lamb, you can't let a few old bits of clothing get you down.'

My breath caught in my throat, and I stopped crying. She hadn't spoken to me like that for what felt like an eternity.

I lowered my hands in surprise, and looked at her through the blur of my tears. A soft smile danced around her lips, and then I saw something swinging from her wrist. She stretched out her arm, and I recognized her thin, black shift dress. There was a time when I had seen her wear it often, but ever since her plaits had fallen to the floor, it had hung untouched in her wardrobe.

'Your father gave it to me a long time ago. I think it should fit you.'

I kissed her on her cheek, then jumped up from the bed, slipped into the dress and ran to the large mirror in the hallway. It was a bit loose around the hips, but otherwise perfect. Overjoyed, I flung my arms around my mother's neck and whispered, 'Thank you' into her ear. In truth, I was thanking her less for the dress, which she would never wear again in any case, and more for the fact that she had finally shown an interest in my life again, expressing a little of the maternal tenderness I had so missed and longed for. My beloved Maman that I had lost years ago was back – even for just a few moments. But I didn't tell her that. Instead, I told her about the man who had invited me tonight – Christian.

'Oh no, a *goy*,' she sighed and looked into my eyes, deep worry lines appearing on her forehead. 'Do not see him again. The Germans won't like this relationship.'

'But, Maman,' I insisted. 'We are just going to the theatre.'

She shook her head in disapproval. 'I'm warning you. This is a bad idea. Under normal circumstances, I would have been happy for you. But not any more. We're living in dangerous times. You never know who collaborates with the *Boches*. Things will get a lot worse for us, I'm telling you.'

I understood her; I was worried myself. But my connection with Christian had been so strong. So powerful. He was a good person, I could feel it. And my desire to get to know him better was stronger than my fear.

'Promise me to be careful, Judith,' Mother said, sensing she wouldn't be able to stop me from seeing him again.

'I promise,' I quickly assured her.

*

With his tall, straight shoulders, Christian towered above the crowd of chattering people. He wore a long trench coat, which made him look very sophisticated. His white shirt collar was held together with a knotted tie.

As he caught sight of me, his face brightened and he hobbled over. 'You look beautiful,' he said, bending over to greet me with a kiss on the cheek. This time I returned his greeting, touching, for a fragment of a second, his smoothly shaven skin, which carried the fresh scent of a cologne.

The theatre was completely sold out, the usher informed us as he checked our tickets. After the tense summer months, Parisians seemed to have taken back control of their lives.

Christian led me into the auditorium and to our seats, the best in the theatre. 'My parents have these seats for the entire season,' he said as he sank into the upholstered chair. 'But their many other social engagements rarely allow them to come.'

I could no longer hide my curiosity. 'What do your

parents do?' I asked, hurriedly sitting down and pressing my knees together.

'My father runs a large private bank. In the evenings, they're hopping from one cocktail party to the next. While my mother exchanges Parisian gossip with the wives, my father does business over cognac and cigars.' Christian shook his head and gave me a disarming smile. 'That kind of life isn't for me.'

He moved in a world that I knew only from books. A world that was galaxies apart from mine. And yet, despite that, fate had brought us together. Gazing at his gentle face, I noted how much I enjoyed his company. With him, life was buoyant; I felt light-hearted and happy. He was nothing like the superficial male students I had met at the Sorbonne before the war, back when there were still young men who weren't soldiers.

Christian's handicap didn't bother me in the slightest. When I had known him only by sight, in the library, I had felt sorry for him. His anonymous messages had bewildered me initially – but now, knowing his story, I was so impressed by him.

We were still gazing at one another. Then I remembered my mother's warning – *these are dangerous times* – and my heart sank. I looked away. How would he react if I told him I was Jewish? That Mother and I had red stamps now in our identity cards, singling us out from all the other French citizens? Maybe he wouldn't want to see me again. I trembled inside. And yet, I had to tell him soon. It was better to straighten this out right away. I didn't want to cause him – us – any trouble. I had to be prudent, just as I had promised Mother.

More and more people came streaming through the entrance and pushed their way past legs, feet and bags to their seats. A few rows behind us sat a group of Germans in uniform. They had female company, and were conversing loudly. Sitting so close to them made me nervous, and I wished I could hide myself away in an unseen corner. But once the lights went out and Michel Francini stepped onto the stage, I tried to forget them. With sharp humour, the comedian depicted everyday life in occupied Paris. The auditorium roared with laughter. Did the Germans behind us not understand they were being mocked?

*

After the performance, Christian suggested we get something to eat. I hesitated and looked at my watch. Of course, I wanted to have dinner with him. Maybe that would also be the occasion to reveal my heritage. But it was already late, the Metro didn't run that frequently in the evening, and many of the stations were closed.

'Please, Judith,' he said. 'At least for an appetizer.' As though he had read my thoughts, he added, 'You'll be back well before the curfew. My chauffeur will take you home.'

Before I could object any further, a black limousine appeared from around the corner and stopped in front of us. The driver jumped out, gave a hint of a bow and opened the door to the back seat. I stared in speechless amazement at the gleaming automobile. Christian gestured to me to get in. Ignoring my worries, I followed.

'This is the new Traction Avant by Citroën,' he explained, as though in passing, climbing in next to me on the seat and dragging in his lame leg. 'My father is obsessed with cars. Most of the French had to drive their luxury automobiles to the Vincennes Hippodrome and hand them over to the Germans. But Father somehow kept the Citroën and his Delage too.'

I nodded raptly. In the women's magazines that were laid out at the newsstand, these cars sometimes appeared in photographs behind famous actors. My parents had never owned a car. In awe, I stroked my hand across the dark leather seats as the vehicle roared through the city.

The bistro Chez Jérôme was brightly lit. In front of the door stood a blackboard displaying the austere menu of the day. Turnip soup, cabbage salad and lentil bake. A few tables had been laid outside, even though it was already much too cold to eat out in the open. Christian held the door for me, and as we stepped inside, an elderly waiter with a long, white apron came to greet us.

'Monsieur Christian, *bonsoir*! What a pleasure! I have a wonderful table for you. You'll be completely undisturbed.' He shook Christian's hand, greeted me too and then led us through the small, lively restaurant to a separate room. 'How is your father?' he asked, pulling the serviettes from the plates, unfolding them with a deft flick of his wrist, and handing them to us. 'We have a fabulous Montrachet, a 1930 vintage, highly recommended,' he continued, without waiting for an answer. Then he gave Christian a conspiratorial wink and asked, 'Which menu should I bring you?'

'The black one, of course,' answered Christian, also with a wink, as he pressed a folded 500-franc note into the head waiter's hand, who swiftly tucked it into his waistcoat pocket, thanked him profusely and disappeared to fetch the menus.

'The black one?' I asked, wrinkling my brow. 'Is that something special?'

Christian put his hand to his mouth and leaned across the table. 'It's the menu with the things that are only available on the black market,' he whispered. 'Many restaurants now have two menus, a good one and a miserable one. Or in other words, an expensive one and a cheap one.'

I laid the serviette on my lap and smoothed it out. 'I had no idea.' Immediately, I regretted my words. How naive and provincial I must have sounded to this elegant, upper-class young man.

'Who cares about all the new German laws and regulations.' Christian chuckled and tossed a packet of Gauloises onto the table. 'I want us to savour the best food our country has to offer – by hook or by crook.'

I stretched my hand out towards the cigarettes, but Christian got there first and held the packet gallantly towards me.

The waiter hastened back to our table, balancing in one hand a silver tray with two glasses of champagne, and holding in the other a black leather folio. 'With the compliments of our sommelier. On the house, of course.' He placed the glasses in front of us and pulled two menus out of the black folio. As I read through the dishes on offer, my eyes grew wide.

Christian seemed to be enjoying my astonished expression. 'So, what are you in the mood for? Ox shoulder with carrots in red wine sauce, or guinea fowl breast on fresh morels?'

My mouth began to water, my stomach rumbled heftily. Even in peacetime, I had never held a menu like this in my hands.

'And for dessert, we have to try the crêpes with hot apples and homemade chocolate ice cream,' Christian suggested, lighting himself a cigarette.

Feeling giddy, I lowered the menu. 'I'd like everything,' I said with a husky voice.

Christian nodded. 'Good, then we're in agreement.' He raised his glass with a celebratory flourish and took a long sip. 'How about we toast to us, to getting to know one another?' He held his glass out towards mine.

I clinked my glass against his but felt like a traitor – I had to tell him who I was, the truth about my family's heritage.

'I'm Jewish,' I blurted out. I did not feel any shame admitting it. On the contrary, I was proud of my roots, but still – the words sounded like a confession. My hands were trembling as I took a deep drag of my cigarette, waiting for Christian to react.

He looked at me with a bright smile. 'I have great respect and admiration for your people, especially given all the threats through history to your very survival.'

My heart swelled at his words. How special it was to find someone who made me even prouder to be a Jew. Mother would be pleased to know.

'What about your parents?' I enquired. 'Do they think like you? Would they let you see me if they knew about my religion?'

His face clouded over at once. 'Let's not worry about my parents right now,' he said evasively. 'They hardly show any interest in me or what I'm doing.'

I had expected a decisive 'of course they won't', but not this. Why were they so indifferent? But then, my mother rarely asked about my life either, even on her decent days. The sudden realization that Christian and I shared a similar pain, feeling neglected by our parents, brought me even closer to him.

Our waiter came back to the table and placed a large platter of fresh seafood, overflowing with oysters, langoustines and mussels, between us.

'What about *your* parents?' Christian returned the question. 'Would they accept you going out with a Christian man?'

I nodded confidently. 'My father left us long ago, I lost all contact with him. And my mother is not very observant. She goes to the temple on high holidays and celebrates our Jewish traditions, but otherwise is quite open-minded, just like me.' The warmth returned to his eyes. He reached over the table for my hand and squeezed it. 'I'm so glad you told me all this.'

Looking at the rare delicacies in front of me, my thoughts went back to Mother once again. While I was dining out like a queen, she was home alone, eating the remaining bit of the potato soup I had cooked yesterday.

'Most people have had very little to eat since the beginning of the occupation and can't afford the black market,' I couldn't refrain from saying.

'I know, Judith,' Christian replied. 'It is heartbreaking. My parents don't know, nor do they care, I suspect, but I've been raiding our pantry whenever I can and delivering food to poor families with small children.'

His parents didn't seem to be nice people, I thought to

myself, and frowned. They didn't care about anything but themselves. What would they say about *me*, if they met me one day? Again, I felt uneasy and out of place at this fancy restaurant that he used to frequent with them.

Christian noticed my tense expression and grabbed my hand. 'Stop worrying, Judith. Tonight, let's just enjoy all of this. Who knows for how much longer we'll be able to get away with it?'

I nodded and relaxed. He was right. It was too early to think about meeting his parents.

I watched Christian as he skilfully picked up an oyster shell from the platter, drizzled a little lemon juice onto it and slurped its contents down in one gulp. He glanced at the door and called the waiter who re-emerged at once. 'Hervé, would you mind bringing us a bottle of the 1930 Montrachet?'

'Certainly, monsieur.'

'Now eat, Judith,' Christian said with an inviting gesture, then an impish grin spread across his face. 'If we don't eat the oysters, the fat Germans will scoff them all instead. Would you prefer that?'

*

Every time I held a copy of Proust's *In the Shadow of Young Girls in Flower* in my hands, my heartbeat accelerated. I would flick dreamily through the pages, and imagine a small, folded note fluttering out. Not because I was expecting one, but because I loved the memory of the mysterious letters which had led to our first encounter. Since our dinner, Christian hadn't written any new notes. Instead, I received from him something even more beautiful: his undivided attention.

Most days, we met in one of the small cafes on the Place de la Sorbonne, between lectures or before I began my shift in the library. Almost as soon as I got up in the mornings, I longed for it to finally be midday, so that I could set off on my way to wherever we'd planned to meet. He was always there long before me; I could tell from the cigarette stubs in the ashtray, and the crumpled state of the newspaper which lay on his lap. The second I saw him, I was bursting with words and emotions. I would sit down, drop my bag on the floor and tell him everything that was swirling around in my mind, everything I had experienced since we had last seen one another.

We also discussed the current political situation and shared our anxiety, always making sure nobody was close by listening. Within a few days Christian became the only person I confided in.

When we were together, over cups of chicory coffee, I no longer feared the uniformed occupiers as much and my daily worries faded away. With Christian by my side, I simply felt safe and happy. I had forgotten what that was like.

We could talk for hours, laugh about the silliest of things, debate literature and other serious matters, or just sit quietly next to one another and read. When he spoke, he did it with a confidence and intimacy I had never come across in anyone else before. But he was also an attentive listener, showing me that, to him, I was the most important person in the world.

And he was so thoughtful! Recently, I had complained about the grassy taste of ersatz coffee. The very next day, when no one was nearby, he handed me a pound of real coffee. An entire pound! At home, Mother and I kept opening the bag and sticking our noses into it, breathing in the delicious aroma. We couldn't get enough of it.

However, it wasn't his parents' wealth that made him so alluring. Quite the opposite. I always felt uncomfortable when he bought me presents, ordered expensive wine in restaurants, or when his chauffeur drove me home in the black Traction Avant, holding the door open for me as if for a diva. I didn't need any of this. No, it wasn't that. Something else made me long to be around him: the absolutely irresistible blend of jadedness and curiosity, of intellect and empathy, of audacity and fear. The scintillating, adventurous world of ideas and thoughts that he had dreamed and read into life fascinated me. In his imperfection and solitude, to me he seemed complete. All I wanted was to be part of this world.

*

'Once the war is over and I'm through with my studies, I want to leave Paris and do something completely different,' he said one day, as we sat in the cafe and he stirred a little saccharine into his cup. 'Breed horses, make wine and write books, for example.'

I couldn't help but laugh. 'You? A future lawyer and heir to an impressive fortune? Aren't you expected to follow in your father's footsteps?'

Christian shook his head fiercely and threw me an indignant glance. 'My selfish, profit-hungry father is the last person whose footsteps I want to follow.'

Regretting my words, I became serious. His father was not only self-absorbed and indifferent, there clearly had to be other issues between them, too.

'Would you . . . would you go with me? Away from Paris, I mean,' asked Christian, not looking at me as he spoke. His fingers fidgeted around on the table, knocking against the coffee spoon, which fell to the floor with a clatter.

Before I knew it, it burst out of me: 'I would go anywhere with you.' When I realized what I had just said, a sharp pain shot through my chest. What a confession! And so soon. I looked down in embarrassment.

Christian squeezed my hand, bent forward, and softly pressed his lips on mine. His kiss was dizzying, fleeting. A kiss like a gentle breeze brushing against a dandelion, without the strength to scatter its seeds. But it was a kiss. A magical moment changing everything between us. How I had yearned for this to happen – and feared it at the same time.

I thought back to our first encounter, his trembling hand. We both had anticipated it from the beginning, this overwhelming feeling that was blossoming between us. Would we call it love someday?

Christian gently parted his lips. 'My lecture begins shortly,' he said. With clumsy movements, as if he was still shaken by what had just occurred, he stuffed books and cigarettes into his bag and got up. 'Will I see you tomorrow?'

I nodded and watched him limp towards the door. He waved at me, then stepped out onto the street.

*

At last! Six o'clock. My shift at the library was over, and I could go home. I had spent the entire afternoon thinking about Christian; about his question of whether I would go with him. He and I. Were we a couple now? A tingle ran down my spine.

The Boulevard Saint-Michel was shrouded by a dense blanket of fog. It got dark earlier now, and because the city was suffering from a chronic electricity shortage, our elegant avenues and boulevards were barely lit in the evenings. The street lamps glowered at the sides of the streets like sinister giants. Only a few cars still traversed the city at night, their headlamps covered with a dark blue fabric, in accordance with the new regulations. I had to walk slowly and carefully to make sure I didn't accidentally stumble over something or walk into a protruding wall. On one recent evening, it had been so dark that I'd even got lost.

I switched on my small torch and followed its faint beam as I walked along Rue Saint-Jacques. What had become of our magnificent Paris? *Ville Lumière*, city of light and passion. It was black and silent now, like a grieving widow.

Suddenly my torch flickered, then went out completely. I cursed, coming to a halt. I didn't have any spare batteries. In these dark days of autumn, all Parisians were reliant on their torches, and batteries could only be found on the black market.

I stuffed the useless object into my shoulder bag and stretched my arms out in front of me, stumbling through the streets. A few pedestrians crossed my path, the glow of their lights helping me to orientate myself. I wondered what Christian was doing right now and thought again about when his lips had touched mine.

Eventually I reached our building. I stepped through the entrance hall into a small courtyard and greeted Jeanne, our concierge, who was standing in front of her lodge. At her feet sat a basket full of kittens.

'Look at these poor creatures,' she said in a tired voice, bending down and lifting the basket. 'I just found them in the street. Ever since rationing started, people are abandoning their pets left, right and centre. It's a disgrace.' She approached me with the basket. 'Please, take one.'

Her imploring gaze fixed upon me, and I felt cornered. I took a step backwards and shook my head. 'I'm sorry, Jeanne . . . but I can't.'

'Please,' she whispered, stepping even closer. 'I don't know what to do with them. I can't bring myself to turn them out on the street.'

The kittens looked up at me attentively, as though they knew their fate hung in the balance.

'All right.' I gave in, moved by their big shiny eyes. 'I'll take the white one.'

'God bless you,' whispered Jeanne, as she grabbed the white kitten by the scruff of its neck and put it in my arms.

I nodded at the concierge and climbed up the dark stairwell to the fourth floor.

When I flipped on the light in our apartment, I saw Mother's bag lying in the hallway. She had arrived home before me again! Presuming that she'd gone to lie down, I opened the door to her room, the kitten still in my arms. And there she was. In the dim light from the hallway, I could see my mother's slender silhouette.

She sat up with a start. 'Where have you been?' she cried, promptly bursting into tears.

'What's the matter?' I asked timidly, sitting down next

to her on the bed. The kitten hopped out of my arms onto Mother's leg and began to purr softly.

Mother let out a sharp cry. 'What's that?'

'Don't be scared, Maman. It's just a cat. Jeanne asked me—'

Mother pushed the kitten away. 'You've taken in some stray animal even though we barely have anything to eat ourselves?' she interrupted. Her tone was cutting, but I could sense the panic concealed within it.

'I'm sorry,' I interjected and picked up the cat again. 'But isn't she sweet?'

'We've no room for pets,' Mother yelled, wiping her face with her sleeve. 'There's not even room for us here any more. It's over.'

'What do you mean?' I asked. 'A little thing like this doesn't eat much.' Seeing that the kitten was cowing in fright, I scratched its neck.

Mother balled her hands into fists and pounded them against her pillow. 'The school let me go,' she cried.

'Let you go?' I repeated. What was she talking about? On her good days, she was without a doubt the best teacher the school had ever had.

Mother slumped back down on the bed, sobbing relentlessly into her pillow. I set the kitten on the floor and stroked Mother's arm. 'Maybe it was a mistake,' I tried to console her, 'and next week everything will be back to normal.'

When her crying finally subsided, I passed her my handkerchief. She blew her nose numerous times and sat back up again.

'There's a new law,' she explained with a broken voice,

bunching up the handkerchief. 'Jews are no longer allowed to work in the public sector. And they are no longer allowed to teach.'

My shoulders sagged. 'What? Why? What have we done?' I tried to steady my breathing. 'Does that also mean I won't be able to work in the library any more? Or study?'

Mother shrugged. 'They'll tell you soon enough. Just like with me. I was completely unprepared.' She ran her fingers through her hair, sniffling. 'When I went to class this morning, the head came and pulled me out in front of all the children. He told me that he thought very highly of me and my work, but as the head of a public school, he has to follow the law. That he was sorry, and so on.' She buried her face in her hands and started crying again. 'What are we supposed to live off now?'

'Maman, don't worry,' I said, trying to sound confident, though fear was stirring in the pit of my stomach. 'I'm still earning, a little at least, and soon you'll find something else. You don't have to be a teacher.'

Mother paused and looked at me, her eyes flashing. 'If you think I'm going to work as a kitchen maid or scrub floors, you're wrong.' She pushed off the blanket and jumped to her feet. 'I've lost my employment, not my pride.' She stormed out of the bedroom and slammed the door behind her.

For a few minutes, I just sat there, then I pulled the kitten out from under the bed, where she had hidden herself away. Holding her in my arms, I followed Mother into the kitchen. She was standing at the sink with her back to me, rinsing a plate. I turned on the radio. Tino Rossi was singing his melancholic 'J'attendrai'. '*I will wait, day and night, for your return.*' What were *we* waiting for? I wondered. And what was awaiting us?

'Why don't we ask Madame Morin whether you can help out in her fur shop,' I suggested. 'I mean . . . just until you find something you like.'

'We still have some savings in the bank,' Mother replied, without commenting on my idea. Her voice was firm. 'Hardly enough for six months.' Her shoulders began to shake again. 'And then what?' She brought her hands back up to her face. 'Believe me, this is just the beginning. They hate us.' I looked at her pale, slender neck and felt helpless.

They hate us. I decided not to respond. Any word I said would only make her more agitated. The idea that, from now on, Mother would spend day after day inside our apartment, depressed, unsettled me. Thoughts of what she might do to herself. Thoughts of somehow losing her. No – I wouldn't go there.

I decided to send her out on errands every morning, to ensure she got some fresh air. And tomorrow, on my way to the Sorbonne, I would stop by to see Madame Morin and ask whether there might be any work for Mother in the sewing room. We would figure this out. We had to.

9

Béatrice

Washington, D.C, 2006

Béatrice often wasn't sure what she looked forward to most – leaving the stressful office life and her pompous boss behind her on Friday evenings, to spend two days recovering from it, or, on Monday mornings, exchanging her mostly unsatisfactory weekends as part-time girlfriend in McLean for her job in the international development arena.

Today, it was definitely the latter. As she placed her security badge against the small glass surface in the World Bank lobby at half past eight that morning, and a green light blinked, prompting the security guard to give her a friendly nod, she felt freed. Freed from having to share Joaquín's worries and responsibilities, freed from the claustrophobia of his house, with the 'must read' books that lay around everywhere, and freed from Laura's small but complicated teenage world.

Béatrice stepped cheerily into the lift, greeted a few colleagues with a smile and chatted to them about their weekends. On the eighth floor, she headed towards her office. Just as she was about to open the door, she saw

Veronica hurrying towards her from the other end of the corridor, her hair waving behind her. Béatrice gave her an encouraging smile. It wasn't even nine yet, and Michael clearly already had her rushing around.

But Veronica didn't return her smile. Instead she stopped, gesturing for Béatrice to come to her. As soon as she'd reached Veronica, the Brazilian woman pulled her into an empty office and closed the door.

'You have to see the boss right away. He's totally mad. Something must've happened. He got in really early this morning and keeps asking if you're here yet.'

Fear fluttered through Béatrice's stomach, triggering one of her irrational anxiety attacks. 'Did he say what it was about?' she whispered.

'No,' murmured Veronica, 'I have no idea. Just wanted to warn you.' She opened the door, poked her head out and looked to the left and right. 'He's in his office,' she said quietly, before stepping out.

Béatrice ran her hand nervously through her hair and unbuttoned her coat. Then she went to Michael's office. After a hesitant knock, she stepped in. Michael whipped around in his revolving chair and looked her up and down.

'Have you read the paper?' he asked, his voice filled with contempt.

'Not yet,' she replied, gripping her handbag tightly. She knew that this confession would immediately unleash a storm of outrage from her boss. Then she saw the *Washington Post* lying open on his desk. Daniel Lustiger, she remembered, suddenly feeling hot, as the journalist's deep, vibrating voice and the clicking of his keyboard flooded her memory.

'I'd fire you on the spot if I could,' said Michael, pushing the newspaper across the table. 'But in this crazy bureaucracy, even that takes an eternity.'

Fire me? Béatrice blanched. Terror coursed through her veins. She picked up the paper and sank down on the chair in front of the desk. There it was, in large threatening letters: World Bank falsifies numbers and squanders millions. She swallowed and read on. Haiti project – a prime example of bureaucratic mismanagement. The article stretched across the entire page. In the centre was a large photo showing children of colour in school uniforms. *An entire page!* Adrenaline pumped through her body. Her scalp prickled.

Michael leaned across the desk and wrenched the paper from her hands. Then he stood up, came right over to her, stretched the paper out in front of him and read slowly and loudly: 'Béatrice Duvier, a spokesperson for the World Bank, wasn't able to give any indication of how the number of pupils currently receiving an education in Haiti with the World Bank's support has been calculated. But this sloppy work by the press department is only one example of the fundamental mismanagement in the Washington-based development organization.' He broke off and looked at her.

Béatrice sat there, appalled, fear clawing at her throat.

'This is scandalous, Béatrice. Absolutely scan-da-lous!' he shouted, before reading on. 'The Partnership for Global Development, PGD, an NGO based in London, has gained access to internal and confidential World Bank documents.' He snorted. 'These show that the actual number of school pupils in Haiti lies far below the bank's expectations. According to the PGD, the numbers were massaged, in collusion with Haiti's education minister, in order not to endanger the approval of further credits and the World Bank's reputation.' He threw the newspaper onto the desk. 'Fucking hell!'

Béatrice, paralysed, stared at Michael's protruding belly, so large it made his white shirt strain at the buttons. He pulled out a handkerchief and dabbed his glistening forehead. 'Do you have any idea of the mess you've gotten us into?' he snapped.

'*Me?* I've never had anything to do with the PGD.'

'So where else would they have got the documents from? I mean, you knew about it.'

She shook her head adamantly. 'No, I didn't!'

'And why didn't you tell me about Daniel's call?' Michael cleared his throat and swallowed heavily. 'I know him well, I could have prevented all of this shit.' He flopped back into his chair, his face red. 'Sloppy press department, that's what the asshole wrote. Fuck!' His fist banged down on the table. 'You get hoodwinked by a journalist and don't say a word to me. And now I have to take the rap for it.'

'I didn't get hoodwinked, Michael,' Béatrice replied, her voice shrill with fear as she desperately tried to recall the details of her conversation with Lustiger. 'All I did was explain what he already knew.'

'You could have prevented this article from coming out,' he responded curtly. 'Next month, an international donor conference is taking place here, to discuss further financial aid for Haiti. Ministers from twelve European countries have confirmed their attendance. After this article, it's going to be a complete catastrophe.'

'I also offered Lustiger an interview with Alexander,' Béatrice continued. 'But he refused.'

'Of course he did,' yelled Michael. 'Because what he wanted was some idiot like you to give him the exact quote he needed for his shitty story. And instead of switching on your brain, talking to me first and then calling him back, you added oil to the fire.' He slapped the palm of his hand against his forehead. 'How can anyone be so stupid! So unprofessional.'

She straightened up and looked at him. 'I didn't say it like that. He completely misquoted me.'

'Oh really?'

Béatrice could clearly hear the cynical undertone in his voice. 'So, I'm assuming you'll be able to prove that. I trust you recorded the conversation, like we discussed.' Michael had provided the press team with recording devices and instructed them to record conversations with major media outlets. This had helped them in the past to have inaccurate quotations corrected and to clear up misunderstandings.

Béatrice lowered her gaze. 'No, I didn't. It all happened too quickly.'

Her boss's mouth contorted into a grimace, revealing his yellow teeth. 'Once again you completely failed, Béatrice Duvier. But this time you've put our entire team in a miserable position. Not to mention how the bank looks publicly now.' He tapped his pen against the desk in a staccato beat. 'I have an emergency meeting with the vice president and the senior managers in twenty minutes. This is going to have severe consequences for you.'

'Michael,' began Béatrice, '*you* were the one who wanted the number in the title. I pointed out that—'

Michael didn't let her finish. 'Excuse me? So now it's

my fault? If you'd told me even once that there was any doubt about the number, we would have changed it. But I was relying on you,' he hissed.

'I *did* tell you,' Béatrice defended herself, 'and in the original release I didn't even mention these numbers. But that wasn't good enough for you.'

Michael waved his hand. 'The only thing that matters now is what's written here in the paper in black and white. And that's *your* fault! Now get out of my sight, before I get really angry.'

Béatrice fell silent. Then she grabbed her handbag and fled his room. She rushed off to her office and sat at her desk. Her body was shaking. How could this have happened? What was the goal of this NGO? And who had passed on internal bank documents? Had the numbers really been falsified? And what would happen to her now? She was entirely responsible for the 'sloppy press department'. The thought that the bank's whole senior management team was now reading her name in the *Washington Post* made her face run red with shame. As she realized the full extent of the unpleasant implications this could hold for her, an undefined, dark fear overcame her.

Béatrice picked up the telephone and dialled Joaquín's number. He answered with a curt 'Yes?'

'Why didn't you tell me about Lustiger's story?' asked Béatrice, without a word of greeting.

'Whose?'

'This awful article that I'm misquoted in. About the falsified numbers.' She was so full of despair and rage that she could barely formulate her sentences.

'What are you talking about?'

'You know very well.'

'Start at the beginning, honey. What's happened?'

Did he really have no idea? Had Lustiger's article not been discussed at his editorial meeting?

Béatrice hastily told him everything. He interrupted several times, whenever she spoke too quickly and he lost the context.

'I'm the economics editor. Every department has their own editorial meeting. I've got no idea what Lustiger wrote.'

'What should I do now?' cried Béatrice.

'Calm down. Don't let anyone see it's bothering you,' he advised her, clearly trying to stay positive. 'Get some fresh air and a coffee. In a few days' time, it'll be water under the bridge. You know yourself that nothing ever turns out as bad as you think. Hon, I have to get to a meeting now. If you'd like, we can talk it over properly this evening, okay?'

He never had time for her. Everything else was always more important. Béatrice slammed the telephone down angrily. Then she buttoned up her jacket, which she still hadn't taken off, picked up her bag and did exactly what Joaquín had recommended.

*

She grabbed a coffee at the Starbucks on 18th Street, sat down by the window and thought about how she could save herself from the uncomfortable situation Daniel Lustiger had catapulted her into. One thing was clear: Michael would never forgive her, and he would take every possible opportunity to remind her of it.

Perhaps Joaquín was right, she thought. Perhaps all she could do was wait it out and hope it would swiftly be forgotten. Perhaps a new article would soon criticize the bank's work in the Sudan, in South Africa or Peru, and no one would mention Haiti any more. That's how it was in the press business: yesterday's news was yesterday's news. Besides, Cecil would soon be announcing her promotion, and Michael would finally be a thing of the past.

When she got back, a yellow post-it note was stuck to her office door. *Boss wants to see you.* V. Béatrice screwed it up and tossed it in her bag.

She entered her office, threw her coat and handbag on a chair and was just about to go to see Michael when her telephone rang. She glanced at the display. Her mother, from Paris. Unable to bring herself to reject the call, she answered. Her mother sounded tired and worn down. Ever since she had taken early retirement five years ago, she had little contact with friends and acquaintances and spent most of her time alone in her one-bedroom apartment in Rue Dareau. Béatrice sent her money every month so that she could live more comfortably; her pension was barely enough to cover the rent.

Her mother reported that she had fallen in the stairwell and cut open her knee. It was very painful to walk, and she could only just make it to the grocery shops in the building next door.

Béatrice was overcome with guilt. She felt bad that she lived so far away, that she only saw her mother rarely and couldn't be of help to her now. She tried to calm her down and promised to call more often. 'Should I speak with your doctor? I can try to take a few days off and fly over,' she proposed.

'Don't worry, *ma chérie*, everything will be fine,' answered her mother. From her voice, Béatrice could tell that she was making an effort to sound cheerful. 'You have an important job with lots of responsibility. I'm just keeping you from your work.'

Béatrice swallowed. She longed to confide in her mother and tell her what had happened just now. But she couldn't. Her mother would only worry more and make all kinds of impractical suggestions.

'I'm so proud of you,' gushed her mother as they said goodbye. 'Of what you've become!'

If only she knew! After Béatrice had hung up, she went to see Michael, her gaze lowered.

'About time too,' he called out brusquely as she stepped in. He was sitting in front of his computer, his glasses pushed down low on his nose. His suit jacket hung over a chair. 'I've spoken to the senior management team,' he said, crossing his arms over his chest.

Béatrice stood there expectantly.

'The phones are ringing off the hook. We've already had over a hundred and fifty interview requests regarding Lustiger's story. In a few hours' time, the president's office will issue a statement and take a stance on all of this.' Every few seconds, a pinging tone sounded out from Michael's computer, announcing the arrival of a new email. 'It's a complete nightmare.' He ground his teeth and frowned at her.

Béatrice said nothing. Her arms hanging by her sides, she stood in front of his desk and barely dared to move.

Ping, came the sound from his computer.

'The vice president is going to launch an investigation to find out who passed on the information,' Michael continued, scratching his ear. 'That will take a few months. In the meantime, you are no longer allowed to respond to phone calls from journalists. Ricardo will take on your press work. I'll give you some other tasks. The archive needs to be organized, there are reports to be corrected and press lists to be updated.'

Béatrice struggled for air. The scumbag wanted to send her into the archive to tidy up? 'You can't be serious.'

Michael stroked his chin. 'I sure am. At least you won't be able to cause any major damage there. Your work trips to Haiti and the Dominican Republic are obviously cancelled. Patricia will attend the conferences on your behalf.'

'But . . .' He couldn't just shunt her off like this!

Another loud *ping* from the computer.

'No buts. Veronica will explain what you have to do.' Michael's expression hardened further still. 'And when it comes to Lustiger's comment about the sloppy press department – you'll pay for that, mademoiselle.'

His telephone rang, and he signalled to Béatrice with an angry wave to leave the room.

*

Veronica unlocked the door and flipped on the light switch. A dim ceiling light came on with a flicker, revealing the large, cold room which was located next to the lifts. Through the thin walls, Béatrice could hear the rushing sound and the constant opening and closing of the doors.

She looked around her. The walls were cracked, the carpet worn. Somebody had pushed an old photocopier into the centre of the room, and leaning against it was a discarded CRT monitor. On the shelves, which stretched across two long walls and up to the ceiling, were piles of folders and books with dusty covers, cardboard tubes, empty CD covers and video cassettes. The archive bore as little resemblance to an archive as Murray Park did to a park.

Béatrice sighed. 'And what am I supposed to be doing in this junk room?'

Veronica went over to one of the shelves and pointed at a row of files. 'The participant lists from the most recent development conferences are in there. You have to go through all of them and make electronic copies.'

'What?' Béatrice rolled her eyes.

'And the material in the other files has to be sorted through and arranged chronologically.' Veronica raised an eyebrow and looked around. 'Well, and while you're at it, you might as well have a proper tidy up. It looks really bad down here.'

She pressed the key into Béatrice's hand. 'This is yours now. Going through all this paperwork – it's sure to take weeks.'

Béatrice groaned. The idea of having to spend the near future in this room filled her with embarrassment, rage and indignation. She hadn't even done anything wrong! She had merely supplied a quote that wasn't exactly ideal. A slip like that could happen to even the most experienced of press officers. Making it into an international crisis and locking her away down here was completely unjustified.

Veronica gave her a friendly pat on the shoulder. 'Cheer up.' She smiled. 'I'll bring you a coffee from time to time.'

Once Veronica was gone, Béatrice closed the door and sat down on the chair next to the old CRT monitor. She couldn't let this get her down; she had to speak to Cecil as quickly as possible to find out how long it would take for the selection committee to announce their decision. She pulled her Blackberry out of her handbag and dialled his number.

'Cecil Hansen's office,' announced a clipped female voice.

Béatrice paused. She had dialled Cecil's direct number; normally he either answered it himself, or let it go to voicemail.

'This is Béatrice Duvier. I'd like to speak to Cecil, please.'

'Mr Hanson is on duty travel,' replied the woman.

'Ah . . . And when is he back?'

'In a week, but then the donor conference for Haiti will be almost underway, and he'll barely be in the office,' said the woman.

At the mention of Haiti, Béatrice recoiled. She had to talk to him as soon as possible and explain the circumstances behind Lustiger's horrendous article. She thanked his office assistant and ended the call. Then she pulled one of the old files off the shelf and opened it.

*

'What a surprise,' exclaimed Jacobina as she opened the door. She was wearing a black tracksuit made of shiny fabric, with the zip pulled right up to her neck, and was clutching her walking stick in her right hand. 'I didn't expect you at all today.'

'Just wanted to say hi,' Béatrice replied with a smile, walking through the door. She noticed at once that something wasn't right. Jacobina's facial expression looked different to usual. Her eyes were swollen, and red blotches covered her cheeks.

'Are you okay?' asked Béatrice, worried.

Jacobina collapsed on the sofa and threw her stick on the floor. 'Nothing is okay,' she replied, rubbing her hand across her belly. Her face was contorted with pain.

Béatrice knelt down next to her. 'Oh my God, what happened?'

The old woman pressed her lips into a narrow line and stared at her toes.

'I just found out I have cancer,' she said then.

As was always the case when she heard bad news, for a moment or two Béatrice was unsure how to react. She stroked Jacobina's hand, which rested on the arm of the sofa. Her skin felt rough and chapped.

'For months now, I've been getting pains in my belly and the small of my back,' said Jacobina tonelessly. 'At first, I thought it was my arthritis, then I suspected a bladder infection or something. Last week I went to the doctor, and today he told me what's wrong.'

She coughed, and it sounded like a bark. 'Cancer. Ovarian cancer. My whole life long, these things were good for nothing. And now they're chasing me to the grave.'

Béatrice straightened up and sat so close to Jacobina that their legs were lightly touching. 'Slow down, Jacobina, and take me through it. What treatment options did the doctor suggest? Will you have chemo?'

'No idea,' answered the old woman, tugging at a loose thread that hung from the sleeve of her tracksuit top. 'I have to do a few tests first. Then they're going to operate.' Her eyes glazed over, her eyelids fluttered. She buried her head in her hands and let out a loud sob.

Béatrice put her arm around Jacobina's shoulders and hugged her. 'Everything will be okay,' she said gently, knowing full well that there was no way this empty phrase would calm Jacobina down. 'Modern medicine has beaten cancer many times.'

Jacobina didn't answer. Her shoulders quaked.

'I'll make us a cup of tea,' said Béatrice, going over to the kitchenette and putting water on to boil.

A few moments later, Jacobina straightened up and wiped the tears from her eyes. 'Were you on your way to the theatre or something? Why are you all dolled up?' she asked, sniffling, as Béatrice handed her a cup of chamomile tea.

Béatrice stroked her hand over her black and white dress in embarrassment. 'Oh . . . I came straight from the office.' She sipped her tea. 'I was – how shall I put it? – suspended from my usual work today and banished to the archives.' In order to take Jacobina's mind off things, she told her about the article and the tragedy it had unleashed. 'Enough now about all this bad news,' she finished up. 'We'll get through this, one way or another.'

Jacobina had been listening intently, staring down at the floor. All of a sudden, she looked Béatrice directly in the eyes. 'There's something else I have to tell you,' she said hesitantly. 'Something that's bothering me much more than my cancer.' Her voice was gravelly. She ripped the thread off her sleeve. 'Many years ago, I made a promise to my father. On his deathbed . . .' Jacobina fell silent and bit her lip. 'A promise that I haven't kept.'

She paused again. Béatrice could feel the intense effort it was taking for Jacobina to talk about this. She touched her arm compassionately.

'At the beginning, I was reluctant. For a long time, my father and I hadn't been on good terms,' Jacobina went on. 'But even later, after my hard feelings had passed and I understood his pain, I continued to put it off. I always thought I'd still have plenty of time.' She reached for her cup and took a few sips. 'Until this morning, when I realized I didn't. My time has run out.'

Béatrice opened her mouth to say something reassuring. That Jacobina shouldn't assume the worst, that they had to wait and see, that she was sure to have many more years left to live.

But Jacobina lifted her hand like a crossing guard with a STOP sign. 'Don't say anything, Béatrice. We don't know what will happen. I'm approaching seventy – and am ready to go. What's the point of staying in this dump for another ten, fifteen years and keeping my head above water with charity handouts? That's no life.' A shadow descended over her face. 'But whatever happens . . . I have to keep my promise.'

Béatrice had never heard Jacobina speak with such insistence.

'I've been feeling guilty about it for years. Day and night, my ageing father haunts my mind, with the memory of what he asked me back then. It's like a curse.' Jacobina closed her eyes, as though she were trying to summon the image of her father into her mind. 'It was 1982. In Montréal. Back then I must have been about the same age as you are now, or slightly older.'

'What did you promise him?' asked Béatrice.

Jacobina slowly opened her eyes. 'He wanted me to find my half-sister Judith. She lived with her mother in Paris. In the confusion of the war, he lost contact with her.' Jacobina swallowed. 'They never saw each other again.'

She spread out her fingers and studied her cracked nails. 'I never met Judith. I didn't even know she existed. He only told me about her just before he died.' With a groan, she heaved herself into a different sitting position. Then she took Béatrice's hand and looked into her eyes. 'When you told me that you're from Paris, it felt like it was a sign! You were sent from heaven, or by whatever it is that guides our fate. I was so stunned.' She gave a dry cough. 'Do you think you can help me find Judith? I can't do it alone.'

'Me?' Béatrice looked at her in astonishment. 'How?'

Jacobina shrugged. 'We have to start somewhere. There's a lot on the internet, but I don't know my way around all this modern technology. I don't even have a computer.'

Béatrice felt a surge of emotion. She had no idea where to start such a search, but the challenge sounded inspiring. This was something that Jacobina needed much more than a clean apartment or fresh linens. By helping Jacobina find her half-sister, Béatrice could heal this woman's soul and bring her the peace of mind that had eluded her ever since she had made that promise over twenty years ago.

'I'll bring my laptop next time and we'll get started right away,' she said. 'How does that sound?'

Jacobina smiled. 'Thank you, Béatrice.' Her gaze wandered over to the window. 'You know, I've failed a few times in my life. I quit my studies, I didn't save any money or build a huge career. But I must keep this promise.'

*

After three days in the archive, Béatrice understood the extent of the mess she was dealing with. It could take months to set this room back to its original state – if, in fact, it had ever been organized in the first place.

Nonetheless, she tried to carry out the task as efficiently as possible, and only allowed herself to look at her laptop once every quarter of an hour, to stay informed on the events in her department. She noticed that she was receiving fewer emails than usual. Was it a quiet week, or had Michael struck her name off the distribution lists? Then she realized that she was no longer being invited to the team meetings and status report discussions. And when she ran into her colleagues in the corridor, they didn't stop to chat like they usually did, but kept walking past her with just a brief greeting.

Eventually, Béatrice understood – and the realization was as simplistic as it was shattering: Michael had sidelined her. He had banished her to this dusty archive to keep her out of the way. She felt despondent and completely humiliated.

Yet, what worried her far more was the fact that Cecil hadn't come back to her. He hadn't responded to any of her emails, in which she'd asked to have a quick chat.

Perhaps he was travelling in a country where his Blackberry didn't work. In Mongolia, for example, or Russia, or Ghana. But that was nonsense. He must just be too busy.

Béatrice walked up and down the cool room, preoccupied and jittery, pulling out brochures and books from the shelves, only to put them back elsewhere. Then she called Cecil's assistant again, but the woman was unwilling to give her any more details. He would get in touch once he was back, she said, adding in a slightly accusatory undertone that she'd already explained this on the last call.

A day in the archive without meetings and deadlines was wearing and oppressive. The time simply refused to pass. But frustration wouldn't help, Béatrice told herself again and again. Until eventually she believed it.

To distract herself, she decided to start the research into Jacobina's mysterious half-sister.

'I'm so proud of you, Ms World Banker.' That had been Lena's commentary when Béatrice told her she would now be looking in on Jacobina regularly. 'I knew you'd be a wonderful addition to our team,' she'd added, giving her back her blazer.

Jacobina wasn't asking for much. A bit of attention, a few biscuits and another pair of eyes on the hunt for her half-sister Judith, who she wouldn't be able to track down alone. It made Béatrice happy knowing she could help this lonely lady. A feeling that was almost stronger than her frustration at being trapped in the archive.

She flipped open her laptop and tried to remember what Jacobina had told her about Judith during her last visit. There wasn't much to go on. Judith had been born in Paris in 1921 or 1922. When she was eleven years old – or perhaps even twelve, or thirteen, Jacobina wasn't sure – her parents had divorced. Lica Grunberg returned to his Romanian homeland, while Judith stayed in Paris with her mother, Claire Goldemberg. During the first year, Lica had visited his daughter. After that they wrote, until the letters became shorter and eventually petered out entirely. And then came the war, and with it the brutal genocide of six million Jews by the Nazis.

Had Judith survived the Holocaust? If she had, was she still alive now? She had to be well over eighty. And where could she be? Still in France? Béatrice typed 'Judith Goldemberg' into the search engine. She found a chemistry lab worker in Tel Aviv, a fashion boutique in New York and a horticulturalist Justin Goldemberg in Fort Worth, Texas. She tried 'Judith Grunberg'. But this name didn't seem to exist, at least not on the internet. There was a Judith Greenberg, a Judy Grunberg, and eventually Béatrice found a Dr Judith Grünberg, who had written a history of early Palaeolithic archaeological finds.

Béatrice opened the *Pages Blanches*, the online version of the French telephone book. There was no Judith either, only a Maryse Goldenberg. But that didn't mean anything, because perhaps Judith hadn't made her telephone number public.

Béatrice closed the laptop. She wouldn't make any progress like this. Then she remembered the Washington Holocaust Museum. It wasn't only a historical memorial, movingly documenting the extermination of the Jews under Nazi rule, but also housed an extensive database with the names of Jews who had been deported to concentration camps. The museum was just a short walk from her office.

Béatrice glanced at her watch: a quarter past two. She hadn't taken a lunch break yet, and no one would notice she was gone. She would make up the borrowed hours tomorrow.

10

Judith

Paris, November 1940

Even when they weren't in uniform, I could immediately recognize them. Their strides were longer than ours, their shoulders broader. Everything about them exuded certainty of victory. They marched on their robust legs through the streets, carrying the *Deutsche Wegleiter*, a German-language city guide. Sometimes they browsed through the book stands of the *bouqinistes* on the Quai du Louvre, photographed the Seine and bought postcards, as if they were normal tourists. They tried to speak French, but it sounded harsh and throaty. Yes, the Germans had conquered our city and our country. They rode first class in the Metro and drank champagne in the best restaurants. But Paris would never belong to them; they would never become natives. Of this I was certain.

Whenever a German soldier came towards me, I made it clear through my body language that he wasn't welcome here. I would never respond to his greeting or smile. I would simply ignore him, stare straight ahead or quickly cross the street. Recently, one had offered me his seat on the bus. 'Mademoiselle,' he called in a friendly tone, getting up from his place. I turned around and acted as though I hadn't even noticed him.

When I passed them on the street, they weren't pushy and dictatorial, as I had first feared, but reserved and – one could almost say – polite. But as hard as they tried to conquer not only the architecture but also the soul of this city, they would never succeed.

A few weeks before, the first frost had arrived, autumn giving way to a bitter winter. There was very little coal available, so we had to be frugal and heated the kitchen only once a day. We kept the door firmly closed, and as soon as it got dark, hung a blanket over the window. That was now mandatory, due to the possibility of air raids, but it also prevented precious warmth from escaping outside.

When I was at home, I constantly wore the thick, grey woollen coat, the one with the big white buttons that mother had given me for my sixteenth birthday. Sometimes, I even slept in it. It felt scratchy around my neck, making me itch, but at least it kept me reasonably warm.

In the evenings, Mother and I tucked hot aluminium bottles into our beds, in the hope of falling asleep before the water had cooled. The kitten that Jeanne had given me slept in with me. We hardly had anything to feed her with; often I could only give her oat gruel, and she wasn't particularly fond of that. She had quickly won my heart, and even Mother now seemed happy to have the company during the day. We had named the kitten Lily.

When I felt Lily's furry little body breathing soundlessly next to me at night, I was no longer afraid. She helped me to believe that, someday, everything would be okay again.

*

This morning I woke up earlier than usual and ran my hand over the blanket. It felt stiff and cold, and every time I exhaled, thin swathes of breath rose up into the air.

It took a great deal of effort to get up. Mother was still asleep, the apartment silent. I wiped the sleep from my eyes with my numb fingers, pulled the woollen coat more tightly around my hips and padded out into the kitchen to light the stove and set water on to boil.

Our coal provisions had almost run out, and even though we had a coupon for our monthly ration, there was little prospect of renewed supplies. I rubbed my hands up and down my arms, shivering. How I hated this biting cold! It had penetrated my life, silently and deeply. At night it robbed me of my sleep, and in the day, my wits. It was worse than hunger. Hunger I could numb with cigarettes and chicory coffee. And we always found something to eat, even if it was only stale bread, potatoes or turnips. But the cold we were powerless against. I feared it more than I feared the Germans.

I pulled the blanket down off the kitchen window and studied the white ice crystals on the glass, which the frost had stitched together into a surreal, dream-like landscape. The kettle began to whistle and my energy gradually returned. I switched on the radio. On Radio Paris, which had become the German occupiers' propaganda channel, a carefree Maurice Chevalier trilled a silly song about a baby's dummy.

*

After my lecture, I made my way to the 6th arrondissement. Christian and I had made plans to meet in the Café de Flore. The Sorbonne was poorly heated, and cafes had become the only places where, as well as being able to chat undisturbed, we could read and work without freezing.

As I walked along the Boulevard Saint-Germain, I saw that the Belle Époque had been repurposed as a restaurant for German officers. It was now adorned with large swastika flags and the sign: *Entry strictly forbidden for civilians*. I quickly walked on.

When I entered the Flore, Christian was already there, as always. I sat down with him at the table, eyeing a coffee pot and his half-full cup. Three cigarette butts lay in the ashtray, which meant he had probably been waiting for me for at least an hour. Christian beamed at me, and I immediately forgot the cold and my empty stomach. He took my icy hand, squeezed it and didn't let it go. We looked at each other. Yes, I would follow him anywhere.

'Let's watch a movie,' he suggested, pulling me out of my reverie.

A movie – what a sweet idea! Ever since I'd told Christian that Mother had lost her job, that we were living off our savings and my meagre library salary, he had been trying to help us out with thoughtful gestures. He brought me bread, chocolate and candles, wrapped in thick newspaper, or he smuggled a few packages of lentils with a pound of real butter, tucked inside a woollen scarf, into my bag. He had wanted to bring us more when he was out with his driver on their weekly tours, delivering food supplies to families in need. But when I told Mother about his offer, she proudly refused. 'We'll get by just fine without any donations.'

And now he was surprising me with a trip to the cinema. I hadn't watched a film in months.

'They started showing *Monsieur Hector* yesterday, the new Fernandel film,' explained Christian. 'A kind of mistaken identity comedy.'

'Where is it showing?' I asked, while finishing Christian's half-full cup. 'In the Grand Rex?'

'No,' he replied, tossing a few coins on the table. 'The Rex is now a military cinema for the Wehrmacht, only showing German tearjerkers. It's on at the Panthéon and starts in ten minutes. Let's go!'

We left the Flore, and almost as soon as we were standing outside on the boulevard, the black Traction Avant glided up.

'Unbelievable!' I blurted out. 'He always knows when you need him.'

'Years of training.' Christian chuckled and greeted his driver, who had swiftly jumped out to open the door for us.

*

The cinema was full to bursting, but barely heated. I was astounded at the number of Parisians who evidently felt the longing to escape the humdrum routine of an ordinary Wednesday afternoon and immerse themselves for eighty minutes in the world of the comedian Fernandel.

We sat down, keeping our coats on, in the last two adjacent seats. Sixth row on the left. A few moments later, the auditorium darkened. War updates were shown first. Marshal Pétain appeared on the screen and gave a blazing speech to the French people.

A latecomer sat down on the seat right in front of me.

'I can't see anything any more,' I whispered, craning my neck to the left and right.

Christian leaned across and put his arm around me. 'I promise you haven't missed anything so far,' he said, touching my neck. As I felt his fingertips on my skin, I trembled. My heart jumped, my mouth went dry. Christian kissed my cheek, then turned my head gently towards his and touched his lips against mine.

'To all those who are waiting for the true spirit of France to be restored, I say that above all else, this lies in our hands . . .' called Marshal Pétain from the cinema screen.

'I love you, Judith,' whispered Christian.

His words pierced me like a sweet arrow. I wanted to cry and smile all at once. Then he kissed me. His mouth was soft and delicious. Strange and yet so familiar. I was afraid of making a wrong movement, of destroying this blissful moment, and froze beneath his lips as though I had turned to stone.

'I love you, my angel,' he repeated. 'And I will always love you.'

'Keep your faith in eternal France,' cried Pétain. The entire auditorium began to cheer hysterically, and I heard a few onlookers take up 'Maréchal, nous voilà', the unofficial hymn of the non-occupied part of France.

'I love you too,' I said back into the darkness. Only now did I find the courage to open my lips and return Christian's kiss. His mouth tasted of coffee and tobacco, but to me, more than anything it tasted of longing and love. A feeling of happiness I had never known before streamed through my body. This kiss was so much more than the erotic adventure of a nineteen-year-old literature student. It opened a secret door to a new life, where previously there had only been a wall. And while, on the screen above us,

Fernandel, with his horsey face and racy little song, sweet-talked the chambermaid of a luxury hotel, Christian and I gave in to our feelings, exploring this new, burning land of our love; one I never wanted to leave again.

Paris, December 1940

Mother pulled and tugged at the blanket which we hung over the kitchen window every evening until even the narrow crack in the lower right-hand corner was covered. With a celebratory look on her face she went over to the cabinet, took out our copper-coloured tube radio and placed it on the table. I was standing at the sink, washing the dishes.

'Is it time already?' I asked, reaching for a towel.

The radio emitted a loud whistling and rushing sound. Mother nodded and concentrated on finding the channel, slowly turning the large silver dial. All of a sudden, the static stopped, and I recognized the drumbeats. Three short ones, one long one. Three short; one long. Then the crisp tones of Jean Oberlé, the speaker at Radio Londres. 'This is London,' he said. 'Frenchmen speaking to Frenchmen.'

Mother beckoned for me to come and sit next to her, then turned the volume down so low that I could no longer make out Oberlé's voice until I held my ear right next to the speaker. 'First, a few personal messages. The blue horse is walking on the horizon. I repeat: the blue horse is walking on the horizon.'

After the personal messages, the real meaning of which I didn't understand, we heard about the successful counteroffensive made by the British against the Italians in Egypt and that the British air raid on Berlin had caused one and a half million Reichsmarks worth of damage. As

Oberlé sang softly, to the melody of the old Mexican revolutionary song 'La Cucaracha', 'Radio Paris lies, Radio Paris lies . . .', there was a sudden knock at our apartment door.

Mother gave a start and looked at me, her eyes filled with panic.

'Who could that be so late?' I asked, dread gnawing at my insides.

'Radio Paris is German . . .' sang Oberlé.

Mother put her index finger to her lips and turned off the radio with her other hand. Another knock. We stayed sitting at the table, motionless. A tangle of thoughts rushed through my mind. Had Mother's dark premonitions come true? Were the police at our door?

'Judith,' called a voice from outside in the stairwell. 'Judith, it's me! Please open the door!'

A warm stream of relief flooded through me. *Him? Here?* 'Christian!' I whispered to Mother and jumped up from my chair to go to the door. But then I came to a sudden halt. I wasn't prepared at all. He had never come to our home before, and he hadn't said a word yesterday about visiting me. I nervously ran my fingers through my hair. What would he think when he saw our small, humbly furnished apartment? My gaze swept through the kitchen, over the old gas stove which Mother had bought from a junk dealer many years ago, and over to the rusted, cold iron oven. In the milky light of the ceiling lamp, everything looked even more dreary than by day.

'What does he want so late?' Mother asked. 'If Lemercier gets wind of this, tomorrow the entire building will know that you're receiving male visitors at night.'

Monsieur Lemercier was an old widower with wisps of hair and incisors so widely spaced he could have squeezed a cigarette between them. He lived on our floor and loved to poke his nose into matters that didn't concern him.

'I have no idea,' I said, before turning around and calling, quietly but firmly, 'I'm coming.' I unbuttoned my grey woollen coat and took it off. I couldn't let Christian see me in this tatty thing. Even though the pullover I was wearing beneath it was also made from thick wool, I immediately began to shiver.

I went over to the door and opened it. There he stood, wrapped up in his warm winter coat, smiling at me. My face lit up, and I longed to throw myself into his arms. But then I got a grip of myself. 'What are you doing here?' I whispered, peering out of the corner of my eye at Monsieur Lemercier's door. Everything looked quiet. I took a step back and beckoned Christian in hastily.

'First, help me to bring the things in,' he said.

Only then did I notice the numerous parcels lying by his feet. As quick as a flash, I bent over and pulled and pushed them through the door into the hallway. Then I grabbed Christian's hand, which was tucked into a glove, and pulled him into the apartment. As the door fell into the lock behind us, I exhaled with relief. Only then did I turn around to him. 'What's in the packages?' I asked, before I'd even properly greeted him.

He stepped up to me silently and put his arms around my waist. 'Hello, my angel.' Then he kissed me gently on the mouth.

The thought that Mother was watching us from the kitchen made me uneasy, and I edged away from him.

'Tonight is Christmas Eve,' said Christian, kissing me on the top of my head and pulling his hands out of the gloves. 'I've been out on the road all day, delivering Christmas gifts to the families I'm looking after. And now I wanted to bring *you* a few surprises.'

'Christmas?' I repeated in astonishment, staring at him. 'I'd completely forgotten.' The cold, the hunger, the war. Who besides the rich still had the energy to think about holidays in these times? But I didn't say that; it was simply too wonderful that he was here.

'I had a feeling you'd forgotten.' He grinned and limped towards the kitchen. Only now I saw that he was carrying a bulging rucksack made from coarse canvas on his back. I picked two packages up from the floor and followed him. Mother was standing stiffly and solemnly behind her chair, her hands clenching the backrest. Her face was pale, and her shorn hair made her high cheekbones stand out even more.

'Good evening, Madame Goldemberg,' Christian greeted her smoothly. 'It's an honour to finally meet you.' He stretched out his hand.

'Christmas isn't celebrated in this home,' commented Mother dryly, pointing at the menorah on the kitchen table. Then she hesitantly took his hand. 'Your unannounced visit gave us an incredible fright.'

'I'm sorry, madame,' answered Christian, taking off the rucksack and putting his gloves on the table. 'But the idea of visiting you only came to me this morning, and I had no way of telephoning Judith.'

'Well, not everyone can afford a private telephone,' remarked Mother pointedly.

Christian pulled the leather straps out of the buckle and opened the rucksack. It was filled with pieces of black, shiny coal. 'Let's get this place properly heated up, shall we?'

Mother clapped her hand in front of her mouth and took a step backwards. 'You didn't steal them, did you?' she asked nervously.

'Don't worry,' said Christian calmly. 'Jean Michel, my chauffeur, took them from my parents' cellar. He helped me to bring them up to you. No one at home will notice a few missing pieces of coal.' He laughed to himself. 'And Jean Michel can keep a secret.'

'You . . . you call that a few?' I stuttered, running my fingertips over the sack. 'That will last us for at least a month.' I looked over at my mother uncertainly.

She had regained her composure and sat back down. 'We can't accept it,' she said, her gaze fixed on the table. 'Please pack them away again.'

'There'll be no question of that,' replied Christian, undeterred, as he set to work. He tore up a few sheets of newspaper and placed them together with a log in the stove. Then he pulled a box of matches out of his trouser pocket and lit the paper. A bright flame immediately flickered up. The wood began to crackle, and a few moments later biting smoke drifted through the kitchen.

Mother remained at the table, motionless.

'Judith, open the packages,' Christian instructed, coughing as he pushed the poker around inside the stove.

The smoke burned my eyes. But I paid no attention to the itching sensation, instead lifting one of the packages onto the table and undoing the bow. As soon as I had lifted the lid just a little, a sweet, heavy scent rose to greet me. An oblong cake roll, covered with dark nougat cream, and bedded in silk paper, gleamed up at me.

'A *bûche*,' I cried in delight. 'A real *bûche de Noël*!'

'It's from Angélina, on Rue de Rivoli. They're the best,' explained Christian proudly.

I leaned back, took a knife out of the drawer behind me and cut into the moist, soft cake. Some of the nougat cream stuck to my fingers, and I immediately licked them greedily. The sensation of the velvety sugary mass on my tongue unleashed an indescribable feeling of happiness. Beneath Mother's disapproving gaze, I launched myself on the cake like a wolf on freshly killed prey. I stuffed it into my mouth with both hands, chewing and swallowing all at once and noisily licking my fingers. My sticky mouth sent just one single message to my brain: more of this cake! More, more, more! I forgot everything around me: Mother's dark expression; the stinging smoke; even, for a moment, the fact that Christian was sitting on a footstool in front of our stove, trying desperately to get the fire going.

Eventually I came to my senses, cut another piece of the cake and offered it to Mother. 'No, thank you,' she said icily.

I rolled my eyes with a sigh. Mother and her unbreakable principles. Why could she never accept a gift? What must Christian think of her? Then I pushed the piece of cake into my own mouth and cast the thought aside.

Mother turned to Christian, her eyebrows raised. 'Say, young man, you don't seem to have much experience in lighting fires.'

Sighing, Christian screwed up another piece of newspaper. 'Indeed.'

Mother stood up. 'Right, give it to me, it'll never light

like that. Such a waste of beautiful wood.' She took the poker from his hand, peered into the hatch and mumbled something beneath her breath. Then she pushed the wood upright, and a few minutes later, laid some of the fresh coal into the embers.

I listened to the contented gurgling of my stomach. The sugar in my blood had warmed my entire body. I leaned back and placed my hands over my belly. I was just about to shut my eyes when Christian said, 'Judith, there are a few more packages there.'

I went back into the hallway, brought the presents into the kitchen and opened one after the other. Smoked fish, cheese, coffee, butter, champagne truffles and a bottle of wine came into view. Tears flowed down my cheeks. 'Thank you,' I muttered over and over. 'Thank you.' Those were all the words I could get out.

I no longer cared where the things were from, or how his parents had got such delicacies in the first place. I just wanted to eat as much as I could until I was full to bursting. I stole a glance at Mother. Hopefully she wouldn't ask Christian to pack everything up and take it away again. Before she could say a word, I swiftly cut into the cheese. But then I saw that she had taken three glasses out of the cupboard, and was handing Christian a corkscrew.

Lily ran back and forth beneath the table, her tail raised, meowing loudly. She was hungry, too. I quickly placed a few pieces of cheese on the floor, and she pounced on them.

With a loud *plop*, Christian uncorked the bottle and filled our glasses. 'May your holidays be blessed,' he said, lifting his glass festively.

The ice now seemed to be broken with Mother. She lit the *shamash*, the central candle on the menorah, which was slightly higher than the others. Then she took it out and used it to light the candle on the far right-hand side. '*Baruch atah Adonai Eloheinu Melech ha-olam* . . .' I heard her chant softly. Blessed are you, oh Lord, our God . . .

Christian listened reverently.

'Coincidentally, today is also the first night of Hanukkah,' she explained, smiling briefly and clinking her glass against ours. 'It rarely starts this late.' She emptied the glass in a few sips and topped it up. I was pleased that, in these dark times, she hadn't forgotten the beautiful tradition of the Festival of Light.

'Do you read the *Petit Parisien*, Christian?' she asked, a little later.

Christian shook his head. 'I used to. But not any more. Ever since it's been published in Paris again, the tone has changed.'

Mother's eyes flashed. 'I completely agree. The Dupuys should be ashamed. They've turned the paper into a Nazi propaganda engine.' She took a long drink of wine. 'But the fact that Colette is writing for the *Parisien*, that really is a disgrace.'

Christian nodded and lit himself a cigarette. 'You mean her weekly column?'

'Yes,' cried Mother, her cheeks flushed by the wine. 'And that's despite her being married to a Jew.'

Christian shrugged. 'Everyone gets by in whatever way they can.'

'And the things she writes,' exclaimed Mother indignantly. It was a long time since I had seen her this talkative. 'About stockings, hats and cake recipes. And about this damn winter, as if we hadn't already had enough of it in our day-to-day life . . . it's terrible, how lowbrow she's become.' She shook her head, picked up a piece of cheese and shot me a conspiratorial glance which betrayed the fact that she liked Christian.

As a cosy warmth unfurled in the kitchen, Mother and Christian debated André Gide's critique of communism and analysed Jean-Paul Sartre's debut novel *Nausea*.

I wasn't even properly listening. I was simply happy. This evening was complete. Coal glowed in the stove, and the table was filled with exquisite food. Christian was with me, and Mother once again resembled the lively Claire Goldemberg my father had fallen in love with. The surprise Hanukkah of 1940 was the greatest celebration of my life.

11

Béatrice

Washington, D.C., 2006

A queue had formed in front of the security check at the Holocaust Memorial Museum. Béatrice lined up along with chatting school kids, tourists with cameras around their necks and Holocaust researchers with laptop bags. After she had passed through the metal detector and one of the security staff had searched her handbag, she walked across the museum's large, glass-roofed lobby to the lift. The Registry of Holocaust Survivors, which administrated the names and biographical information of the survivors, was located on the second floor.

Two years ago, shortly after she had moved to Washington, Béatrice had visited the museum as a tourist. She still had the small booklet that one of the staff at the entrance had pressed into her hand. As she had walked through the exhibition rooms, she had read in it the personal story of one of the victims during the Nazi era. The visit had shaken Béatrice to the core; for days afterwards, she had been unable to get the haunting images and artefacts out of her head. But only now, in the hope of stumbling across a clue about Judith Goldemberg, was she able to grasp the historical significance of this archive in all its tragic enormity.

In the corner of one room, two museum employees sat at narrow desks. The man was leaning over a file, talking softly on the phone. Béatrice decided to speak to the woman, a fragile-looking old lady with snow-white hair fastened up in a small bun.

'Excuse me.'

The woman looked up and smiled at Béatrice. Her eyes were friendly and sea-blue, like aquamarines. Her white blouse looked freshly starched, and tiny diamonds sparkled on her earlobes. Her perfume was unobtrusive, her hands perfectly manicured.

'Can I help you?' she asked.

'I'm searching for someone. A woman. I only have her name,' explained Béatrice in a low voice.

The old woman interrupted her: 'We can certainly help you but it's best you speak with my colleague. He'll be with you in a moment, if you'd like to wait.' She smiled warmly as she stood up and reached for her woollen cardigan, which hung over the backrest of the chair. 'End of my shift for today.' Then she went over to her colleague, her steps small and a little shaky, and said goodbye to him.

The man ended his phone call and the old lady, who was walking to the lift, bent forward slightly. 'Bye, Julia. See you tomorrow.' Then he looked at Béatrice. He had sparkling green eyes. A softly arched mouth. Classic facial features.

Béatrice felt as though the ground wavered beneath her feet.

'That was Julia,' he explained, in a strong French accent. 'She comes here a few afternoons per week to help out. An extraordinary woman. She survived Auschwitz. But over to you. What can I do for you?'

'I'd like to help a friend find her half-sister,' answered Béatrice in French, once she had regained her composure.

'Ah, *une française.*' The man smiled broadly, visibly delighted to be able to speak his native language. 'Take a seat. I'm Grégoire Bernard. Call me Grégoire.'

'Béatrice Duvier,' she answered, cursing inwardly as she felt herself blush. She sat down on a stool, shifted forward to the edge and pressed her handbag on her knees. 'We don't know whether she survived.'

'What's the sister's name?' asked Grégoire, looking Béatrice so directly in the eyes that she squeezed her bag even more tightly against herself.

'Well, I think she's called Judith Goldemberg, if she has the same surname as her mother.' Béatrice told Grégoire the few facts she knew about Judith.

'Let's have a look in the reference books,' he suggested, brushing his almost shoulder-length hair behind his ears, 'and see if we can find her. You should contact the ITS, the International Tracing Service, in Bad Arolsen. The ITS coordinates the search for Holocaust survivors.'

'Bad Arolsen?' She had never heard of the place.

'It's in Germany. In 1946, when the ITS was founded, the town was selected as a base because it was exactly in the middle of the four occupied zones, and almost untouched by the war. The ITS is currently in the process of digitizing everything. Next year, the documents will be released to the public, and we'll receive the data from all the files.

Then the search will be much easier.' He smiled at her. 'But I'm sure you don't want to wait that long.' He stood up and pulled a thick, well-thumbed volume from a shelf.

Only now did Béatrice notice how tall Grégoire was. He was well built, around her age, and looked as though he kept himself in good shape.

'I suggest we start with this.' He sat back down, laid the book on the table and pushed it across towards her.

Serge Klarsfeld, *Le Mémorial de la déportation des Juifs de France*, read Béatrice. *Memorial to the Jews deported from France.*

Grégoire leaned back and crossed his legs. 'Klarsfeld himself almost became the victim of a Nazi raid. He and his family hid behind a wardrobe and evaded discovery. But the Gestapo caught his father. He was arrested, deported and murdered in Auschwitz.' Grégoire reached into his trouser pocket and pulled out a packet of chewing gum. 'Klarsfeld and his wife devoted the remainder of their lives to tracking down Nazi criminals and collaborators. It's thanks to them that many were brought to trial.' He popped a piece of gum in his mouth and grinned. 'I'm trying to give up smoking. It's forbidden everywhere here. You almost feel like a criminal if you're carrying cigarettes in your pocket.'

Béatrice giggled. 'I'm guessing you haven't been here very long.'

'Almost six months,' he replied. 'It feels like a very long time. But I still haven't got used to the severe discrimination against smokers. That's why I've decided to give it up altogether.' Grégoire picked up the book and leafed through it. He read something, frowned a little and mumbled a number.

Béatrice stared at him, raptly.

He traced the lines with his index finger, turned the page and pulled his finger down it once again. He did the same thing multiple times. 'There!' he cried out.

Béatrice jumped.

'Judith Goldemberg.' He showed her the page, which contained hundreds of names. In the middle, where the tip of his index finger rested, between Jacques Goldbaum and Yvonne Goldenberg, was Judith's name. 'She was in convoy sixty-three, which left Paris on the seventeenth of December 1943. Final destination Auschwitz.'

'So she died in the camp?' Béatrice's pulse accelerated.

'Not necessarily. But it will be harder to find out what happened to her afterwards.'

Béatrice was flustered. Shaken. Happy. She didn't know whether it was because of this unbelievable discovery or Grégoire's eyes.

'Here's what we do know so far.' He pulled the book back towards him and read out loud: 'On the eleventh of December, SS-Obersturmführer Heinz Röthke sent a telegram to Berlin, informing Adolf Eichmann that on the seventeenth of December a convoy with eight hundred to a thousand Jews would be ready for departure. On the fifteenth of December, Röthke received the response from Berlin, authorizing the transport for a thousand Jews. On the seventeenth of December, Alois Brunner, leader of the Gestapo special command unit in the Drancy internment and transit camp, sent a further telegram to the capital city, confirming the departure of convoy sixty-three at 12.10 hours from Paris-Bobigny. Eight hundred and fifty Jews were on the train.'

Grégoire looked over at the bookshelf. 'There are additional sources we can search through to get more information on the convoy. But unfortunately, right now I have to see to a few other things first.' He brushed his hand through his hair again. 'Leave me your telephone number. Then I'll ring you as soon as I know more. Or just come by again tomorrow. By then I may have found something.'

*

His gaze. His hands. His mouth. Béatrice sat in the archive, next to the old computer screen, and chewed on a pencil. She didn't understand why she couldn't get Grégoire out of her head, and why she felt no inclination to call Joaquín back, even though he had left her a voicemail and sent two text messages. She only knew that she was planning to slink out of the office at two o'clock again today, to go to the Holocaust Museum.

'If you carry on like that, you won't even be done by Christmas,' came a sudden bark from behind her.

She spun around in shock and saw Michael standing in the doorway. He stepped in, giving her a disapproving look. The bitter smell of cold cigarettes met her nose.

'What's up?' she asked coolly.

'I've spoken to Alexander,' he said.

'Glad you did,' she replied before leaning back in her chair. Finally, the misunderstanding was sorted out. Alexander had approved the press release with the number in the headline.

'He said he had made it clear to you, numerous times, that the number of pupils was under no circumstances to appear in the release. Because there were differences of opinion among the experts.'

'What?' Béatrice jumped up. Her throat sealed shut. What a disgusting liar Michael was! Alexander had told her the exact opposite. Béatrice remembered his words very clearly.

'That's not true,' she asserted with an angry stare. 'He told me to do what you had suggested. And that was to use the thirty thousand.'

Michael sneered condescendingly. 'You are mixing up truth and reality,' he declared softly, as if he was talking to a child. 'The only thing I ever suggested – which I *always* suggest, by the way – was to be careful and double check. No, no, Béa, don't blame other colleagues now for your irresponsible behaviour.' He narrowed his eyes. 'You *deliberately* damaged the bank's reputation.'

'I did not,' Béatrice shrieked. 'Let's call Alexander and clarify this.'

'I'm not done yet,' Michael continued. He pulled his lighter out of his trouser pocket and played with it. 'Alexander also asked me whether *you* might perhaps have given Lustiger the internal documents.' He tucked the lighter back into his pocket and eyed her. 'I said that I wouldn't rule out the possibility until it's proven otherwise.'

Béatrice was simmering with fury. Her hands cramped up. How could he dare say something like this! What an arsehole. An obnoxious, vindictive arsehole. 'I have nothing to do with the documents,' she cried. 'Nor with the PGD.'

Michael's face was expressionless. 'You should have clearly explained to me why these numbers couldn't go to press,' he said. 'If you can't cope with deadline pressure, Béatrice, then you're in the wrong place.'

Béatrice fell silent. She had only done what they had asked her to do and raised her concerns repeatedly. And what if *Alexander* had lied to Michael? Alexander? That couldn't be. He had always impressed her as a friendly, charismatic leader. Everybody around here knew he was a favoured candidate to succeed the current vice president who was about to retire. What was she missing here?

Michael grunted snidely and crossed his arms in front of his chest. 'By the way, Cecil contacted me. You applied for a job with him?'

Béatrice's cheeks grew hot.

'He asked me for a reference.'

She held her breath.

'As you can imagine, I don't have anything positive to say right now.' He went to the door. 'I expect your detailed account of your conversation with Daniel Lustiger. VP needs it for the investigation. In the meantime, you'll stay here in the archive. In a few months' time, we'll reevaluate.' Then he left the room. Only the cigarette stench remained behind.

*

'I've good news,' said Grégoire, waving Béatrice over as soon as he saw her at the entrance. She thought she noticed his gaze rest on her just a little longer than necessary. She had made an effort with her make-up, and her light blonde hair, soft and full, cascaded over her shoulders. She was wearing a close-fitting, black suit, which emphasized her slim waist and concealed her slight tummy.

'What have you discovered?' she asked, forgetting, for a moment, Michael's visit to the archive and the terrible things he had said.

'Let's go to the museum cafe, then I'll tell you everything,' suggested Grégoire, reaching for his coat. 'I urgently need a coffee.'

He walked beside her with large steps, led her down a flight of stairs, out the exit and across the small square to the cafe. 'So, what brought you to D.C.?' he asked as he held the door open for her.

'I work for the World Bank.' She was about to explain what the organization was, because mostly people had either never heard of it or thought it was a normal investment bank, but Grégoire nodded knowingly.

'How exciting!' he said, visibly impressed. 'And you can just take off in the middle of the day like this?'

Béatrice sighed. Michael's grim face appeared in her mind's eye. 'Not really. But that's a longer story.'

'Well, then I'll get us something to drink first. Take a seat.'

Apart from two women who were sitting at the counter and chewing their sandwiches, the place was empty. Béatrice looked for a spot at one of the small, square tables by the window and rubbed her cold hands together.

A few minutes later, Grégoire returned with two paper cups and sat down opposite her. He removed the plastic lid from his coffee and shook in a sachet of sugar.

'So tell me. What have you found out about Judith Goldemberg?' pressed Béatrice as she dunked her plastic spoon into the milk foam and stirred the coffee beneath. It felt as though she had known Grégoire for ever.

He leaned back and brushed his long hair out of his

face. Then he reached into the inside pocket of his jacket and pulled out a bundle of folded papers. 'Here, I've copied the relevant Klarsfeld pages for you.' He pushed two sheets of paper towards her. 'I also checked in Danuta Czech's text. Czech worked in the Auschwitz Museum in the fifties and created a meticulous chronicle about the camp. A thousand pages long. It is called *The Auschwitz Chronicle*. She carried on working on it even after she was retired.'

Béatrice listened, spellbound.

'Remember what we found in Klarsfeld's book?'

She nodded enthusiastically.

He unfolded another piece of paper. 'Convoy sixty-three left the train station in Paris on the seventeenth of December. Czech writes that it arrived in Auschwitz three days later.' He smoothed the paper flat and read: 'The twentieth of December. Eight hundred and fifty Jewish men, women and children arrive from Drancy in the sixty-third transport from France. Two hundred and thirty men and one hundred and fifteen women are accepted in the camp and allotted numbers. The remaining five hundred and five are gassed.'

Béatrice let out a harsh breath. And Grégoire read commentaries like these every day. She saw that he had underlined numerous sections.

He tapped his finger on the Klarsfeld copies. 'Here it says that of the three hundred and forty-five people, thirty-one survived. Six of them were women.' He sipped his coffee and looked intensely at Béatrice.

Unable to hold his X-ray gaze, she concentrated on the copies.

'But there's more: at the end of the 1980s, a man called George Dreyfus put together a similar list,' he went on.

'Admittedly this list is more detailed. It contains the names of almost seventy thousand Jews who were deported between 1942 and 1944.'

'Where did he get the names from?'

'We presume he looked at the original deportation lists that can now be found in the Mémorial de la Shoah, the Holocaust Memorial in Paris.' He shook another sachet of sugar into his coffee. 'The Shoah Memorial is, by the way, another good point of call. You should contact them.'

She nodded again. This search for Judith required more work than she had initially presumed. Would she have the time and energy to do this? But then Béatrice remembered Jacobina's despair as she'd told her about the promise she had made to her father. *It's like a curse*, she heard the woman say. She would help Jacobina – no matter how much effort this would involve.

'But I haven't even told you the really good news yet.' Grégoire briefly laid his hand on hers, a fleeting touch, giving his words more emphasis. 'In Dreyfus's list, Judith Goldemberg is recorded as a survivor. Here, look for yourself.' He pulled out the copy.

There it was: *Rescapée*. Survivor.

Béatrice beamed. She wondered what Jacobina would say when she told her this fantastic news! Perhaps everything would be simpler than she had imagined just a moment ago. The Holocaust Museum had already helped so many families.

Grégoire folded the papers up again. 'That was the first step. But now it gets more complicated. Where do we search next? We don't know whether she went back to Paris after the war.'

'Why wouldn't she? She was French.'

Grégoire shook his head. 'Perhaps she emigrated to the United States. Or to Israel. Perhaps she married and took another name. Sometimes the tracks just disappear into nothing.'

The possibility that Judith might have a different surname now was something that Béatrice hadn't even considered. Her hope crumbled again, like a clod of earth in the sun. She blew out her cheeks and exhaled loudly.

'Don't give up so quickly,' said Grégoire encouragingly, touching her hand again briefly. 'We'll think of something. In any case, you should write to the Shoah Memorial and, of course, the International Tracing Service. Another idea is to contact the registry office in Paris. Perhaps there's a marriage certificate.'

He scrunched up his empty coffee cup. 'Now to you and your long story. Would you like to talk about it?'

*

At five o'clock on the dot, Béatrice left the World Bank and took a taxi to U Street, to Jacobina's.

In front of the building entrance, two boys were playing with a dented tin can. They kicked it back and forth, cheering whenever the can collided with the door. Béatrice hurried past them, trying to avoid being hit by it, and rang the doorbell. A few moments later, the door opener buzzed – this time without Jacobina having croaked her usual 'Who is it?' As soon as the door had fallen shut behind Béatrice, the tin can clattered against it again, unleashing exuberant shouts from the boys.

When Jacobina opened the door, a smile fleeted across

her face. She looked different, thought Béatrice, better somehow. It was her hair, she realized. Jacobina had washed it. The black locks no longer clung to her head, but instead framed her face in gentle waves.

'You look nice today,' she said.

'Thank you. It's because my back is getting better,' Jacobina responded, waving her in. 'I can move again, slowly.'

Béatrice unpacked a small chocolate cake she had bought at Poupon in Georgetown, a French patisserie she always went to when she wanted to treat herself to something special. 'What did the doctor say today?' she asked.

Jacobina eyed the cake longingly. 'They're going to operate. And after that I have to do chemotherapy for five months.'

'Gosh.' Béatrice sighed and looked at her friend sympathetically. 'Do you know when the operation will be?'

'No, they won't tell me until next week. But the doctor said my chances are good.' Jacobina looked calm and composed, not as desperate as she had a few days ago. The doctor's words must have given her hope.

'I'll be there for you all the way,' Béatrice assured her with a smile. 'And now I absolutely have to tell you what I found out about Judith.' As Béatrice narrated the story of her research in the Holocaust Museum and her encounter with Grégoire, she cut the cake into six pieces. Two of which she put on a plate and handed to Jacobina.

'You like him, this Grégoire, don't you?' remarked Jacobina with a grin.

'Sure, he's nice.' Béatrice tried to make her tone sound casual.

'You can't fool me,' giggled Jacobina. 'You've got this

mysterious gleam in your eyes.' She bit into the cake and rolled her eyes with pleasure.

'Do you have anything of Judith's that could help us with the search? A picture perhaps? Or a birth certificate?' asked Béatrice.

Jacobina shook her head. 'By the time my father told me about her, he was already very weak. He died that same night. But then, you know that already.'

Béatrice nodded and went over to the kitchenette to boil some water for tea.

'The only thing he left me is the *mezuzah* outside my door and a small box full of junk. I haven't looked in it since his death.' Jacobina devoured the remaining crumbs on her plate, then took a third piece of cake out of the carton.

'What's in it?' Béatrice came back to the sofa with two steaming cups of tea and sat down.

'Old letters from my mother, photos and so on. Nothing exciting.'

'Where is the box? Could I see it?'

'No idea,' answered Jacobina, munching away. 'Why are you so interested in it?'

'Perhaps we might find some clue about Judith,' Béatrice replied.

'I don't think so, I would have seen it. But take a peek under my bed, there's all kinds of stuff down there that I banished from my life.'

Béatrice went into the tiny bedroom. She knelt down on the floor, reached under the bed and pulled out an assortment of clutter: a mangled broom, checked curtains, a coat with a faux-fur collar and a heavy box with a torn lid. The whirled-up dust settled on Béatrice's face, tickling her lungs. She coughed. With her fingertips, she opened the box and peered in. Papers, video cassettes, books, a broken mirror. As she pushed the papers aside, her fingers collided with something hard. She groped them further in and pulled out a tin container the size of a shoebox. Triumphant, she took it back in to Jacobina. 'Is this it?'

Jacobina wiped her hand across her mouth and nodded. 'Papa Lica's collected works.'

Béatrice sat down and tried to open the box. The lid was jammed, and she spent a while jiggling around with it. Suddenly it sprang open, and a colourful flood of postcards, letters and black and white photos with serrated edges poured out over the sofa. Some slipped to the floor.

'Well, have fun clearing that up,' grumbled Jacobina, limping over towards the bathroom. 'You won't find anything about Judith in there.'

Béatrice pulled off her shoes and pushed a cushion beneath her head. Then she began to read.

The handwriting was barely decipherable, and much of it was in Romanian. One of the photos showed a tall, dark-haired man. He stood there, ramrod straight and with a solemn expression on his face, his stiff hat pulled down low over his face. The chain of a pocket watch poked out of his waistcoat pocket. Next to him, just as serious-looking, stood a girl in a white lace dress, holding a baby doll that was missing a leg.

When Jacobina came back, Béatrice showed her the picture. 'Is that you?'

Jacobina snorted a mocking, 'Yes,' and turned on the television.

Béatrice studied the remaining vestiges of this past life, spread out before her. Jacobina was right. She wouldn't find anything about Judith here. All of this had been written much later. She began to push the pile back together and returned it to the box. As she bent forwards to pick up the papers which had fallen to the floor, two French words caught her gaze: *Mon amour.*

Béatrice paused. Then she pulled a flimsy piece of paper out from between two postcards. The handwriting was elaborate and, in many places, faded and smudged. Béatrice read.

> Paris, 8th December 1943
>
> My beloved,
>
> We've been sitting in the cellar since the early morning hours, waiting for something to happen. Outside in the city, the sirens wail without pause, but no bombs have fallen yet.
>
> Three days ago you disappeared, and all the light has vanished from my life along with you. My heart is silent with agony. I cannot forgive myself. If only I had not left you alone, so soon before our escape. You mean everything to me. Everything!
>
> In my despair, I'm writing to your father's address, which I found in your diary. I'm praying for you, my beloved, and for a new world, in which there is a place for our love.
>
> With all of my heart,
>
> C.

Béatrice read the letter through once more. Then she lowered the piece of paper and stared into the distance. Her hands were cold and clammy.

'Jacobina,' she whispered, 'I think I've found something.'

Jacobina's eyes were fixed on the TV screen. 'What did you say?'

Béatrice stood up and pressed the letter into Jacobina's hands. 'Have you ever read this? I think the letter was intended for Judith.'

Jacobina looked at the sheet of writing paper and shrugged. 'I've no idea who wrote it. I've never seen it before. Isn't there an envelope with it that says the sender?'

Béatrice went through the entire pile again. She looked at every envelope closely, but none had the same unmistakable handwriting.

'This letter could only have been written to Judith,' said Béatrice, pacing up and down in front of Jacobina. 'Everything fits. Paris. The date. This C mentions that he sent the letter to the address of Judith's father. So your father must have received it. And that's why it's in his box.'

Jacobina cocked her head to one side. 'Judith never turned up at our home in Romania, in any case. And how could she have! In the middle of the war, as a Jew. And at the beginning of 1944 we fled to Canada.'

'We have to contact the Shoah Memorial and a few other organizations which Grégoire told me about,' said Béatrice, folding the letter carefully. 'We're going to find Judith. I can feel it.'

*

Laura put her mobile phone down beside her and stretched out on the sofa. It was almost midday, but she was still wearing her pink pyjamas with the unicorn print; an outfit that made her look not like the sophisticated teenager she wanted to be, but the little girl she sometimes still was. A bowl of cornflakes stood on the coffee table in front of her.

Béatrice, who was sitting next to Laura's feet, looked up from her book and briefly glanced through the terrace doors into the garden. It had rained all night long, and huge puddles had collected on the lawn. In the bird house, which hung lopsidedly from a branch, two sparrows were fighting over a few grains.

The morning had passed calmly. After she and Joaquín had woken up, their bodies still lethargic and the sheets warmed from sleep, they had made love. Not passionately – their sex life had never had been like that – but gently and intimately, like a couple who knew each other's preferences and reactions completely. Every touch was routine, every movement predictable. After the disagreements of the past weeks, the rediscovered intimacy had done Béatrice good.

'We're going to see *Underworld Evolution* today, aren't we?' Laura asked, letting out a yawn.

Joaquín put down the newspaper he was reading and took off his glasses. 'Of course, sweetheart, we promised you we'd go. What time is the film on?'

'It's showing in one hour, in Tyson's Corner,' said Laura, sitting up and pouring a thick layer of sugar over her cornflakes.

Rudi came trotting out of the kitchen, licked up a few crumbs from the floor and laid down beneath the table.

Béatrice remembered their movie plans all too well, but she felt lazy. The couch was cosy and Irène Némirovsky's novel *Suite française* – an account of 1940 France, when the country fell to the Nazis – so fascinating that she could hardly put it down. Némirovsky died two years later in Auschwitz, but her novel was only published in 2004.

After her visit to the Holocaust Museum and finding the mysterious letter in Jacobina's apartment, Béatrice immediately immersed herself in this book that Monique had recommended so vividly when they last spoke. The read was gripping and brilliant. It brought Béatrice emotionally closer to Judith Goldemberg and the horrific pain she and millions of other Jews endured during those years.

'Do you mind if I stay here and read?' she asked.

'Spoilsport,' cried Laura, looking at her father with wide, pleading eyes.

'Oh, Béa, please come with us,' cooed Joaquín. 'And this evening we'll go out for dinner in D.C. together, just you and me, okay?'

She turned to him. 'Sorry, but I really don't feel like watching a movie today. I'm totally absorbed by my book. And later this afternoon I want to visit an older friend I'm helping out from time to time.' She'd been wanting to tell him about Jacobina for a while. But it simply hadn't come up.

Joaquín raised his eyebrows in surprise. 'You? Since when?'

'A few weeks ago now,' she replied. 'I got involved with a charity.'

'A charity? Why?'

'It gives me something I don't get at the office.' She

looked back out into the garden. The bird feeder was now empty. 'In the bank we try to improve systems. We don't even come into contact with the people we want to help.'

'Improve systems,' he repeated, with a derisive laugh. 'I thought everything at your bank was about eradicating poverty.' Then his tone turned serious again. 'You can go see this lady tomorrow.'

Béatrice already regretted having mentioned Jacobina. She got up and stood by the window. 'I really don't want to go to the cinema today,' she insisted, crossing her arms in front of her chest. 'Please, try to understand.'

'Don't be so stubborn, honey,' said Joaquín. He no longer sounded gentle and pleading now. 'It's only a couple of hours.'

At the word 'stubborn', something tore inside Béatrice. She stopped short and looked at him. 'Me stubborn? I'm the one who usually gives in. No matter how often you change or cancel our plans.'

Joaquín tossed the newspaper onto the table. 'You're overreacting, Béatrice. I always have to justify myself to you whenever my job gets in the way of your leisure plans. I always have to fight with you whenever Laura suggests something. I've had enough.'

Béatrice was shaking. She hadn't expected such a strong reaction. Joaquín rarely lost his temper.

'You're the one who's overreacting,' she cried, 'just because I don't want to watch this film.'

'It's not about the damn film, Béatrice,' he fired back. 'It's about us doing something together with my daughter.' Dark-blue veins protruded on his forehead, running together in the middle like a web.

Laura, meanwhile, had drenched her sugary cornflakes in milk and was spooning them into her mouth. She crunched and chewed away, acting as though the adults' exchange of blows didn't interest her in the slightest. But Béatrice knew she was listening attentively.

'I don't want to argue about this any longer.' She grabbed the book and her handbag and went into the hallway.

'Wait!' Joaquín ran after her.

Béatrice pulled her coat off the hook.

'If you leave now, don't bother coming back,' he said with quiet anger.

The finality of his words stunned her. For a brief moment, Béatrice stood there feeling unsure. Then, with a decisive gesture, she opened the front door. 'I'm not intending to,' she said. 'You don't really care about our relationship anyway.' She slammed the door loudly behind her and heard Rudi's agitated bark behind it.

12

Judith

Paris, February 1941

With the reserved smile of a servant, Christian's chauffeur handed me the dress. '*Voilà, mademoiselle* . . . Have a pleasant day.' Nothing about his calm voice betrayed that he had just dashed up four flights of steps. He made the hint of a bow and went back towards the stairs.

'Thank you so much,' I muttered into the hallway, feeling overcome as I studied the black garment bag which concealed the dress. *Atelier Jacques Fath* was written on it in twirling gold script. My dress! My first proper evening gown! It was finally ready.

The memories of that cold January morning rushed back into my mind. When Christian had pulled me past a group of German soldiers along the grand Rue François Premier. He paid no attention whatsoever to the Germans. 'We'll get a dress made for you,' he said, gazing at me with a tenderness that sent a tingle down my spine. For days he had spoken of nothing else. He had got this idea into his head, so that he could take me out in proper attire. 'Jacques Fath is the best,' he explained with a radiant smile. 'He'll immediately know what will suit you and turn you into a princess, my angel.'

I knew there was no point trying to talk him out of it. But I already feared Mother's reaction when she would see me in this dress one day. Would she let me wear such a custom-tailored extravaganza? Would she accept that the money Christian was ready to spend on it could have fed us for several months? All Mother was thinking about during these dark days was our survival. And although I understood and shared her worries, I wanted more than to just survive. I wanted to escape our dreadful reality for a few hours and live this splendid dream with Christian, my beautiful love. He was the joy of my life. My future.

Everything in Jacques Fath's realm was sumptuous. The immense door knocker made from polished brass, which had a wolf's head engraved into it. The tall chairs upholstered in leopard skin. The young assistant with the squirrel-like face who rushed towards us as soon as we stepped into the atelier. The snow-white peppermint bonbons that were placed everywhere in large silver bowls.

'Unfortunately, silk isn't getting through at the moment,' said the squirrel when Christian asked for it, the corners of his mouth turning down. 'An import ban, you understand?' He coughed behind his hand a few times as he strutted up and down in front of a cabinet where large bolts of fabric lay organized by colour. Eventually he pulled out a dark-blue sheaf of fabric and unrolled it in front of us on the cutting table. 'But what about this?' he asked, his gaze resting on Christian, running his hand over the material then tugging at his tie. 'The finest rayon.'

*

As excited as a child on the first day of school, I carried the gown on my outstretched arms into my bedroom. With every step, the material rustled inside the cover. I laid the made-to-measure gift on my bed and carefully unbuttoned the garment bag. The silky, shimmering fabric immediately came into view. *The finest rayon*, I heard the squirrel say in my mind. Brimming with excitement, I pulled off the cover completely and lay the dress out across my bed. Stunning! Elegant and sleeveless, with a wide, long skirt and a close-fitting waistline, accentuated by a leather belt with a silver buckle. The neckline was trimmed with lace. On my checked bedspread, which was darned in numerous places and flecked with coffee stains from where I'd been careless while reading, the gown looked like something from another, more beautiful world. A world in which women who lived in expansive apartments in the 16th arrondissement, with coiffed hair and pearl necklaces, organized receptions for their husbands and their business partners. But me? Could I wear something like this? Filled with awe, I brushed my fingers along the wavelike folds of the skirt, feeling like a modern version of Charles Perrault's *Cendrillon*.

My thoughts wandered back to the atelier. To the squirrel's nimble fingers. To how he had wrapped the measuring tape around my hips, my arms and my neck, with economical movements, murmuring numbers, letting go of the tape and jotting them down in a notebook. In this boutique, where people from the finest circles in Paris came in and out, I was nothing more than a shabby little thing with frozen hands. As white as chalk and deeply embarrassed, I stood before the merciless wall-to-wall mirrors in the atelier of this rising fashion God, and tried to ignore the assistant's knowing glances as he eyed my woollen tights.

We saw Jacques Fath himself only once. At the second fitting. Immaculately dressed, he strode into the room with a smooth smile, and without introducing himself kissed my hand gallantly and greeted Christian like an old friend. He looked likeable, with large teeth, a tall, arched forehead and friendly eyes.

'Christian, what a delight! How is your beautiful mother?' he asked.

Only then did it occur to me that Christian's mother must come to the boutique several times a month, and that made me feel all the more uneasy. I wondered what she'd say if Monsieur Fath told her that her son had come in accompanied by a pale young girl in woollen stockings. A *Jewish* girl!

But then I relaxed again. Knowing Christian's resistance to his parents and his reserved feelings for them, he had probably asked Monsieur Fath to handle my gown with the utmost discretion.

Jacques Fath spoke a little about his new boutique and why the location was so much better than that of his old studio in Rue la Boétie. Then he concentrated on my dress, with the focus of an archaeologist who had just discovered an ancient Egyptian scroll in a rock crevice. He gathered some fabric at the waist, lectured the squirrel because the buttons at the back had been placed too far apart – even though to me they looked perfect – and checked the length of the seam. Suddenly he paused, frowned and eyed the belt, which was fastened so tightly that I could only take shallow breaths.

'Pardon, mademoiselle,' he murmured, pulling the belt from its loops with a sweeping motion and holding it out in front of the assistant's nose.

'How wide is this belt, Edouard?' he asked threateningly, as though he already knew the answer.

Edouard grimaced and placed his measuring tape against the belt. 'Exactly five centimetres, monsieur,' he answered, coughing in embarrassment.

'And how wide is it supposed to be?' asked Monsieur Fath, raising his eyebrows in a scowl.

Edouard tucked the measuring tape back into his trouser pocket and shrugged.

Monsieur Fath slammed his fist down on the table, making the silver bonbonniere hop to the side with a clatter. 'Did we not discuss this at length a few weeks ago?' he yelled, throwing the belt to the floor. 'Four centimetres, Edouard. Four!' He ran his fingers through his hair, then composed himself and smiled apologetically at Christian. 'I'm sorry. But these are the new rules from Vichy,' he explained, gesturing to me that I could get changed. 'Leather is a very scarce commodity. It all goes to Germany. Belts cannot be any wider than four centimetres. If I don't keep to that, they'll close down my shop!' I read genuine concern in his expression.

Edouard apologized profusely and a few moments later Jacques Fath went to the door.

'The dress will be ready in two weeks, Christian.' He winked. 'And as promised – no word to your lovely mother about this.' Then he turned to me: 'It was a pleasure, mademoiselle.' With a brief wave, he left the fitting room.

*

Now this magnificent example of the finest occupation haute couture, with a belt of precisely four centimetres in width, lay before me on my bed. After I had thoroughly admired it and brushed my fingers across the fabric, I could no longer hold myself back. My teeth chattering from the cold, I undressed and slipped into the gown. It fit as though it had been poured on. The material nestled against my slender form, the belt gave me shape and hold.

Shortly after six that evening, I stood next to Christian, freezing cold yet as opulent as a film star, in front of a bust of Napoleon III which rested above us on a head-high white marble pillar, and sipped from a glass of champagne. Beneath Fath's floor-length gown, I was wearing my thick, scratchy woollen tights, without which, in this cold, I wouldn't have managed the walk from the car across the square and up the steps into the Palais Garnier.

'You look breathtaking, my angel,' whispered Christian with a loving gaze, touching my arm gently. 'Your eyes are two aquamarines. Your skin is shimmering like porcelain.'

I smiled at him, feeling like Michèle Morgan, the French actress who had just been offered a film contract in Hollywood. We were standing in the Salon du Glacier, the magnificent rotunda on the first floor of the opera house, its decor reminiscent of the Belle Époque. A heavy chandelier illuminated the room, which was ornate with elaborate gold accents; and on the ceiling, libertine bacchantes stretched before fluffy clouds towards the evening sky. Elegantly dressed ladies and gentlemen stood around us in small groups, greeting one another with insincere kisses on the cheek, raising their champagne glasses to each other or studying the programme. To complement their evening gowns, the women wore lavish headbands and embroidered gloves that stretched up to their elbows. The men were in white tie.

Although it was fascinating to watch, the decadence on display also triggered a feeling of revulsion in me. While people like Mother and I were barely getting by and constantly fearing the increasing pressure of the Nazi regime with its ruthless discrimination against the Jews and other minorities, Parisian high society simply greeted its German occupiers with indifference.

They did not speak about Admiral Darlan, our new head of state, who had only been in office for a few days, nor did they talk about the German, anti-Semitic film *Jud Süss*, which had just arrived in the cinemas of Paris. No, on this evening, politics didn't exist. Instead, they debated animatedly whether the dancer Suzanne Lorcia was perfect for the role of Swanilda because who else could hold their own alongside the genial Serge Lifar?

A tall man with dark hair and an angularly shaped moustache broke away from a group of Wehrmacht officers and headed towards us. His military jacket was hung with insignia, crosses and epaulettes, indicators of high military rank and esteemed service. His bolt-upright posture, gold buttons and narrow, tall patent leather boots lent him a stiff, well-bred appearance.

Dread twisted in my gut. I had never spoken to a German before. What did he want from us?

'*Heil Hitler.*' The uniformed man greeted us in a commanding tone, shaking Christian's hand. I immediately noticed the thick, golden signet ring with an engraved coat of arms that was resplendently displayed on his finger.

Christian nodded and while he did not return the salute he replied promptly, yet with an undertone of surprise, 'Good evening, Monsieur Militärbefehlshaber.'

I looked at Christian. The ease with which he had pronounced the officer's long title in German unsettled me. He must have met this man before. Why had he never told me about him? Did he have something to hide? Dark thoughts pierced my mind: Christian, dating a Jewish girl during the day and courting the Nazis at night. Christian, a collaborator? I put down my champagne glass and dug my fingernails into the soft leather of the tiny, dark-blue clutch bag Monsieur Fath had given me as a gift to match my dress.

The officer fixed his fog-grey eyes on me, and it felt as though a gust of Arctic cold swept through the room.

'Allow me to make the introductions,' said Christian with a dry smile, putting his hand on my arm. 'Marie Lavigne, my fiancée.'

I shivered. A whirlwind of emotions gripped me. Why had he given me a false name? What if the German wanted to check my papers? But my panic was joined by a surge of happiness. Christian had introduced me as his fiancée. It was official. We belonged together. My thoughts tumbled over one another. The officer stared at me. My shoulders tensed with anxiety beneath the intensity of his gaze.

'It's an honour, mademoiselle,' he said finally, in his toneless German accent, holding his hand out towards me.

I hesitantly placed my hand in his and felt the cold metal of his ring beneath my fingers. He introduced himself as Otto von Stülpnagel.

The name sounded familiar.

'It promises to be a splendid performance this evening,' said Christian, visibly trying to lighten the atmosphere, with a wave of his programme.

Von Stülpnagel ran his hand across his receding hairline and nodded. 'I completely agree. The *Coppélia* is breathtaking. Graceful and precious, just like the ladies in attendance this evening.'

A waiter came over to him and held out a tray with a glass of effervescent champagne. Von Stülpnagel took it, accidentally spilling a little over his hand, and drank it down in one gulp.

'I'm sure you know that Delibes based this ballet on a German novella?' he asked, looking at Christian. He seemed to have no interest whatsoever in including me in the conversation, which was fine by me. In the presence of this occupier, with all his medals and insignia, I wouldn't have been able to get a single word out.

Von Stülpnagel pulled a white handkerchief from his trouser pocket and wiped his hand with it. 'The novella is called *Der Sandmann*, by E. T. A. Hoffmann, an extraordinary German writer.' He nodded, as though agreeing with himself, and signalled to the waiter to bring him another glass.

I frowned and looked at Christian, disconcerted. I didn't know what to make of this conversation. But Christian only paid attention to the military officer.

'Well,' continued von Stülpnagel, who visibly enjoyed the conversation, 'what very few people know is that *Coppélia*, back in its day, at its 1870 premiere here in the Parisian Opera House, was performed together with *The Marksman*, an opera by the German composer Carl Maria von Weber.' He emptied the second glass in just a few swallows and looked at me sternly.

Had he noticed my unease?

He turned back to Christian. 'So, you can see the extent to which French culture is influenced by the German.' He smiled complacently.

'Without question, monsieur,' Christian hurried to assure him, putting his hands in his pockets.

Von Stülpnagel let his gaze wander around the room, and it seemed to me that his interest lay more with the Parisian women than the tapestries. 'Every time I come here, it's as though I'm seeing the place for the first time,' he said, tugging at his handlebar moustache. 'Simply magical. As our Führer aptly remarked: "An opera house is the benchmark by which a civilization can be measured."' With a melancholic expression on his face, he looked past us into the vague distance. 'There's no other place in Paris the Führer has spent longer in than here, the Palais Garnier.' He sighed.

A bell began to ring piercingly, and a murmur rippled through the hall. Chairs were moved around, making scraping sounds; footsteps resonated against the parquet floor.

'The performance is about to start,' announced Christian, taking my hand.

Von Stülpnagel awoke from his thoughts, stretched his back and said goodbye with a firm handshake. 'Please give my best to your esteemed father,' he called to Christian once he was already a few steps away, looking around searchingly for his fellow officers. 'And tell him he did an excellent job.' Then he disappeared.

'Who on earth was that?' I hissed, as soon as his black hair had been swallowed up by the crowd.

Christian put his index finger to his lips. 'Not now,' he whispered.

Only later, after we had been sitting for a while already in Christian's parents' box, and Serge Lifar was spinning a captivating Suzanne Lorcia through the air like a white feather, to the rhythm of the cascading semi-quavers, did Christian whisper to me, 'The MBF is the leader of the German military in France. He has an account at my father's bank.'

I lowered the programme and looked at Christian. My doubts had been foolish and unfounded. How could I have thought badly of him, for even a moment?

He leaned over to me. 'Another thing. It's better if no one knows you're Jewish,' he whispered. 'We have to be extremely careful.'

As I looked back at the stage, I thought about what he had just said. I had heard the rumours, of course, that the German occupiers were putting Jewish refugees from the Ukraine, Poland and Russia in labour camps. My mother talked about it constantly. But they were only taking the men. I was a woman, and I had a French passport.

I pushed my hand beneath Christian's, and as I touched his skin, which was always so warm despite the cold, I once again felt safe and secure.

13

Béatrice

Washington, D.C., 2006

After Béatrice had climbed into a taxi, she decided not to visit Jacobina this Sunday after all. She was far too upset and disappointed to listen attentively to her or to think clearly about Judith.

She stared out of the window, lost in thought. Cherry trees, dabbed with white blossom, streamed past her. The car rolled across Key Bridge and turned right towards Georgetown. This back-and-forth with Joaquín had been going on for a year now. A constant high-wire act between needs and confessions, between Washington and McLean, between Yes, No and Maybe Later. One step forward, two steps back. A morning together, five nights alone. Béatrice felt like a tightrope walker without a net. Always under pressure, emptiness looming beneath her like a dark crevasse. She had to keep her balance. Understand him and look ahead.

But for how much longer would she be able to do that? Would they ever overcome the bitterness that had settled between them? She yearned for the early days of their relationship. The months before Joaquín's big promotion. When he had more time for both Laura and her, when their differences were easy to defeat and their weekends in McLean something to look forward to: blissful family time.

Now, the atmosphere between them was constantly tense. Even the smallest things erupted into conflict. They needed to learn to communicate better and rekindle their romance, or it was over.

The taxi driver spoke non-stop on his phone, in a language she didn't recognize. He seemed to be embroiled in a heated debate, was cursing loudly and shaking his head violently. Béatrice was relieved when he finally dropped her off at her building.

She stepped into her apartment and went straight towards her telephone. The small lights on the stand were blinking in short, regular intervals. Without taking off her coat, she sat down to listen to the new messages. The first was from her mother. She was feeling better, she said. She still couldn't walk without the cane, but the pain had subsided. Béatrice sighed with relief and resolved to call her back right away. Then came the next message. A deep, melodic male voice, speaking French. It took a second before Béatrice recognized it was Grégoire's. He had been to the weekly market at Dupont Circle that morning, he said in that relaxed chatty tone which had got under her skin already in the museum. He hadn't been able to resist all the tempting produce for sale and had bought way too much. Did she feel like coming round for dinner this evening?

Béatrice listened to the message a second time. Then a

third time. It had been a while since a man had offered to cook for her. Joaquín was too intellectual to peel carrots without cutting his finger in the process, and too busy to go to the market on Sundays. He depended upon her and the deep-freeze aisles in the supermarket.

A dinner with Grégoire, prepared by him – what a lovely idea. They could talk in detail about how to proceed with the search for Judith. But Béatrice also wanted to learn more about him and the work he was doing at the Holocaust Museum.

However, before she'd call him back to confirm, she had to speak to Joaquín and clear the air. Their fight was weighing heavily on her; she wouldn't be able to forget about it easily and enjoy dinner with another man. *Another man* – maybe she shouldn't accept Grégoire's invitation. She was in a committed relationship, albeit a complicated one. But still, she wasn't the kind of person who'd look for another partner before breaking up with the existing one. It wasn't fair to anyone. Her father had done this to her mother, before abandoning them completely, and generated a profound anxiety in Béatrice. She would never forgive him for that.

She dialled Joaquín's number, thinking about what to say. Voicemail. 'It's me,' Béatrice recorded after the tone. 'We need to talk.' She paused. How to frame it? How to put her shattered expectations into a few sentences without sounding accusatory? She took a deep breath. 'It's time to re-evaluate our relationship, Joaquín. We need to think about what we both need and want from this. Let's get together, just you and me, as soon as you can, okay?' She hesitated on how to end her message. With a short 'love you'? No, that didn't feel right. Not any more. 'Enjoy the movie,' she finally said and hung up.

A few moments later she called Grégoire back and made plans with him for early that evening.

*

Grégoire filled the pear-shaped glass up halfway and tilted it back and forth. Then he poked his nose almost entirely into it, closed his eyes and breathed in the aroma. 'Blackcurrant . . . plum . . . cedarwood . . . and a hint of semi-sweet chocolate,' he mumbled, giving an approving nod. He took the first sip.

Béatrice watched, mesmerized, as he performed his ceremony. Internally, she was anything but calm and composed. Her body pulsed and tingled. Grégoire's presence had plunged her into a state of feverish euphoria.

There was something sensual about the way he placed his upper lip to the edge of the glass, letting the wine flow into his mouth, moving his tongue back and forth before he swallowed.

Grégoire put the glass back on the kitchen counter and poured some for Béatrice. 'It's far too early for this bottle,' he said. 'But I was curious. A friend of mine made this wine. 2002 was an average vintage, even though we had a wonderful late summer.'

Béatrice knew about a lot of things – French literature, international affairs, development aid – but she had no idea about wine. The wine she drank was usually red and rarely cost more than fifteen dollars.

'You really know your stuff,' she said, taking a sip from her glass. The wine felt smooth and delicious against her tongue.

'It's my job. We own a vineyard near Bordeaux. In Pomerol, to be precise. Château Bouclier. My father bought it shortly after the war.'

Béatrice's eyes widened. 'You're a vintner?'

'Not directly. We have a winemaker who takes care of the production. But over the years I've learned a great deal from him.'

She wrinkled her brow. 'So what are you doing at the Holocaust Museum then?'

Grégoire picked up a handful of spinach, which lay freshly washed in a sieve, tossed it in a pan and poured some oil over it. 'I took a year off to finally finish my doctoral thesis. The museum gave me a research fellowship.' He distributed the spinach evenly across the pan with a wooden spoon. 'I was halfway through my doctorate when my father had a stroke, and I had to take his place all at once. You know, we're a small family business. He didn't want to hand over the reins to a stranger.'

The spinach crackled loudly in the hot oil and, within a few seconds, shrunk into a small heap. 'It took many months before Papa was feeling better again.' Grégoire sipped from his glass. 'But after that he didn't want to go back to work any more. So, in a sense, I became a businessman overnight.'

Béatrice watched as he was cooking: draining rice, pulling a huge piece of aromatic white fish out of the oven and simultaneously stirring a lemon-butter sauce. He moved deftly and skilfully, as if it required no effort whatsoever.

The world was full of wonders, thought Béatrice, letting the delectable wine dissolve on her tongue. Here she was on a wet and cold March evening, drinking the best wine of her life and being cooked for by a fascinating man.

As she let her gaze roam around the kitchen, she couldn't help but notice an envelope on the countertop, addressed to Grégoire Pavie-Rausan. But that wasn't the last name he had introduced himself with at the museum, she remembered. Why was he using another name? 'Sorry for being nosey,' she said, pointing at the envelope. 'But didn't you say your last name was Bernard?'

Grégoire nodded. 'That's right. When my parents got divorced, my mother took back her maiden name, Bernard, and obtained my legal custody. It was easier for us if I carried her last name as well, with school and so on. But since I've moved back to Château Bouclier and now run the wine business, most people call me by my father's name. I'm his son, his name represents our brand, and it's logical to them. I'm actually thinking of changing it back too, for my passport at least. Just to avoid any problems.'

'You should, especially if it's on your bottles,' Béatrice agreed. 'Pavie-Rausan is an unusual name. People will remember it.'

She took her glass and sat down at the kitchen table. It was set in style. Candles burned within silver candlesticks, and broad linen serviettes had been placed on the plates.

'And your mother? Where's she now?'

'She lives in Paris, happily remarried to a fine man.'

Grégoire topped up her glass, even though it was still half full. 'You know, cooking relaxes me,' he said, 'but this whole Fahrenheit nonsense completely throws me off. Yesterday everything ended up burned.'

Béatrice laughed. 'I can't stop thinking in Celsius and kilograms either, even after two years in the US.'

Her Blackberry buzzed. She pulled it out of her handbag. A text message from Joaquín.

Thanks for your voicemail, I really appreciate it. Yes, we do have to talk. I'm confident we can figure this out. I'll call you. Love, J.

Béatrice sighed as she thought again about their fight earlier that day. It wouldn't be a pleasant conversation, but they couldn't avoid it any longer.

'Problems?' asked Grégoire.

She waved her hand. 'No, just the office. My colleagues work around the clock.' She turned off her phone and put it back in her bag. She didn't want to think about Joaquín and their relationship problems any more today, she just wanted to enjoy this special evening.

'What's the topic of your thesis?' she asked, watching as he chopped a bunch of herbs into green dust at lightning speed.

'I'm writing about the French collaboration with the Nazis.' He cleaned the knife and wiped it dry on his apron. 'And how the French processed it later. There's still a lot of work to be done in that sense.'

'What do you mean by that?' Béatrice could only vaguely remember her history lessons. Her school days were all too long ago.

'Well, we've suppressed this topic for a long time. Chirac is the first president who officially apologized to the Jewish people for the Nazi collaboration. It was *him* who opened the Shoah Memorial in Paris last year.'

'You're right.' Her eyes followed Grégoire's supple movements. 'And why does this topic interest you so much?'

He stirred the herbs into the sauce. 'Because of my family. My father often told me about the war and what it was like during the German occupation. He claims that his father – my grandfather – destroyed his family back then. Something really bad must have happened.' Grégoire squeezed a lemon and drizzled the juice over the salad.

'And how did your grandfather see it?' Béatrice wanted to know.

He tipped the rice into a bowl. 'No idea, I never met my grandparents. My father broke off contact with his family right after the war and left Paris. Initially he got a job in Bordeaux, then he bought our vineyard near Libourne. But to this day I've not been able to find out what happened back then. My father simply won't talk about it.'

'Why not?' Béatrice felt the wine going to her head, reddening her cheeks. Or was it Grégoire who held her senses enthralled? His muscular arms, his voice, his smile . . .

'I don't know,' he replied. 'I guess no one likes talking about things that are close to their heart, do they?' His intense gaze shot through Béatrice like a lightning bolt. 'Your friend, Jacobina, only found out about Judith very late too, right,' Grégoire continued. 'In any case, my father's memories and his rift with the family inspired me to study the Second World War.'

He set the steaming fish on an oval platter and placed it between the candles on the table. '*Voilà.* I hope you like it.'

Béatrice felt like a queen. He continually served new wines, placing freshly polished glasses on the table. In awe, she read the labels. Meursault, Domaine des Comtes Lafon, white Burgundy. Haut Bailly, Pessac-Léognan, Bordeaux. Faiveley, Chambertin Clos de Bèze, red Burgundy. The names began to spin before her. She didn't care where the wines came from and what grape variety they were. As long as Grégoire didn't stop talking to her and topping up her glass.

'These are all just tasters, of course,' he emphasized with a laugh, revealing his white, strong teeth. 'The most important rule amongst us wine professionals is to never empty the glass. We only ever take a few sips.'

'And you just leave it in the glass? What a waste,' said Béatrice indignantly.

'True.' He nodded. 'It takes discipline.' His green eyes twinkled with pleasure. 'Mostly we spit it back out. We cannot just get drunk all the time.'

Their conversation was relaxed and familiar, sharing experiences about being in America as Europeans and telling stories from their lives.

'Washington is an exciting place, of course. The White House, the Pentagon, CIA and so on. But I couldn't live here long term,' declared Grégoire once they had reached the cheese course, which he presented in the form of wafer-thin shavings of Ossau-Iraty, drizzled with honey.

'I'd like to be back home by summer at the latest.' He took a piece of baguette from the bread basket and bit into it. 'Then it will soon be harvest time. I definitely have to be there for that.'

Béatrice felt sobered all at once. 'That's . . . that's really soon,' she murmured, lowering her gaze in order to hide her disappointment. All of a sudden, the cheese on her plate seemed dry and pallid.

Grégoire leaned back. 'Yes, thank God. By then my research will hopefully be complete. I'll finish writing it up at home.' He brushed a few breadcrumbs from the table. 'Would you like dessert?'

Béatrice looked at the clock. It was just before midnight. 'Thank you, but it's getting late. I really must go. Tomorrow is Monday.' She had hoped that Grégoire would protest, and at least try to talk her into an espresso. Instead, he merely nodded in agreement and dismissed her offer to help tidy up with a smile to soften his words. With a heavy heart, she stood and picked up her bag.

Grégoire folded his serviette together and got up too. 'I'll email you a list of organizations that you can contact to find out more about Judith,' he said, helping her into her coat and accompanying her to the front door. 'And of course, you can visit me any time in the museum.'

She stepped out and turned towards him, waiting for something. A word that would keep her from going. An arm stretching out towards her.

But Grégoire merely lifted his hand to wave. 'Get home safe.' He stifled a yawn. 'Time for me to go to bed too.' Then he closed the door.

*

Béatrice sat at the small table in the middle of the archive and worked listlessly. She recorded addresses, ordered files which in all probability no one would ever touch again, and compiled data no one was interested in. Through the walls, she heard the lifts rush up and down within the shafts. Another month in this room and she would have to see her therapist due to acute claustrophobia and workplace depression.

Her thoughts circled back to her dinner with Grégoire. What a wonderful evening. Everything was so easy with him. So lovely and familiar. She pictured him before her, effortlessly opening rare bottles of wine, setting a glass to his lips, the way he moved as he cooked. And soon he would disappear from her life and return to France.

Her Blackberry rang. Béatrice looked at the display. Cecil. Panic gripped her throat. Only after the fourth ring she finally took the call.

'Cecil, hello,' she said, trying to keep her tone casual. 'How was your trip?'

'Excellent, thank you. You called?' He sounded busy and distracted. In the background Béatrice heard a woman's voice, probably his assistant.

'Yes.' Her pulse raced. Her tongue felt as heavy as lead. She had been waiting for this call for weeks and had memorized what she would say down to the last detail. And now that the moment had come, her mind was wiped empty, like a school blackboard before the start of a lesson. 'I . . . I wanted to explain what really happened during the *Washington Post* interview.' She paused.

'Such a nuisance, the whole thing,' commented Cecil, 'but the investigation is underway. Believe me, I will find out what went wrong in the Haiti office.'

Béatrice breathed out with relief. Her pulse slowed. So Cecil hadn't allowed himself to be led astray by Michael, and knew very well that not she, but someone in Haiti had passed on the internal emails to the Partnership for Global Development.

'I didn't know anything about it,' she emphasized.

'I totally believe you. But your quote, Béatrice,' Cecil continued, letting out a whistle, 'that shouldn't have happened. It makes our press department look very bad.'

His words pierced Béatrice's limbs like a stiletto. 'He completely misquoted me, Cecil. Lustiger always writes extremely negatively about the bank.'

'Yeah, he's a total manipulator. I hate dealing with him. But that's why we have skilled people like you handling the press. So that it *doesn't* happen.'

Béatrice's throat closed. 'Will this now change anything about me joining your office?' she asked timidly, even though she knew very well what he was about to say. She had already suspected it for a long while. Otherwise, he would have called her back quickly, like he usually did. Having her darkest suspicion confirmed by him in the next few seconds was like an arrow headed straight for her.

'Well, I did my best,' he spoke slowly, as though wanting to delay the actual message a little more, 'but the selection committee has taken a firm stance against you since that article came out. People like Lustiger call here all the time. The air is pretty thin in the president's office. You always have to give a hundred and fifty per cent there. Every day. Every minute.'

She nodded silently.

'We've offered the job to your colleague Ricardo. He also applied. The guy is pretty impressive, and he was highly recommended by Michael.'

Handsome Ricardo with his black, gelled hair. Always

well dressed, always well prepared. Béatrice felt nauseous. The shelves in the archive blurred before her eyes, merged together and crumbled. As though from a great distance, she heard Cecil say how much he regretted all of this, and that he wished her all the best. She choked out an 'I understand, Cecil. Thank you for your call,' and hung up.

For a long while Béatrice just sat slumped in her chair, staring into nothing. She listened to the humming of the lifts and the footsteps of passing colleagues. Tried in vain to grasp the consequences of this phone call.

It could take one or two years before another job was advertised that she was both qualified for, and which would also mean moving up the career ladder.

Economists had an easier run of things. They were constantly in demand, both in Washington and in the regional offices. But for employees in the press department, it was different. There were only a few positions, and of those, even fewer became vacant; and they were supposed to be reduced even further in the years to come. What's more, the Lustiger fiasco had branded her indefinitely. Michael wouldn't pass up the opportunity of recording the incident in her personnel file.

Béatrice bit her finger until it bled. But she didn't feel the pain. Her worst fears had come true: she had lost the support of Cecil, her only ally, and her fate now lay entirely in Michael's hands. In the best-case scenario, he would eventually release her from the archive and let her do her old job again. In the worst case, he would get rid of her. Even though it didn't happen very often within the bank, there were still convenient ways of letting staffers go. For example, Michael could declare her position 'redundant' in the course of drastic budget cuts. Or he could refuse to renew her contract at the end of this year. The idea of no longer being able to support her mother and searching for a new, certainly less well paid job in Paris sent a shiver down her back.

Béatrice sucked at her bleeding finger, then wrapped a tissue around the wound. She couldn't take that risk; she had to get back in Michael's good books. Appease him. Win back his trust. He was and remained her boss. It was up to her to make the best of this situation.

She looked around despairingly. She would transform this bleak room into a first-class archive. She would take the task he had given her and fulfil it in such a way that he couldn't not be satisfied, no matter how much the work frustrated her. Right now, it was her only chance. She took a breath and got to work.

*

Towards six o'clock, Béatrice packed away her laptop, left the office and set off to Jacobina's. She jumped out of the taxi a street before, to pick up something for dinner. Jacobina had requested Indian.

The building entrance was open; a young woman was cleaning the stairwell. Béatrice passed her briskly. As she reached Jacobina's apartment and put out her hand to ring the doorbell, her friend opened the door.

'I heard you. Come in,' she said, fumbling with her walking stick. 'Hmm, that smells lovely.'

'Biryani rice.' Béatrice unpacked the shopping bag.

'Delicious. I haven't eaten properly yet today.'

She watched Béatrice as she filled two plates with rice.

'By the way, did you pay my phone bill by any chance?' she asked. 'It is working again. I got a sales call today.' She chuckled. 'The sudden ringtone totally scared me. I hadn't heard it in months.'

'Yes, I did. You need a phone, Jacobina, especially now.'

'You're such a sweetheart, Béatrice. Thank you!'

Once Jacobina had satisfied her appetite, she leaned back on the sofa and looked at Béatrice curiously. 'What's wrong? You've hardly touched your food.'

Béatrice pushed her fork morosely around her rice and told Jacobina about her job situation.

'There's some silly saying about this,' Jacobina replied, dunking her naan bread into green chutney sauce. 'If you don't like something, change it. And if you cannot change it, then change your perspective of it.' She shoved the bread into her mouth. 'My mother always used to say that,' she mumbled, chewing.

'You mean I should convince myself that my horrid boss isn't so bad after all?' Béatrice put her fork down. 'But I hate the bastard.'

'I mean that you shouldn't just give up. Your life doesn't depend on this man and this bank. There are endless other opportunities.'

'No, there aren't,' protested Béatrice. 'You have no idea what a battle it was to get that job in the first place.'

'Sure, but you're not happy there anyway.'

Béatrice sighed. 'You're right.' Jacobina's words comforted her. Visiting this lady did her good in general, she had realized. She enjoyed helping her, but there was more: Jacobina had become someone she could confide in – a friend.

Jacobina stroked her bony hand over Béatrice's arm and smiled. 'I'm sure something new will turn up soon. Keep your head up.' Then her expression turned serious. 'My operation is the day after tomorrow.'

Béatrice slapped her hand over her mouth in shock. 'And here I am banging on about my work. Which hospital?'

'George Washington.'

'That's not far from my office. I can visit you there every day.'

Jacobina nodded and looked at Béatrice in silence.

'I brought my laptop with me,' said Béatrice, in an attempt to distract her, and pulled the computer out of her bag. 'I'd like to write a few emails with you before I go home. Grégoire has done loads of preliminary research and sent me the addresses.'

Jacobina wiped a serviette across her mouth and straightened up. 'Then let's do it. Where do we start?'

Béatrice opened her email account and scanned the message Grégoire had sent her that morning. 'He says we should first fill in the enquiry form for the International Tracing Service in Germany,' she explained. 'Then we should write to the veterans' ministry in Paris, and to the Shoah Memorial. That's in Paris too, and they have an extensive archive there.'

At the very end of his message, Grégoire had written that he would love to see her again soon. Nothing more. The brevity of the sentence had initially disappointed Béatrice. It sounded like a pleasantry. But after she had read the message multiple times, she began to wonder. Perhaps Grégoire really meant it the way he had written it? Otherwise, he could have signed off without saying anything. Béatrice stared at the screen, and once again her mind began to dissect the final sentence and its significance.

'Hey, I have to get up early tomorrow,' said Jacobina, tugging Béatrice's sleeve. 'Let's get stuck in.'

*

On Tuesday morning, right after Béatrice woke up, Joaquín called. 'Are you free this evening to come to McLean and stay overnight?' he asked. 'I'd like to sit down and discuss what went wrong last Sunday.' She could hear him pouring tea. 'I can finish work a little earlier today and pick you up.' Normally, Béatrice only spent the night at Joaquín's on weekends. She was pleasantly surprised he wanted to free this time for her.

'What about Laura?' she asked. 'Will she be around?'

'She can do something else. Read, or watch a film.'

'Sure, sounds good. I'll be down in the street at six and wait for you.' She had a long shower, got dressed and packed her nightshirt and a fresh blouse for the following day. She also put on the necklace with the teardrop-shaped pendant that Joaquín had given her. It would make him happy to see her wearing it.

Still, she worried all day that Joaquín would call her back because something important at the office had come up, and that he had to cancel their evening plans. But, contrary to her expectations, at six o'clock sharp, his car pulled up right in front of her at the entrance to the bank.

'I'm sorry about Sunday,' she said, as soon as she sat next to him.

'I'm sorry, too,' he mumbled, steering the car out into

the traffic. 'I shouldn't have exploded like that.' They fell silent for a while, listening to the news. Then Joaquín switched off the radio. 'In the future, please let's try not to argue in front of Laura,' he said. 'I want her home to be peaceful.'

Béatrice chewed at her fingernail. 'So why did you make such a fuss out of me not wanting to go to the cinema?' she asked. 'If you hadn't got so worked up, it wouldn't have escalated like that.'

'All I wanted was that the three of us do something together,' groaned Joaquín. Light drizzle began to fall. He turned on the windscreen wipers. 'Is that so hard to understand?'

Her stomach cramped. 'I miss how we were with each other when we met,' she said, searching for his hand.

Before she could touch it, his mobile rang, and within seconds he was engrossed in a conversation about rising energy costs and the expected rise in interest rates. A call from the editorial team, Béatrice presumed, and sighed. Joaquín only ended the call after he had parked his car in front of his house.

'Shall I cook something for us?' Béatrice asked in a conciliatory tone, as he opened the front door.

Rudi dashed towards them, wagging his tail, barking joyfully and jumping up at his master.

'Only if you don't mind,' answered Joaquín, rubbing Rudi's belly. He sounded tired. As usual, his daily grind, with all its deadlines and responsibilities, had exhausted him. Would he have enough energy now to discuss their relationship problems? Béatrice doubted it.

'Hi there,' Laura greeted them from the kitchen table.

She was wearing headphones from which loud pop music boomed as she hummed along quietly. Her bare feet tapped to the beat.

Joaquín gently took off the headphones and kissed her. 'Hello, sweetheart. How was school?'

'Horrible,' muttered Laura as she buried her hands in the pockets of her hoodie. 'I failed the math test,' she announced, not looking at her father. 'Ms Hoffman wants to see you.'

Joaquín shook his head, sighing, then pulled up a chair and sat next to her. 'How could that have happened?' he asked in exasperation. 'We went through everything.'

Laura shrugged. 'I guess it wasn't enough.'

Meanwhile, Béatrice had taken a box of spaghetti out of the cupboard and put water on to boil.

Joaquín proceeded to lecture Laura about the virtues of ambition and hard work and how important a role they play if you want to succeed in life.

Béatrice cooked away silently. She knew it wasn't his fault, but still – she found it hard to contain her disappointment. This was supposed to be *their* evening. A long-needed opportunity to voice their feelings and frustrations and to come up with a few things they both could do to change and make things better. Yet, as so many times before in recent months, his other priorities crowded her out.

Twenty minutes later, they were sitting around the table. Joaquín shovelled a large portion of spaghetti onto his plate and continued his requirements-for-achievement monologue. He decreed tutorial sessions and forbade her from watching early evening TV. Laura sat slouched next to him, her head propped on her arm, silently spooning up her tomato sauce.

'Don't you think it's enough now?' Béatrice intervened, feeling sorry for the girl. 'Let Laura enjoy her dinner. Tomorrow is another day.'

Laura shot her a grateful glance and blinked – there it was again, a glimpse of the old complicity they once had. Béatrice smiled.

'You don't get it,' Joaquín insisted. 'If she starts falling behind now, she'll never make it up again.'

'Don't be so negative,' Béatrice retorted. 'Severe punishment will only make things worse.'

'What do *you* know about education?' Joaquín mumbled as he shoved in the noodles.

How did he dare say something like this? Just because she didn't have children, she wasn't entitled to have an opinion? Anger was welling up inside her. Here they were again, fighting, hardly twenty minutes after they had arrived. Then she looked at Laura and pulled herself together. Joaquín had just asked her not to argue any more in front of his daughter. Béatrice wanted to respect that.

'I was a child once, too,' she said abruptly and decided to leave it at that.

It was Joaquín who picked up the topic again, later, after Laura had gone to bed. 'It's my fault,' he said. 'I have to help her more. I just hope she won't get held back.'

Béatrice, stacking the crockery in the dishwasher, paused. 'But not because of *one* bad result.'

Joaquín sighed. 'It happens quicker than you think. That school is super tough.'

Béatrice poured liquid dish soap into the machine and turned it on. The device immediately began to vibrate, gurgling gently.

'I got some bad news too,' she said. 'I didn't get the job.'

'Which job?' Joaquín put on his glasses and picked up his mobile phone.

'How could you forget?' She threw the damp kitchen towel on the worktop and stared at him. 'My dream job! I've been talking about it for weeks.'

'Well, I guess then you'll have to apply for another one,' he replied absent-mindedly, reading through his messages.

Béatrice wanted to make a quick comeback, but she fell silent. He wasn't listening anyway.

'Shall we talk about us now?' she asked after a while.

Joaquín looked at her bewildered. 'Didn't we already do that in the car? It's quite late already and I still have work to do.' He stepped over to the countertop and looked through the mail that lay there, still unopened. 'By the way, I have to fly to New York on Saturday to attend an economic policy symposium,' he announced, opening an envelope with his thumb. 'Not clear yet for how long. Laura will stay at Sarah's.' He unfolded the letter and read. 'A bill reminder,' he called out impetuously. 'I already paid that stupid thing last week.'

Béatrice hung the tea towel up to dry and watched Joaquín, as he went up the stairs, cursing.

No doubt. It was over.

*

Béatrice had given the George Washington Hospital her name and number as Jacobina's emergency contact and asked the nurses to call her with an update after the surgery.

The call came the very next morning, a short while after

Béatrice had arrived in the archive. The radical hysterectomy had gone well, the nurse informed her; the ovarian carcinoma could be removed successfully. Jacobina was still a little weak but would be able to receive visitors in the coming days and would probably be discharged at the weekend.

Radical hysterectomy, Béatrice repeated in her mind after she had hung up the phone. The surgeon had found a tumour the size of a lemon and, in the process, removed both ovaries and the womb. As soon as Jacobina had regained enough strength, a lengthy chemotherapy awaited her. She would probably lose her hair, struggle with nausea, and everything to her would taste of metal. Béatrice shivered at the thought of the ordeal that lay ahead for her friend.

She called Lena, told her the results of the operation and assured her she would take excellent care of Jacobina, for which Lena was very grateful.

Then she concentrated her attention back on her work. It was the week of the Haiti donor conference. Finance and development ministers from across the world had gathered at the bank's headquarters in D.C. to decide over additional funding for the Caribbean island state. Normally, Béatrice would be buzzing industriously around Michael, finalizing speeches, trying to get a quote from the Haitian finance minister and organizing the press conference. She would have greeted the government delegation from Port-au-Prince, corrected the final translations into French and might perhaps have been invited to a cocktail reception at the embassy. Everything would have been planned down to the precise detail, and a thick file with stage directions,

Q&As and other background information would have been sent to the president's office.

But nothing was like it used to be. Béatrice was no longer an active player in the drama of international development assistance; she had been banished to a musty room full of old files. Now her mission was to display a positive attitude. She could not simply feign interest in her new assignment to Michael; she had to actually develop it and make sure she made swift progress. Lunch breaks were a thing of the past, as was turning up late in the morning and leaving a bit earlier in the afternoon. She had written up a few recommendations for reorganizing the archive. Because Michael loved these types of initiatives, she meticulously recorded everything she had done during the day.

And then there was the chaos that dominated her heart. All the feelings she could possibly experience were strewn like a colourful heap of Mikado sticks. At times, Grégoire's green eyes would come to her mind, evoking both happiness and longing. Feelings she hadn't had in a long time.

But these would dissolve into pain when her thoughts turned to Joaquín, their quarrels, struggles, and his never-ending work obligations. She had to end this relationship. As soon as he returned from his symposium in New York, she'd summon up her courage and do it.

And Grégoire? Should she call him? Did he have feelings for her? Her logical mind answered with a definite 'No'. Her heart countered with a more measured 'Perhaps'.

But when it came to matters of the heart, logic always had the upper hand. She still *was* in a relationship – how inappropriate, even foolish, to consider another one. She needed more time. Time to get to know Grégoire better. Time to recover from all the pain with Joaquín. However, time was the one thing she *didn't* have. In just a few months, Grégoire would move back home to France.

Besides, she couldn't rule out the possibility that he had a girlfriend waiting for him. That he had just invited Béatrice for dinner as a friend. This wasn't a topic she wanted to bring up with him, because then she too would have to tell him about Joaquín.

Better not to call Grégoire at all. He would soon be gone, anyway.

*

On Sunday, he called *her*. This time she recognized Grégoire's voice at once. As soon as he began to speak, Béatrice felt the endorphins course through her belly and down to the tips of her toes. He just wanted to see how she was doing, he said. That sounded promising, thought Béatrice. He sounded interested. But then the left side of her brain immediately intervened, suggesting convincingly that Grégoire had waited far too long to call her for him to be seriously interested. She tried to push aside the pesky thoughts, and told him about the mountain of work she had on her plate this coming week.

'Hey, do you fancy coming to the Cherry Blossom Festival with me?' he asked. 'The trees are supposed to be at their most beautiful this weekend.'

Spontaneous, enthusiastic and available. What an alluring mixture. Béatrice immediately accepted.

Half an hour later, she was strolling blissfully alongside Grégoire through an ocean of delicate pink blossoms.

The Cherry Blossom Festival in Washington, D.C. had existed since 1912, when Tokyo had made a gift of three thousand seedlings to the American capital. Every year, towards the end of March or the beginning of April, the trees around the Tidal Basin in the West Potomac Park were in full bloom, giving the city a romantic spring flair, which was in stark contrast to the hard-hitting world politics that were made here every day.

'Cherry blossoms – a symbol of beauty and transience,' sighed Grégoire theatrically, popping a piece of chewing gum into his mouth. 'I could almost start to like this city.'

'You'll have to hurry, then. It only lasts a week,' replied Béatrice dryly.

'That's what I mean. Transience.' He plucked a few blossoms from a tree and put them in Béatrice's hand. 'Let us enjoy the beauty of the moment.' His eyes flashed mischievously. They both laughed.

'But I'm not renting a pedal boat,' said Grégoire as his gaze drifted over the Tidal Basin, which was covered with little boats. 'That really would be too tacky.'

Béatrice regretted his decision, but didn't say a word. The warm sun, the tall, handsome man next to her amid the white and pink splendour, it was like a dream. All he'd have to do now was take her hand and hold it tight.

But he didn't.

14

Judith

Paris, February 1941

More snow had fallen during the night, gathering in menacing piles on the windowsills, pressing against the panes like an intruder. There was a time when I had loved the snow. It slowed the hectic bustle of the city and gave Paris a magical glow. In the wartime winter of 1941, however, snow was nothing but a paralysing threat. It crept inside our worn-out shoes and turned our feet into blocks of ice as we queued in line for hours. It blocked the streets and stopped food deliveries from reaching the shops on time. To escape the snow, people crowded into the Metro tunnels, bringing the subterranean transport system to a standstill.

I walked down the hallway into the kitchen. As I passed the wall mirror, I caught sight of my pale face and was startled: my lips were blue with cold, and my brown locks had lost their fullness. My body looked stiff and hunched, like an old woman's. What had this devilish winter done to me?

The only comforting thought on this icy morning was that, thanks to Christian, we had enough coal to survive another few weeks of this merciless cold. Lily circled around my legs. I picked her up and scratched her neck, then lit the fire and brewed some coffee.

At around seven o'clock, Mother set off with our coupons. She looked weak. Since the beginning of the year, her mental state had declined rapidly. She was uncommunicative and lethargic, still struggling with the fact that she couldn't work in her school any more. For a few weeks, she had helped out at Madame Morin's in the evenings and on weekends, in the sewing room out back. But then, overnight, the fur shop had been sold. Madame Morin hadn't wanted to talk about it. The last time I saw her, she said something about a forced sale, and tears shot into her eyes. I didn't understand what had happened. But in the display window of the shop, which had been in their family for generations, the yellow sign saying *Jewish Business* had been replaced by a red one. And before long, there was no sign at all.

I glanced out of the window and saw Mother stamping through the snow in her thin boots to line up at the bakery in Rue Rambuteau, for half a pound of bread, and then at the grocer's in Rue des Archives for a few potatoes and a handful of lentils. We were getting less and less for our food coupons. A few courageous students had begun to forge coupons and sell them in the bathrooms at the Sorbonne. But I didn't dare use them – police checks were popping up everywhere. By now we were short of everything. We had no wool to darn stockings with, no leather to repair our shoes, and no batteries for our pocket torches. We had only hunger, fear, and the vague hope that at some point the spring would come.

Paris, March 1941

'So, when are you going to introduce me to your parents?' I asked, trying to sound as casual and natural as possible. I was sitting tensely on the outer edge of a black rattan chair in a cafe on Place Saint-Sulpice, playing with the straw that protruded from my glass of lemonade. The question had been burning on my tongue for a while now, and today I finally found the courage to ask Christian.

Ever since we had first met, his parents seemed to be a topic which he, for reasons I still didn't understand, tried to avoid at any cost. Besides making disparaging remarks about his father from time to time, he never spoke about them. When, occasionally, a reference to them escaped his mouth, he would get a dismissive look on his face and quickly and casually continue talking, as if he regretted having mentioned them. Over time he had given me brief, disjointed insights into their wealth and their many societal commitments. These snippets of information had imprinted themselves in my memory like puzzle pieces. That his parents were at a cocktail party in Neuilly, that they had recently bet fifty thousand francs at the horse races, or had a disagreement at breakfast about the starters which they would serve their guests that evening. But the puzzle pieces didn't fit into a proper whole. As soon as I asked any questions, Christian would change the subject, and I was left feeling guilty and uneasy.

Christian folded the newspaper on his lap and smoothed it out. A few unruly pages slipped to the floor.

'I mean . . .' I continued, taking the straw out of the glass and rotating it in my fingers. 'You've known my mother for almost six months now, you introduced me to that Nazi bigwig as your fiancée . . . So I thought . . .' I looked at him inquiringly, but he evaded my gaze and leaned over laboriously to pick up the fallen pages. 'We could—'

'I can't,' he interrupted me, rolling up the newspaper and tossing it on the table. He took a sugar spoon and stirred his coffee so vigorously that it slopped over the edge of the cup.

'Why not? Is it because I'm not sophisticated enough for them?'

He didn't answer. So I went a step further. 'They expect you to be spending your time with the daughters of their affluent friends, not some poor student who lives in a shabby little apartment with her unemployed mother?'

'Stop that right now!' he exclaimed, his lips closing into a tight line.

'Only if you tell me what the problem is,' I retorted.

Christian continued to avoid my gaze. He brushed the hair off his forehead, sighed loudly and looked across the square. His eyelids twitched. 'I don't want to talk about it,' he mumbled.

I lit myself a cigarette, the fourth already since we had been sitting here, and leaned back. 'Shall I tell you what the real problem is? It's because I'm Jewish.' The words shot out of me. Angry, I took a deep drag of my cigarette and blew the smoke in his direction. I wanted to provoke him so that he would finally come out with the truth.

For a fraction of a second, our gazes met. His eyes looked dark and sad. A pigeon flew through the open window. It fluttered wildly around our table, trying to pluck up a few crumbs. The waiter hurried over and flapped the menu around until the bird found its way back outside.

Christian took a long breath and waited until the waiter had disappeared. 'I'm afraid you are right,' he finally replied, looking cautiously around him. Then he pulled his chair so close to mine that our legs were touching. 'Introducing you to my father would be complete insanity and could put you in danger,' he said tonelessly.

I stared at him in amazement. My hands began to shake. 'What do you mean exactly?' I asked, terror raring up within me.

He looked around once again to make sure no one was nearby. 'My father agrees with what's happening in the German Reich,' he said. 'And he's a supporter of Admiral Darlan, who is collaborating more closely with the Germans than his predecessor.'

His father an anti-Semite! A *collabo*! My ears were filled with a rushing sound.

'High-level politicians and officers come to see us, including many Germans,' explained Christian.

I felt the colour draining from my face and wanted to tell him to stop. But I couldn't move my tongue.

'I don't know exactly what they discuss,' he continued, crossing his weak leg over the healthy one, something he always did when it began to hurt. 'Except recently . . . The door to his office was ajar. I was sitting in the living room and overheard a few scraps of conversation. It was about the commissioner's office that's being set up. A department for Jewish issues, or something like that. But then someone closed the door, and I could no longer hear anything.'

It was as if I had bought a bag of sweets, and as I opened it, instead of the longed-for bonbons, thick hairy spiders were tumbling out. I gulped down the rest of my lemonade and put the empty glass on the table with a trembling hand.

'I suspect my father is passing them confidential information,' Christian explained, undeterred. After having shied away from telling me the truth for so long, he now seemed unable to hold himself back. 'Perhaps they're pressuring him, I don't know. In any case, as the director of one of France's largest private banks, he's in a key position.'

My throat was burning. Up until this moment, everything had been so perfect. Almost unbelievably wonderful and easy. Like a fairy tale. And now?

Christian went to put his arm around my shoulders. But as soon as I felt his touch, I pushed him away.

Although he didn't let it show, I sensed his confusion.

'So long as he doesn't know who you are, nothing will happen to you,' he said after a pause.

'Von Stülpnagel saw us together,' I interjected. 'He might tell him.'

Christian waved his hand dismissively. 'I don't think so. A general like him has other problems and huge responsibilities. I'm sure he's long forgotten running into us at the opera a few months ago.' He drank down his coffee in small, quick swallows. 'Remember, my angel, as soon as all this is finally over, then . . .' His hand reached for mine, and this time I didn't pull away. 'Then we'll go south. You and I.'

I didn't doubt for even a second that his feelings for me were genuine. But since that day, my stomach tangled into knots whenever I thought of his father.

Paris, May 1941

Dripping in sweat, Christian and I hurried across the Pont Neuf. The sun was so bright I had to lower my gaze and shield my eyes so I could see. On the other side of the bridge, I made out the Quai du Louvre, which in the shimmering light had blurred to a single bright line of houses. Heavy military trucks rolled alongside us. I pulled Christian along, trying to get him to move faster. But he couldn't. His lips tight, he was dragging his lame leg behind him like an unwieldy cane.

Then I woke up. For a moment, I wasn't sure where I was. Opening my eyes, I stretched out my fingers and, in the darkness, felt the familiar contours of my rough pillow and the blanket. But the engine noise from the trucks was still there. It grew louder, until the entire room was humming and vibrating, and my windowpanes were clinking. The noise was coming from outside, four storeys below me. Doors slamming. Footsteps. Male voices. Dazed with sleep, I sat up and looked over to the window. A thin, pink strip of light threaded through the black sky. The first sign of the rising sun. Suspecting that it was around half past four or perhaps even a little earlier, I clambered out of bed, my limbs stiff.

I stumbled over to the window and saw the shadowy silhouette of the houses on the other side of the street. The roar of the engines pushed its way up towards me. I pressed my face against the windowpane and gazed down, but still couldn't make anything out.

After a while, I opened the window and stuck my head out into the darkness. Cold morning air greeted me. Shivering, I crossed my arms over my chest and rubbed my shoulders. The rumbling pulsed in my ears. Men were shouting out brusque commands. I stretched my head out even further and saw dim spheres of light. Were they the covered headlamps of parked buses? What were they doing here at this early hour? On the other side of the street, lights went on across several floors of a building. Shadows flitted past the windows. I stared at the soundless figures.

A window was flung open below me. 'Over here!' shouted a loud male voice.

As quick as a flash, I pulled my head back. The police! They were coming to get us! I didn't dare shut the window through fear it might squeak. A bolt of panic hit me. What should I do now? Wake Mother? Pack? Get dressed? Or hide in a wardrobe?

I listened out for the sounds from downstairs. Clattering. A few screams. Then everything went quiet. Minutes passed. They felt like hours. Down on the street, the idling engines of the buses groaned.

I had to wake Mother. To be on the safe side, I listened out for a while longer, but no more sounds came from the apartment below us. Nonetheless, I still didn't dare walk across the creaking parquet floor and decided to let her sleep.

Once the band of light on the horizon became broader, I could wait no longer. Cautiously, I went back to the window and looked down. In the grey morning light, I saw French police officers guiding men into two long buses. Many were still wearing their pyjamas. Others had hastily pulled something over them. Some were barefoot.

I recognized a few of the men, having seen them at the grocer's or on the street.

The policemen hurried around, using truncheons to push the men ahead of them and force them into the buses. Monosyllabic instructions like 'Stop', 'Go' and 'Quickly' rose up to me. Two *gendarmes* brandishing guns stood on the pavement, watching over everything.

I stood there and watched, my mouth open in a silent scream.

In the apartments on the other side of the street, I saw curtains moving. Women opened the windows and watched in silence as their neighbours were forced into the buses.

A whistle was blown. The policemen jumped into the vehicles, doors closed, a horn shrilled. Then the two buses set off, trundling down the street and disappearing into the urban canyon. The din subsided, and everything became completely silent again, like after a thunderstorm. The women in the apartments on the other side of the street were still staring downwards. One by one, they stepped back from the windows, drawing the curtains.

A new day began.

15

Béatrice

Washington, D.C., 2006

The first response from Paris came more swiftly than
expected. Béatrice was just pulling on her jacket to leave
the bank and visit Jacobina, who was back home from the
hospital, when her computer buzzed, signalling the arrival
of a new email. Re: Judith Goldemberg.

Her heart pounding, Béatrice sank back down onto the
chair and opened the message. It was from Marie-Louise
Diatta at the National Archives.

Dear Madame Duvier,

   The Ministry of Veterans' Affairs received your
enquiry and forwarded it to the National Archives. For
your information: after 2nd June 1992, the majority of
the files which could be retrieved from the Drancy
assembly and detention camp were relocated to the
National Archives.

   I am pleased to inform you that we have found two
documents in our files relating to Jacobina Grunberg's
half-sister, Mademoiselle Goldemberg. I'm attaching a

copy of a photo of Judith Goldemberg, as well as
a copy of her registration form at the Drancy camp.
We hope that this proves helpful in your search.

Please do let me know if you have any further
questions.

Kind regards,

M. L. Diatta

Béatrice opened the file with the photograph first. It was
a black and white picture. A young girl with fresh cheeks
stared out at her. Her face was pretty, her expression
seemingly unsuspecting of the terrible journey into the
abyss which stood before her. Judith's gaze wasn't open
or childish, however, but instead held a deep sadness, and
pride too. The seriousness in her eyes was softened by her
delicate round cheeks. She had a small, heart-shaped mouth
and sensuous lips. The hint of a smile gave her an impenetrable, melancholic air. Her face was framed by dark,
wavy hair that stretched down to her shoulders.

Béatrice studied the picture and tried to read into
Judith's gaze. When and where might this photo have
been taken? In the Drancy camp? Shortly before Judith's
deportation to Auschwitz? And who had taken it?

Béatrice opened the second email attachment. It was a
copy of a form that had been filled out by hand. At the
top stood a registration number: *9613 B*. Beneath it were
the particulars of Judith's birth.

Surname: Goldemberg
Forename: Judith
Date of birth: 19th October 1921

Place of birth: Paris
Nationality: French
Occupation: Student
Residential address: 24, Rue du Temple, Paris

Béatrice couldn't wait to surprise Jacobina with this information. Now she had a photo, a date of birth and an
address. That was sure to lead them to further clues. She
printed out the two pages and set off to see her friend.

*

Jacobina looked pale and tired. She was wearing a short-
sleeved, blue nightshirt with black leggings beneath. Her
skin hung loosely from her thin arms, as though it didn't
belong to her. From her right wrist dangled a dirty dressing,
the clip loose. Seeing Béatrice, her mouth twitched into a
pained smile. Béatrice followed her into the living room.
Leaning on her walking stick, Jacobina laboriously made
her way to the armchair and fell down into it with a loud
groan. She was holding her belly like a pregnant woman.

'How are you feeling?' asked Béatrice, unpacking the
groceries she had bought for her friend. Fruit, a bottle of
juice and some bread.

'So-so,' murmured Jacobina, stroking her stomach. 'I
have a check-up in a few days, then the chemo starts.'

She didn't have any appetite, but Béatrice persisted until
Jacobina eventually tried the cherries.

'I also brought you something else,' said Béatrice. She
laid the printout of the photo on Jacobina's lap. 'I just
received this from the National Archives in Paris. A picture
of Judith.'

Jacobina gave a start. Her eyes widened, she raised her hands to her cheeks and her mouth dropped open. 'Oh my God,' she cried, 'oh my God.' She stared at the picture in shock. When a tear dropped down onto the photo, she buried her face in her hands and began to cry softly.

Béatrice stroked her arm gently. 'Your half-sister was a beautiful woman,' she said.

Jacobina pulled a tissue from a crevice in the armchair and wiped her face. 'You have no idea how much she looks like my father . . . She's the spitting image of him,' she murmured. 'It's . . .' She broke off and suppressed a sob. 'It's quite overwhelming.'

'Look, the archives sent something else too.' Béatrice pulled out the copy of the registration form. 'It even gives Judith's last address in Paris. Rue du Temple.'

Jacobina studied the information on the form closely. Then she took Béatrice's hand and squeezed it tightly. 'Thank you, Béatrice,' she said. 'Thank you. This is a big day for me.' The tears overpowered her once more.

'Now we can make an enquiry with the registry office in the 3rd arrondissement to see if there's a marriage certificate for Judith,' Béatrice said. 'We have her birthday and an address. Grégoire thinks we should also write to the rabbi who looks after the Jewish community in the Marais.' She made a mental note to contact the registry office and the Jewish community by email that evening.

Jacobina nodded. 'And what about the residents' registration office?'

'We don't have anything like that in France,' explained Béatrice, filling two glasses with orange juice. 'Residential addresses are noted on our IDs, but we're not obligated to notify a change of address when we move. So that means there can be several people with the same address.'

They sat next to each other in silence. Jacobina was still transfixed by the photo. 'What a shame my father never saw her like this,' she said eventually. 'So grown-up and pretty. When he separated from her mother, Judith was still a girl. And then . . .' She sighed. 'Then he lost contact with her.'

'Yes, some fathers are good at that,' quipped Béatrice, letting out a short, bitter laugh.

Jacobina frowned. 'Lica didn't just take off,' she retorted, a little indignantly. 'He was homesick, but his first wife didn't want to live in Romania. They got divorced and he moved back alone. And then he met my mother. He said he wrote to Judith regularly. Later, he was arrested and interned in a labour camp because he was a Jew.'

'I'm sorry, I didn't mean it like that,' Béatrice apologized. 'I was just thinking about my own father. He left us when I was very young. I wrote him letters for years, but he never replied.'

'Perhaps he didn't receive them?'

Béatrice shrugged. 'I think he did.' Her expression darkened. 'My mother even had to take him to court to get alimony. It must have annoyed him that I was studying, because it meant he had to pay for longer.'

Jacobina looked at her gently. 'You and Judith were both abandoned,' she said in a whisper. 'Each in different ways. Your fathers left you long before you could even understand it. I'm sure it will never stop being painful. You'll both always carry something unresolved within you.'

She took a deep breath and slowly exhaled. 'But do you know what? It also makes you strong. Nothing will ever be able to hurt you that much again.'

Béatrice swallowed. The living room began to swim in front of her eyes. Embarrassed, she rubbed her tears away.

'What a wonderful person you are, Béatrice. You have done so much for me,' Jacobina went on. Her voice sounded strained. 'Without you I'd still be that lonely old lady feeling sorry for herself. I would never have had the courage to search for Judith. And I wouldn't have survived the operation. I probably wouldn't even have gone in for it.' Her eyes radiated warmth and a contentment Béatrice hadn't seen in them before. 'Now I have hope again that somehow my life won't end as badly as I expected.' Jacobina smiled. 'You've brought kindness and humanity back to me. I want to thank you for that.'

Béatrice lowered her gaze. The gratitude made her feel self-conscious.

'Come on, let's eat some more cherries,' said Jacobina. 'I'm starting to feel hungry.'

*

As Béatrice stood in front of the lifts the next morning, waiting for the doors to open, a heavy hand landed on her shoulder. Startled, she turned around and stared into Michael's face. The whites of his eyes were bloodshot, his expression unapproachable.

'So, how's it going in the archive?' The biting smell of tobacco hit her nose.

Béatrice took a step back. The lift chimed, and people coming out crowded past them.

'All well,' she answered, forcing out a half-smile. 'I'm making good progress,' she added hurriedly.

He sniffed. 'I sure hope so.'

They stepped into the lift. The doors closed, and Béatrice was enveloped in a cloud of smoke. She pressed the button for the eighth floor.

'The Haiti conference was a disaster, by the way,' he said, pushing his hands into his coat pockets and jingling a few coins.

Béatrice fixed her gaze on the illuminated numbers indicating the floors. She didn't want to hear what he was about to say.

'We were counting on at least one million dollars in additional aid. But after your outstanding *Washington Post* fiasco, we barely scraped together two hundred thousand. Peanuts!' He cleared his throat loudly, letting the coins clink in his pockets.

'Donor countries' priorities don't just change from one day to the next because of a newspaper article,' Béatrice objected.

'You are greatly underestimating the power of the media, mademoiselle,' he countered.

Floor number seven lit up. Almost over; in a moment she'd be liberated. Béatrice tried to breathe evenly. The lift stopped again. Eighth floor.

'Even if you refuse to acknowledge it,' said Michael, giving her a meaningful look, 'you have half the Haiti programme on your conscience.' The doors opened. He promptly walked out and, without a further word, strode off along the corridor.

Béatrice stared after him until he had disappeared into his office. Then she hurried into the archive, slammed the door behind her and dropped onto her chair. She couldn't cope with his animosity any longer; it was unacceptable. But what were her options?

Once again, Béatrice ran through the individual stages of the dreadful scenario awaiting her if she quit or, worse, her contract wasn't extended. She'd lose her diplomatic visa, meaning she'd have to leave the United States within a few weeks and return to France. She'd probably move in with her mother, at least for the first few months, search for a new job and live off her savings. Everything she had thought she'd achieved would be destroyed.

You have half the Haiti programme on your conscience, Michael's voice echoed in her head. No matter what she did here in the archive, it would never be forgotten. Béatrice let out a deep sigh and listened to the rushing sound of the lifts. After a while, she gave herself a jolt and powered up her laptop.

*

The second email from Paris arrived early that afternoon. The sender was a Monsieur Kahn, an employee of the Shoah Memorial. Her email had been forwarded to him, he wrote. He had searched for Judith in the historical files and found her name in Serge Klarsfeld's book. A copy of the relevant page was attached. Unfortunately, there was nothing else in the archive about Judith.

Béatrice was disappointed that Monsieur Kahn wasn't able to give her any new information. She had already received the pages from the Klarsfeld book from Grégoire. She read on:

I have also attached a copy of the original telegraph from SS-Obersturmführer Heinz Röthke to Adolf Eichmann, in which he announces the departure of convoy sixty-three to Auschwitz. Klarsfeld cites this communication on page 484 of his book.

Béatrice clicked on the attachment. When the hand-signed telegram from 1943, written in German, opened in front of her, she shivered. A brief French translation was also joined.

The Commander in Chief of the Security Police and Security Service for the attention of the Military Commander in France. Communication. 17th December 1943.
Telegram:
a)   To the Reichssicherheitshauptamt, for the attention of Obersturmbannführer Eichmann.
b)   To the Chief of Staff at Concentration Camp Oranienburg.
c)   To Concentration Camp Auschwitz, for the attention of Obersturmbannführer Hess.
Subject: Jewish transport from Bobigny station near Paris to Auschwitz/OS on 17.12.1943
   On 17.12.1943 at 12.00 hours, transport train DA 901/54 left departure station Bobigny headed for Auschwitz with 850 Jews on board.
   The deported Jews correspond to the remitted evacuation guidelines. The transport will be accompanied from Paris to Auschwitz by a protective police command force of 1:20.

All traces and references to Judith ended in Auschwitz. But why, then, was Judith included in George Dreyfus's list as a survivor, a *rescapée*? Had there been a mistake? Or had an important source of information been over-looked?

She had to talk to Grégoire about it. He had invited her to visit him at the Holocaust Museum any time. Now she had an important reason to go and see the handsome vintner with the beautiful green eyes again.

*

The next day, as Béatrice swept into the museum during her lunch hour, with glistening Dior lips, designer handbag and perfectly styled hair, Grégoire wasn't there. She should have called beforehand, she thought with disappointment. Perhaps he had taken the day off.

Then she spotted his beige coat hanging on a hook by the door. Relieved, she walked through the room, looking around, but couldn't see him anywhere. She decided to wait a little. Perhaps he had just popped out to grab a coffee.

A few steps away from her stood the elegant elderly lady with the white hair Béatrice had briefly talked to on her very first visit; she was showing a young man with horn-rimmed glasses a file. Today, she was wearing a black woollen jacket, from beneath which a stiff, white collar poked out. Her hair was gathered into a bun. Her name was Julia, if Béatrice remembered correctly. Julia, a woman who had experienced first-hand the horror of the Holocaust, and survived it. As she spotted Béatrice, she mumbled something to the man and stepped towards her. 'Hello, are you looking for anything in particular?' she asked in a friendly tone. She smelled of lavender, and once again Béatrice noticed her light-blue eyes.

'I'm actually waiting for Grégoire,' she replied, looking around to strengthen her statement.

'Oh, Grégoire has been down in the archive for a while now. But he should be back any moment,' explained Julia. 'Can I help you in the meantime?'

Why not? thought Béatrice, unbuttoning her jacket. Perhaps this lady would think of something that hadn't occurred to her and Grégoire. 'I'm looking for a woman,' she began. 'She was deported in 1943. A few days ago, I received a photo of her, but now I'm not exactly sure where to look for further information.'

As Julia heard the year, she flinched slightly.

Béatrice rummaged around in her handbag for Judith's photo.

Then Julia laid her hand on Béatrice's arm and nodded her head towards the door. 'He's back now,' she said with a smile. 'I'm sure he can help you quicker than I can, given he's already familiar with your case.' Julia waved Grégoire over and went back to the visitor with the glasses.

Béatrice pulled her hand from her bag, turned towards the door and saw Grégoire coming towards her, his footsteps buoyant. Her heart throbbed, her cheeks burned and her mind once again became a tangled mess. It was almost unbearable, this emotional whirlwind of desire, tormented restraint and happiness. Then Grégoire was standing in front of her, leaning forward and greeting her with two kisses on the cheek – *à la française*. As his stubble tickled her cheek, Béatrice felt slightly dizzy. And then it was over already, his fleeting touch a thing of the past.

'What brings you back today?' he asked in a business-like tone, turning away and going over to his desk.

That didn't sound very enthusiastic. Had she come at an inconvenient moment? She lifted her chin and followed him. 'The National Archives in Paris sent me a photo of Judith.'

He turned back towards her at once. 'Fantastic! Do you have it with you?'

Béatrice laid the picture and the Drancy registration form on his desk. Grégoire studied the documents closely.

'What should I do next?' asked Béatrice. 'I've written to the rabbi and the registry office in Paris, but haven't heard anything yet. Should I call them?'

Grégoire smiled at Béatrice and handed the copies back to her. 'Patience, patience. A search like this can take months, sometimes even years,' he said. Now he sounded like he always did – warm, attentive and sincere. His green eyes shone like the water of a mountain lake. Béatrice felt reassured again.

'Years?' she echoed, wrapping a strand of hair around her finger. 'Jacobina may not have that much time.' Her gaze wandered over to the bookshelves where Julia was standing, now talking to an elderly woman.

Grégoire pulled a chair up for Béatrice, gestured for her to take a seat, and sat down on his revolving chair. 'I'm sure the registry office will be in touch soon. But as we don't know whether Judith returned to France after the war, it couldn't hurt to involve the International Red Cross too. The Red Cross runs a search service that undertakes investigations into prisoners of war and civilian prisoners in the Second World War. They're very well connected, and, of course, they also work with the French Red Cross and the ITS in Bad Arolsen.'

Béatrice sighed. 'Good, I'll do that.'

'I have a contact there for you. The office is in Baltimore.' Grégoire flicked through a file, scribbled a name and email address down on a notepad, tore off the page and handed it to Béatrice. 'Hey, don't look so downbeat. You're on the right track.' He brushed his hair behind his ears. 'Shall we go for a coffee?'

She nodded eagerly.

*

Initially, the fact that she hadn't got her period didn't worry Béatrice in the slightest. It had never been particularly regular; sometimes it came early, but more often than not, it was late. It would announce its arrival with mood swings and intense cramps that came and went as swiftly as a summer storm. But this time, there was nothing. And by the time Béatrice was a week late, she was quite worried, and picked up a pregnancy test on her way into the office.

Just half an hour later, she was standing in front of the sink in the eighth-floor bathroom, staring at the plastic stick in her hand. First, it had just stayed white. Slowly, two narrow, pale-pink strips appeared. Two – positive! No, no, no. It couldn't be. It just couldn't! Her mouth went dry, her pulse pounded at her temples.

The bathroom door opened and two women stepped in, conversing loudly about the pros and cons of fully funded pension systems in Latin America. Béatrice threw the test stick into her handbag, washed her hands and fled the bathroom without drying them.

Outside, a sudden dizziness overcame her. She saw glittering stars, everything was spinning. Béatrice breathed heavily, groping her way slowly along the wall so as not to fall. She stumbled back to the archive, sat down and closed her eyes. Gradually, the feeling passed and her breathing returned to a normal pace. She opened her eyes and pulled the test stick out of her bag, secretly hoping that, back in the bathroom, the chemical colouring process hadn't been entirely complete. But in the stick's tiny window, the two lines were clearly visible. By now they had even become more pronounced, the pale pink intensifying to a deep, loud one.

A baby! She was going to have Joaquín's baby. A man she would never be happy with again. A man with whom she was about to break up.

While she believed in a woman's right to choose, she would never be able to bring herself to have an abortion, she knew that at once. She had friends who had undergone abortions and never regretted them. But she couldn't forget the many conversations she'd had with Monique, who chose to terminate her pregnancy years ago and had never gotten over it. When Monique tried to have a baby last summer, she was no longer able to conceive. Since then, her friend was suffering from insomnia and a feeling of emptiness that no therapy could alleviate. Béatrice was afraid that, if she had such a procedure, she would one day be plagued by a similar crisis of conscience. Even her mother had influenced her on this. 'God, I'm so glad I kept you back then,' she often said to Béatrice. 'You're the thing I love most in the world.'

But Béatrice wasn't in her thirties any more. A pregnancy at forty-three was considered 'high risk' and could entail all sorts of complications and health problems, for both the baby and her.

And what if this was her *last* chance to ever have a child? The thought of soon approaching the end of her reproductive years sent a chill down Béatrice's spine. What a brutal ultimatum!

Still staring at the two pink stripes, she played out the various scenarios of motherhood. She saw herself stuck in McLean with a baby in her arms, heating up macaroni for Laura and arguing with Joaquín about money. The single-parent alternative was no less daunting. Leaving her baby in a crèche early each morning. Trying to hold her own by day in a stressful job she could barely cope with even now, and soothing her crying child by night. Béatrice knew a few single mothers at the bank. They never had time for anything and always looked stressed. The pressure had to be enormous.

Then Béatrice pictured herself pushing a pram through Paris. At the thought of returning to France with a child in tow her stomach tied up in knots. She would be forced to take the first job she could find in order to support the baby, her mother and herself. Just like her mother had once done for her, after her father had left. The whole cycle would repeat itself.

Béatrice tried to suppress the nausea rising within her, but in vain. She ran as quickly as she could back to the bathroom, and threw up.

*

Béatrice took the lemon wedge that was pressed into the rim of the glass and squeezed a few drops into her water. For days now, she had barely been able to keep down even a bite of food. She didn't know whether it was the first signs of her pregnancy, or her general malaise at the state of her life.

'Your red wine is on its way, *bella* Béatrice,' Lucío called to her from the counter, as always in his perfectly rehearsed Italian accent.

'No, thank you, Lucío. I'll stick with water today,' she said with a tired smile.

Lucío gave her a look of playful shock. 'Water? Are you pregnant or something?' He laughed.

Béatrice recoiled.

'Just kidding, signorina,' called Lucío good-humouredly, coming out from behind the counter and topping up her water glass.

In a few moments, Joaquín would be here. She had called him early that morning, before breakfast even, and asked him to meet her at Lucío's after work. He had returned from New York two days before and agreed without hesitation. Yet, instead of a break-up, she would now announce her pregnancy.

Should she tell him as soon as he sat down? Or over dessert? How would he react? They had only ever spoken about *his* child, never about the possibility of having one together.

'It's okay, Béa, stay calm,' Jacobina had said soothingly when Béatrice had turned up on her doorstep the evening before in an agitated state.

It had felt entirely natural for Béatrice to pour out her heart to Jacobina. But her friend hadn't said what she had wanted to hear: that she would be able to cope as a single mother.

'You're having a baby, Béatrice! That's a huge responsibility,' she had preached instead. 'And you . . . you're only talking about *you* and what *you* want.' Jacobina fell into an authoritative tone that was entirely at odds with her fragile-looking body.

Béatrice had slumped down on the sofa, feeling abashed.

'Think back to your own childhood,' Jacobina continued sternly, and Béatrice began to cry. 'Do you want your baby to grow up without a father, just like you did, and spend his or her whole life suffering from his absence? You have to find a solution *with* Joaquín.'

Béatrice had thought about Jacobina's words the entire night, and eventually dialled his number.

He arrived a quarter of an hour late. And he wasn't alone. Behind him, a short, hoodie-clad figure trudged through the door. Laura. Her hands were tucked in the pockets of her jeans, and her face hidden under the hood. Béatrice could only make out the downturned corners of her mouth. She rolled her eyes and sighed loudly. With Laura around she wouldn't be able to tell him anything at all. But she *had* to! This couldn't wait another day. It had been hard enough to hold out until now.

Joaquín walked over to the table, leaned across to Béatrice and gave her a brief kiss on the mouth. 'Sorry, hon,' he breathed. 'Laura was supposed to be staying the night at Sarah's, but something else came up and Anne cancelled at the last minute.' He sat down and smiled. 'How lovely that we're seeing each other today, all spontaneous like this.'

Laura uttered a throaty 'Hi' and sat down on the empty chair next to her father. Then she pulled her mobile phone out of her pocket and began to tap around on it.

Joaquín glanced at the menu that Lucío had already left on the table before their arrival. 'Are you in the mood for pasta, sweetheart?'

Béatrice was about to say yes, when she realized that his words were directed at Laura. 'Sounds good,' the girl replied without looking up.

'I worked from home this afternoon and helped her with her schoolwork,' Joaquín explained as he unfolded the serviette and placed it on his lap. 'We had a few spats, but I think it was a good start.' He lovingly tussled Laura's hooded head then turned to Béatrice. 'Let's order, I'm starving.' He craned his head around, looking for the waiter.

Béatrice gazed at the glass salt cellar, which was shaped like a hen's egg. Beneath the table, her hands balled into fists. How long would she have to wait now before she could tell him? Another week, until he'd be free again to see her?

Laura dropped her phone onto the table. 'I need to go to the bathroom,' she announced. 'I'll be right back.'

As soon as she was out of sight, Béatrice leaned over the table. 'I really need to talk to you in private,' she said.

'What is it?' he asked.

It wasn't the right moment, but she had to use the few minutes they were alone and tell him. She couldn't keep this news to herself any longer. 'I'm pregnant,' she blurted out.

'Pregnant?' Joaquín repeated loudly. His pupils shrunk to the size of pinheads. He stared at Béatrice, motionless, his mouth half open.

'Lower your voice,' she hissed, already regretting her bluntness. She *should* have waited.

'Are you sure?' he asked.

What a stupid question. But before Béatrice could say anything, Laura was standing in front of them, her face as white as a sheet. Was she already back from the bathroom? Or did she never go? Béatrice had no idea, but one thing was clear – Laura had overheard everything.

'I don't want any brothers and sisters,' she cried, tearing the hood off her head. The diners at the neighbouring tables fell silent and looked over at them.

'Calm down, sweetheart!' Joaquín said softly, stretching his hand out towards Laura.

But she pushed his arm away. 'No way,' she howled and stormed out of the restaurant.

'How incredibly thoughtless of you,' Joaquín snapped at Béatrice, throwing his serviette on the plate and standing up too. 'Couldn't you have waited until we were alone?' He grabbed Laura's phone. 'I'm going to look for her and take her home. This is a huge shock . . . And not just for her.' He pulled his jacket from the back of his chair and clamped it beneath his arm. 'We'll talk later.' With those words, he was already gone.

The people behind her were whispering. Glasses clinked; cutlery fell to the floor. Someone giggled. A short while later, the normal background noise resumed. Béatrice stared at Joaquín's crumpled serviette. He was right. She couldn't have chosen a worse moment to break this news. The poor girl. How could Béatrice ever make this up to them?

Lucío came rushing over and placed on the table an oval-shaped platter of pasta in a mussel sauce. '*Prego, signorina. Pasta alle vongole.* It helps with everything.' He wiped his hand over his damp forehead and looked at her expectantly.

As the scent of white wine and garlic rose up towards Béatrice, her stomach turned. A swell of acid shot up through her oesophagus into her mouth. Pressing her hand to her lips, she pushed past a baffled-looking Lucío and dashed to the bathroom.

16

Judith

Paris, May 1941

I put down my bag and went into the kitchen. It smelled good, of soap and fresh laundry. Mother stood at the window with her back to me, ironing. I was glad to see her like that; it was something she hadn't done in a long time. Hearing me come in, she turned around briefly and gave me a tired smile. Then she dampened a cloth, laid it over a blouse and placed the hot iron onto it. The cloth immediately began to hiss and steam.

How was I supposed to tell her? I wondered, stepping over to the sink and filling a glass with water. I couldn't get out of my mind the uneasy premonition that Mother wouldn't cope well with the news. For three days now, I had been avoiding this conversation. But I had to tell her today.

It was early afternoon. In these late May days, Paris was showing its most beautiful side. The city shone, bright and sublime in the warm spring light; maple and chestnut trees blossomed on the large boulevards; and behind the golden-leaf-adorned gates of the Jardin du Luxembourg, the lilacs were in full bloom.

I sat down at the kitchen table and flicked through the paper, without reading anything.

Mother continued to iron. 'There's a button missing on your blouse,' she murmured. 'Do you still have it?'

I drummed my fingers on the table. Then I summoned all my courage. 'Our bank account has been blocked,' I said, staring at Mother's apron strings, which she had tied into a bow behind her back.

She put down the iron and turned towards me. 'What? What are you talking about?' she asked. Her lips were quivering.

'I went to the bank. They said we can't make any more withdrawals.'

'That's impossible!' she exclaimed, waving her hands in agitation. 'There's enough in the account.'

'It's not about the money,' I replied, looking straight at her. 'It's because we're Jewish. The account has been blocked. Orders from above, that's all the bank employee said. Then he closed the counter.'

Mother sat down at the table next to me. 'Those pigs!' she whispered. 'They're trying to break us. Tomorrow I'll file a complaint with the bank manager.'

'You can try, but they still won't pay out any money.' I could smell burning from somewhere. A flame licked up from the ironing board.

'Heavens! My blouse,' I cried, jumping up and pulling the hot iron off the material. Then I grabbed a cloth and beat out the flame.

Mother remained at the table, her face in her hands.

I sat back down. 'We have to keep a clear head.'

She looked up and her mouth contorted into a mocking grimace. 'A clear head! You and your wise advice. Have you still not grasped what's happening?' She took off her apron and flung it on the table. 'Pétain wants to exterminate us, that senile old traitor. Step by step. Jews have to register, Jews are no longer allowed in public service, in law or medicine. Soon we won't be allowed to work anywhere. And now he's taking away our own money.' She slammed the palm of her hand against the table. 'What are we supposed to live on now?'

The more agitated she got, the calmer I became. As always when I sensed that Mother was slipping down into the depths, my role shifted from daughter to that of parent, or at least to responsible carer. I was convinced of Christian's unconditional loyalty and knew he would stand by us in our time of need. I spoke my thoughts out loud. 'Christian can get food for us. He—'

She didn't let me finish. 'All I ever hear is Christian, Christian, Christian,' she rebuked me. Her gaze held a trace of contempt. 'You've become completely dependent on your *goy*.' She pushed both hands into her hair and closed her eyes for a moment. 'And what do we do if your Christian wakes up tomorrow and decides not to slip you any more coffee beans?' she continued mockingly. 'If he falls in love with another, more suitable girl? A girl that belongs to the master race. A girl that is *not* Jewish.' She glared at me. 'I've told you from the beginning that this relationship was a bad idea. These people treat Jews like scum. To them, we're nothing but lepers.'

At the mention of his parents, I flinched involuntarily. Even though I hadn't told her what I'd found out about

Christian's father, her poisonous remark hit a nerve. I looked down with embarrassment.

'*Work, Family, Fatherland.*' Mother parroted Pétain's slogan and stood up. 'Makes me sick.'

In that moment, she seemed like a stranger to me. An aged, embittered woman who expected nothing more of life.

Lily jumped down from the windowsill and landed right in front of Mother's feet. She lifted the cat, who thrashed her legs stubbornly, from the floor and went into her bedroom. I watched as she closed the door behind her.

Somehow, we had to keep going. I pondered what I could swap on the black market for food. The big clock in the living room, which had been Father's. The heavy silver cutlery from Mother's trousseau, which lay in the cupboard beneath a velvet cover and was never used. Grandmother's bronze letter opener. With a heavy heart, I decided to sacrifice my evening gown from Jacques Fath too, should the situation escalate.

Through the open kitchen window, I heard an accordion player launch into the sloping harmonies of 'Je n'en connais pas la fin' – I don't know the end. Fine particles of dust danced in the white sunlight. It was a long time since I had felt this lonely.

Paris, June 1941

As I stepped into the apartment early in the evening, I was met by oppressive silence. Exhausted, I set down my bag. My feet hurt, and my stomach was growling like a rabid wolf. I had spent the entire afternoon queueing in front of the garment store, in sweltering heat, to get new nightshirts for Mother and me.

Because all our natural resources had to be sent to the German Reich, leaving barely anything for our people, at the beginning of the summer the *cartes de vêtements* had been introduced. These clothing cards were small, tear-off coupons with different point scores on them. It was, however, utopian to believe that this system would meet our needs. I had another forty points left until the end of the year, but for a dress alone I needed fifty points.

I crept down the corridor on tiptoe. Ever since Mother had stopped the wall clock several days before, she hadn't left the bed. As always when the clock was no longer allowed to tick, everything was painful for her. Listening and seeing, talking and walking. The only thing she could tolerate during those days was silence. And I knew it was best to make myself invisible.

I slipped soundlessly into the kitchen. It looked exactly as it had when I left that morning. On the table was the remaining half of a loaf of bread I had bought several days ago. By now it was so stale that cutting it was a struggle. Alongside it lay a knife and a few crumbs. Then I spotted the coffee cup. Earlier that morning, I had put it in front of Mother's door, filled with freshly brewed, real coffee, in the hope that the aroma would lure her out of bed. Now the cup, the coffee dregs dried on, stood in the sink. So, she had got up after all, I thought, pleased with the marginal progress.

For Lily, I shook a few oat flakes out onto a plate, softened them with water and placed it on the floor. The cat immediately jumped out from behind the oven and sniffed the oats. Then she threw me an accusatory stare and disappeared, without eating them, back beneath the cupboard. 'I'm sorry, little one,' I whispered. 'But I'm afraid I don't have anything better.'

As long as Mother wasn't taking part in our life, the kitchen remained cold and the radio turned off. I spent most of my time in the Sorbonne, sat in my lectures with a rumbling stomach or working silently in the library. When I finally left the reading room in the late afternoon, the shelves in the grocery stores were already empty. Sometimes, spurred on by good intentions, I got up really early in the morning and joined the queue at the bakery at around half past five. But even at that hour, the line was already despairingly long. The first women in it must have arrived earlier still; some of them with exhausted children in their arms, sleep dust still clinging to their eyes.

Thank God that Christian continued to give me provisions. Yesterday two packets of rice and some apples; this morning a bag of biscuits, plus a jar of jam. The food shortages the Parisian population had been enduring since the beginning of the occupation completely passed him and his family by. In his apartment in the elegant 16th arrondissement, they wanted for nothing. The girls from the black market came to his home every morning, bringing meat, coffee, butter and bread in excess, and leaving again with a carton of cigarettes and a pile of tightly bound banknotes, which they concealed in their shopping baskets beneath chequered hand towels. And almost every afternoon, he slipped off with his driver to distribute as much as he could to people who had even less than Mother and me. He liked to call me 'my angel', but it was him, the angel. Mother was entirely wrong about him. He wouldn't let us down. Ever.

This morning, I had told him about our bank account being blocked. To my surprise, he hadn't reacted in his usual calm manner.

'I've been fearing as much,' he said instead, looking heavy-hearted. 'Recently my father has been receiving numerous visits from Vichy government advisers and German officers. Von Stülpnagel has come a few times too. They shut themselves away in his office for hours. I have no idea what their secret talks are about.' He frowned. 'But if my father is involved, it can't be anything good.'

His words plunged me into intense worry. We were sitting in a brasserie on Quai de Bourbon, in front of small, saffron-yellow omelettes and bread. I looked around cautiously, but no one was paying any attention to us. 'Did Von Stülpnagel say something to you? Did he mention me?' To my relief, Christian shook his head. 'Can you find out what else they're planning?' I wanted to know. My voice was edged with fear. 'It's been happening to all Jewish accounts. Mother read that they're after our money. Someone is passing her underground newspapers.'

Christian dabbed his mouth with a serviette. 'My father never talks about his business affairs. His office is always locked. Not even my mother is allowed in there.'

I pushed my food listlessly around my plate, then set down the fork.

'Let's leave the country!' whispered Christian, leaning close to me and gazing tenderly into my anxious face. 'To the Italian zone. To Lake Geneva or Grenoble. You'd be safe.' He stroked my cheek. 'I have friends there.'

His suggestion came so out of the blue that, for a while, I just stared at him in disbelief. But after a few moments, I could picture it all. Christian and I by the banks of the lake. A small house, just the two of us. Perhaps a garden. An apple tree. The Alps in the background. It sounded so tempting. Then reality caught up with me. 'I can't,' I said soberly. 'I have to take care of my mother.'

'We'll bring her with us, of course,' Christian replied, without hesitation.

How I loved him for saying this! And yet, his idea sounded too wonderful to come true.

'She would never leave Paris,' I said, struggling to conceal my disappointment. 'She's lived here her entire life.'

'Ask her anyway, will you?' he pleaded. 'Perhaps she would . . . For you.'

How little he knew! My father had tried in vain to convince her to move to Romania with him, when she was young and full of energy. And Christian had no idea about her constant anxiety and dark premonitions.

'Yes, of course I will,' I nodded sadly.

*

I tiptoed over to Mother's door, which stood slightly ajar, and listened for sounds coming from inside the room. Nothing. Tentatively, I pushed the door open by a hand's width. Mother lay there curled up like an infant, staring at the drawn curtains through which the dim evening light fell. Lily's head peeped out from the hollow curve of Mother's belly. As soon as the cat saw me standing at the door, she jumped out of the bed, meowing. Mother groaned and reached her hand out to her.

Determined to speak with her, I stepped into the room. It was hot and smelled of stale air. 'How are you feeling?' I asked softly.

As she heard my voice, she gave a start. Then she turned towards me. Her eyes were sunken into their sockets, her skin grey and crumpled like old newspaper. 'Tired,' she croaked, clearing her throat.

After so many days of silence, it was good to finally hear her voice again.

'Would you like something to eat?' I asked, going over to the window and opening it. I didn't pull the curtains. I knew she wouldn't be able to bear that much light.

Mother shook her head and gestured for me to go over to her.

I sat down on the edge of her bed.

'Oh, child . . .' she sighed, straightening the pillow beneath her head. 'I'm terrified.' She swallowed. 'We can't go on like this. We don't have a centime left. And with me not allowed to work any more, how—'

'It will be over someday soon,' I interrupted, in the motherly, upbeat tone which I had grown accustomed to using in recent years, whenever she was seized by her depression. 'We'll sell some things and get through it somehow.'

'Someday . . . somehow,' she repeated slowly. A tear ran down her cheek. She studied the pale lilac flower pattern on her blanket. 'Judith,' she said, reaching for my hand. 'There are awful rumours.' She ran her hand across her face. 'They're saying that the police are now rounding up French Jews as well and handing them over to the Germans. And then . . .' Her eyes were filled with panic and horror. 'Then they're deported to Eastern Europe and exterminated like sick cattle.'

I didn't know whether to believe her, or whether the loneliness of her room had made her hallucinate. 'Mother, they're labour camps,' I said, squeezing her hand. 'Not death camps.'

She looked at me insistently. 'I'm afraid for you, Judith. You have to get away from here.' Her voice sounded like brittle glass.

I immediately thought about Christian's suggestion. Perhaps he had been right, maybe she would come too. Now was a good moment to speak to her about it. Once again, I pictured us strolling along Lake Geneva. 'Christian offered us a place to stay with friends in the Italian zone,' I said, doing my best to sound cheerful and encouraging.

Mother lowered her gaze. The curtains billowed softly in the breeze that was coming in through the open window. 'You trust him, don't you?' she asked, swallowing heavily.

I nodded silently.

'Then go with him,' she said without hesitation. 'Get yourself to safety.'

'You mean . . . without you?' I asked, stunned. 'No way.

I'm not leaving you here alone,' I added, before she could respond.

Mother sighed. 'You have your whole life ahead of you. Go and make the best of it. But for me . . . it's too late.'

'It's not too late, Mother,' I countered, jumping up from the edge of her bed. 'You're coming with us.'

She closed her eyes. 'I can't. I don't have any strength left, Judith. I can barely manage to get up.'

'And that's precisely why I am not leaving you here,' I said, feeling overwhelmed and helpless.

Mother put her arm over her eyes; even the scant light coming through the curtains was blinding her. 'Nothing makes sense any more.' Then she turned to the wall. 'I'm tired, so tired . . . I want to sleep now.'

I positioned myself at the foot of her bed and studied her bristly short hair, which made her look like a curled-up hedgehog. 'Either we go together, or I stay here with you,' I declared. 'But I am not leaving you alone.'

She didn't answer.

'Look at me, Mother!' I demanded.

But she didn't stir.

'Talk to me!'

Nothing.

I was about to grab her by the arms and shake her. But then I came to my senses, swallowed down my rage and left the room, my head hanging. It was pointless. My decision had been made – we would stay in Paris. If I left her here alone, the guilt would haunt me for the rest of my life.

17

Béatrice

Washington, D.C., 2006

The sports section of a daily paper and a few tattered magazines. That was all there was to pass the time in the sparsely furnished waiting room. And it was simply refusing to pass. For over two hours already, Béatrice had been fidgeting around on one of the orange plastic chairs, waiting for Jacobina. She crossed her legs one way and then the other, even though that didn't make the chair any more comfortable, inspected her fingernails and googled 'maternity clothes' on her phone.

Meanwhile, Jacobina was sitting somewhere behind the wide opaque-glass doors which separated the waiting area from the treatment rooms, receiving her first intravenous chemical cocktail. Terrified of the infusion, she had asked Béatrice to accompany her to the early morning appointment. But once Béatrice was sitting next to her in the consultant's room, Jacobina had changed her mind. 'Wait for me outside,' she said, her eyes wide with fear. 'I don't like crying in front of others.'

Béatrice was the only person in the waiting room. She

picked up one of the magazines from the table and flicked through it. Willowy Hollywood actresses in bum-skimming shorts smiled out of its pages at her. It's a boy, announced a headline on page 11. Béatrice studied the spherical belly of Gwyneth Paltrow, who was apparently about to give birth, and looked as though she had swallowed a basketball. Before, Béatrice had always skipped over the stars' pregnancy news in magazines. Now she greedily devoured every line. She read how much weight Paltrow had gained over the past months, and how long it had taken her to lose it all again after her first baby.

For the first time, Béatrice was overcome by tender anticipation for the life growing inside her. She smiled. No matter how complicated life would get with a child, she would handle it. She touched her belly. Hopefully, everything was all right. A pregnancy at forty-three involved considerable health risks and wasn't to be taken light-heartedly. But with the right medical care she'd get through it.

Her Blackberry rang. Joaquín. His name on the display gave Béatrice a stab of pain. Ever since he had stormed out of the restaurant a few days before, they had communicated only by text message. Béatrice placed the magazine back on the table and hesitantly took the call.

After a brief hello, he got straight to the point. 'Béa, I've been giving this a lot of thought . . . I'm not quite sure how to say it, but seeing you at home with Laura, I sometimes wonder if you actually *want* a child.'

Everything in Béatrice tensed up. 'What do you mean? I always try my best.'

Joaquín sighed. 'Well, not as much now as before. Lately, you two have been quite distant from each other.'

A sudden surge of adrenaline pumped through her body, making her feel dizzy. 'Are you suggesting I should have an abortion?' she blurted out, jumping up from her chair so abruptly that it almost tipped backwards.

'Please – calm down,' Joaquín implored.

'Calm down?' Béatrice shouted. 'How can I? You've been avoiding me for days. And now you're telling me to get an abortion!' Her voice cracked with rage and disappointment.

The receptionist leaned over the desk to look at her. Béatrice avoided her gaze and sat down in a corner of the waiting room that was out of her line of sight.

'I'm sorry I didn't call sooner,' said Joaquín, 'but I needed a little time. It was all too sudden for me in the restaurant.'

'Too sudden for *you*! You don't even care how I'm doing,' she snapped back. 'I feel like you've completely abandoned me.' Her head began to pound.

Joaquín exhaled forcefully. 'I'm worried about you. Giving birth at your age . . . It's risky.'

He sounded like a stranger. How could she have ever believed that she knew this man? 'Everything in life is a risk,' Béatrice countered. 'Do you actually know how many women over forty have babies nowadays?'

'And besides that,' Joaquín added, 'there's a pretty high chance that your baby will have genetic problems.' He cleared his throat. 'Statistically speaking, of course.'

'*Our* baby, Joaquín. It's our baby, not just mine.' Béatrice laid a hand on her belly. She was close to tears.

Someone tapped her on the shoulder from behind. She turned around and found herself looking into the receptionist's kohl-rimmed eyes. The woman pointed at a sign bearing the illustration of a telephone with a line through it.

'I'm almost done,' Béatrice said without apology.

'Well, and . . . I just turned sixty-one,' Joaquín said quietly. 'I don't want to start back at the beginning again. Changing nappies. Sleepless nights. I simply don't have the strength for this any more.'

'So why didn't you tell me that before?' asked Béatrice flatly, suddenly feeling very alone. 'Before you went to bed with me.' He was constantly playing the über-Dad for Laura, and yet now that it was about *their* child, he wanted to leave her in the lurch.

The glass doors glided apart, and a nurse in blue scrubs led Jacobina in. The old woman was limping more heavily than usual, gripping the nurse's arm with both hands.

'I'm simply too old for a baby,' asserted Joaquín. 'Also, older fathers are more likely to have autistic children. The statistics are really worrying.'

'Stop with your statistics shit!' cried Béatrice. The nurse helped Jacobina to sit down on a chair.

'I made it,' mumbled her friend, giving Béatrice an exhausted grin.

Béatrice gave her a quick nod and a smile, mouthing an apology for being on the phone, before going over to the window and studying the soundless traffic on K Street. 'There's no way I'm getting rid of this baby. Not ever.'

'But don't you understand, Béa?' persisted Joaquín. 'I love you. I want to live with you and be happy together. Laura will be our daughter. But I can't bring up another child . . . I just can't.'

Tears welled up in Béatrice's eyes. She wiped them away

with the back of her hand. 'Laura doesn't want to be my child. You know that very well.'

'Is there any water?' Jacobina asked the nurse croakily in the background. 'My throat's so dry.'

Béatrice turned around to her, put her hand on the phone and whispered, 'We're about to leave.' Then she put it back to her ear. 'I can do it on my own.'

'Béa, please. Let's make this decision together,' pleaded Joaquín.

'There's nothing to decide,' she replied in a tear-choked voice before ending the call.

'That piece of shit,' snorted Jacobina, once Béatrice had explained their conversation. 'But trust me: as soon as the baby's here, he'll change his mind. They always do. You wait and see.'

Béatrice pulled a handful of paper towels out of the cardboard box that stood on the table beside the magazines, and blew her nose. 'Who knows,' she said morosely. She bent over to her bag, pulled out her water bottle and handed it to Jacobina. 'Here.'

Jacobina took it gratefully and drank.

'And how are you?' asked Béatrice as she put on her jacket. 'Was it very hard?'

Jacobina shook her head. 'It was easier than I thought. I barely noticed anything.'

The nurse in the blue scrubs came back and pressed a small bag containing medication and a note into Jacobina's hand. 'So, sweetie, now get yourself home and rest,' she said, smiling broadly and giving Jacobina a friendly stroke on the shoulder. 'If you feel nauseous, take two of these tablets. And if it gets really bad, take a couple of these.

You can eat normally. And don't forget, sweetie: drink lots of water.'

Jacobina nodded obediently, interlaced her arm with Béatrice's and let her guide her to the exit. 'Calling a stranger sweetie,' she said, once they were in the lift. 'Only in America.' They couldn't help but laugh.

*

Béatrice pulled the lid off her yoghurt pot and licked it, just like Laura always did. Yoghurt wasn't among her favourite foods, but right now it was the only thing she could eat without feeling sick. All those stories about pregnant women ravenously attacking their refrigerators and stuffing themselves with sour gherkins and chocolate ice cream were utter nonsense. Béatrice pushed a spoonful of strawberry yoghurt into her mouth and eyed her Blackberry indecisively. For the past hour, she had been thinking about whether to call Grégoire.

Even though they hadn't spoken in a while, she didn't mind. The new direction her life had taken since the appearance of the two pink stripes on that test stick had been far too radical to also deal with Grégoire. But she felt she should at least tell him what was going on.

Really? she wondered, as she contemplated the shiny, ripe strawberries depicted on the yoghurt pot. He had cooked dinner for her once and always treated her politely, but nothing had happened between them. He'd never tried to get closer to her or confessed any feelings. And they weren't real friends either. She hardly knew anything about him and his private life. Why would she tell him about something as confidential and intimate as an early pregnancy?

But while she couldn't guess what was going on inside Grégoire's head, she knew her own emotions only too well. She was falling for this man, as hard as it was to admit. And at an impossible moment – with Joaquín's baby growing inside her and everything else in her life falling apart. If she didn't do it for *Grégoire*, she should tell him for her *own* sake. It would help her regain mental clarity and avoid any potential misunderstandings in the future. Better now than later.

She put the half-empty pot on the desk and boldly grabbed her phone.

Grégoire answered right away.

'Lovely to hear from you,' he said, immediately chatting away as though they had spoken only yesterday.

As always when she heard his voice, Béatrice felt a magnetic pull that she had never experienced with any other man. After a few moments, she was able to restrain her emotions and invited him to dinner on Thursday evening. 'I'd love to,' he answered at once, adding that he would bring an excellent wine.

She had just ended the call when she heard someone behind her. Béatrice spun around in her chair and saw Michael leaning in the doorway with his arms crossed, his mouth twisted into an obnoxious sneer. 'Long lunch breaks and private calls. I guess you think that because you're sitting here alone, I won't notice?' he said.

How long had he been standing there? She felt her face turn flame-red.

'I've got some news for you.' Michael closed the door and pressed his back against it, as though wanting to make sure it was properly shut. Then he sat down on a chair next to the old CRT monitor. The chair groaned and creaked beneath his weight. He took off his glasses and rubbed his eyes.

'We – in other words, the senior management team – had a meeting yesterday to discuss the budget for the coming two years,' he began, stroking his chin. 'It's not looking good. The executive board has decided on new reforms over the next few years. We need to save at least fifty million dollars.' He lifted an eyebrow. 'To put it plainly: heads will roll.'

Béatrice stared at him in shock.

Michael, visibly enjoying the impact his news was having, studied her silently. 'Given that your current performance leaves a lot to be desired, the obvious step would be to start with you,' he continued, stroking his hand over his stomach.

Words like fist punches. Béatrice closed her eyes for a few seconds. She knew he couldn't simply fire a pregnant woman. There were rules and regulations that forbade it. But she would tell him about her pregnancy another time. First, she had to speak to the staff association.

Michael stood up and went over to the door. 'I have just one piece of advice for you: take your work here in the archive seriously. It's your last chance.' The door slammed shut behind him.

*

Thursday evening. Béatrice was standing at the window of her living room, staring down at R Street. The sun hung low over Georgetown, bathing the city in a warm orange light. The day before, intense rains had whipped the final, withered cherry blossoms down from the trees, blanketing the sides of the streets. Now the cars were turning the wet petals into mush. That's how quick it was, thought Béatrice wistfully. Just a short while before, the trees had bowed beneath the weight of the lush, white-pink splendour, and now it was all over.

She glanced at her phone and saw that Jacobina had tried to reach her several times. She would call her back tomorrow morning. Ever since Jacobina had begun chemotherapy, she was calling constantly to tell Béatrice how bad she was feeling and that she'd completely lost her appetite. Béatrice was always happy to listen and encourage her to keep going. But not tonight. This evening belonged to her. To her and Grégoire, who should be arriving any moment now.

She turned off her phone and her thoughts strayed back to the Sunday afternoon she had spent with him, strolling around the Tidal Basin. She remembered how he had made light of the transience of beauty and pressed the plucked cherry blossoms into her hand. It had been a perfect moment, filled with desire and hope. The hope that Grégoire would rent a pedal boat, kiss her passionately out in the middle of the lake and decide not to go back to France. Fleeting, foolish dreams. Now fate had guided Béatrice in a completely different direction, and she felt ashamed of her secret Grégoire fantasies. She was pregnant by Joaquín. A man she no longer wanted in her life, and who didn't want their child in his.

The doorbell rang. Béatrice felt giddy with excitement. She had prepared feverishly for Grégoire's visit, cleaning her apartment, poring over cookbooks, buying French cheese at Whole Foods for him and winding her unco-operative hair into hot rollers.

The entire time, she had been thinking about how to deliver the news. The three words that would put an end to anything that could have been between them – but mainly to her fantasies. *I am pregnant.* It still felt so new, even to her. Beautiful and strange at the same time.

When would be the appropriate moment for her confession? Right away? Or better later, when she would serve the cheeses? No, that was too late. Most likely, he'd already ask her during the main course why she wasn't eating. She needed to tell him then.

Yet, just a moment later, while setting the table, another conclusion dawned upon her. She wouldn't say anything at all tonight. It was too early. Not even Monique or her mother knew about the pregnancy yet. Her doctor, whom she had seen a few days ago, had also advised her to be cautious. 'The first trimester is the hardest,' he had said. 'Anything can happen, especially at your age. Hopefully, at your next visit in a few weeks we can detect the heart-beat.'

The words still echoed in Béatrice like a silent warning. No, she couldn't tell Grégoire. Not yet. Not before she had heard her baby's heartbeat for the first time.

This evening they'd just enjoy a carefree dinner. She wanted to watch him again as he swished the wine back and forth across his tongue in a state of deep concentration. Listen as he explained the particularities of the vintage and the blend of grapes. Fantasize a little more before this man would disappear from her life for ever.

Béatrice was wearing a close-fitting black dress, which

she had ordered online the day before her pregnancy test. Now she wanted to impress Grégoire with it before her belly swelled to unimaginable dimensions. It fit perfectly, thought Béatrice contentedly, catching a glimpse of her slim figure as she passed the wall mirror.

Grégoire's appraising glance as she opened the door didn't escape her. There he stood, so close and yet beyond reach, in his beige coat. His hair casually tousled. A bottle of wine in each hand. Béatrice's stomach tightened in excitement. He kissed her on both cheeks, put down the bottles and tossed his coat over a chair. 'What a lovely place you have here,' he said, falling back onto her sofa. His presence filled the entire room.

Béatrice sat down next to him and poured water into the glasses she had placed on the table.

'I like how you haven't overdone it with the furniture,' commented Grégoire, looking around curiously.

She had furnished the two spacious rooms of her light-flooded apartment, which was situated on the second floor of a Victorian building, only sparsely. Opposite the wide grey sofa stood tall bookshelves, overflowing with French novels, and in between, a coffee table. The living room was next to a white open-plan kitchen with a huge stainless-steel refrigerator. From the two high, arched windows on the west side of her living room, she had far-reaching views across Dumbarton Oaks Park, where Béatrice liked to sit during spring, when it wasn't yet too muggy and the temperature still bearable.

A dream location in the most upscale neighbourhood of the capital city, where magnificent historic buildings with turrets and rose gardens could be found alongside cute, colourful little houses. Georgetown was a piece of tranquil old world, where houses were under conservation protection and metro stations unwanted. Being able to call this apartment her own meant everything to Béatrice. Two years ago, when she had jubilantly and proudly put the key in the lock for the first time, she had believed that she had finally arrived.

Grégoire tilted his head to make out a few of the book titles on her shelves, then stretched his legs out in front of him and spread his arms across the back of the sofa. 'Any news on Judith? Has the Red Cross been in touch yet?'

'No, unfortunately not,' answered Béatrice with a sigh. 'I'm not making any progress at all right now. No one has responded to my emails. Neither the rabbi nor the registry office, nor the ITS in Germany.' She propped her head in her hands and studied the bubbles of air rising up in her sparkling water.

'Don't lose hope. Remember, these things take time,' said Grégoire, looking at her from the side. 'They are dealing with a huge number of enquiries – thousands – and have to research in the archives first before they answer. A third of the employees in Bad Arolsen are in the process of digitizing everything. Soon it will become easier.'

Béatrice nodded absent-mindedly.

Grégoire touched her arm. 'How are you otherwise, Béatrice? You look troubled somehow.'

Whether it was his warm tone, or the pregnancy hormones that were doing somersaults through her body – Béatrice didn't know. But when she heard his question, something unravelled within her. It was all too much:

her horrible phone conversation with Joaquín, the pregnancy, and now Grégoire by her side, so close. Before she could answer, tears were running down her face.

'Hey, what is it?' whispered Grégoire, moving closer and putting his arm around her.

As she felt his hand on her shoulder, all of the pain stored inside her burst out, in loud, staccato sobs.

Grégoire held her tighter. 'What's happened?' he repeated, stroking her back.

'That . . . I . . .' was all Béatrice could get out. She buried her face in her hands.

'Do you feel like talking about it?'

Should I? Béatrice wasn't sure about anything any more and in her helplessness continued to cry with abandon. The scent of Grégoire's aftershave and the warmth of his body made her feel completely dazed.

He gently touched her hair, then the back of her neck. 'Béatrice . . .' he breathed, holding her neck and pulling her gently towards him.

Béatrice stiffened briefly, then gave in. Her heart hammered with anticipation. 'Béatrice,' he repeated, as he kissed her damp cheeks, her eyelids and finally her lips.

It felt as if gravity ceased to exist. She floated in his arms, intoxicated by his tenderness and by this confusingly wonderful, absurd fantasy which had suddenly come true. She didn't want to think or question any more. She only knew that she was ready to let herself fall and give in to him completely. Béatrice closed her eyes and returned his kiss.

They kissed for a long time, clinging to one another as though they were afraid of being torn apart again.

Eventually Grégoire broke away and looked at her, caressing her cheek. 'This might sound like something from a bad novel, but . . . ever since I first saw you in the museum, I've been wanting to kiss you,' he said, smiling shyly.

'You hid it pretty well,' Béatrice replied, trying to dab away the smeared mascara beneath her eyes. 'I didn't have the slightest idea.'

'It's just that I'm old-fashioned, I wanted to get to know you a little first. You know, I'm not twenty any more.' He took her hand. 'Will you tell me now what's wrong?'

Béatrice turned serious. She knew it wasn't right, but how could she possibly destroy this heavenly moment now? 'Oh, well . . . it's my boss, this vindictive macho type,' she said instead. 'Everything I do makes him mad. I'm worried that he's not going to extend my contract.'

Grégoire frowned. 'Should I have a little word with him?' he said jokingly.

Béatrice couldn't help but laugh, and decided it was time to change the subject. 'Can I pour you a glass of the wine?' she asked, standing up to fetch the corkscrew from the kitchen.

Grégoire jumped up too and pulled her back into his arms.

'Forget the wine. We have to think up a strategy for dealing with your boss. You can't let a guy like that ruin your career.'

'I'll find a solution,' sighed Béatrice. 'But not now.'

He kissed her. 'I never want to let you go again.'

Béatrice moved close to him. Then she took him by the hand and led him into her bedroom.

*

Sex with Joaquín had been good. Not passionate, exactly, but intimate enough to patch their ailing relationship back together for a while after particularly bad arguments. Sex with Grégoire was out of this world. Béatrice finally understood what it meant for everything to feel right: the chemistry, the hormones, and all the other inexplicable things that flooded their bodies with pleasure and joy.

And yet, at the same time, everything felt so wrong. Instead of revealing what was going on in her life as she should have, she remained under the spell of the moment, hypnotized by her feelings, the magic of their first night together and an attraction she had never felt before. And now it was too late. Once again, she had failed. At the restaurant with Laura and Joaquín she had said too much, too soon. And now too little. But it was even worse this time. What had been left unspoken, now carried the weight of a lie separating her for ever from Grégoire like a thick, invisible wall.

Béatrice tossed and turned all night, listening to Grégoire's steady breathing and reproaching herself for her behaviour. Towards dawn, she eventually fell asleep, too.

But soon afterwards she awoke again, gripped by sudden panic, and sat up with a jolt. Had she been dreaming? Where was she? What had happened? Béatrice felt as though she couldn't catch her breath, brought her hands to her neck, and coughed loudly. Pale morning light spilled through the curtains.

Grégoire lay sleeping beside her. He really was here. And it really had happened. Béatrice shivered a little and pulled the blanket up to her chin. What would happen when she came out with the truth *now*? He'd despise her, no doubt, and never see her again.

She gazed at him. Loose strands of his hair fell across his forehead. His upper body was bare, his chest rising and falling as he breathed almost soundlessly. Now and then, he let out a small sigh as he exhaled. She realized that Grégoire was the first man to have slept in her bed here in Washington. She'd often asked Joaquín to stay over, but he had never agreed, worried that Laura would be scared at home alone.

Béatrice pulled her hand out from beneath the blanket and stroked his arm tenderly, tracing the soft shadows of his muscles. He stirred and looked at her, tired. 'Let's sleep some more,' he murmured, closing his eyes again and turning over.

Béatrice sat there silently and listened until his breathing became steady again. Then she brushed her hair behind her ears and crept carefully out of the bed. On tiptoe, she padded across the creaking parquet floor into the kitchen. Filling the kettle with water, she put it on the stove. The untouched cheese plate from the previous evening was still on the counter. *Petit Basque*, *Saint-Nectaire* and *Brillat-Savarin* lined up alongside one another like dried pieces of cake. Seeing it made her feel sick. She grabbed the plate and shoved it into the refrigerator, then switched on her phone. Six a.m. Béatrice bit her lip. She had to tell Grégoire before he left this morning. No more excuses. The blinking Blackberry in her hand, she sat down on the stool next to the oven and listened as the water came to a rolling boil. Once she'd poured it through the old-fashioned coffee filter, just as she'd learned from her mother, she would wake him. She looked at her phone and was startled to see seventeen missed calls from

Jacobina and twelve messages. Béatrice put the phone to her ear and listened.

In the first couple of messages, her friend babbled as though she'd been drinking. She was saying all kinds of confused things. She was feeling ill, she spluttered, and wanted to speak to her father. She knew he was there. She choked several times and coughed. Nothing made sense any more, she said then, and hung up. From the third message on, Jacobina's voice became more insistent, more despairing. It was the punishment, she screamed, followed by a whimpered, 'Everything, everything was in vain.' Then Béatrice just heard muttering, and then a sudden dial tone. On one message, it sounded as if the receiver dropped out of Jacobina's hand; Béatrice heard a loud thud and rustling sounds. The last message was a male voice: 'Good evening, this is the emergency room at George Washington Hospital. Ms Jacobina Grunberg has been brought in and requires immediate surgery. You are listed as her emergency contact. Please call us as soon as you can.'

Béatrice ran back into the bedroom and shook Grégoire by the shoulder. 'Grégoire! Wake up!' He opened his eyes and smiled.

She sat down on the edge of the bed. 'Jacobina had surgery last night. I have to go to the hospital right away and check on her.'

His expression immediately turned serious. 'I'll come with you.'

Béatrice looked at him in amazement. She wasn't used to having a man by her side who had time on his hands. Joaquín always got up long before her, made hot cocoa for Laura and then prepared himself for the working day ahead. Often his secretary would call him even before eight a.m.

'Don't you have to go to the office?' asked Béatrice.

'This is an emergency. And today's Friday, so it's not busy anyway. I just need a coffee, then I'll be ready,' he said, scratching his head and rolling out of bed. 'Do you have a toothbrush I can use?'

Now definitely wasn't the right time for the big confession. She would do it later. Béatrice went into the bathroom and rummaged around in her cosmetic bag for a travel toothbrush. As she turned around, Grégoire was standing in the doorway.

He clasped her shoulders and looked lovingly into her eyes. 'Last night was wonderful,' he whispered. Then he grinned playfully. 'Even though you practically let me starve.'

18

Judith

Paris, July 1941

'I'm really sorry, Mademoiselle Goldemberg' – Monsieur Hubert looked at me sorrowfully over his round glasses – 'but I'm no longer able to keep you on as my employee.' The elderly man, who always placed great importance on his appearance, looked different today. Unshaven, with dishevelled hair and dark rings beneath his eyes, he sat there in his brown leather chair. His bony white hands played with a piece of paper, continually rolling it up and then unrolling it again.

I set the books I had been holding down on the table. 'I don't understand,' I stammered. 'Have I done something wrong?'

Monsieur Hubert, who publicly praised my work so much that I often blushed. Who, whenever Mother was suffering from one of her depressive episodes, always turned a blind eye and let me go home before my shift was over. Monsieur Hubert, who had never reprimanded me, even though I frequently brought my books back long after they were due. Monsieur Hubert, who always listened when I complained about the inattentiveness of the students in the lecture theatres, and whose longing for intellectual depth somehow reminded me of the beautiful Lucien Chardon in Balzac's *Lost Illusions*. He had always watched over me with a fatherly benevolence. And now he wanted to dismiss me? Just like that?

With a sigh, he rolled out the piece of paper and smoothed it flat. 'No, no. Your work is excellent, as always. But . . .' He held the paper out towards me. 'Here. Read it for yourself. I . . . I'm no longer allowed to have Jewish employees.'

I felt a flash of terror. Suddenly everything was clear. My mother's work ban. The policemen in our street early in the morning. Our blocked bank account. And now it had caught up with me. I heard my mother's words. *We're nothing but scum to these people. Nothing but dirt.* For a long time, I hadn't wanted to acknowledge it. But now the picture had slotted together. Mother had been right all along.

'I see,' I whispered. Beads of cold sweat formed on the palms of my hands. With trembling fingers, I reached for the piece of paper, and recognized at once the official letterhead. I stumbled over to the chair by the desk, sat down and stared at the lines. In the top left was the emblem of the Sorbonne, and beneath it the name of its president. In the text, again and again, I saw the word *Jew*, underlined each time. 'Why?' I asked, not expecting an answer. Not from him. What did Monsieur Hubert know about our fate? About our relentless societal descent?

Just a year ago, Mother and I had been well-regarded citizens. French, like everyone else, and treated as such.

And now, since the Germans had taken over our country, we were nothing but dirty Jews. Persecuted. Beggars who could only survive thanks to the groceries which Christian smuggled out of his kitchen, because his parents had so much that even in wartime they didn't notice if something was missing. *Work, Family, Fatherland*. Hang Pétain and his propaganda! I had lost my work and my family, and my fatherland had betrayed me.

'Mademoiselle,' said Monsieur Hubert, pulling me back from my thoughts.

I lowered the letter. All at once, my pent-up rage directed itself at him. Because I suddenly understood that Monsieur Hubert wasn't at all the kind, protective father figure I had thought him to be. No, he was among those who followed these indiscriminate rules without questioning them. He was among those who made this insanity possible. He was nothing but a follower.

Monsieur Hubert scratched his head and straightened his glasses. 'There's a new law,' he said in a wavering voice. 'A Jewish statute . . .'

'Another law,' I hissed.

'Mademoiselle, listen to me now,' he pleaded. 'There's . . . there's nothing I can do . . . Otherwise . . .'

'Otherwise what?' I cried, standing up and putting my hands on my hips.

'I . . . I have a wife . . .' he stammered, 'and three children.'

'And what about me?' I snarled. 'I have a sick mother. What'll happen to us now?' I felt like spitting at him, the coward. I tore up the letter and let the pieces fall to the floor in front of him.

He propped his head in his hands and sighed. 'Please . . .' He looked up at me from his watery, brown eyes. 'Please listen to me.'

All I felt for the old man was disappointment and rage.

'I tried everything . . .' he protested, wiping his shirt-sleeve over his mouth. 'I asked the president for permission to let you work in the archive, out in the back. Where no one would see you. Until this whole thing with the Germans is finally over. But he refused my request.'

'Where no one would see me?' I repeated. 'So you're ashamed of me?'

'No, mademoiselle, of course I'm not.' He leaned back in his chair and took off his glasses. 'Unfortunately, that's not everything. There's something else I have to tell you.'

'Something else?' I echoed flatly.

He cleared his throat. 'Please have a seat.'

I pulled myself together, went back to the chair and sat down.

'The second Jewish statute . . . this new law . . .' He swallowed. 'Well . . .'

I focused on the small woven strands in the carpet, waiting to hear what else he had to say.

'You are also no longer allowed to study at the Sorbonne.'

I felt as though someone had poured scalding hot water over me. Everything was hurting, burning, spinning around. 'Excuse me?' I cried, looking at him.

He pulled a handkerchief out of his trouser pocket and laboriously cleaned the lenses of his glasses. Then he briefly held the spectacles up to the light and put them back on. When he finally looked at me again, tears shimmered in his eyes. 'The president has introduced a numerus clausus.

I mean . . . he had to. He had no choice. The law is the law. With immediate effect, only three per cent of our students can be Jews.' He sniffed loudly and wiped the handkerchief across his nose. 'Believe me, I did my best for you. But your grades in the past months were . . .' He coughed into the handkerchief. 'Well, there are Jewish students who've been performing much better than you.' He put the handkerchief away and placed his elbows on the armrests. 'For me you will always be the best. I know that you've been having problems at home.' He ran his fingers through his sparse hair.

I jumped up from my chair. 'Problems at home? What are you talking about?' It wasn't like me to argue with a superior. But the despair and pain were so great that it tumbled out of me. '*Now* I have a problem. Now! I'm no longer allowed to work, or study. What am I supposed to do now? My life is over.' My voice failed me. My mouth was so dry, my throat so swollen that I could barely swallow. Tears shot into my eyes. It was as though Monsieur Hubert had simply thrown my life into the Seine, and now it was being swept away like a piece of driftwood. I stood there in the middle of the room, frozen to the spot. Then I felt Monsieur Hubert's arm on my shoulders. I wanted to push him away, but didn't have the strength.

'Mademoiselle . . .' I could hear that he was crying too. 'I'm so sorry . . . If only I could help you somehow! But I'm powerless against the numerus clausus.'

Powerless, I thought, filled with contempt. There was always a way. Even in these brutal times. I brushed my hand across my face and wiped away my tears. Then I pulled myself straight and jerked free from his arm. I hurried over to the door and opened it, then turned around once more. He stood there in front of his chair, helpless like a blind man who had lost his walking stick. The lenses of his glasses were fogged, his shoulders slumped.

'You're no better than the Germans,' I said, full of contempt. Then I left the room.

19

Béatrice

Washington, D.C., 2006

Shortly after seven o'clock, Béatrice and Grégoire arrived at the hospital at bustling Washington Circle, on the corner of 23rd Street. The sky was grey and overcast, portending a rainy weekend. The Circle was already jammed with commuters coming in from Virginia, and a few joggers were making their way along 23rd Street towards the Watergate Steps, which led down to the riverbank.

Grégoire and Béatrice had showered quickly and drunk their coffee standing up. On the way to the hospital, Grégoire had briefly dived into a Starbucks and emerged again with a pale, squashed croissant. 'Sorry, but I have to get something in my stomach,' he apologized. He ripped the croissant in two and handed her half.

Béatrice pulled a face and declined.

Grégoire smiled. 'Hey, don't be so worried. Jacobina's in good hands. Afterwards we'll go have breakfast somewhere together, okay? And perhaps we can get something to bring her later too.' He put his arm around Béatrice. 'I'm sure she'll be feeling better again soon.'

They entered the hospital lobby and asked the young man at the reception for Jacobina's room number. He reluctantly looked up from his newspaper, tapped something into his computer and shook his head. 'It's not in the system.' He pulled a doughnut out of a paper bag and bit into it.

Crumbs rained down onto the keyword of his computer.

'But she has to be here,' persisted Béatrice.

The man looked up from his screen, chewing, and shook his head again. Then he put the doughnut on the bag and had them spell out Jacobina's name.

'Ah. Grunberg, not Greenberg,' he mumbled. 'Room 712.' He asked for their drivers' licences and studied them closely. Then he gave them each a square sticker which said *visitor*.

When Grégoire and Béatrice stepped out of the lift on the seventh floor, a nurse approached them. Béatrice paused and asked her about Jacobina.

'Ms Grunberg? Yes, right here,' said the woman, pointing to the opposite side of the corridor. 'But she's not at her best right now. We've given her strong pain-killers.'

'What happened to her?' asked Béatrice, taking a step to the side to make room for an elderly man in a wheel-chair.

'Sorry, I'm not able to answer that,' replied the sister. 'You have to ask the doctor. He's not in yet, but if you want to wait here, I'll tell him as soon as he arrives.'

Béatrice nodded, and the sister headed off.

Once she was out of sight, Béatrice opened the door. Warm, stuffy air greeted her. She took a few steps into the room, which contained three beds. The first was empty. The woman in the centre bed was wearing headphones and staring at a tiny television which was attached to the ceiling. On her nightstand was a tray with a half-eaten bagel.

In the last bed, towards the back, Béatrice thought she could make out Jacobina's curly black hair. She nodded to the woman with the headphones and went over to the bed by the window. It *was* her. As pale as chalk, the corners of her mouth in a sullen grimace, as though she could feel the pain even in her sleep. Multiple bruises had created a bizarre pattern on Jacobina's arm, which was attached to a drip. She was also hooked up to a machine which made regular beeping sounds.

Seeing Jacobina there, so tiny in the huge bed, Béatrice felt sorry for her. How sad that all her close friends had moved away, including Nathalie, her best friend whom Jacobina had mentioned several times. A few social contacts could do wonders for her now.

Béatrice left the room, closed the door quietly and sat down next to Grégoire, who was waiting for her in the corridor.

'Let's go have breakfast and come back afterwards,' he suggested, putting his hand on her leg.

'I'd rather stay. The doctor should be here any minute,' answered Béatrice, who felt nauseous even at the thought of scrambled eggs on toast.

'Then I'll wait with you,' said Grégoire, crossing his legs.

Béatrice stared at his brown shoes; the leather was a little worn around the toes. Now or never! There was no point in delaying any longer what she had to say. She fidgeted anxiously on her chair.

'Shall we go to New York for the weekend?' Grégoire interrupted her thoughts and put his arm around her shoulders. 'I feel like doing something special with you.'

Béatrice looked at him, frowning quizzically.

'Are things going too fast for you?' he asked, pulling his arm back.

'Grégoire, I . . .' *No more excuses.* 'I . . .'

'Don't worry,' he said reassuringly. 'We don't have to go anywhere. I don't mind what we do. As long as we're together.'

Béatrice shifted her gaze to the door of Jacobina's room. 'I'm . . . I mean, I *was* until very recently . . . in a relationship with someone else.' She felt Grégoire flinch slightly alongside her.

Silence. The nurse they had spoken with earlier pushed a food cart to the entrance of room 712 and entered.

Béatrice gripped the armrests of the chair so tightly that her knuckles turned white. Still staring at the door, she drew in a long breath and finished her sentence. 'And I'm pregnant.'

Her handbag, which she had hung on the back of the chair, fell to the floor, and her lipstick rolled out. Neither Béatrice nor Grégoire bent over to pick it up.

The sister came back with a tray, put it on the cart and pushed it to the next room.

'But we're no longer together,' added Béatrice softly. 'I'm sorry. I wanted . . . I should have told you earlier.' What a struggle to get the words out. It was worse than facing Michael. Worse than anything.

Béatrice looked at Grégoire out of the corner of her eye trying to read the expression on his face.

He was sitting there in stony silence. Béatrice stood and picked up the lipstick. As she turned around, their gazes met. All the warmth from his green eyes had vanished. Béatrice quickly leaned over to her bag. As soon as she had sat down again, Grégoire got up.

'Why didn't you tell me sooner?' he asked, jamming his hands in his pockets.

He sounded neither accusatory nor angry. His tone was composed, almost friendly, giving Béatrice some hope.

'I know I should have. But I felt it was too early. We just met . . . and last night everything happened so quickly.'

'Way too quickly, indeed.' Grégoire glanced out of the window, then looked directly at her. 'This changes everything. You're about to start a family.'

'No, Grégoire. No,' cried Béatrice, jumping up. 'The baby wasn't planned.'

Grégoire's face was expressionless. 'There's no need,' he said. 'You know I'm soon going back to France anyway.'

'Please let's talk about it,' implored Béatrice. Once again, she was unable to hold back the tears.

But Grégoire only shook his head and walked down the corridor towards the lifts.

'Wait!' Béatrice followed him. 'My relationship is over,' she repeated in despair.

With a loud ping, the lift doors opened. A woman hobbled out, pushing in front of her a metal frame, from which an infusion bag swayed back and forth. Béatrice and Grégoire stepped aside to make room for her.

'You're pregnant!' explained Grégoire. 'None of it's over.

On the contrary – for you and the father of your child, it's only just beginning.'

Father of your child. At these words, she shuddered. She wiped the tears from her face and took his hand. 'Please believe me, it's over. He doesn't want the baby. I . . .'

Grégoire pulled away from her. 'Sorry, but I've got to go. You need to concentrate on your family now! I'm sure you two will work it out and I wish you all the best.'

Béatrice sobbed loudly. 'Stay,' she pleaded, stretching her arms out towards him. 'Let's talk.'

'No, Béatrice, I don't want to. There's nothing else to talk about.'

As she watched Grégoire get into the lift, hot tears were streaming down her cheeks. She knew she should not follow him.

The doors closed.

*

When it rains, it pours, as the American saying goes. Béatrice reeled back down the corridor to the row of chairs and slumped onto one of them. She searched for her phone and dialled Grégoire's number. However, much as she had expected, he didn't answer. Béatrice stammered a few clumsy sentences on the voicemail, but while she was still searching for words, his mailbox automatically ended the call. She immediately called again asking him to return her call.

A tall, balding man in white scrubs came towards her. *R. W. Adams, M.D.* was sewn onto the chest pocket. Around his neck hung a stethoscope. He greeted Béatrice briefly, asked whether she was with Jacobina, and sat down next to her. 'Your friend is doing well under the circumstances,' he said in a friendly manner. 'Mechanical bowel obstruction. It's very rare, but not unusual after her operation. Sometimes scar strands form in the abdomen, which in the worst-case scenario can exert pressure on the intestines from the outside. The chemotherapy should have been delayed until later.'

He spoke swiftly and used words that Béatrice didn't quite understand. Obstruction of the small intestines. Spiral CT. Leukocyte values. She struggled to follow him. While her thoughts were full of worry for Jacobina, she was also replaying the last moments with Grégoire again and again, seeing his face disappear behind the closing doors in the lift.

The doctor shook her hand. 'Take good care of her. She's going to be okay.'

And as Béatrice was still thinking about what Grégoire had said to her, Dr Adams was already on his way to the next patient.

*

Béatrice was lying in bed, staring at the crack on the ceiling. Since Grégoire had left her on Friday morning, she hadn't heard a single word from him, just as she had feared. Above her, her neighbour was crashing around the apartment with the vacuum cleaner, constantly knocking against things. Béatrice was too worn down to get annoyed about it like she usually did. Once again, she dialled Grégoire's number. But after a seemingly endless number of hopeful-sounding dial tones, the mailbox clicked on again. She hung up immediately.

That morning, she had paid Jacobina a brief visit in the hospital. Her friend was starting to take notice of things again and complaining about the tube in her nose that was providing her with artificial nutrition. In five or six days, once she was able to eat properly again and her blood values had stabilized, she could go home, they had promised her.

On the way back from the hospital, Béatrice had gone past Grégoire's building and rung the doorbell several times. No response. She had tried to peer through the window at the entrance, but hadn't been able to see anything. Then she had gone home, peeled off her clothes, pulled on her nightshirt and collapsed onto her bed.

She no longer had the strength even to cry. The pillow still carried a little of Grégoire's scent, of his aftershave. It almost drove her mad with longing and grief. She pulled off the pillowcase and threw it onto the floor. She would wash it tomorrow.

Upstairs, her neighbour turned the vacuum off and the television on. Unintelligible scraps of dialogue made their way down to her in the bedroom. Irritated and desperate, she pressed the pillow over her head. Eventually she fell asleep.

The following days rolled past slowly. In the mornings, Béatrice went to the office over an hour earlier than usual, in order to avoid running into any of her colleagues and having to answer aggravating questions. Questions like 'So, when are you coming back from your special mission?' Or 'Have you heard? Ricardo nabbed himself a top job at the president's office.'

The week passed quietly. No one strayed into the archive; even Michael didn't bother her. But on Thursday, just before five o'clock, when she was about to set off home, she suddenly heard the dreaded *click clack, click clack*. The corridor which led to the lifts was carpeted, muffling the steps of those passing by. But over time, Béatrice had learned to recognize Michael's swift pace, which was totally out of keeping with his portly figure, and she heard immediately whenever he was approaching.

He flung open the door. 'You're in your coat? Were you planning to take off early or something?'

Béatrice exhaled. 'I got in very early today.'

Michael put his mobile phone away and looked around the room grimly. He smelled of aftershave, but even that couldn't overpower the pungent odour of the cigarette he had probably just smoked.

'This place still doesn't look much different. Some effort!' he said, even though one could clearly notice that the room had been transformed from the dusty cave it had once been into a well-organized archive. The conference folders were labelled and placed in alphabetical order, all the other documents were classified, and no stray papers or rolled-up posters could be found. The clutter had disappeared entirely, and the random collection of books that had been piled up everywhere was now arranged thematically by development topic on the shelves that dominated the room.

'Don't you see the huge change?' Béatrice defended herself, gesturing at the walls of books. 'Everything here has its place now. Everything makes sense.'

'Hmm, hmm,' he grumbled, lost for words, which was an unusual occurrence.

Béatrice rejoiced over her small victory, but was wise enough not to show it.

'Anyway,' Michael went on, 'I came here to tell you that I'm flying to Ecuador tonight for a week with the VP. As soon as I'm back, we'll sit down and talk about your performance. In the meantime, I expect a detailed report from you about what you've done here so far.'

She nodded. 'Sure thing, Michael. The report is almost ready. You'll have it on Monday.'

Michael snorted loudly and disappeared.

Béatrice had already concocted a plan. While her boss was away on duty travel, she would speak to the staff association and notify them of her pregnancy. The bank took maternity rights very seriously. No one would be able to fire her.

Then her mobile rang. Grégoire! At last. She quickly grabbed her Blackberry. But it wasn't Grégoire; it was Joaquín, the last person she was expecting would call. Disappointed, she let the phone ring a few times, then picked up.

'Hey, it's me. I'm in the lobby downstairs. Do you have time to grab a tea?' he asked.

'What do you want?' she replied coolly.

'I'd like to talk to you.'

Reluctantly she agreed, took her bag and rode the lift down to the ground floor.

Joaquín was standing in the entrance in his dark brown anorak and the chequered shawl he always wore during the colder months. Over his shoulder hung the heavy, sagging leather bag containing his most sacred possessions: his laptop and notebook.

Béatrice walked towards him. As she drew closer, she was taken aback by his appearance. He seemed to have aged years since she had last seen him. He looked tired, with dark circles around his eyes, and hadn't shaved. As he smiled at her and kissed her on the cheek, Béatrice felt as if she were getting back into an old car she had left somewhere along the road because it had stopped working. Her old life.

They went to the Starbucks on I Street. It was filled with young people sitting in front of open laptops and drinking venti latte macchiatos from paper cups as large as coffee pots. Béatrice and Joaquín got a tea each and sat outside on the scratched metal chairs.

They dunked their teabags into the hot water, their movements synchronized, and Béatrice knew that, in a few seconds, Joaquín would put his teabag on a spoon and then wrap the string tightly around it in order to squeeze out the final drops. She didn't know why, but she had always found this ritual incredibly stuffy.

A moment later, he did exactly what she had feared, then laid the spoon and teabag carefully on a paper serviette. In silent defiance, she pulled her teabag out of the paper cup and slapped it, saturated, on the table.

'Is everything okay?' asked Joaquín, wiping up the splatters of tea with another serviette.

'What kind of stupid question is that?' Béatrice shot back, already regretting having agreed to meet him at all. 'You know perfectly well that absolutely nothing's okay.' She opened two sachets of sugar at once and poured the contents into her cup.

'I've been thinking all night, Béa,' said Joaquín, in the gentle tone of voice that always came across so mature and composed that Béatrice felt like putting her hands over her ears.

He smiled hesitantly. 'Please forgive me for the horrible things I said the other day. I reacted like a complete idiot. Of course we're having this child together.'

She was speechless. For the first time ever, he hadn't said what she'd expected him to.

'Bringing up a child is a huge responsibility, yes . . . but it's also the most extraordinary and beautiful thing that can happen in life.' He drank a sip of tea. 'And I want us to experience that together.' He smiled hesitantly.

'And . . . what about Laura?' asked Béatrice, who could barely believe what she had just heard.

Joaquín waved his hand dismissively. 'Oh, Laura. That was a knee-jerk reaction in the restaurant, just like mine. We were both overwhelmed by the news and I feel terribly sorry for that. She's going through a difficult phase, you know, like all the kids her age. Don't take it personally.'

'I still don't think she'd want a half-sibling.' Béatrice was unsure whether to trust this sudden change of heart. But she was even more unsure about how she would fit into this increasingly uncomfortable future family scenario.

'To be honest, she's a bit jealous and afraid you'll take her place in my heart. That's pretty normal, right? But it'll pass. She feels bad about it, she told me so herself.' Joaquín pulled his chair closer to Béatrice's and stroked her cheek. 'She'll get used to the fact that there'll soon be four of us. It will be good for her to not be home alone any more and to be part of a real family.' He moved to kiss Béatrice, but she turned her head away.

'And how do *you* picture it? Life as a four?' she asked instead.

'Easy. You'll move in with us and we'll turn the guest

room into a nursery. You'll have to economize, of course, especially in terms of space, but also financially. You'll have to sell your furniture. And you won't be able to work as many hours. You know, I'm away a lot, so someone has to be home looking after the kids. But we can make it work.' He sighed and stirred his tea. 'When you have a child, your priorities change, Béatrice, you'll see. Clothes, fancy restaurants, travel . . . all of that becomes unimportant.'

Béatrice raised her eyebrows, but didn't comment. She still couldn't visualize it. Her being a mother, the four of them together. 'Do we have to live in your house in McLean?' she asked then, reluctantly pulled along by Joaquín's plans for their family life. 'I wouldn't feel at ease raising our child there. I mean, you bought this home for your former wife. Why couldn't we look for a new place together here in D.C.?'

He sighed. 'Firstly, because I can't afford it. The prices have sky-rocketed. Secondly, because the public schools here in the District are awful. It wouldn't be the right choice for Laura. And besides, I can't just take her away from her friends.'

Move in with Joaquín. Give up my own life, including my apartment and furniture. Ferry Laura around to parties and friends' houses. Go shopping in the Safeway in McLean. Prepare dinner every evening. Spend the weekends with people like Anne Parker in some suburb or other. Grilling hot dogs on Memorial Day in Joaquín's small garden. The pictures darted through Béatrice's mind like a lightning storm. But – did she *like* what she saw?

It would be good for their child and that was all that

mattered. That was what Jacobina had said too. *Good for the child.* This was the sentence she had to get used to. She nodded. 'Hmm.'

Joaquín pulled her against him, and this time Béatrice didn't resist. 'I'm glad we've talked things out,' he said. 'I missed you so much, honey.' Then he looked at his watch. 'Heavens, I have to go. The editorial conference is about to start.' He stood up and shouldered his leather bag. 'We'll see each other at the weekend, okay? So we can sit down with Laura and discuss everything.' He kissed her on the forehead and zipped up his anorak. Then he walked across the pavement, raised his arm, and within seconds a taxi had pulled up. Getting in, he gave her a quick wave, and the vehicle sped off, its tyres screeching.

*

After Joaquín's surprise visit, Béatrice stopped trying to get in touch with Grégoire. She had decided on keeping the baby. And her baby needed its father. So now she had to bear the consequences and stop running after a broken dream.

But how on earth was she supposed to switch off this all-consuming longing for Grégoire? How could she stop herself from thinking about him constantly? The image of his gentle face and sea-green eyes had imprinted itself on her brain. In her apartment, the memory of him was everywhere. On her sofa with outstretched legs; sleeping next to her on the left side of the bed; barefoot in her kitchen with a cup of coffee. She took the two bottles of wine he had brought with him from the fridge and hid them away at the very back of her wardrobe, where she never looked. She couldn't bring herself to pour them away.

*

When she woke up on Saturday morning, Béatrice felt a strange pulling sensation in her lower abdomen. It came and went and felt like the beginning of her period. No need to worry, her doctor said, when she finally reached him on the phone. It was normal. After a few hours, it really did feel better; reassured, Béatrice left her home to go grocery shopping.

She was dreading the evening ahead at Joaquín's house, with a family dinner at the kitchen table and the inevitable make-up sex. Afterwards, he would promise to make more time for her, and then everything would probably stay as it was. For a while she would be able to avoid intimacy by claiming that she was nauseous and tired because of the pregnancy. But what about after that?

With two full shopping bags in her hand, Béatrice stood in front of the Whole Foods supermarket on Wisconsin Avenue and looked around for a vacant taxi. She had bought the kinds of things her doctor had recommended: lots of fruit and vegetables, everything organic so that the growing life inside her would be properly nourished.

All of a sudden, an intense pain shot through her lower abdomen. She dropped the bags in shock, bent over and gripped her belly. She had read about cramps and stitches, that they were part and parcel of the first trimester. But could they really be this strong?

Béatrice remained doubled over until the pain slowly began to subside. A packet of biscuits and a few loose potatoes had fallen out of the bags. She gathered them up and tried to take a few steps. Then another stabbing pain shot through her. Béatrice cried out, put the bags down again and pressed her hands to her belly. The pain subsided again. Then came more dragging, stabbing and tearing pains. She groaned. An elderly woman stopped and asked, 'Are you okay, honey?'

Béatrice nodded silently and bent over, her face contorted with pain, until all she could see was the asphalt.

A strong contraction tore through her, stronger than the previous ones. She let out a sharp cry and stumbled against the shopping bags. Onions, apples, potatoes and broccoli tumbled out, rolling across the pavement and into the street. *My baby*. The words pounded inside her head. *I'm losing my baby!* Whimpering, she slumped to the ground and curled up on the pavement.

The woman leaned down to her. 'Hang in there, I'll ring an ambulance.'

'Thank you,' Béatrice gasped through her tears.

After that, everything went very quickly. An ambulance came and took her to the Georgetown hospital.

The A&E doctor asked lots of questions and then explained the procedure to her. 'I'm afraid you've had a miscarriage. We'll have to perform a minor operation to prevent any infection.'

Béatrice closed her eyes with a groan and nodded. She didn't care what happened to her now. So long as the pain finally stopped. She signed the paperwork with trembling hands and handed her credit card to the ward sister.

'Who can we call for you?' asked the nurse. 'Someone will have to pick you up afterwards.'

Béatrice gave her Joaquín's number.

She had to undress, then she was guided to a bed and pushed along a corridor into an ice-cold room. At long last, the redemptory anaesthesia came, allowing her to escape from it all.

*

When she opened her eyes again, she was lying in a hospital room. Joaquín was sitting next to her. She had no pain any more.

'How did this happen?' he asked, sounding seriously concerned.

'Just like that,' she replied quietly. The torture was over. All she wanted right now was to hold on to this comforting thought. Her tongue felt swollen and dry. 'Can I have some water?'

'Of course. Here.' He passed her a glass.

She drank a few sips, then gave him back the half-empty glass. 'I lost my baby,' she whispered, staring at the wall. 'Do you understand? It's gone.' Then she turned away from him and cried into her pillow. Cried for the child she had accepted so reluctantly. A warm, overpowering feeling for this being that she hadn't been prepared for, yet had somehow already loved, overcame her.

Joaquín silently stroked her back.

'Take me home,' she whispered. 'I want to get out of here.'

The door opened, and a nurse came in. 'How are you doing?' she asked with a friendly smile.

'Okay,' lied Béatrice, lifting her head and dabbing her tears away with the blanket.

'You can leave now. Please take it easy over the next few days, you need to heal.' The nurse opened the band that was wrapped around Béatrice's wrist, pulled out the needle and stuck a plaster in its place. 'Please don't be too discouraged by this,' she said, giving Béatrice's arm a reassuring pat. 'Neither of you should lose heart. A miscarriage certainly doesn't mean that you can't get pregnant again.'

*

'Should I pick up something to eat?' asked Joaquín a short while later, as they turned into R Street in his car. Until then he had barely said a word, and Béatrice was grateful she didn't have to talk.

'I'm not hungry,' she muttered, staring out of the window.

'You have to eat something. Come on, I'll go past Lucío's.'

'No,' said Béatrice. 'I don't want anything.'

He stopped the car in front of her building and turned off the engine. The headlights immediately went dark. A cyclist rode past them. 'May I come up with you? There's a free parking space over there.'

Béatrice didn't answer for a while. 'We don't belong together, Joaquín,' she said eventually.

He sighed loudly and fell silent. After what felt to Béatrice like an eternity, he whispered, 'I know. I've known it for a long while.'

'It's . . . it's better if we don't see each other any more.' In the dim light from the street lamp, she saw Joaquín nod.

'Okay . . .' he responded, his voice choked.

'I'm going up now,' Béatrice said before opening the car door. Without turning around again, she climbed out and shut the door behind her.

Joaquín turned on the engine and drove off.

Béatrice watched the car as it trundled along R Street and, together with the past year of her life, disappeared into the darkness.

20

Judith

Paris, August 1941

It was early evening. The city was as hot and still as the bouillon I was greedily spooning into my mouth. My first proper meal in days.

Christian and I were sitting on the terrace of Mille Couverts, a popular brasserie on Rue du Commerce in the 15th arrondissement. The spacious three-storey restaurant, which, at the turn of the century, had been a ladies' fashion boutique, was one of the few establishments to still offer the Parisian population an affordable menu in spite of the food shortages. Before the war, most of the diners here had been workers from the automobile industry. Now, it was sought out by all those who could no longer bear the depressing solitude of their apartments. I preferred it to the fine restaurants Christian liked to frequent, where you were handed starched white serviettes and lived in constant fear that a group of German officers would sit down at one of the neighbouring tables.

The bouillon was delicious. Instead of the tender beef which was traditionally included in a consommé, it just contained a few pieces of carrot and potato, but the salty broth was wonderfully invigorating and, for a moment, helped me to forget my worries.

Christian was smoking and drinking wine. Through the haze of the cigarette smoke he smiled at me.

It was a long while since he had asked after my mother. He knew I was uncomfortable talking about her, because I never had anything good to report. Mother spent the whole day lying in bed, pale and gaunt, and only left it to go to the bathroom. She rarely touched the buttered bread or any of the other food Christian continued to supply us with. And if she did, she would push it aside after just a few bites. Ever since the evening when I had suggested to her that we flee together, I hadn't been able to have even one proper conversation with her. She didn't listen; instead, she stared through me and started sentences that she didn't finish. She seemed to feel most comfortable when Lily was lying next to her, pressing the soft scruff of her neck against her face. Then she would sometimes hum a little melody, laughing to herself and whispering into the cat's ear.

Her depressed state made me feel sad, angry and helpless all at once. A few weeks ago, I had been on the brink of calling out the doctor, but Mother had begged me not to until, eventually, I relented. Admittedly a doctor wouldn't have been able to do much. The blue sedatives which Docteur Fabri, our family physician, had previously prescribed for her may have been able to send her to sleep for several hours, but they were by no means capable of healing her depression.

Sometimes I felt as though I were being pulled down

with her into the deep, dark hole from which she couldn't escape. Since my dismissal from the Sorbonne, I felt surrounded by a threatening emptiness. I got up each morning at half past five, like always, and for the first few moments everything seemed normal. It would be bright in my room, and I would look forward to my first cup of coffee. But then, at the latest by the time I was on my way into the kitchen, I would remember everything: that I no longer had an income; no plans, no goals and no tasks. That it didn't matter whether I got up or stayed in bed. Sometimes I would turn around on the spot and get back in under the covers. Stare at the ceiling, watch the flies buzz in great arcs through the air, and smoke a few cigarettes. Or I would pull the blanket over my head and try in vain to sleep a little longer.

In these quiet moments, when the pointlessness of my existence and the hopelessness of my situation descended on me like a thick, black coat, when my breaths lengthened and my heartbeat slowed, I could empathize with Mother's suffering. I felt compassion for her wounded soul and wished I could free her and myself from the evil of this world.

A year before, when the Germans had marched in, I hadn't been afraid. *They can't harm us*, I had thought. France was a free country. A republic that had saved the lives of thousands of Jews who had fled here at the beginning of the century from the pogroms in Eastern Europe, making many of them French citizens. France would protect us. I had really believed that. How stupid and naive! Now we had lost everything. A few days before, we'd even had to give up our radio, my last connection to the outside world. Jews were no longer allowed to possess radio sets. What a ludicrous system we had to conform to!

My days dragged by onerously; long and empty. I sat around in the apartment with my gloomy thoughts, tidying things here and there without even knowing what I was doing. In order to escape the deathly silence and kill time, I sometimes wandered aimlessly through the streets. But even that brought no relief. I kept looking over my shoulder, feeling as though someone was watching me. The fear was so ever-present that I was even afraid of the clipping sound my own soles made on the pavement.

Christian was the only glimmer of light in my life. His love carried me and kept me going. This evening, sitting here with him in Mille Couverts, looking at him and knowing that our love was alive, gave me courage to return to the heavy isolation of my home.

Christian touched my hand. 'You like the soup, my angel?' he said, stroking my fingers.

I nodded keenly, spooned the final drops out of my bowl and leaned back contentedly. The air seemed suffused with the lightness of summer. Couples strolled past us. Two children ran after a ball. A newspaper vendor waved the latest edition of *Paris Soir* in the air. 'German advance into the Ukraine,' he yelled. 'German troops occupy Kherson harbour.'

'Stay with me tonight,' said Christian.

I looked at him in surprise. He had never suggested that before.

'My parents are in Vichy, the staff have the evening off . . . We will have the apartment to ourselves.'

I straightened up, the soup heavy in my stomach. 'You mean . . .'

He took my hand and looked deeply into my eyes. 'Yes,' he said. 'I want us to spend the night together.'

It felt as though my heart were about to burst with love.

'I don't want to just think about you all the time,' he said. 'I want to lie next to you and hear you breathe.'

A sinuous warmth spread through my body. I felt an intense longing to be alone with him. How often I had dreamed of falling asleep beside him, his voice in my ear and his lips on my hair. Of seeing him when I opened my eyes in the morning. What was just one night? I thought to myself. Mother wouldn't even notice if I didn't come home. And tomorrow morning at six, as soon as curfew was lifted, I would go home. The neighbours would think I was coming back from the bakery.

'*Paris Soir*,' yelled the newspaper vendor. 'German victory in the Ukraine! Just one franc, messieurs-dames.' Passers-by crowded around him, holding out coins and stretching their hands towards the newspapers.

'I want to be with you too,' I whispered.

Christian squeezed my hand, beckoned the waiter and put a few food coupons on the table. A short while later, we were roaring past the Eiffel Tower in his dark Traction Avant, over the Pont de Passy and the Seine, through the 16th arrondissement to the elegant Avenue Victor Hugo, where his parents' apartment was located.

Christian pulled a bag out from beneath his seat and took out a hat, a thin silk tunic, a pair of shoes and some sunglasses. 'Here, put these on,' he said. I saw Jean-Michel, his chauffeur, look at me in the rear-view mirror. What did he know? Would he keep quiet?

'What's this?' I asked hesitantly.

'They belong to my mother. Just to be on the safe side, in case someone runs into us.'

I paused. What had I let myself in for? Jean-Michel parked the car. Outside, darkness was falling.

'Nothing will happen,' Christian assured me. 'The concierge has the day off and has gone out to the countryside.' He put his mother's hat on me and straightened it. It was stiff and heavy and had a wide brim which was decorated with large red feathers, covering half of my face. Christian gave me a wink. '*Voilà, madame.* It suits you wonderfully.'

I took the tunic and slipped my hands through the wide sleeves. I had never felt anything so soft against my skin before. The fabric carried the scent of a fruity, sweet perfume; of roses, jasmine and apricots.

Christian studied my swift transformation and nodded. 'Perfect! Now just the sunglasses and the shoes. I'll go ahead and make sure no one's in the entrance hall. As soon as I signal to you, come after me.' He winked again. 'Don't worry, Judith. Most people are on holiday this month. And the ones who are still there live further up and use the lift.'

As I tried to squeeze my feet into his mother's narrow shoes, Christian clambered out of the car and limped over to the building entrance. I put on the sunglasses and stared after him, biting my lips nervously. It was less the risk of running into other residents that worried me, and more the fact that, in just a few minutes' time, I would be

entering the lion's den, the home of one of the most influential anti-Semites in our republic. A man who had made
it his goal to destroy people like me.

Christian reappeared at the entrance and waved me over.
Jean-Michel sprang out of the driver's seat, dived around
the car and opened the door for me. I hadn't managed to
entirely squeeze my heels into the narrow patent leather
shoes, so I padded and stumbled on tiptoe across the
pavement to Christian.

'No one's here,' he whispered, leading the way.

The entrance hall was an expansive, oval room. Elegant
and immaculate. The walls and the floor were clad with
grey-veined marble. The windows to the concierge's lodge
were darkened.

'I'll take the lift and you the steps,' whispered Christian,
stepping into the wrought-iron lift cabin, which was
adorned with leaf-shaped ornaments and reminded me of
a birdcage. Two broad staircases, like conjuring snakes,
wound their way up to the right- and left-hand side of the
lift. The steps were covered with dark red runners. 'We
live on the second floor,' Christian murmured. 'See you in
a moment.' Slowly, the birdcage rattled upwards.

I slipped off the shoes, stuffed them into my bag and
hurried up the steps, taking two at once. By the time I'd
reached the second floor, without running into anyone,
Christian was just getting out of the cabin.

'You see how easy that was?' He triumphantly pulled
his key from his trouser pocket and opened the door.

I stepped inside, my legs wobbly from excitement and
fear. The scent of cold cigar smoke and women's perfume
hit me. I removed the hat and sunglasses, pulled off the

silk tunic and laid them on the narrow bench by the entrance door. Then I followed Christian barefoot over the wooden parquet, which carried the slight scent of floor wax, into the reception room. Its imposing vastness and grand furnishings took my breath away. This wasn't an apartment; it was a palace! Huge chandeliers suspended from intricate chains gave a ceremonial atmosphere. Hanging resplendent on the walls were heavy tapestries, depicting hunting scenes filled with horses and dogs. I glanced at the group of dark green chairs: six of them arranged around a Louis XV-style smokers' table, all at the same distance from one another. Further behind was a white wall-mounted console table with gilded carvings, upon which stood crystal carafes of wine, spirits and cognac, as well as glasses of differing sizes.

Christian pointed towards a dark oak door. 'That's my father's office,' he said.

We went into the drawing room. Filled with awe, I studied the eighteenth-century oil portraits. Bloated male faces and plump, white-powdered women in long robes stared out at me. On the other side of the room, between wide casement windows, stood artfully made walnut commodes in a sophisticated rococo style, adorned with inlays and gilded fittings. I curiously approached the fireplace and studied the bronze candlesticks on the mantelpiece, then carefully stroked my finger across one of them.

'Please don't say anything,' observed Christian dryly, sitting down on a grey, kidney-shaped chaise longue in the middle of the room. 'It's embarrassing how much greed and money there is in here.'

I walked across the thick carpet and sat down next to

him. The fragile-looking chaise longue let out a sigh. I moved to get right back up again, but Christian put his arm round me.

'Stay with me, my angel,' he whispered as he kissed my hair.

For a long while I just sat there, my head nestled against his shoulder, filled with happiness about this moment in our small, longed-for reality.

Barely a sound could be heard through the closed windows, which were tucked behind ivory-white silk curtains. It was as though the outside world had simply ceased to exist. War, darkened streets, curfew, passport checks, fear and hardship were taking place somewhere else; in the newspapers and on the radio, between *chansons* by Maurice Chevalier and Tino Rossi. But here, in this little Versailles on Avenue Victor Hugo, a bygone world lived on. A world whose splendour, abundance and excess I found both alluring and repulsive.

Christian stood up and limped back into the reception room. A short while later, he returned with two full wine glasses and handed me one. We drank in silence. Shyly, I rotated the glass in my hand. I didn't know why we suddenly couldn't find the words. Was it because we were on forbidden terrain? Because he believed I didn't feel comfortable in this ostentatious palace? Because we were afraid that his parents might stroll in unexpectedly? Or was it perhaps that for the first time since we had met, we were completely and utterly alone?

As I studied the unhappy stares of the faces on the oil paintings, I felt Christian's eyes rest on me. A strange tension had built up between our bodies. A crackling, erotic energy whose existence I had first sensed as we sat next to one another in the dark cinema, back in winter, kissing for hours. But now this feeling was much more intense and exciting. It prickled and tingled in my body, as though every one of my cells were electrically charged. My hand trembling, I brought the glass to my mouth and drank a little more.

Christian put his glass down on the side table and placed his hand on my arm. 'Come,' he said gently. 'Let's go to my room.'

I choked on the wine and coughed. Then I put my glass down too, shaking, and looked into his eyes.

His gaze was warm and loving. 'Are you afraid . . . about the first time?'

I nodded silently.

'Me too,' he admitted, standing up and taking my hand.

We silently crossed first the drawing room and then the reception room – past the powdered women, wine carafes and hunting scenes. I saw a galloping horse, a grazing deer and then the small bench again where I had laid Christian's mother's hat. All around me, these unfamiliar colours and scents. I felt vertigo.

Christian pulled me through a door. It was dark inside his room.

'Please don't turn on the light,' I pleaded, my voice toneless. I didn't want him to see me, nor did I want to see him. I wanted the darkness to hide my embarrassment.

Christian put his hands on my hips, his lips on my mouth, his touch discharging the tension between our bodies into the dark.

'Judith . . .' he whispered. 'Judith.' While kissing me,

he unbuttoned my blouse. His lips wandered down my neck towards my breasts.

I felt hot, my blood was churning. Being this close made me afraid. It was so new and unfamiliar. Everything was going much too fast. But at the same time, I yearned for his body like nothing else in the world. I knew that what I was about to do wasn't some rash, unconsidered act.

'I love you, Judith,' I heard Christian saying, again and again.

My inhibition evaporated like morning mist over the fields, until all I could feel was deep, burning desire. My head and my heart had belonged to him for a long while. Now I would give him every fibre of my body. And at that moment, I stopped thinking.

21

Béatrice

Washington, D.C., 2006

When Béatrice awoke the next morning, for a moment everything seemed like normal. But then the images came rushing back. The blood. The cramps. The pain. *My baby is gone*. A profound sadness overwhelmed her. For a long while, she was unable to get up, her limbs felt heavy and stiff.

Eventually, she found the strength to leave her bed, trudged slowly into the bathroom and splashed cold water on her face. She didn't dare look in the mirror. Then she went to the kitchen, made herself a strong coffee and called the office to say she would be off sick for a week. She simply wouldn't be able to bear the bleakness of the archive in her current state.

A little later, she called Jacobina to ask how she was, and told her what had happened.

'Oh my goodness,' murmured her friend, full of sympathy. 'That's terrible! And I can't do anything to help you. I'm so sorry.'

Then Béatrice reached out to her mother and later to

Monique, opening up to them about the miscarriage. They were both compassionate and knew how to comfort her. It felt so good to connect to her home, to be able to let everything go. Béatrice was saddened, as she so often was, by the thousands of kilometres that separated them.

She stayed in her apartment for days. She couldn't summon the energy to get dressed and go shopping. In her cupboard she found a few packets of pasta and a jar of apple sauce, the use-by date several weeks past expiration. It didn't matter. She ate it anyway.

She had expected Joaquín to call, to ask how she was doing and whether he could bring her anything. That was the least he could have done. But he didn't. On the one hand, Béatrice was disappointed by his indifference, and caught herself muttering a bitter 'typical' into the silence. On the other hand, with every minute that went by, the relief grew that she had finally separated from him.

Her thoughts also revolved around Grégoire. She kept wondering where he was and what he was doing. Was he thinking about her?

On the third day, she rummaged around in her wardrobe and pulled out one of the two wine bottles from behind her ski boots. She poured herself a glass and drank it. Not in a restrained way, relishing it as he had shown her, but quickly and thirstily. The alcohol immediately went to her head, and after a few more sips the living room began to spin before her eyes. Spurred on by her tipsiness, she called the Holocaust Museum and asked for Grégoire. He had gone out, they told her. And he still wasn't answering his mobile. Later on, she wrote him an email and asked whether they could meet. She did not bring up the miscarriage, which she found too personal to be mentioned in an email.

Her message remained unanswered.

*

Two days later, on Thursday morning, the rainy spring weather gave way to a sudden, humid start of summer. In Washington the seasons tended to change very abruptly. As Béatrice stepped out of her building, she was met by warm, muggy air. She pulled off her jacket and tied it around her waist. Soon the cumbersome air conditioning units would be rattling on all the house walls; young people in flip-flops would stroll through the neighbourhood; and sweat-soaked joggers with bright red faces would lumber their way past.

Jacobina was due to be discharged from the hospital today, and Béatrice had promised to pick her up and take her home.

Her old friend looked frail and exhausted. She had lost a lot of weight, most noticeably around her face: her cheeks were sunken, and her eyes had been almost swallowed by the sockets. Her black tracksuit flapped loosely around her legs as she shuffled her way through the exit, leaning against a walking frame. Béatrice took her arm and helped her into a taxi.

'That fennel tea they gave me every morning – what utter swill,' complained Jacobina.

'Once we get you home, I'll make you a really good coffee,' suggested Béatrice.

'Not allowed. For the time being they've forbidden me from almost everything.'

'Okay, then we'll find something else you like,' said Béatrice encouragingly.

Jacobina leaned closer. 'And how are you doing, sweetie? You've been through a lot.'

Béatrice shrugged. 'Hanging in there. It's hard to deal with such a loss.'

Jacobina squeezed Béatrice's hand. 'I'm here for you. Any time. Don't forget that.'

Béatrice smiled. 'Thank you.'

Jacobina instructed the taxi driver not to take the route over Dupont Circle, because it was a detour that would cost at least two dollars more. Then she turned back to Béatrice. 'And your handsome vintner? What's going on with him?'

'No idea. He hasn't been in touch.'

Jacobina sighed. 'Men. They're so much trouble. I've always got along quite well without them.'

The apartment in U Street was dark. A sour smell hung in the air, as though someone had spilled a bottle of milk several weeks ago. Béatrice held her nose and marched straight into the living room to open the shutters and windows.

'Don't open them too far,' commanded Jacobina as she made her way towards the armchair, leaning on her walking frame. 'I hate it when the sticky heat comes in.'

'Just for a moment. You can hardly breathe in here,' replied Béatrice.

Jacobina sat down, grumbling, and pulled the medication she had received in the hospital out of the plastic bag. 'Oh, good heavens.' She put the little bottles in front of her on the table. 'Look at everything I have to take.'

Béatrice got to work. The apartment was in a bad state. In the bed, amongst the sheets, she found damp, mouldy hand towels; the floor was covered with discarded clothes and crumpled-up paper towels. As she stepped into the bathroom, she discovered the source of the horrible smell: around the edge of the toilet was a thick crust of vomit, which had leaked down onto the floor and dried. 'Ugh, what happened here?' she asked, holding her nose.

'You have no idea how bad I was feeling. I couldn't stop throwing up. The pain was so intense I thought I was about to meet my maker,' called Jacobina from the living room.

Béatrice slapped a hand over her mouth. 'Oh God! And I didn't return your calls.' Only now did she realize the extent of what had happened with Jacobina the night that Grégoire had stayed at hers.

'Don't feel bad. It's done now,' said her friend in a relaxed tone, turning on the television.

Béatrice loaded up the washing machine, cleaned the bathroom and made the bed with fresh sheets. Then she folded up the clothes and wiped down the kitchenette. She had hoped that busying herself like this would distract her. But as hard as she tried, after every few minutes, her thoughts kept returning to the baby she had lost, and eventually to Grégoire.

'I'm not completely back on form yet, Jacobina,' explained Béatrice after an hour, throwing the cleaning cloth into the wash basin. 'But next week I'll do a thorough clean, I promise.'

Jacobina waved her hand. 'There's no hurry, Béa. I'm so grateful for everything you're doing. Just stay with me a little longer, okay?'

Béatrice made some herbal tea and came back with two full cups. She sat next to Jacobina and unlocked her Blackberry, which had been blinking for a few minutes. She scanned through the newly received emails. Several bank-related messages, a new offer from Air France and

– oh God! – the Red Cross. Finally! Her pulse quickened. 'Guess what? Baltimore answered.'

'Who?'

'The search service of the Red Cross.' Béatrice opened the message and read it out loud:

Dear Ms Duvier,

We are writing in reference to your enquiry about Judith Goldemberg and your supposition that she survived the Holocaust. Unfortunately, we have to inform you that this is not the case. Ms Goldemberg did not survive the Auschwitz concentration camp. She is not a "rescapée", contrary to the assertion of George Dreyfus, whose work you quote in your letter.

Ms Goldemberg's name is on the list of Jews who were deported to Auschwitz on the seventeenth of December 1943 in convoy sixty-three. We have enclosed a copy of page 473 from Serge Klarsfeld's book, Chronicle of Jews deported from France. As you will see, Klarsfeld put a small dot next to the survivors' names. Unfortunately, there is no dot after Judith Goldemberg's name.

We are very sorry to give you such distressing news and remain at your disposal should you have further questions.

With kind regards,

Linda Evans

Béatrice lowered her phone and looked at Jacobina anxiously. 'I'm sorry. I really hoped we would find her.'

Jacobina didn't reply and kicked her foot against the walking frame.

'I don't understand why Grégoire didn't know that,' said Béatrice in disappointment, standing up and going over to the window. 'He showed me both books at the Holocaust Museum. We talked about Klarsfeld's work for a while. Then he brought me the Dreyfus list and said it meant that Judith had survived.'

'Your Grégoire can't know everything,' replied Jacobina, playing with the sash of her bath robe. 'The Nazis have six million Jews on their conscience. Six million! And we're looking for one single person. It's obvious there will be differing results. I'm surprised we found out anything at all, after such a long time.'

Béatrice sat back down.

'And . . . what the Red Cross writes is pretty clear,' Jacobina added. 'We know exactly when Judith was deported to Auschwitz. But we have nothing to prove that she was freed.'

Béatrice agreed, although she found it hard to accept this abrupt ending.

'I'm happy that I finally know what happened to Judith,' said Jacobina after a while. 'Thanks to you and your help, I've kept my promise to my father – that's all that matters.'

Béatrice nodded sadly. 'I was just hoping—'

'It's fine, Béatrice,' Jacobina interrupted her. 'It's all fine. We knew it was unlikely that she survived in any case.' She crossed her ankles in front of her. 'This evening I'll light a candle and say the Kaddish prayer for Judith. Then at least somebody from our family has given her a blessing, by way of goodbye.'

*

The next day, Béatrice returned to the office. The uncertainty over the future of her career was worrying her. If Michael really did manage to fire her, using the new budget cuts as justification, with a small redundancy payment and just a few months' notice, she would have to look for a new job as quickly as possible. *Heads will roll*, he had said. And hers could be one of them. Jacobina was right. She had to look outside the bank. At the United Nations, for example, in New York, Geneva or Rome. There were so many international organizations and sub-organizations, and each one of them had a press department. From now on she would refocus all her attention on her career.

As she stepped into the lift, she bumped into Veronica. The exuberant Brazilian carried an angular carton in her hand, the takeaway breakfast from the cafeteria. The delicious aroma of toasted bread streamed out of it.

Veronica looked at Béatrice curiously. 'Hey, are you feeling better?'

Béatrice nodded. 'Yes, all good.'

'What did you have?'

'Some horrid virus,' fibbed Béatrice, because her private life was none of Veronica's business. 'I was really knocked out. And how are things here?'

'Same old, same old,' her colleague replied. 'Just Michael is different.'

Béatrice raised her eyebrows in disbelief. 'Michael? Change is not in his DNA,' she commented sarcastically.

'You'll see.' Veronica blew a strand of hair out of her face. 'Ever since he got back from Ecuador, he's been running from one meeting to the next. And if he's not in a meeting, he locks himself up in his office. He looks stressed all the time and hardly pays any attention to our team any more. I noticed he's receiving a lot of calls from the Haiti office. Something weird is going on.'

'The Haiti office?' Béatrice's mind was racing. 'Did they turn in the findings of the investigation?' Would she finally be acquitted, her innocence re-established? Or, and the thought made her stomach cramp, was he plotting a ghastly lie to get rid of her for good?

Veronica shook her head. 'Not yet, but it'll come soon enough. In a couple of weeks or so.'

The lift stopped with a ring; the doors opened. 'I gotta run, see you later.' Veronica stepped out and hurried down the corridor.

As soon as Béatrice entered the archive, she reached a new low. The silence, the isolation, the grief over her lost baby – it was unbearable. And Michael, of course. Who knew what he was fabricating right now to hurt her? Should she call Cecil and ask about the investigation? *Believe me, I will find out what went wrong*, she remembered him saying. But she quickly discarded that idea. After everything that had happened, he would probably not give her any confidential information. All she could do now was get on with her work and seek out a new job somewhere else.

*

As her lonely days turned into weeks, Béatrice grew increasingly anxious. By day, she updated her CV, composed application letters, and searched online for positions in the press industry. There weren't many vacancies around, and for most of them she would have to accept a significant drop in income.

At night, she lay around listlessly in bed, drank wine and grieved. She had lost everything. Her baby, Grégoire, Joaquín, and now there was a high chance she might even lose her job.

In the hope of tackling her solitude by reinvigorating old connections, she made dinner plans with a friend from the bank. But just a few hours later, the woman cancelled, because she still had so much work to do before flying to a conference in Africa.

And while the air conditioning in the archive blew an icy wind against the nape of Béatrice's neck, outside it became hotter and muggier with every day that passed.

At least Michael was leaving her in peace for once. He didn't stop by any more to check on her, nor did he send any instructions by email. He also didn't comment on the reports he had requested before his trip to Ecuador – the detailed account of her conversation with Daniel Lustiger and the list of activities she had carried out to tidy up the archive. She had sent this information some time ago but never heard back a word. It was as if Michael had vanished. She didn't miss his hostile, arrogant gaze or the smell of cold smoke at all. At the same time, this uncharacteristic silence worried her, like the uneasy quiet before a major storm. He hadn't just forgotten about her. Something else was going on. Something that could have lasting and negative implications for her.

*

Every other day, on her way home, Béatrice checked in on Jacobina and brought her something to eat. Bland fare. Nothing fatty, nothing raw, no nuts, no vegetables. Jacobina was still in pain and spent most of the day sitting apathetically in front of the television. She was as happy as a child when Béatrice came by with rusks and yoghurt.

One hot evening, towards the end of June, Béatrice had just reached Jacobina's apartment when the door was pulled open, and her friend greeted her with a big smile. 'Come on in, Béa, hurry,' she called out, leaning on her walking frame and gesturing with her arm. Her eyes were full of life and energy. Béatrice had never seen her this euphoric. 'What's going on?' she asked, following her friend inside.

Jacobina dropped onto the couch. 'I can't tell you how excited I am. A miracle happened.'

Béatrice put the carton with hot porridge she had just bought for Jacobina on the glass table and sat next to her. 'I'm all ears.'

'Remember that mail you found in the cupboard on one of your first visits?'

'How could I not?' Béatrice chuckled. 'Such an impressive pile.'

'Well, this morning I was so bored that I took it all out and opened each letter, one by one. And guess what?'

Jacobina's eyes were gleaming. 'Among all the bills and ads there was a letter from Nathalie. From December of last year, can you imagine? She had tried to call me, but the line was shut down, nobody could reach me.'

'That's wonderful,' Béatrice exclaimed. 'And how's she doing?'

'She lives in a cute little town in Maine now, with her daughter and granddaughters nearby, and she is doing a lot of charity work for children from underprivileged families. She became part of a thriving community there, she writes, where people still care for each other.'

'I'm so happy you two are reconnecting again,' Béatrice said.

'Wait,' interjected Jacobina, 'I haven't told you the best part yet.' Her cheeks turned pink with elation. 'Nathalie wants me to visit her in Maine when I'm well enough. She even said I could stay with her for good. Or if I prefer, she'd help me find an affordable place nearby.'

'Fantastic!' Béatrice smiled. 'And what do you think about this idea?'

'I'll visit her as soon as I'm done with the chemo, provided all goes well,' Jacobina declared. 'Nathalie and I already spoke this afternoon. If I like it up there, I might stay longer.'

She turned serious again and sniffled. 'It's all because of you. If you hadn't found the mail and mentioned it, I'd have never looked at it again. You have changed my life in so many ways.'

For a while they just sat there, holding each other and sharing this special moment of friendship. And as she relished her friend's renewed happiness, Béatrice felt that she, too, was now ready to move on. Jacobina's joy had also filled *her* with light and energy.

Friendship. There was such a power to it.

*

Thursday morning. Béatrice walked into the archive, put the paper cup with takeaway coffee she had bought on her way to the office on her desk and wiped the moisture from her face. Even at this early hour it was already brutally hot and humid outside; would she ever get used to this insane climate?

Another long day of confinement in the archive confronted her. And still no news from Michael. At least American Independence Day was coming up next Tuesday, and the bank offices would be closed both Monday and Tuesday. Plus, tomorrow she planned to take the afternoon off to accompany Jacobina to her first follow-up doctor's appointment and to finally clean her apartment. Something she had promised Jacobina quite some time ago.

Béatrice was looking forward to the mini holiday, freeing her from the unpleasantness that surrounded her here. At least for a few days.

The sound of steps reverberated from the corridor. They were forceful and fast, but thankfully they differed from the feared *click clack* announcing a control visit from Michael. A second later, the door swung open and Veronica stormed in. She was breathing heavily, her long hair hanging in dishevelled strands over her shoulders.

'Have you heard the news?' Veronica gasped.

'Which news?'

'The Haiti investigation,' Veronica uttered, still panting. 'They came out with their findings, just now.'

Béatrice straightened up at once. 'And?'

Veronica shook her head. 'You won't believe it,' she cried, raking her fingers through her hair.

Béatrice felt the palms of her hands growing damp. 'Tell me!'

Veronica closed the door and sank into a chair. 'A whistle-blower who's based in our Port-au-Prince office opened up to the investigators. He overheard – and even recorded – a phone conversation Alexander had with Michael.'

Béatrice stiffened. Had the two men been plotting something against her?

'As you know, Alexander was hoping to become our next VP for Latin America. But his performance in Haiti isn't that great, and the senior management voiced some objections. To counter their opposition and show off with a big success story, he instructed Michael to use the exaggerated student numbers. And obviously, it was that same whistleblower who handed the documents with the real numbers to the Partnership for Global Education.'

Béatrice stared at Veronica, her eyes wide open. She had expected a lot of things but not this.

'In return Alexander promised Michael he would create a director position for him, as soon as he was in his new job.'

It took a moment before Béatrice was able to open her mouth again. 'And now?' was all she could say.

Veronica smiled, clearly satisfied with the strong impact her news was having on Béatrice.

'Michael has to step down from his current position, effective immediately! He'll be demoted to an adviser to some low-key partnership the bank is involved in, but you know what that means.' She rolled her eyes and grinned. 'Sitting around in an office without any responsibilities whatsoever. And Alexander has accepted an early retirement package and will be leaving the bank.'

Veronica jumped up again and strolled towards the door. 'You see, Béa, there *is* some justice in this world after all.' She opened it, waved and off she went, leaving behind a dazzled Béatrice. Only after her first shock had finally subsided was Béatrice able to fully grasp what had just happened. Heads *had* rolled, indeed! And Michael was gone.

A deep feeling of triumph streaked through her body like a comet. Béatrice let out a long, loud and liberating shout. The first shout of joy the walls surrounding her had ever witnessed.

*

A second major surprise came in the early afternoon. And again, Veronica was the messenger. Our new boss wants to meet you, she texted.

Who is it? Béatrice wrote back immediately, not knowing what to expect.

Catarina Serrano, Veronica replied. She'll be acting head until they've hired a new manager. She'd like to see you now.

Béatrice knew who Catarina was and had heard her speak at meetings but never worked with her directly. The Peruvian had an excellent reputation and had only recently moved from the bank's Paris office to the D.C. headquarters to run the central press office.

'Nice to meet you, Béatrice,' Catarina greeted her when Béatrice walked into Michael's former office. What a relief to see this woman instead of him, Béatrice thought as she sat down. No more anxiety, no more panic attacks. Just the faint smell of cigarette smoke that still hung in the air. But that would soon be history, too.

Catarina had to be in her mid-fifties; she looked very elegant in her dark-blue suit with the big glossy buttons. Her raven-coloured hair was tied into a classy bun, and her eyes looked warm and friendly.

'I've heard good things about you,' she said.

'Thank you.' Béatrice's face flushed. It had been a long time since a superior at the bank had told her something like this.

'So, what exactly are you doing in the archive?' Catarina wanted to know.

'Michael asked me to organize it.'

Catarina creased her forehead. 'Organize the archive? A highly qualified and experienced professional like you? What utter nonsense is that?'

Béatrice shrugged. 'Michael and I . . . We had . . .'

Catarina gave a dismissive wave of her hand. 'I know about the whole Daniel Lustiger thing. Trashing the bank is Lustiger's trademark. The only way this could have been avoided is if our two esteemed colleagues hadn't come up with their own success number.' She crossed her legs and picked a piece of lint from her sleeve. 'In any case, Béatrice, this whole archive thing is over now. I'd like you to get back to your office at once and do your real job.'

A heavy weight lifted from Béatrice's soul, and a mixture of joy and relief bubbled up inside her. 'Of course!'

Catarina leaned back in her chair. 'There's something else I'd like to talk to you about. As you can imagine, I have to hit the ground running; this whole change came rather suddenly. I need a few days to get started in my new role here and identify the most pressing priorities.'

Béatrice listened attentively. What a fantastic woman! With her here now, Béatrice would get things done *and* enjoy it, too.

'Therefore,' Catarina went on, 'I won't be able to attend the OECD development conference in Paris next Tuesday. I'd like *you* to go on my behalf. Could you make that work?'

Béatrice looked at her, perplexed. Did she hear that right? Catarina was sending her to Paris and asking if that was okay?

'I'm sorry for such a last-minute request,' Catarina apologized. 'This will obviously get in the way of any Fourth of July activities you might have planned. But someone needs to go. And I have the presentation ready.'

Béatrice gave Catarina a gleaming smile. She was treated again with respect, like a professional. 'I'd be delighted to go to Paris and do this presentation.'

'Terrific,' said Catarina. 'Veronica will make your flight and hotel arrangements now and I'll email you all the other necessary information shortly. Good luck.'

Paris, Béatrice thought, as she floated down the corridor to pick up her belongings at the archive. What an incredible opportunity! Not only would she get her career back on track, make new contacts and deliver a great presentation, she could also see her mother. If she left tomorrow night, after helping Jacobina during the afternoon, she could spend the weekend at home. It couldn't get any better. She would call her mother right away to announce this unexpected visit.

*

At lunchtime the next day, Béatrice left the bank building with a flight ticket, her laptop and a presentation on inclusive growth. She went home, packed, picked up some cleaning supplies and took a taxi straight to Jacobina's place. The flight departed late in the evening. She had plenty of time to get everything done.

Once Jacobina and she returned from the hospital and Béatrice had served her friend a glass of water, she pulled on her cleaning gloves with determination.

'Are you on some big mission?' asked Jacobina.

'Absolutely,' replied Béatrice. 'Remember, I'm leaving for Paris tonight. I want this place to be nice and tidy before I go. Even though the doctor was pleased with how you're doing, you're still much too weak to do any strenuous activities.'

She opened a big plastic sack and stuffed into it everything that crossed her path: the old newspapers which were piled up on the floor, empty boxes, dusty dried flowers, and all the other clutter that had collected on the shelves, in cupboards and in other overlooked corners.

Jacobina protested. 'You can't just throw everything away!'

'No worries, just the rubbish. You don't need any of this.'

'I trust you,' Jacobina grumbled and retreated to her tiny bedroom.

The afternoon sun shone with all its force through the living room window, and although the air conditioning unit was buzzing at full strength, it simply wouldn't cool down the apartment. Sweat ran down Béatrice's back, and she wiped her arm over her damp forehead. Then she pushed the sofa aside in order to hoover up the thicket of spiderwebs and dust that had been allowed to flourish there undisturbed. Her gaze fell on a yellow envelope. She pulled it out and was about to throw it into one of the bags as recycling. But then she recognized the curving, generous handwriting; she had seen it once before. The letter was addressed to *Mademoiselle Judith Goldemberg*. Beneath it was an address in Galati, Romania.

The envelope she hadn't been able to find back then! It must have slipped under the sofa when she'd emptied out Lica's box.

As she turned it over, her heart skipped a beat in shock. The tips of her fingers felt numb. This was impossible. These kinds of coincidences didn't happen!

'Jacobina,' she called out, rushing into her bedroom. 'I found the sender.'

Jacobina peered out from between her pillows in confusion. 'Which sender?'

'I know who wrote the letter to Judith.' Béatrice waved the envelope excitedly. 'I've got C's full name! You won't believe it, he—'

'Just a minute,' Jacobina interrupted her, 'I have to sit up properly first.' Groaning, she pulled her legs out from beneath the blanket and straightened up.

'His name is Christian,' cried Béatrice, darting around the room in a frenzy. 'Christian Pavie-Rausan.'

Jacobina ran her hand through her curls and yawned. 'Never heard of him.'

'Listen, that's Grégoire's surname too!' Béatrice pressed the envelope into Jacobina's hand. 'It's probably just a huge coincidence but what if he's somehow distantly related to Grégoire?' She looked at Jacobina expectantly.

But her friend seemed unimpressed by Béatrice's euphoria, and only wrinkled her brow. 'With your vintner? But why?'

'Grégoire's family comes from Paris, he told me.'

'Paris is a big city.'

'But this name, it's not very common at all,' persisted Béatrice. She feverishly contemplated the various ways in which Grégoire and Jacobina's families could be connected. A mystery which she would now get to the bottom of, sixty-three years on.

Jacobina yawned again and gave her back the envelope. 'Sweetheart, this man has really turned your head. You're seeing everything in relation to this Grégoire.'

'I have to go to him at once and show him the letter. He's not answering my calls.' Béatrice bent over, pulled Lica's box out from beneath the bed and rummaged through it for Christian's letter. Then she put it into the envelope and held it up triumphantly. 'It fits.' She ran back into the living room and grabbed her bag. 'I'll clear the rest up later, when I come back. First I have to find out whether Grégoire and Christian are related in any way.'

'Knock yourself out,' replied Jacobina, lying back down. 'Well, they do say lovesickness is incurable.'

22

Judith

Paris, August 1941

When I awoke, everything smelled different to usual, of intensely sweet flowers and cold smoke. Where was I? Opening my eyes, I blinked in the morning sun that was streaming directly through the open window onto my face. Once I had adjusted to the light, I discovered furniture that I'd never seen before. A bureau with curved legs, topped with a bouquet of blossoming lilies. Next to it, a grand armchair with thick, dented cushions. And open books everywhere.

Then I remembered everything. Last night. Christian, his lips on my shoulders. The pain that had made me into a woman and rearranged the stars in the universe. A delicious shiver ran through me.

I sat up and rubbed my eyes. Only then did I realize that I was naked, and shyly pulled the blanket up to my shoulders. Christian lay alongside me, still sleeping. His dark blond hair fell in long strands over his forehead; his sinewy arm gripped the eiderdown against him, as though he didn't want to let it go.

My gaze fell on his gold watch on the nightstand. Seven o'clock already! Long after I'd meant to be home. I jumped out of bed and gathered up my things, which lay scattered across the floor. Hurriedly, I slipped into my skirt and blouse and looked around for my shoes but couldn't see them anywhere. Then I remembered that I'd stuffed them into my bag the previous evening. I reached for the lacquered wooden comb that lay next to the watch and quickly ran it through my hair.

The bedspread rustled behind me. 'Good morning, my angel,' said Christian, his voice thick. I turned around and immediately lost myself in the soft, almost boyish features of his handsome face. His eyes were half closed, his hair had taken on a reddish gleam in the early-morning sun.

'How long have you been awake?' I asked with a smile. Hopefully he hadn't watched me walking around the room stark naked.

'Why are you dressed already?' he asked sleepily, yawning behind his hand. 'Coffee?'

'No, it's late already. I have to go home right away. Mother will worry.'

'Wait a minute.' He sat up. The blanket slipped, revealing his smooth, youthful upper body. 'I'll get dressed and take you home.'

'No, it's fine. I'll take the Metro.'

'I won't hear of it,' he protested, rolling first his healthy leg, then the lame one out of the bed. 'Could you hand me my robe, please? It's hanging behind the door.'

As I stretched out my wrist to pass it to him, he pulled me towards him. 'Judith . . .' He paused.

Sensing that he had something important to say, I sat down next to him.

He looked into my eyes earnestly. 'Perhaps this isn't the right moment, but . . .' He blinked. 'Will you marry me?'

A profound happiness flooded through my body, making me feel complete and wonderfully alive. My eyes filled with tears; my hands were trembling. 'Yes . . .' I whispered. 'I will.'

Christian tenderly stroked his thumb across my lower lip. 'We belong together,' he said. 'For ever.' Then he kissed me.

*

Twenty minutes later, we sat holding hands on the back seat of the Traction Avant, behind a cheerfully whistling Jean-Michel, driving through the empty streets.

A beautiful late summer's day was beginning. It was warm, the first leaves were turning yellow, and waiters in long white aprons were positioning chairs on the pavements and wiping down tables. Christian wound down the window a little and fresh morning air streamed in. A joyful energy filled my heart, making me feel invincible.

We drove past bakeries and grocery stores, women and children with hungry eyes standing before them. I sympathized with these people, knowing only too well how it felt to wait in a queue for hours with an empty stomach.

Eventually the car steered into Rue du Temple. As soon as I caught a glimpse of the street's buildings, I felt guilty. I had never left Mother alone for so many hours before. Hopefully she was still sleeping.

I looked down at my crumpled skirt and longed for a

damp washcloth and fresh clothes. Christian squeezed my hand, smiling at me. He had packed bread, butter and marmalade. Soon we would have a quiet breakfast together, and afterwards perhaps stroll along the Seine, and in the late afternoon go to a reading in Adrienne Monnier's bookstore in Rue de l'Odéon. I realized how hungry I was and looked forward to the first sip of coffee.

Just before our building, Jean-Michel stopped the car and turned around to us. 'Monsieur, mademoiselle. I can't go any further, the street is cordoned off. May I ask you to get out here?'

I looked out of the window. A throng of people had gathered around our building, making it impossible to see it.

'What's going on?' I wondered, suddenly filled with a sense of foreboding. The haunting images returned of the morning when the French police had driven innocent people out of our surrounding apartment buildings and transported them off in buses. An event which no one on our street had mentioned since.

Before Jean-Michel could get out and open the door for me, I jumped out of the car. 'Wait here!' I called to Christian. 'I'll be back in a moment.' I made my way around the wooden roadblock and ran towards our building. Some ominous instinct told me that something had happened to Mother.

I slowly worked my way through the crowd of people. There were sombre faces everywhere; some people were whispering to one another behind their hands. I asked a young woman who I'd seen a number of times in the bakery what had happened.

She gave me a quick glance, then lowered her gaze. 'Somebody . . . somebody . . .'

'What? Tell me!' I urged, my voice shrill.

But the woman only shook her head, pressed her lips together and disappeared into the crowd.

I pushed onwards, past the shoulders and arms, until I had reached the entrance. There was Jeanne, our concierge. Finally, a familiar face! I waved at her anxiously. But she didn't notice me.

She was standing in her grey work overalls, her arms crossed in front of her chest, talking to a policeman. He was clearly interrogating her. She shook her head back and forth before she answered. The policeman wrote something in his notebook. Then her gaze fell upon me. Her eyes widened in horror, and while the *gendarme* was still busy taking down notes, Jeanne surreptitiously motioned towards me. Not understanding what she meant, I pointed my finger at myself. She nodded emphatically and pointed towards the street, signalling for me to disappear. Her mouth soundlessly formed some words that I couldn't decipher. Then the policeman looked up from his notepad, and Jeanne immediately acted as though she were deep in conversation.

Terror stabbed my heart. I drew away from the door and back into the crowd. What should I do? Where was Mother? Someone put their hand on my shoulder, and I spun around in shock. Madame Berthollet stood before me, the elderly lady from the fifth floor. I had barely seen her since the Germans had conquered our city.

'Good God, Judith,' she cried, taking me by the hand and pulling me without a further word through the tangle of people. She was surprisingly nimble for her age. As soon as we had reached the other side of the street, she pushed me through an open gateway into a small courtyard. Her face was red and strands of hair had come loose from her bun. 'Judith . . .' she croaked, gasping for air. Her eyes were glassy, her eyelids twitched. 'They came this morning . . . really early.'

I leaned against the building and stared at her in confusion. Then I understood: Mother! They had taken Mother away. It felt as if a knife was cutting through my heart.

Madame Berthollet looked around her. No one had followed us. 'One of these raids that they're doing regularly now,' she said. Her breathing had calmed again. 'It was almost six. I think they wanted to get both of you. But then . . .'

My eyes were fixated on her lips. Had I heard right? A glimmer of hope rose within me. 'But Mother got away, didn't she? They didn't find her.'

She evaded my gaze.

'Say something!' I demanded, grabbing her by the shoulders. 'Where's my mother now? I have to go to her at once.'

Madame Berthollet let out a sigh. When she looked at me again, I saw that she was crying. 'Your mother . . . she . . .' A sob escaped from her throat. 'She jumped out of the window to get away from them and died immediately . . .'

A dense fog enveloped me. Madame Berthollet's face faded, then I could no longer see her. Mother was dead. And I the only person who could have prevented her fatal jump – but I had been in bed with Christian.

My stomach clenched, I couldn't catch my breath, and

let out a choked cough. Weeks ago, we could have fled peacefully to Lake Geneva. Christian had offered to organize everything. And now Mother was gone.

Dazed, I stumbled along the wall of the building and gasped for air. The nausea intensified. I bent over and spat up bile. Yellowish droplets ran down my chin in long threads. They tasted of vinegar. My back slid down the wall until I was squatting on the floor. I closed my eyes and covered my face with my hands. *She died immediately.* The old lady's words kept ringing in my head. How did she know? How in God's name did she know that Mother hadn't suffered terribly, as death slowly and torturously ate its way through her ruptured flesh, oozing entrails and shattered bones? Until she eventually died a wretched death in a pool of her own blood? And it was my fault. I had left her alone. God, I wanted to die too!

Someone touched my shoulder. I buried my head in my arms and hunched my upper body. I wanted to be left alone.

'Judith,' called a voice, as though from a great distance.

Mother, I thought, and saw her sad face before me again as she lay there in bed, stroking the cat. *I don't have any strength left*, I heard her say.

'Judith,' cried the voice.

It wasn't my mother's. I opened my eyes and saw Madame Berthollet kneeling alongside me. She edged closer. 'You have to get out of here,' she urged me. 'They'll come back. And then they'll take you with them.'

I pushed her away from me. 'I want to see her,' I sobbed, staring at the wide, ochre-yellow stones of the courtyard paving. 'I want to see my mother.'

'Don't you understand, Judith?' hissed Madame Berthollet, grabbing my head with both hands and brusquely turning it towards her. 'You have to get out of here. Right away! You're in extreme danger.'

'My mother is dead,' I responded flatly, closing my eyes. 'I want to go home.'

'Judith, look at me!' she commanded.

I reluctantly opened my eyes. 'The police were in your apartment,' she explained in a trembling voice. 'You can't go in there now, not under any circumstances. Do you hear? As soon as someone sees you there, you're done for.'

'Where else am I supposed to go, for heaven's sake?' I snapped, glaring at her, even though I knew she was only trying to help me.

'Is there anywhere you can hide away?' she asked.

I stared at her and, slowly, the meaning of what she was trying to tell me dawned upon me. But where should I go? I had no place to hide. My fear spiked. Then I remembered Christian. He must still be sitting in his car, waiting for me to come back. I needed to be with him. He would help me to find a hiding spot. I got up, my joints cracking. 'Where have they taken Mother?'

'I don't know,' replied Madame Berthollet, standing up too. 'A car from the mortuary picked her up earlier.'

Brave. I had to be brave. I breathed in and out, swallowing down a barrage of tears. Then I sneaked back to the courtyard entrance and peered out. The street was still cordoned off. But the crowd had begun to dissipate, and I could see part of the pavement which, earlier, had been hidden by all the people. My gaze fell on a dark red puddle which had flowed down onto the street, and I vomited.

Once I was able to look at the street again, I saw residents, neighbours and onlookers standing together in small groups, talking in hushed tones. The policeman who had been questioning Jeanne was nowhere to be seen. I leaned forwards a little more. The Traction Avant was still in the same spot.

You have your whole life ahead of you, I heard Mother's words. *Go and make the best of it.* I swallowed down the sour taste and wiped the bile from the corners of my mouth. Then I turned around, stepped back over to Madame Berthollet and embraced her. 'Thank you for your friendship,' I whispered. 'I will never forget what you just did for me.'

'Now go, my child,' she replied in a soft voice, pushing me gently out onto the street.

In the shadow of the building walls, I padded my way along Rue du Temple, frightened down to the soles of my shoes. I couldn't go too slowly, because then I would draw attention to myself. But I couldn't hurry either; that would be noticeable too. I didn't dare to turn around even once. Any unnecessary movement could be my downfall.

Suddenly, Christian was standing before me. I jumped.

'What happened?' he asked, looking at me wide-eyed. 'I saw you rushing across the street with a woman.'

My eyes immediately flooded with tears again. 'Mother,' I stammered, falling into his arms. 'She's dead.'

'Oh my God,' he whispered, pulling me tightly against him. Then he took my hand. 'We have to get out of here,' he said with resolve. 'Quickly!'

I nodded and hurried over to the car. Christian stayed back behind me. As soon as I had reached the Traction

Avant, I wrenched open the door and jumped into the back seat. Jean-Michel got out and helped Christian, who was wheezing, into the car.

'Drive!' I shouted at Jean-Michel once he was back in his seat. 'Drive away from here as fast as you can.'

'Where to?' asked Jean-Michel, turning around the vehicle.

'Anywhere,' I cried, pressing my face against Christian's chest. Then I let out all my pain and tears.

23

Béatrice

Washington, D.C., 2006

Béatrice ran out onto the scorching-hot street. She hailed a taxi and asked the driver to take her to the Holocaust Museum. Every few minutes, she glanced at her watch. The museum was closing in an hour's time. If the early weekend rush-hour traffic on 14th Street wasn't too bad, she would have enough time.

When she reached the museum and tried to pass the security control at the entrance, they told her that it was closing earlier than usual today. In less than a quarter of an hour, all visitors would have to leave the exhibition rooms. Béatrice claimed that she had an urgent appointment and placed her handbag on the conveyor belt of the X-ray machine. She nervously shifted from one foot to the other, watching her bag slowly disappear into the device. As soon as she had been waved through, she ran through the lobby, up the stairs and onto the second floor, to Grégoire's workplace.

Already from a distance, she could see that his desk had been cleared. She stopped in confusion and looked around.

Instead of Julia, who she usually saw here, today a bald, middle-aged man was helping the visitors.

'Excuse me,' murmured Béatrice. 'I'm looking for Grégoire.'

'Greg?' said the man. 'He doesn't work here any more.'

His words were like a slap on the face. Béatrice stared at him in such distress that he took a step back.

'Are you not feeling well?' he asked with concern.

'Why . . . why doesn't he work here any more? I have to speak with him urgently. Where is he?' The room began to spin. The heat outside, the cold inside the museum, the discovery of the envelope and the news of Grégoire's departure – it was overwhelming. The man in front of her began to blur, she lost her balance and felt the ground below her feet disappear, as if she was in a free fall.

Someone grabbed her by the shoulders and helped her onto a chair. As her vision began to clear again, she saw the bald man standing in front of her.

His hand was still resting on her right shoulder. 'I'll fetch you a glass of water,' he said, walking away and coming back a few seconds later with a small plastic cup.

Grateful, Béatrice drank it down in one gulp.

'As far as I know, Greg had to go back to France earlier than planned,' said the man. 'He left over a week ago.'

A dull pain flooded Béatrice's head. Tears rose in her eyes. Embarrassed, she lowered her gaze and wiped her face.

'Are you feeling any better?' asked man, taking the cup from her and throwing it into a basket.

A museum employee loudly requested that all visitors leave the building.

'You have to go now, unfortunately,' he said, without waiting for her answer. 'We're closing in a few minutes.'

Béatrice looked at him through watery eyes. 'Why are you closing so early today?' she asked. In truth, she didn't care, she just wanted to say something in order to distract this man, who clearly felt uncomfortable in the presence of a crying visitor.

'We're having a small memorial for a staff member who died a few days ago. She worked with Greg, actually.'

'Do you mean Julia? The old lady?'

'Yes, Julia. An incredible woman, when you consider everything she went through. Her death was a shock to all of us.'

'I'm very sorry to hear that,' Béatrice said, regretting now that she never had the opportunity to get to know Julia a bit more. How enriching it would have been to hear about her life. Béatrice remembered that day when she had come in looking for Grégoire and almost showed Julia the photograph of Judith. If Grégoire hadn't appeared that very moment, she might have had a longer conversation. And now it was too late. How quickly life could change. Her thoughts returned to Grégoire, and a new wave of pain lanced through her.

The man turned around and picked up a note from his desk. 'Here. This is an obituary for Julia we laid out in the museum today.'

Béatrice took the piece of paper, which showed a photograph of Julia smiling, and scanned the text without reading it. Then she put the paper in her bag and got up. 'I'll get going now. Thank you for your help,' Béatrice said, before steering towards the exit. As she passed

Grégoire's desk, she paused and studied the tidy work surface. There was nothing to suggest that, not long ago, he had been sitting here.

She stepped back out onto the street. The air was hot and moist as Washingtonians prepared for the big holiday. The weekend rush hour was in full swing; traffic moved at a snail's pace. From afar, sirens could be heard, quickly becoming louder. The cars drove to the side, forming a lane in the middle of the street. Just a few seconds later, three black limousines escorted by numerous police cars raced through towards the White House. Then everything quietened again, and the cars pulled back into the queue of traffic.

Béatrice went to the edge of the pavement and stretched out her arm. A few taxis rushed past; none stopped. After several minutes she gave up, crossed the street and stepped into the bright, gravelled avenue of the National Mall. Sweating joggers panted their way past, and a little further away she saw a group of tourists, hooting with laughter, rolling along the path on Segways.

Béatrice sat down on a bench and watched them. A crushing feeling of loss overtook her. The entire time, she had held on to the hope that, somehow, her many attempts to reach Grégoire would spur him to get back in touch. But now she knew that, in reality, he was already back in France, immersed in his old life. And while he had moved on, she had not. Pain ripped through her chest. How on earth had this charming Frenchman managed to break through the protective walls of her heart she had so painstakingly built? How could thinking of him unleash such feelings of longing within her?

A loud scream tore Béatrice from her thoughts. She noticed that one of the tourists had fallen from his Segway. The man straightened up, cursing as he wiped the dust from his jacket. The group's tour guide lifted the overturned vehicle and went to hand it back to the man, but he refused the mount and shuffled over to a nearby bench.

Béatrice glanced at her watch. Five o'clock. Time to get back to Jacobina's and finish the cleaning. She stood up and walked back to 14th Street. This time she was in luck. As soon as she waved, a taxi pulled over.

*

Jacobina opened her door with a mischievous smile. 'So, what did your handsome vintner have to say?'

'Nothing.' Béatrice lifted her shoulders in a half-shrug and stepped in. 'He wasn't there.'

'Never mind,' Jacobina mumbled. 'You'll go back again after your trip.' Leaning on her walking frame, she hobbled to the sofa and sat down.

'No,' Béatrice said as she grabbed one of the rubbish bags. 'He doesn't work there any more.'

'And they didn't have the courtesy to tell you where he is now?' Jacobina asked.

Béatrice turned her face away so her friend couldn't see the tears in her eyes. 'They did,' she sighed. 'He's back home in France.'

For a moment, Jacobina didn't say anything and all Béatrice could hear was the humming of the air conditioning. Then Jacobina cleared her throat. 'Well, my dear, what are you waiting for?'

Béatrice wiped her face and fiddled around with the

string that was attached to the bag, trying to tie a knot. 'What do you mean?'

'Bordeaux can't be that far away from Paris,' Jacobina carried on. 'If you take a connecting flight tomorrow, right after you land, you'll still be back in Paris on time for your conference next week.'

Béatrice dropped the bag and turned around. 'You think I should . . . ?'

'Absolutely,' Jacobina nodded enthusiastically. Her eyes were glinting. 'You really care for this man. Don't lose him! Fight for this love.'

Béatrice stood up and sat next to Jacobina. 'But I cannot simply turn up at his home.'

'Why not?'

'Because . . .' Béatrice chewed on her lip. Her mind was racing. Grégoire's emerald eyes popped up in front of her. So did the sadness and disappointment she had seen in them after her confession. *Why didn't you tell me sooner?* Just thinking back to this moment at the hospital, Béatrice felt ashamed again. Her shoulders sagged. 'He doesn't want to see me.'

'What makes you so sure?' Jacobina insisted. 'My guess is he's been thinking about you just as much as you have been thinking about him.' She put her hand on Béatrice's shoulder and patted it. 'Come on, Béa, take a little risk. You blew it the first time. This is your chance to win him back. You'd be stupid not to take it.' She sounded firm and persuasive.

Béatrice looked at Jacobina and hope crept into her heart. Her old friend was right. *Why not?* She had nothing to lose. Suddenly everything fell into place. This *was* her chance, and if she didn't grab it, she'd regret it for the rest of her life.

She drew a deep breath and smiled. 'Okay,' she said. 'I'll do it!'

*

A few hours later, sitting at the departure gate with her ticket and passport in her hand, Béatrice felt nervous and excited. She leaned back and studied the bustle of activity around her. Mothers with pushchairs containing whimpering babies, young people with bulky rucksacks and men in suits, pulling small travel cases behind them into the business lounge.

Although Jacobina had convinced her to do it, Béatrice was still afraid of turning up at Grégoire's door, so unannounced. How would he react? Would he be pleased to see her? Or would he continue to refuse to even listen to her? But beneath the fear was something else: a premonition that this journey wasn't just a desperate attempt to regain the happiness she had found with him. After finding the envelope today, she believed that her trip to Bordeaux could also help get to the bottom of another secret: that of Jacobina's family and whether Grégoire's was somehow entwined with hers.

Béatrice fidgeted on her seat. All kinds of suspicions came into her mind. She thought back to what Jacobina had said, that Paris was a big place; that many people must share that surname. But perhaps it really would prove to be true that Christian Pavie-Rausan was a distant relative of Grégoire's, one who had fallen in love with the beautiful Judith as a young student. Goosebumps erupted on Béatrice's arms at the thought. But what had happened between Grégoire's father and his grandfather? Something his father had deliberately hidden from his son his entire life. Something so terrible and profound it had torn the entire family apart.

Could it possibly have anything to do with Christian and Judith?

Only long after the aeroplane had taken off and the flight was soaring across the ocean did Béatrice let go of her thoughts and fall into a short, restless sleep.

24

Judith

Paris, October 1941

Six square metres. A mattress, a table and a chair. That was all
there was. I had gone into hiding – just as Madame Berthollet
had advised me. For the past six weeks, I had remained in the
tiny attic on the sixth floor of Christian's building on Avenue
Victor Hugo. The decision had been quickly made.

'You'll be safe at our place,' Christian said after I had
told him about the raid and my mother's suicide. 'The
Nazis and the police are always in and out. This is the
last place they'd expect you to be.'

Jean-Michel had driven us straight back to Christian's
parents' apartment. I had never expected to be there again
so soon. Everything was exactly as we'd left it an hour
before, when life had still been filled with love and tenderness. The rumpled pillows and sheets, the two half-smoked
cigarettes in the ashtray. The lacquered comb set on the
nightstand. I sat down on Christian's bed and stroked my
hand over the blanket. Just a few hours before, we had lain
here, happy in one another's arms. It felt as if an eternity
had passed since then.

What I wouldn't have given to turn the clock back, to save Mother! But there was no time for grief or regret. The house staff would be arriving at any moment, Christian said, to prepare the apartment for his parents' return from Vichy.

He quickly packed some supplies: candles, matches, bottles of water, food, some clothes from his mother's wardrobe, a blanket and a few pillows. Then I followed him up the stairs to the sixth floor, to the door of my solitary cell. The adjoining rooms were used as storage spaces by other apartment owners and bolted with thick padlocks. But nobody ever came up here, Christian assured me. Not even the maids. The sharp scent of moth powder and cat urine filled the corridor. Dust tickled my nose.

'Are you sure we can trust Jean-Michel?' I whispered, uneasy at the thought of how much the driver knew about me.

'Absolutely,' Christian replied, pulling out a silver ring containing numerous keys, and putting one after the other into the lock. 'He hates my father as much as I do. My father wanted to fire him years ago. But I stuck up for him, and he was allowed to stay. He's never forgotten that.'

'Are you really sure?' I repeated, looking nervously down the corridor.

Christian kissed the tip of my nose. 'One hundred per cent sure, my angel.'

The fourth key fit, and from this moment on I made myself invisible. I was good at that: because of Mother's illness, I'd had years of practice in moving around soundlessly.

The housemaids lived one floor below me. Not all the rooms were currently occupied, Christian knew from the concierge. Nonetheless, I had to be constantly on my guard so that they didn't suspect anything. During the day, when the staff were a few floors further down in their employees' opulent apartments, that was when I was safest. They wouldn't be able to hear my footsteps.

At the end of the corridor, in a tiny shack without a door, stood a wooden tub with a lid which I used as a toilet. I quickly learned which of the rotten floorboards to creep across in order to prevent the tell-tale creaking. Right, left, straight, middle and right; that was the code. It meant that I first had to place my right foot on the narrow floorboard directly outside the door to my room. Then, with the other foot, I took a large step to the left, then lifted my right leg to join it. The two middle floor-boards between my door and the neighbouring door were the most dangerous. As soon as they were stepped on, they sank down with a groan. I had to almost jump to reach the next board. Then two steps straight ahead, then slightly at an angle down the middle, and then to the right again into the partition.

Once a week, very early in the morning when the building's inhabitants were still asleep, Jean-Michel stole up to the attic, dragged the tub downstairs and emptied it out somewhere. I felt deeply ashamed and was terrified every time that something could happen. What if somebody saw him? Or if he slipped, the tub bumping down the narrow stairs? It was unthinkable. But Jean-Michel showed neither fear nor disgust. An hour later, the tub would be back in its place, and I used the opportunity to wash my hair over it with a bottle of water and some soap. What I wouldn't have given to sink into a hot, fragrant bath.

It was lonely up here. I had no clock, no radio, and no idea what was going on outside. But the solitude was my friend; it alone could protect me from the Germans and the anti-Semitic decrees from Vichy.

In the beginning, I cried constantly over all I had lost – my mother, my studies, my freedom. Sometimes even over my father. After a while, the tears became fewer, and I carried my grief silently in my heart.

From the way in which the light fell through the tiny, semicircle window, I estimated the rough time of day. I couldn't stand by the window and look out, as somebody on the other side of the street might see me, become suspicious and alert the police. That's why, during the day, I opened the curtains just enough to let in a tiny bit of sunlight. After darkness fell, I would switch off the table lamp, which I kept veiled with a black cloth, pull back the curtains entirely and look at the night sky. Sometimes I opened the window and breathed in the damp scent of autumn. I would think back to the time when I was still able to roam freely through the streets, and long for our home in Rue du Temple. Looking back, I realized that even the trying days which I had spent in our apartment with my silent, depressed mother had been blissful compared to what I was living through now.

At night, fear invaded me, shaking my body. As rats and mice scurried along the corridor outside, I imagined their pitter-patter were the footsteps of policemen who had come to get me. With my eyes wide open and my knees huddled tightly against me, I sat motionless in the darkness, listening and waiting for them to storm into my hiding place, pull me out onto the street in my nightshirt and force me into one of their buses. Just as they had done with my neighbours. By dawn, when the rodents had disappeared into their dens, it became quiet, and I slowly sank back down into my pillow, waiting for another painfully endless day to limp past.

During the days, I lay listlessly on the mattress, smoked and watched the changing light. As the scratching smoke slowly unfurled in my throat, and the nicotine quickened my heart rate, for a few seconds I felt a dizzying lightness.

Yet, once the cigarette stub began to go dark on my plate, my thoughts became confused again and my eyelids heavy. Then I would usually reach for one of the books which Christian had brought me. My beloved *Le Père Goriot* by Balzac, or one of the wonderful novels by George Sand. But I was rarely able to concentrate. The letters swam before my eyes, and my thoughts wandered off – back to the large reading room in the Sorbonne, to my lectures, and to Monsieur Hubert.

Often, I lay there with my eyes closed, but couldn't fall asleep. Disconnected images and feelings whirled through my head. Sometimes I felt sadness, sometimes panic. Then, for a long while, I felt nothing at all, as though my life's candle had been extinguished.

On good days, when I had enough strength, I wrote in the diary which Christian had given me on one of his visits. A thick, leather-bound notebook, knotted with a brown cord.

'What am I supposed to do with this?' I had asked as he handed it to me, thumbing through the empty pages.

'Just write down whatever comes to your mind,' he had suggested, pulling a golden fountain pen from his bag and laying it on the table. 'It'll keep you occupied.' I had pulled a face and put the book aside.

But then, during one of the sleepless nights when all I did was toss and turn, I had the idea of writing down our story. As soon as the rustling from the rats and mice had finally ebbed away, I flicked on the veiled lamp, unscrewed the pen and thought back to how everything had begun between Christian and me.

I quickly realized that I enjoyed writing; that it did me good. It was a better way of passing the time than reading. While reading, my thoughts slipped away from me like a piece of wet soap, but formulating sentences was like a medicine. I dreamed my way back to all the details of our love story with such intensity that I went into a kind of delirium, living through everything once more as though it were happening in that moment. I would suddenly be crossing the street again, my gaze lowered, to go to our first rendezvous in the Café de la Joie. Or I would see Christian's face before me in the candlelight as he explained that there was both a red and a black menu. The past became present again, and my loneliness was numbed for a while. Writing was an exquisite drug. An exquisite escape.

*

Sometimes, around midday, a few pigeons would flutter over and interrupt the silence. I couldn't see their twitching heads, but I heard them hopping on and off the windowsill. Their contented cooing reminded me of a long-gone time, when Charles Trenet trilled jaunty songs on the radio as I stood barefoot in our kitchen, scattering breadcrumbs on the windowsill for the birds. When the pigeons flew away again, all I could hear was my own breathing. Then I would study the pattern of cracks on the wall, which was eating its way through the plaster like a fine cobweb. I saw the corner where the paint had peeled off. In the beginning, I had inked small pen strokes on the wall. One stroke for every day in this hell. But after a while the strokes became too many and I scratched them off with a knife. Losing time hurt less if I didn't measure it. During the first weeks up here, I remained curled up in despair on the mattress, counting the moments until Christian and Jean-Michel would come up the steps.

In the beginning they visited me often, almost daily, and looked after me so tenderly. They brought bottles of fresh water, clean plates and washed sheets, bread, apples, cheese, and sometimes a piece of cold chicken and even a bottle of wine. They also thought of damp washcloths and soap so that I could clean myself a little. I didn't feel properly clean afterwards, of course, but it was better than nothing.

Jean-Michel always helped to carry things and immediately disappeared again in order not to disturb us. What a thoughtful and kind man he was.

Once Christian had put the supplies down on the small, wobbly wooden table, he would look at me expectantly. He so wanted to see me smile again. But I no longer felt the urge to reach hungrily for a piece of bread, like back when Christian had turned up at our door in the depths of winter, with a rucksack full of gifts, and I had licked the sticky, sweet *bûche* from my fingers in order not to waste a single crumb.

Christian also had my skirt and blouse cleaned and brought them back to me freshly ironed. *The clothes I wore when Mother died.* Seeing them unleashed within me a cramp-like nausea. I could taste the bile in my mouth again, and the red pool of my mother's blood flashed before my eyes. *Her death was my fault.* The words hammered inside my head. I turned away, trying to push down the tears.

Christian packed the clothes away again. 'I'm sorry,' he whispered. 'I thought . . . I thought you might want to have something of yours.'

I shook my head violently. 'Not these things.'

The next day, he brought me a bag full of clothes and nightshirts from his mother's wardrobe, a woman who seemed to possess nothing normal or comfortable. 'They should fit you,' he said. 'Mother is the same height as you, just a bit more rounded.'

'And you don't think she'll miss these things?' I asked, pulling out of his bag a silk skirt, an ice-grey nightshirt, a pair of trousers and a dark-blue jersey dress, all by Coco Chanel, as well as white lace undergarments.

'You don't know my mother,' he replied with a wink. 'Her wardrobes are bursting at the seams. And if she can't find the item she fancies, she buys something new.'

The Chanel clothes were my favourite. The trousers and blouse were loosely cut and felt good against my skin. And so I sat there, in the elegant fabrics which Christian had stolen from his mother, in a shabby attic room four floors above Christian's father, a collaborator and anti-Semite, and waited for a better day in the distant future. How absurd, brutal and sad life was!

*

Not long afterwards, Christian reduced his visits and came just two or at most three times a week. 'I have to be more cautious,' he said. 'The concierge saw me on the staircase recently. She started asking me all kinds of stupid questions.'

I agreed with him at once. The concierge couldn't get suspicious. But during the long, empty days which followed his decision, I grew increasingly mistrustful. 'Why are you so late today?' I asked on one occasion.

He put down the rucksack and kissed me. 'I'm sorry, my angel, I couldn't get here any sooner.'

'So what was so important?' I persisted. I was constantly wondering what Christian was doing the whole time without me. Was his life simply continuing as normal? Was he enjoying his breakfast with his parents a few floors below me, while I was longing for him every second? Or did he spend his afternoons, like he used to, in cafes, reading the newspaper?

'Nothing special,' he replied evasively. 'First, I had a lecture, and then I went to the library.'

I frowned. 'But it's Sunday. There aren't any lectures today.'

He stroked my cheek. 'No. Today is Wednesday.'

I fell silent for a few seconds. How could I have lost track of time to such an extent? Then I blurted out the question that had been burning on my tongue for days. 'You're meeting other women, aren't you?'

His eyes went round. 'Why would you say that?'

I straightened the headscarf that I had bound around my hair to conceal its greasiness. 'I mean, now that I'm stuck up here.'

He laid his hands on my shoulders. 'What foolish thoughts are you getting into your mind? There are no other women for me.'

But his words couldn't assuage my fears and doubts. I burst into tears, sank down to the floor and gripped his knee. 'I miss you so much,' I stammered. 'I'm afraid of losing you. If you stop loving me, I'll die.'

It was the first time since my arrival up here that my fear of being discovered paled against the fear of losing Christian. I was fully dependent on him. He was my only contact to life, to a world I had lost. My love for him had become overshadowed by reliance and despair which bore no relation to the butterflies in my stomach from before.

Christian grabbed my shoulders, pulled me back up and wrapped his arms around me. 'Please never, ever think anything like that again, my love. Do you hear me? I love you. Only you. And I live for you. You are my entire happiness, my sun, my one and all.'

I pressed my face against his chest and sobbed into the fabric of his stiff, freshly pressed shirt.

'I'll never leave you,' he said, stroking his hand over my back. 'Never.'

'But I'm so ugly now,' I croaked between sobs. 'I'm so ashamed.'

'Don't be. All I see is your beauty.' He pulled me even closer to him. 'Do you think that with my lame leg I'm not afraid that you'll stop loving me?'

I closed my eyes and clung to him. When he was there, everything was good. His love was the only thing I still had. And so, just like I had become accustomed to the stench of cat urine and moth powder, I would also learn to accept the silence and this endless waiting.

And yet, soon after he had gone, the destructive thoughts returned, circling over me like vultures above their prey. Wouldn't it be better to die than to languish away up here in stolen clothes? Wouldn't it be better for all of us if I turned myself in to the police?

The pigeons answered with a gurgled cooing.

Paris, November 1941

The skies turned grey and overcast; the days became shorter. It rained a lot, and before the clouds cleared, darkness had already fallen over the city again. A long winter was announcing its arrival. At night it was so chilly that I pulled all of the Coco Chanel provisions over me at once. I wore the blue jersey dress over the blouse and wide-leg trousers, and over that, the pale-grey woollen cardigan and dark-brown pleated skirt. I had lost a lot of weight; everything was too big for me now and slipped down over my hips. In addition, Christian had brought me a warm sweater and a thick coat which I rarely took off, especially not at night.

I curled up into a tight ball and pulled the blanket over my head, my teeth chattering. In the mornings my face felt numb with cold, and my stiff joints cracked as I stood up.

With the falling temperatures my fear rose. How was I supposed to survive the long winter months up here? I thought back to the icy nights of the previous year, when we'd had so little coal that we could only heat the kitchen, and only once a day. But in this attic there was no oven, and no hot water. If Christian didn't find somewhere else for me to hide, I would freeze to death.

I lit up a cigarette. Smoking immediately filled my frosted body with new life. What I wouldn't have given to be able to wash my hair, take a bath, put on lipstick and make myself look beautiful for Christian. He was planning to visit me before lunchtime today.

Goosebumps prickled across my skin at the mere thought of pouring a bottle of cold water over my head and rubbing soap into my hair. So instead, I quickly wiped a damp washcloth over my face, pulled a comb through my matted hair and tucked it into a headscarf. The hot bath would remain a wish for a long time.

The wind rattled at the window and an icy draft pushed its way through the cracks. Shivering, I rubbed my palms together and pulled the coat more tightly around my waist.

I dreamed of other things that I longed for. My stunningly beautiful dress from Jacques Fath. If only I could stroke the fine fabric one more time! I remembered our night at the opera, when I was sitting enthroned like a princess on one of the plush red velvet armchairs in Christian's parents' box. Then I thought of Mother's woollen cap, which probably still held the scent of her hair, and our copper-toned tube radio, on which we used to secretly listen to Jean Oberlé on the BBC.

In the first weeks after Mother's death, it would have been unbearable for me to see these familiar things. They would have reminded me too acutely of her tragic death, and of the loss of our home. But now, after all the long days and nights in which I had felt more dead than alive, I longed for these things from my former, free life. I wanted to have something close to me that connected me to Mother. So I had asked Christian, on his latest visit, whether he could fetch me a few items from our old apartment. He had immediately agreed.

'The dress is in the wardrobe in my bedroom,' I told him, pressing the key to the building into his hand. 'Mother's caps are in the top right-hand drawer in the commode, right next to the entrance door. And don't forget the scarf.' At the thought of soon having some personal mementos of our life, of being able to smell and touch them, my mood brightened.

'I'm sure Jeanne has taken good care of our apartment and looked after Lily,' I chattered on. 'She was always very reliable.'

I asked him to bring the photos of me and Mother from her bedroom. In particular, the one of my first day at school, which I loved, and, of course, the photo taken in front of the synagogue, showing us together with the rabbi. My father had taken this picture, after Mother and he had got divorced. It was his last visit to Paris to see me. After that I never saw him again. I also asked Christian to water the little tree in the living room and give Jeanne my best regards. My cheeks began to glow. For the first time in weeks, I was looking forward to something.

He stroked my head. 'I will, my angel. Tomorrow. I promise. I'll bring it all to you on Thursday.' He looked at me tenderly, and I pressed myself against his lanky body.

*

Finally, the time came. I recognized Christian's footsteps by the familiar rhythm of his limp. Filled with anticipation, I jumped up from the mattress and put my ear to the door. His steps became louder; in just a few moments he would be here. But I couldn't hear Jean-Michel. Normally he came with Christian, to carry the heavy bags containing my supplies. Why wasn't he there today? Had something happened? I stepped back from the door and waited until Christian pushed down the door handle.

He walked into the room, his lips pressed into a thin line. His face was slightly flushed from climbing the staircase, but I could see at once that something wasn't right. Without a word, he closed the door and let a dark-blue rucksack slip down off his back. It landed on the floor with a crash.

'Careful,' I whispered. 'People can hear this!' My voice was edged with fear. 'Where's Jean-Michel?'

Christian opened the bag, unpacked three bottles of water and placed them on the table, his movements jittery. 'He's running a few errands and will be here later,' he mumbled.

I shot him an anxious look.

Christian took a deep breath and ran his hand through his hair. 'I . . . I went to Rue du Temple.' He stepped towards me, gripped my wrists and looked into my eyes. 'Your apartment . . .' He loosened his hold and bit his lip.

'What's wrong?' I urged. In my mind I was picturing a kicked-in front door, ransacked cupboards and shattered crockery on the floor. 'Our things have been stolen, haven't they?'

Christian shook his head. 'Somebody else lives there now.'

It was as though all the blood drained from my veins. My spine stiffened; my ribcage clenched. 'What?' I asked, stumbling over to the mattress.

Before I could break down, Christian grabbed me by the shoulders and wrapped his arms around me. 'I'm so sorry,' he whispered, pressing his lips against my hair.

For a long while we stood there, motionless, clinging to

one another. My cheek buried in the soft fabric of his coat, I tried to process the news.

Eventually I untangled myself from his embrace and brushed from my face some strands of hair that had strayed from the headscarf. 'Who's living there now?'

A moment passed before he answered. 'An elderly couple.' He took off his coat and laid it over the chair. 'Your concierge wasn't there when I arrived. So I went up to fetch the things anyway, and the key didn't fit. I didn't even ring the bell, and then the door opened.' He paused and looked at me, as though wanting to be sure I was ready to hear the rest of the story.

With a brief nod, I signalled to him to continue.

'A woman, in her mid-sixties, French. She moved in a few weeks ago with her husband, she said. Apparently, they're paying rent and have a proper contract. She didn't know who had lived there before, she told me, and she wasn't interested in finding out.' Christian leaned against the wall and crossed his arms. 'She also said that when they moved in, the apartment was completely empty. Then she asked me to leave.'

I collapsed onto the mattress, shivering, and pulled the blanket around my shoulders. A cap, a scarf and a few photos. It wasn't much that I'd wanted. But even this last piece of home had been taken from me.

Christian sat down next to me, put his arm beneath the blanket and searched for my hand. 'Forget the past,' he said. 'Let's focus on the future.' His voice sounded thin, as though he couldn't convince even himself.

Later, we made love, anxiously and heavy-hearted. But this room wasn't a good place for such things. Out of worry that someone might hear us, I moved with inhibition, and covered Christian's mouth with my hand.

'Focus on the future,' I repeated in a whisper as we lay there afterwards, our limbs entangled on the narrow, musty mattress. His hand stroked my back, and his heartbeat vibrated through my body. 'The future.'

But in my heart was only darkness.

25

Béatrice

Pomerol, France, 2006

The taxi turned off the main street and into a wide, cypress-lined private road. The narrow trees stood to attention with their tops soaring into a cloudless sky. Béatrice sat anxiously in the back seat of the car and stared out of the window. Everywhere were grapevines, stretching in strict symmetrical order over the bare soil, across kilometres of hilly landscape. Their growth and direction was controlled by wooden posts at shoulder height, knocked into the ground and linked together by taut wire.

The taxi steered towards a sandstone archway. *Château Bouclier* was chiselled into the stone in large letters. Grégoire's world. She had arrived. A shiver went down Béatrice's spine.

The car entered the open gateway and navigated across a gravel path, between olive trees, reaching an expansive forecourt that was encircled by a perfectly pruned hedge. Béatrice looked out at an elegant estate with a manor house and numerous adjoining buildings, all built from pale sandstone. In the centre of the forecourt stood an old acorn tree, its thick, green leaves like splayed-out hands reaching for the sun.

The driver came to a halt directly in front of the large marble steps that led up to the main house, each one narrower than the one preceding it.

Béatrice studied the house, which looked as immaculate and well maintained as the vineyard. It must have been painted recently. The immaculate plaster gleamed in the afternoon sun; the red roof tiles shimmered. The entrance door and window shutters were also painted red, giving the house an inviting air. Next to the entrance stood fat-bellied terracotta pots with rose bushes. A cat was sitting at the edge of one of the steps, licking its paws.

Nostalgia welled up in Béatrice. For years, she had devoted all her energy to building her career abroad, contemptuous of everything that was familiar, longing for foreign shores, for newness and uncertainty. And now, at the sight of this friendly sandstone house in the dazzling sunlight, somewhere north-east of Bordeaux, she longed to be back amongst the scents of her homeland, the sounds of her language. She wanted to soak it all in and hold on to it. She wanted to stay.

'Do you need any help with your luggage?' asked the taxi driver, turning around to her.

Béatrice looked at him. She had completely forgotten him. Only now did she notice how young he was. Early twenties, at most. 'No, thanks,' she murmured, opening her handbag to get her purse.

'That'll be exactly ninety euros,' he said.

Béatrice handed him a hundred-euro note and raised her hand in protest when he fumbled around for some coins. 'Keep the change.'

She picked up her travel bag, which lay alongside her on the seat, and got out. As soon as she had shut the door behind her, the taxi set off, the gravel crunching beneath its wheels, and disappeared through the archway.

Béatrice looked up at the red shutters. Was someone watching her, perhaps? The windows on the first floor were open, but she couldn't see anyone behind them. The air was still. Nothing moved. Béatrice slowly climbed the steps. As she walked past the cat, the animal leaped to the side, meowing.

Béatrice put down her bag and rapped the cast-iron door knocker against the large entrance door. It thudded dully. But the house remained quiet.

She knocked again. Shortly after, she heard footsteps. A thin, elderly woman in a grey apron opened the door. Her blonde hair was bound into a loose ponytail, and she was holding a broom in her hand.

'Good day,' said Béatrice, with a tense smile. 'I'd like to see Grégoire, please.'

The woman, visibly disgruntled that Béatrice had interrupted her work, looked at her with raised eyebrows. 'You mean, monsieur?' She spoke in a foreign, hard accent which Béatrice couldn't place.

She nodded. 'Yes . . . Is he here?'

'Please come in,' said the woman, stepping to the side.

Béatrice picked up her bag and walked into a large foyer with a brightly polished parquet floor. From the ceiling hung a chandelier, its lights connected by countless chains filled with crystal teardrops. A wooden staircase with round-topped balusters led to the first floor.

'Monsieur is at the office,' said the woman. 'I'll call and let him know. What is your name?'

'Tell him that his friend Béatrice from America has arrived.' Béatrice followed the woman into the drawing room.

'Take a seat,' said the woman. Then she hurried out.

Béatrice looked around at the valuable paintings, silk curtains and antique furniture. The colours and materials had been curated with care and attention to detail, so despite the different styles, everything harmonized.

Through the ajar door, she heard the housekeeper talking on the phone, probably to Grégoire.

Béatrice studied the white marble open fireplace, above which glittered a large mirror with a gilded frame. Her gaze wandered over the two Louis XV commodes to the dark eighteenth-century oil portraits depicting men with serious expressions and grey locks, and smiling women in flowing robes. She stepped hesitantly towards an antique playing table and stroked the palm of her hand over the chessboard inlay.

Everything was very bourgeois, very traditional. This was obviously the home of someone who relished the past. The pieces of furniture and over two centuries of history that they embodied had an oppressive air to them. Doubts about her impromptu trip arose in Béatrice's mind. Perhaps Grégoire wasn't the intellectual, loving adventurer she had thought him to be back in Washington. What had led her to believe she would be welcome here?

She thought back to the simple world she had grown

up in. The small two-room apartment in Rue Dareau with boring floral wallpaper and second-hand furniture. Her childhood bed from IKEA. As she grew older, she'd had to bend her legs in order to fit.

Béatrice walked soundlessly across the heavy rug and sat down on a velvet-upholstered sofa. She looked out of the window at the hillside, across which the vines stretched in geometric lines, as though they had been set out with a ruler. Not a sound could be heard: no farm engines, no water pipes and no birdsong. Even the housekeeper had stopped talking. The silence felt good. A leaden tiredness descended upon Béatrice. She leaned back and closed her eyes.

Hearing the entrance door slam shut, she sat up with a start. How long had she been sitting here? Had she fallen asleep? Béatrice glanced at her watch and noticed that she hadn't changed the time yet. It took a moment for her to calculate the six-hour time difference. Five o'clock in the afternoon. She brushed the hair off her face.

Then Grégoire entered the room, taller and more handsome than ever. Different. His face was no longer pale, as it had been in springtime Washington, but tanned and angular. His hair was longer, now touching his shoulders, and he sported a rugged, three-day stubble beard. He wore a white shirt, the sleeves rolled up to the elbows, and light blue jeans. Béatrice recognized only the brown shoes, the ones with the worn tips. The light scent of his aftershave filled the room, almost making her lose track of her thoughts.

As Grégoire caught sight of her, he froze.

Béatrice was bursting with anticipation; her pulse

soared. Back in Washington, it had been a torment to constantly think about him without knowing how he was and what he was doing. Seeing him before her, just a few metres away, now living this moment she had ached for, she fully felt the intensity of her passion for him. She had imagined this reunion so often, down to the smallest detail. Her entire body tingled with happiness but also with apprehension. She didn't dare say a word, waiting for his reaction.

But Grégoire said nothing. He stood there, his arms hanging, and stared at her.

She must look dreadful, Béatrice realized, with tired eyes and a face as creased as her blouse.

'Béatrice,' he said eventually. 'What are you doing here?'

At the sound of his voice the feverish anxiety which had accompanied her for the entire journey disappeared. Feeling calm again, she stood up and walked over to him. 'I have been thinking a lot about you and us,' she said, without taking her gaze off him. 'Since you didn't return my calls, I decided to take a chance and come here. I want to explain what happened.'

Grégoire smiled shyly, sending a flare of joy through Béatrice's heart.

'Will you hear me now?' she asked with a pleading look.

His green eyes flashed as he leaned forwards, put his hands on either side of her face and pulled her towards him. 'Every damn minute since I got here, I've been thinking about you and longing for you,' he whispered, pressing her tightly against his chest. 'I'm so happy you came.'

They clung to one another. Happily. Frantically. Then they kissed. At first hesitantly and cautiously, as though they were afraid to get too close. Then their lips became greedy, melting into each other. Béatrice now knew she had been waiting her entire life for this moment. For this kiss. This man.

Grégoire was the first to pull back from their embrace, leading her over to the sofa.

'I acted like a little boy,' he said, holding on to her hands. 'I didn't even let you explain . . . I was so hurt.' He brought her fingers to his mouth and kissed them. 'I, too, had a lot of time to think about us. We'll find a way. With your baby.' He pulled her close to him again. 'I'm sure there's a good stepfather inside me.' His warm breath tickled her ear. 'If you hadn't come, I would have flown over to you,' he murmured into her hair. 'Next week at the latest. I wouldn't have lasted any longer.'

Béatrice curled up against him and breathed in the scent of his skin. 'There isn't a baby any more,' she said. 'I lost it . . . about two months ago.'

He sat back from her and looked at her with widened eyes. 'I'm so sorry.'

'There's no need.' Béatrice shook her head gently. 'It's all okay. Maybe it's for the best.'

'Did you . . . ? I mean . . .' He paused.

'No,' she said. 'It just happened. It happens to a lot of women my age.' She told him about the operation, about her unhappy relationship with Joaquín, and that she had waited far too long to end it.

Grégoire squeezed her hand.

They stayed silent.

Then he smiled and kissed her on the forehead. 'How long can you stay?' he asked.

'Until Monday morning,' Béatrice said. 'On Tuesday I have to give a presentation at the OECD in Paris and see my mother.'

'Wonderful! We'll have an unforgettable time. But first let me give you a tour of the estate and our vineyard,' Grégoire suggested, standing up and pulling her with him out of the drawing room. 'Then we'll do a tasting of the finest wines Château Bouclier has ever produced. The 1995, for example. A vintage year.'

'Perhaps I should shower and change first,' Béatrice interjected, laughing, as she stumbled after him. 'I look awful.'

'You can do that later.' He turned around and kissed her on the mouth. 'And you're always stunning, with or without jet lag.'

In the hall they ran into the housekeeper, who was busy sweeping the floor. 'Béa, this is Ewa, the heart and soul of Château Bouclier. Ewa is from Poland and has been working for my father for almost thirty years now.' Grégoire smiled at Ewa. 'Wait until you try her boeuf bourguignon this evening,' he said to Béatrice. 'A pure delight!' He kissed the tip of his fingers with a smacking sound and winked to Ewa. 'I bet the beef has been braising in your cast-iron pot for an hour already?'

The hint of a smile flashed across Ewa's face.

'I knew it.' Grégoire beamed. 'By the way, everything I know about cooking, I learned from Ewa.'

The housekeeper fiddled with her apron in embarrassment.

'Béa will be staying with us for two days,' Grégoire explained to her. 'We'll eat out on the terrace tonight.'

26

Judith

Paris, December 1941

A few nights before, two narrow icicles had formed on the windowsill inside my tiny room. They had grown larger and larger, until they were so long that they almost touched the floor. By candlelight, they looked like polished crystal. While they were still small, I had admired them – now they scared me.

The cold was everywhere, raw and unforgiving. It had attacked my body like an insidious virus, making its way into my lungs, my hands and my thoughts. My fingers and feet were frozen stiff; I barely dared to move them fearing they might break. I had lost my sense of smell, could no longer sleep, no longer write and no longer think clearly. Cold was everything I felt, everything that surrounded me. Terrible, relentless cold.

I had once believed that the solitude up here could save me. But I'd been wrong. The solitude and the cold had destroyed me; they were impossible to escape. Only death would liberate me.

Perhaps the Germans would have shot me immediately

if I'd fallen into their hands, or maybe I would have been unable to bear the labour in their camps and dropped dead. But here, in this solitary confinement, the price of my supposed safety was a slow, tortuous decline.

The cold drove me insane. I wanted to scream. For Christian. But all that came from my mouth was soundless breath. No one could hear me, and no one would get me out of here. They had forgotten me. I closed my eyes. How long would I have to wait until the pain numbed my senses and gentle sleep embraced me?

Frost flowers shimmered on the window. The thick, puffed-up blossoms were on long stems, interwoven with one another to a web of shadow and light. Harbingers of death, sown in the cold, that had grown into poisonous thistles within my heart. The ice flowers swayed back and forth as though they were dancing a slow waltz. Watching them made me feel light-headed. I imagined being carried by the blossoms, nestled in their leaves. They would rock me back and forth until this damned life finally ebbed away and another began. Something that wasn't cold, wasn't painful. Something that would reunite me with my mother.

*

'Judith.' I heard a voice from somewhere. 'Judith.'

Something warm. Something warm at my feet. What was that? Where had it come from? It hurt terribly, as though somebody were setting my body alight with a burning torch. Now I felt the warmth at my back. I wanted to scream with pain. An arm was placed around me. A hand touched my fingers and wrapped them up in something warm, damp.

'Judith, please say something.' The voice, again. It sounded familiar. I tried to move my lips, tried to speak, but I couldn't.

'My angel, I'm here with you.'

My angel. Christian! How was he suddenly here? Then I heard a rustling. Voices.

'Give me the other bottle. Quickly,' someone urged.

Very slowly, the sensation came back. At first, I could only move my big toe, then my whole foot. The pain was excruciating. Again, I tried to speak, but my lips stuck together. I swallowed. My throat hurt. Something warm touched my mouth. Someone called my name again. I moved my head in the direction the voice was coming from. Then I opened my eyes and saw Christian's face above me. Had he really come back? Was I hallucinating?

'Judith, oh God . . . I was so afraid.' He pressed his lips against my forehead. They felt moist.

A spoon touched my lips. 'Eat this,' he said, placing his hand beneath my neck and lifting my head. I opened my mouth obediently, and hot liquid trickled onto my tongue. I swallowed. The broth ran down my throat, burning like fire. I heard Christian say that I should eat more of it. I opened my lips again, and he immediately pushed the spoon into my mouth.

'My angel, you had almost frozen to death,' he whispered.

I felt the broth scorch my mouth. *Salt*, I thought. *Burning salt.* It stimulated my saliva. Soon, threads of spit tickled my cheeks.

'I couldn't come sooner. I'm so sorry.'

Why was he apologizing? I swallowed. It was a little easier now than the first time.

'My father became suspicious, and I'm pretty sure he's having me followed,' Christian continued.

His father. Avenue Victor Hugo. My hiding place. The thoughts rained down on me in a storm. The dream of the dancing ice flowers was over. I was back again. My life wasn't yet over. The urge to cough overcame me.

'Are you all right?' asked Christian, dabbing at my mouth.

I nodded. Then I looked around me. My hands were wrapped up in damp, warm towels. Beneath my feet lay a hot aluminium bottle. A further blanket was spread out over me.

'Please forgive me,' Christian begged.

Beneath the towels, I carefully balled my hands into fists and stretched them out again. It worked – the fingers moved without breaking. Then I pushed off the towels and touched the blanket.

'From now on I'll send Jean-Michel to you twice a day with hot water bottles and soup,' said Christian, placing his hands over mine. 'This won't happen again.'

I could hear what he was saying, but it was difficult to follow. My thoughts were still focused on my hands, which had become mobile again.

'And on the days when we can't see each other, I'll write to you about what I'm doing, and you let Jean-Michel know what you need. I won't ever leave you alone again for so long.' He pressed his mouth against my cold lips. 'Never again.' Then he turned around. 'Right, Jean-Michel?'

Only now did I notice the shadowy figure kneeling behind Christian on the floor, moving around soundlessly.

In the half-darkness, Jean-Michel was arranging the supplies and unfolding steaming-hot hand towels. Then he stood up and set the small table with a candle, glasses and crockery.

'I have a surprise for you, Judith,' announced Christian with a promising grin, whispering something to Jean-Michel. The chauffeur opened a bag, took out a large box and put it down on the floor next to the mattress with a groan.

'*Voilà*, our portable tube radio,' announced Christian, tapping the box proudly. A radio. A real radio.

I smiled. Even now, he still amazed me. 'The batteries don't last long, but they'll be fine for General de Gaulle's Christmas speech on the BBC.'

'Christmas . . . speech?' I stammered. My first words in a long time. My throat felt itchy.

'Tomorrow is Christmas Day.' He turned back to Jean-Michel. 'Thank you, Jean. You can go now. And from now on, please bring Judith two hot water bottles and a canister of tea every morning and every evening. The cold up here is extremely dangerous.'

'At your service, monsieur,' answered Jean-Michel, his expression impassive. He wished us a good night and left the room.

Slowly I sat up, wrapped the blanket around my shoulders and watched as Christian lit the candle and took a bottle of wine out of his rucksack. The cork sat loosely in the neck of the bottle. He must've already opened the wine down in the apartment.

'I'm so glad that we have Jean-Michel,' he said, pouring wine into the two glasses which the driver had placed on the table. 'My father has been asking me so many questions recently. What I'm doing, where I'm going, where I've been and so on. Before, he never cared what I did during the day.' He sat back down on the floor next to the mattress and handed me a glass.

As I stretched out my hand, I noticed it was shaking.

'He seems to have caught wind of something,' Christian continued. 'Two days ago, when I went to buy the hot water bottles for you, a man followed me. I couldn't get a proper look at him, because he had his hat pulled down over his face. But I had a weird feeling the whole time. I've no idea whether my father has something to do with it, but it all seems very strange.'

I took a sip of wine. As soon as the heavy liquid coated my tongue, I felt nauseous. I swiftly put the glass down on the floor and covered my mouth with my hand, suppressing the urge to gag.

'Are you not feeling well?' asked Christian. I could read the shame and worry in his eyes.

The nausea soon subsided. 'The cold affected my stomach a bit, that's all. Don't worry,' I said, trying to sound relaxed. 'But I'd like some more hot broth.' I didn't want him to feel guilty for having left me alone. He hadn't had a choice.

Christian immediately reached for the metal tureen that lay by his feet, lifted the lid and handed it to me. The aromatic scent rose up and saliva collected in my mouth. I greedily spooned up the bouillon and soon felt a delicious warmth spreading from inside me. Even my hand stopped trembling.

'The last time I saw you eat like that was in Mille

Couverts. Do you remember?' Christian tenderly pulled the blanket, which had slipped off a little, back up onto my shoulders.

I looked up briefly from the bowl. 'My last meal as a free person,' I added, before turning my attention back to the bouillon.

'We have to get you out of here,' said Christian. 'Things can't go on like this. We'll flee.'

The spoon slipped from my hand and fell into the tureen with a clatter.

'Shh!' hissed Christian, putting his index finger to his lips.

'Flee?' I repeated.

'I can't just sit by and watch you suffering up here any longer.' He pushed the hair off his forehead and looked at me from the side. 'And now there's nobody to keep us here.'

At the thought of my mother, whose bones were rotting away in a mass grave somewhere, if she hadn't long since been cremated, my eyes filled with tears. 'You know I cannot leave,' I said, struggling to conceal my urge to cry. 'It says in my ID papers that I'm Jewish. They would arrest me at the very first checkpoint.'

'An acquaintance has put me in contact with someone in the underground. Tomorrow I'll meet with him and ask him to get you counterfeit papers.'

The underground. Counterfeit papers. His words sparked inside me like white phosphorus in the air. I swallowed. So there really was a way out of this hell of loneliness? I took his hand and kissed it. 'You would do that for me?' Tears ran down my cheeks.

'I would do anything for you, my love,' he whispered.

'You're not safe here any more. I've heard terrible rumours about what the Germans are doing to the Jews. We have to get to Switzerland as quickly as possible.'

My lips trembled. 'How long do you think the papers will take?'

He drank a sip of his wine and scratched his head. 'No idea. One or two months perhaps. I'll know more tomorrow.'

'It's sure to be very expensive. Where will we get the money for it?' I asked, even though I knew the answer. I felt uncomfortable discussing money with him, a man who had so much of it.

'Let me worry about that,' he said, as I'd expected, and stroked his finger over my cheek. 'You're the most important thing in the world to me. And besides, I already put aside the money for it a long time ago.'

'Why didn't you tell me about this plan before?' I asked, rubbing my hands together to warm up.

'I didn't want to give you false hope. I needed time to think everything through.' He took the tureen from my lap and put it back on the floor. 'And my acquaintance had to find the right man. We have to be incredibly careful. No one can find out who my father is.'

I was shaking with anticipation. Christian pulled me against him. 'By spring we'll be sitting at Lake Geneva, my angel. I promise.'

I breathed in his scent and felt loved and protected, like I always did when he was near me.

'Soon all of this will be nothing but a bad memory,' he whispered. In the darkness, with my face close to his, his words sounded so clear and plausible. As though we had just decided to take a weekend trip to the countryside, and only had to resolve whether we wanted to have lunch in Honfleur or Deauville.

Christian leaned back, turned on the radio and twisted the large, golden dial. 'Let's listen to the BBC now. De Gaulle's speech has already started.'

At first, all that emanated from the speakers was a gentle crackling and rustling. Christian turned the dial further, and suddenly the white noise stopped. I heard a man's voice – speaking in French.

'Our allies, the English and the Russians, now have very powerful troops,' explained the voice. 'Not to mention those provided by our allies the Americans. The Germans won't be able to defend against all these troops, because in England, Russia and America, countless planes, tanks and ships are being built.' A reverent, almost festive atmosphere filled the draughty attic chamber which, just two hours before, had almost sent me to my death.

Christian looked at me. In the warm glow of the candle-light, his pupils had widened into large, black moons. 'I believe de Gaulle. He will save our country,' he said, with solemn respect in his eyes.

We listened intently to the voice from London. On that icy night of Christmas Eve 1941, safe in Christian's arms and with a warm bouillon in my belly, my heart dared to hope again. We had a plan. Christian would rescue me, and de Gaulle would rescue France.

My gaze fell on the icicles, which glinted menacingly in the candlelight. No, I would not let them conquer me. I would hold out until spring. With shaky legs I stood up, stumbled over to the window and broke them off with my hand.

'My dear children of France,' the General announced over the ether at the same moment, 'soon you will receive a visit – victory is coming to you. And it will astound you with its beauty!'

27

Béatrice

Château Bouclier, Pomerol, 2006

Grégoire led Béatrice out of the house and down the marble steps. They walked along a neatly raked gravel pathway, between fruit trees and rose bushes, to a building with broad, wood-framed glass doors, built in the same style as the main house. *Salle de dégustation* was on the sign next to the right-hand door, *bureau* next to the left-hand one.

Grégoire opened his office. 'This is where I work.'

Béatrice stepped curiously inside. A stunning view over the vineyard opened up in front of her.

Grégoire leaned against a white, modern desk piled with files and loose papers. The corners of his laptop peeped out from beneath opened letters. He pointed towards a large, framed map on the wall. 'That's our land. Five hectares. The dark area on the right-hand side, that's where our best grapes grow.'

Béatrice studied the circles, lines and plots on the map. 'Why are those the best?'

'More clay in the ground and optimal sun exposure,'

explained Grégoire. 'It's the clay which gives the wine its special strength and structure.'

Béatrice nodded absent-mindedly. She was still getting used to the fact that Grégoire was not only the doctoral candidate from the Holocaust Museum, but also the owner of a Pomerol vineyard.

He seemed to have read her thoughts. 'Don't worry, I'm still the same person.' He laughed.

'Did you know that Julia died?' asked Béatrice. She wanted to finally tell Grégoire about the envelope she had found beneath Jacobina's sofa.

Grégoire nodded sadly. 'Yes. Somebody from the museum left a voicemail on my phone. But I haven't had time yet to return the call.' He crossed his arms. 'A lot happened here while I was away. I'm still working my way through the most pressing things.'

'Wasn't anyone standing in for you here?' asked Béatrice.

'Yes, but two months ago Xavier quit, out of the blue. Presumably he got a better offer somewhere else, and I still haven't found a replacement. That's why I had to return earlier than planned to run the day-to-day business.' He sighed, and a worry line appeared between his eyebrows. 'Besides that, our region is in crisis. Wines from California, Australia and Chile are flooding the market, quite literally. Admittedly that's nothing new, but this year the situation has got worse.' He ran his hand through his hair and tucked a strand behind his ears. 'Our bottle sells for eighty euros. The wines from Chile and Australia are cheaper and yet very good. To stay competitive, we have to develop a better marketing strategy.'

'So that means no more trips to Washington?' asked

Béatrice with a wink. She decided to postpone talking about the letter until later.

Grégoire came up to her and put his arm around her waist. 'I'm not worried. We may not be Château Petrus, but Bouclier is still one of the region's finest wines. We will come up with new ideas.' He took her hand again. 'Enough of this. Now you have to finally *taste* our wine.'

They stepped out into the open air and through the other glass door into a room with a dark tiled floor. On the walls, to the left and right, countless wine bottles were stacked on wooden shelves which stretched up to the ceiling. Grégoire motioned her over to a large, horseshoe-shaped bar, over which hung a gleaming red chandelier.

The room was cool. Béatrice rubbed her arms, shivering, and sat down on one of the bar stools.

Grégoire went behind the bar, fetched a woollen stole and handed it to her. 'Put this around you,' he said. 'We have to keep the temperature low, so the wine ages properly.'

Béatrice gratefully wrapped the stole around her and watched Grégoire pull numerous bottles off the shelves and uncork one after the other. Behind the bar was a glass wall, presenting a view of a dimly lit vault filled with oak barrels.

'That's our showroom,' explained Grégoire, sniffing one of the corks. 'This is where we organize wine tastings and sometimes dinners for special clients.'

He took a few glasses out of the cupboard, held them appraisingly up to the light and polished them with a cloth. Then he poured the wine, swirled the glass around and handed it to her. 'Ninety per cent Merlot, nine per cent Cabernet Sauvignon and one per cent Cabernet Franc. Merlot does better in the cool ground of the Pomerol than Cabernet.'

Béatrice stuck her nose into the glass. 'Blueberries and . . . hmm, perhaps plum?' she said, holding herself back from drinking it all down at once.

'And a touch of toasted nuts,' added Grégoire with a chuckle.

Then they drank.

They sat there together for a long while, savouring the wines, comparing aromas and tastes and exchanging loving glances.

Béatrice watched the movements of Grégoire's hands with fascination, and listened raptly as he spoke about the gravelly clay soil of his *terroir*, of the ferrous earth and the vines that grew on it.

She had never been happier.

28

Judith

Paris, December 1943

When spring finally arrived last year, the pigeons returned to my windowsill. In their gentle cooing I had heard a message of hope. I felt as if they had come to wish me luck. But my new papers weren't ready yet, so we had to delay our escape. Only later did we realize that the man who Christian had assured me could provide me with a new *carte d'identité* had simply made off with the money. The second man Christian confided in was shot by the Germans shortly after the handover of money. And the third somehow found out who Christian's father was – and after that wanted nothing more to do with us. Maybe he feared that Christian would betray him.

Three chances for escape, three bitter disappointments. I wasn't sure I could take another, but I had to endure.

Many suns and moons later another atrocious winter came upon us. It brought the Russians a momentous victory, with the devastation of the sixth German army in Stalingrad. To me, it brought only endless cold and misery.

A stormy spring melded into a hot summer. I could recognize the passage of the seasons from the changing light shining through the narrow gap between the curtains. Time passed – but we stayed. Instead of sitting by Lake Geneva, I remained sitting on my shabby mattress in the attic, ever more depressed, ever lonelier. I had long since realized that our plan to flee with forged papers was a pipe dream.

*

The fourth godless winter under German occupation hit me hard. Wehrmacht officers had moved into the building across the street. At night, I heard them staggering back home, drunk and jeering. Through fear that they might see my face at the window, I pulled back the curtains only rarely at night, and even then, never completely.

Back when I had only just gone into hiding, I had thought it would be impossible to live here longer than a few weeks. Marching to Russia on foot or rowing across the Atlantic in a tiny boat sounded more feasible compared to suffering this tomb. Since then, two and a half years had gone by. *Two and a half years*. In my memory, those years blurred into a thick fog of empty days and cold, sleepless nights. If I hadn't stopped counting the days with pen strokes on the wall, it would be covered with slashes now.

*

Outside the attic, life continued. In the newspapers Christian brought, I read that the extremely anti-Semitic Louis Darquier de Pellepoix had been appointed

Commissioner-General for Jewish Affairs. Now every Jew had to wear a yellow star on their chest. Yet another humiliation for my people.

The war, too, had intensified. Last year, the Allied Forces attacked the Renault factories in Boulogne-Billancourt, just outside Paris, and a few months ago, bombs fell on our suburbs once again. Through the gap between my curtains, I saw flames licking on the horizon.

Somehow, Christian remained hopeful. 'Just have a little more patience,' he always said, 'we are not surrendering. Our victory will come.' To me, his words sounded naive, almost absurd.

Did he truly believe that? The swastika was still fluttering high over France, and last year the Germans, together with the Italians, had also occupied the south of our country – the last remaining free zone. With that, the prospect of escape had shifted further out of reach.

Christian saw things differently. 'You wouldn't recognize our beautiful Paris any more,' he told me recently. 'The Germans have given up the city. Museums are empty, apartments dilapidated, the parks overgrown. There are ugly bunkers everywhere, and half the Metro system is dead.' According to him, the Germans no longer acted as arrogant and victorious as they had two years ago. Nowadays, he saw them hanging around in large groups – finding more confidence in numbers – and usually drunk playing with their brandished guns, cursing the Parisians.

For Christian, the tide had turned after the Battle of Stalingrad. He told me about the landing of the Allied Forces in North Africa, forays of the French troops in Italy, and the liberation of Corsica by local resistance groups.

He firmly believed in the imminent downfall of the German Reich.

But Russia and North Africa were far away, I interjected. And Corsica wasn't Paris. For me, nothing had changed.

*

Driven by his unwavering optimism, Christian continued to make an increasing number of contacts in the underground and, together with Jean-Michel, became active in the resistance efforts. He was obsessed with our escape and final triumph over the Germans. Whenever he came to see me, his energy and enthusiasm spilled over, and, for a moment, I believed him. But once I was alone again, his ideas faded into soapy bubbles – large, iridescent and full of air.

I cut off my hair. Just like Mother did when Father left us. She did it because her marriage had come to an end. I did it as a sign of remembrance to her – there was no grave I could have placed flowers on. Only now, after my own life had been torn apart, did I fully understand the magnitude of her pain back then.

I didn't grieve for my lost hair, once golden-brown curls that had become dull and brittle. But I grieved for my previous life. Every second.

*

One day I heard Christian limping up the stairs, faster than usual. I looked at the door, glad to soon be rescued from my solitude – at least for a short while.

'Guess what?' he whispered even before he had fully entered the room.

His coat was only half buttoned, and his scarf hung loosely around his neck. He was breathing heavily, his cheeks crimson. I had never seen him this agitated. Fear welled up inside me. Did something bad happen?

'Your passport is ready,' he said, a bright smile appearing on his face.

'My . . . *passport*?' I repeated in disbelief, wrapping the blanket tighter around my shoulders.

He knelt in front of me on the mattress and took my hands. His eyes were glistening. 'I'm going to pick it up right now. The handover is in a small cafe on Place de l'Étoile.'

I stared at him in shock. My head was spinning as the news slowly seeped in. *It is finally happening.* I would leave this prison and become a free person again, united with my love.

'As soon as it gets dark, we'll leave town,' Christian explained in a low, determined voice. 'Jean-Michel is loading up the car as we speak – blankets, a few items of clothing and provisions.'

My whole body was shaking, a mixture of joy and anxiety thrumming through my veins. I threw my arms around his neck, my eyes swimming in tears. 'My darling . . .'

He wrapped his arms around me and kissed my hair. 'Everything will be fine. A new life is waiting for us.' He cupped my face in his hands and looked deeply into my eyes. 'As soon as we are in Switzerland, we'll get married.'

'I love you,' I whispered, overpowered by happy emotions I hadn't felt in years. 'I love you so much.'

'I love you, too,' he replied softly. Then he got up and buttoned his coat. 'I'm heading off now.' He looked at me and smiled. 'Wrap up warm, have something to eat and be ready.'

I nodded, trying to pull myself together.

Christian opened the door and stepped out.

I roamed through my tiny room, fearful and anxious. The moment of escape. It had finally come. I had anticipated this day for so long; dreading it and yearning for it at the same time. It was hard to believe that soon, my misery and loneliness would belong to the past.

I forced myself to think practically. Dress, eat and get ready, Christian had said. He would be back in an hour at most. I dragged the bag with clothes from beneath the table. In this cold, I would need at least three layers. Over the woollen shirt and stockings, which I never took off during winter, I was wearing a pair of pyjamas. I pulled the black trousers out of the bag and put them on, together with the silk blouse and a thick white pullover. Finally, I slipped into the elegant, grey sheep's wool jacket. Christian's instructions reverberated through my mind, again and again, as though the words themselves could tame the feverish waves of joy and panic coursing through my body.

I sat down at the table and hastily devoured a hunk of bread. It was so hard and dry that it got stuck in my throat. I coughed, retched and gasped for air. Only after flushing it with a gulp of water did the bread finally go down. I leaned back, relieved, wiping away the sweat from my forehead. I had to calm down.

Suddenly I heard steps again – did Christian forget something? But it wasn't his limping gait. These steps were loud and heavy, like the steps of a soldier whose feet were clad in thick boots.

My temples throbbed. My palms grew moist. Driven by an intense surge of dread, I tore open the window and tried to squeeze myself through the narrow opening.

Somebody stormed into my room. 'Stop!' a sharp voice yelled behind me. I felt two hands on my hips, pulling me back and throwing me to the floor.

When I looked up, I saw a tall man. He had a noble, chiselled face with thin eyebrows and high cheekbones. His grey hair was combed across his forehead at a slight angle so it covered the bald spots. The man's lips were thin and tight. In his long, dark coat with the grey-flecked fur collar, he looked like a statesman or an ambassador. It seemed as though I had seen him before.

'Get up!' he shouted.

I rose, shuddering.

The man took a step towards me. My body went rigid. I clawed my fingernails into the fabric of my trousers.

'I finally got you,' he said calmly, glaring at me. 'How long have you been hiding here?'

I bit my lip.

'Speak!'

'A few months,' I mumbled, lowering my gaze.

'Look at me when I'm talking to you!' His words struck me like gunshots.

I stared into his face, my lips quivering – and suddenly I knew who was standing before me.

'Seducing my silly son to live up here in the lap of luxury.' He spat on the floor at my feet. 'Easy job with a cripple, right?' His black, piercing eyes dissected me. Then he grabbed the collar of the jacket I was wearing. 'Oh, what do we have here?' A sarcastic tone resonated in his voice. 'That good-for-nothing stole from his own mother. Take it off! Now!'

I could barely breathe. I pressed my arms against my chest protectively.

'Take off my wife's clothes, I said,' he growled, a sound almost more terrifying than his shouts.

Slowly, trembling, I slipped off the jacket and pulled the pullover over my head. 'Please, monsieur, I . . . I don't have anything else.'

'What do I care?' He barked a harsh, cruel laugh, then I felt his heavy boot crash into my stomach. A jagged pain shot through my body. I tumbled and fell to the ground, curling and whimpering in agony. He kicked me a second time. The pain blinded me.

'Stealing from respectable people, that's what you're best at, you Jewish pest.'

I was sprawled in front of him with gritted teeth and a pounding head. He yanked my arm, wrenched me to my feet and spat in my face. I sucked in a breath, trying not to show my repugnance.

His face was as red as blood. 'Enjoying life up here at my expense! At least my son has come to his senses.' He swished the spit around in his mouth and hurled it at me one more time. 'The coward confessed everything.' He grabbed me by the neck, holding my face close to his. His breath smelled of sweet liqueur. 'Your rich lover betrayed you.'

His words eviscerated me. I felt his spit running down my cheeks and over my mouth. *Could Christian really have . . . ? No, never.* This man was lying.

'Please, monsieur,' I begged, 'let me go.'

'Shut your mouth,' he snarled, loosening his grip as he tore off my blouse. His claws fingered my chest. I heard the cloth rip and the buttons jingling on the floor like marbles.

'No,' I screamed. 'Please don't.'

'Don't worry, you skeleton.' An evil smirk pulled at his lips. 'I'm much too good for a piece of filth like you. Take the trousers off! They belong to my wife too.'

With shaky hands I pulled down the black trousers. As I stood there in front of him, shivering in the pyjamas, his smirk widened to a grin.

'We're going downstairs now. And then I'll call the police.' He raised his hand high, then slapped me across the face with full force. The pain was agonizing. Blood shot out of my nose. He pushed me towards the door, and I stumbled forward, numb. At least numbness was better than pain.

'The game's up, you whore.'

29

Béatrice

Château Bouclier, Pomerol, 2006

After the wine tasting, Béatrice and Grégoire strolled back to the main house, disappeared into his living quarters on the first floor and made love. Even long after they had sated the desire of finally being reunited, they lay closely intertwined in bed and listened to the sounds of the house. The creaking of the ceiling beams, the gentle rustling of the curtains at the open window. Downstairs, Ewa was speaking to a man who kept coughing.

Béatrice was only vaguely aware of the life around her. Dozing contentedly, she absorbed the closeness of Grégoire's warm, pulsating body.

'My father's downstairs,' he said as he stroked her shoulder. 'He's going to have dinner with us.'

Béatrice opened her eyes and stretched. 'Then I just need to have a shower and get dressed.' She yawned, climbed out of bed and went into the bathroom. As she stood beneath the shower, the warm water flowing over her body, she felt fresh again despite the jet lag. After drying herself off, she took a black dress from her travel bag and slipped into it. She wanted to look pretty when she met Grégoire's father.

Béatrice opened her handbag, searching for her lipstick, which, as always, was nowhere to be found when needed. One after the other, she pulled out her purse, phone, boarding cards and breath mints. Her fingers brushed against a piece of paper. She took it out and unfolded it. Julia's obituary. She had tucked it away in her bag and completely forgotten to read it.

'Grégoire, look at this. Somebody gave it to me in the museum.' Once again, she looked at the picture of Julia's face, which despite her age had still been beautiful and smooth.

Grégoire glanced over her shoulder. 'Oh,' he said, 'read it out to me.' He turned away, and Béatrice heard him opening a drawer.

'Julia Rosenkrantz,' she read out loud. 'A courageous woman . . .'

She read how indispensable Julia's personal commitment had been over the past fifteen years to the museum and the Jewish community, and that thanks to her, numerous families separated by the Holocaust had been reunited. As Béatrice reached the last paragraph, she paused. 'This can't be true,' she cried. A shooting pain lashed at her chest. Her heart almost stopped.

'What's wrong?' asked Grégoire.

Open-mouthed, Béatrice turned around to face him. Grégoire was sitting on the edge of the bed, lacing up his shoes.

Then she read the spine-tingling sentence once again,

this time slowly and out loud: 'Julia was born in Paris in 1921 as Judith Goldemberg.'

'What?' Grégoire straightened up and stared at her wide-eyed. 'You can't be serious.'

Béatrice was shivering. Her knees buckled, as she realized the enormity of this coincidence. Feeling light-headed, she leaned against the wall.

'Keep reading!' Grégoire urged.

Her mouth dry, Béatrice swallowed and continued. 'On the seventeenth of December 1943, at the age of twenty-two, Julia, a literature student at the Sorbonne, was deported to Auschwitz via the French transit camp Drancy. In 1945, after being freed, she emigrated to the USA and changed her name. In 1955, she married the architect Moses Rosenkrantz, who died seventeen years ago. The couple had two children.'

Béatrice lowered the piece of paper and looked back at Grégoire.

'It's hard to comprehend,' he whispered, shaking his head.

Béatrice's shoulders slackened. What a merciless, bitter irony of fate. It hadn't been George Dreyfus who'd been wrong, but the Red Cross in Baltimore. The dot intended to mark the Holocaust survivors had been placed after the wrong name – giving one family hope, and taking it away from Jacobina and her.

Béatrice sat down on the bed next to Grégoire and stared at Julia's photo. 'And to think that I spoke with her. It's through her that I met you.'

'Unbelievable,' he murmured.

Béatrice closed her eyes and leaned against Grégoire,

suddenly feeling sapped of energy. He put his arm around her and pulled her close. They sat for a long while. Béatrice tried to recall every detail about Julia. Every word she had said. She imagined what might have happened if she had pulled the photo from the French National Archives out of her bag just a few seconds earlier and shown it to her. The photo of the young Judith.

'I'm looking for this woman,' she would have said. 'That's me,' Julia might have answered, pale, tears shining in her eyes. Béatrice imagined how it might have been if Jacobina and Julia had met, how they would have confided in one another and shared memories of their father. Might meeting her half-sister, a woman so different from her, have delayed Julia's death?

*

The table was set formally, with heavy silver cutlery, candlesticks and stiff, white serviettes which sat enthroned like pointed hats on the immense underplates. Ewa scurried hectically back and forth between the kitchen and dining room, bringing out the finishing touches: a basket filled with freshly cut bread, a butter knife, and a salt cellar containing a silver spoon. It was too cold to eat out on the terrace, so she had decided to set things up indoors instead, she told Grégoire and Béatrice apologetically as they stepped into the room.

By the window, with his back turned to them, stood an elderly man, leaning against a walking stick and gazing out over the vineyard. He had thick, white hair and was wearing a dark velvet jacket.

'*Bonsoir, Papa*,' said Grégoire, going over to his father.

The man turned and smiled. He was a little shorter than Grégoire, with friendly brown eyes and dimpled cheeks. His hair was combed into a side parting. Béatrice noted with surprise that the two men didn't look in any way similar.

'There you are at last, my son,' said his father in a deep, resonant voice. 'I've been trying to call you.'

'I . . . I received a surprise visit today,' replied Grégoire formally. 'I'd like to introduce you to Béatrice. My girlfriend, from Washington.' At the word 'girlfriend', he hesitated briefly and shot Béatrice a questioning glance. But she confirmed with a smile that he had chosen the right word.

She went up to Grégoire's father and stretched out her hand. 'It's a pleasure to meet you, monsieur.'

The old man took her hand and smiled indulgently. 'Call me Christian.'

As quick as lightning, Béatrice withdrew her hand. She felt the colour draining from her face. Confused, she stepped back and stared at the man in shock.

'What's wrong?' asked Grégoire with concern.

'Christian . . .' whispered Béatrice, her voice cracking with shock. 'You're Christian Pavie-Rausan!' The thought was shattering.

'What's wrong?' asked Grégoire again, touching her shoulder gently. 'Are you not feeling well?'

She didn't answer. Instead, she reached her trembling fingers into her shoulder bag, took out the envelope with the large, curving handwriting and handed it to Grégoire's father. 'You wrote this letter, didn't you?'

The old man frowned and took the letter. As soon as

he recognized the handwriting, his breathing became laboured. 'Where did you get this?' he asked sharply. Something wild and confrontational appeared in his eyes.

'It . . . it was by chance . . .' stammered Béatrice. Where was she supposed to begin? His flashing eyes unsettled her.

'How in God's name did you get this letter?' he roared.

Grégoire's eyes darted back and forth between the two of them. 'What's this letter?' he asked. 'You haven't shown it to me.'

'I . . . the moment hadn't come up yet,' she uttered. 'So much else has happened. The trip, you and I, the obituary.'

Meanwhile, leaning on his walking stick, Christian hobbled over to one of the three Louis Philippe armchairs that stood in a half-circle facing the fireplace. He collapsed into it with a groan, tossing the stick aside.

Ewa immediately hurried over and handed him a glass of water. 'Please calm down, monsieur,' she said.

'Jacobina Grunberg is a friend of mine,' began Béatrice hesitantly. 'She is Judith's half-sister.'

As Christian heard the name Judith, he flinched.

'But what does this letter have to do with Judith?' asked Grégoire.

Béatrice took a deep breath. 'Let me start from the beginning,' she said, turning to Grégoire. She moved to sit opposite Christian and crossed her legs. 'The two of them didn't know of the other's existence. Their father only told Jacobina about Judith shortly before his death. He made her promise to find Judith. But Jacobina postponed the search for decades. Only recently did she feel ready to keep her promise.'

Christian sat, slumped in the armchair, motionless. His eyes glassy, he gazed into the cold fireplace.

'I wanted to help Jacobina with her search, and that's how I met your son in the Holocaust Museum,' said Béatrice, encouraged by his silence to continue. 'But what we only just found out, completely by chance, is . . .' – she paused briefly, her gaze firmly fixed on Christian's face – 'that Judith was working with Grégoire at the museum.'

'What are you talking about?' cried Christian indignantly, grasping the collar of his shirt and tugging at it, as though he couldn't get enough air. 'Judith is dead, for God's sake. Dead.'

'Unfortunately, yes,' said Béatrice, 'but she didn't die in Auschwitz. She survived. After she was freed, she emigrated to the USA and lived in Washington.' Béatrice was fully aware of the earthshattering impact her words must be having on the old man. 'Judith died last week,' she added, almost whispering now. 'She was eighty-five.'

Christian's face turned ashen. He stared at her openmouthed. In his eyes lay a worrying mix of denial, doubt and utter horror.

'What are you saying?' he croaked. 'She was alive this whole time?'

Béatrice nodded almost imperceptibly.

Ewa came in with a tray. She placed three glasses and a bottle of white wine in a silver cooler on the low iron table in front of the fireplace, and filled them silently. Taking note of the tense atmosphere, she quickly left the room again.

Christian sat there, paralysed, and stared off into the

distance. 'This whole time,' he whispered, 'all these long years I believed she was dead.'

'Papa,' said Grégoire, going over behind the chair and putting his hands on his father's shoulders. 'What was your connection to her?'

His father didn't react.

Béatrice barely dared to breathe. She felt so sad for this old, broken man.

'Carry on, Béatrice,' requested Christian suddenly.

Béatrice threaded her hand through her hair in embarrassment, worried about making him even more upset. 'Jacobina has a box full of old documents which her father left her,' she said then. 'Your letter was in there. But I only found the envelope with your name on it yesterday.' She looked over at Grégoire. 'I immediately went to the museum to show it to you. That's when I found out that you'd left. And about Julia's – I mean Judith's – death.'

Béatrice pulled the picture of Judith out of her bag and laid it on the table. 'A few weeks ago, the National Archives sent me this picture.'

As Christian looked at the young, oval face with the fresh cheeks, he howled in pain, as if somebody had shot him.

Grégoire kneeled down on the floor next his father. 'What happened back then, Papa?'

'Judith. She . . .' Christian broke off, lowered his gaze and began to cry softly.

Béatrice almost felt like an intruder, as the pain this man had buried in the depths of his heart more than half a century ago suddenly gushed to the surface, splintering apart his well-ordered life. She stood up and went over to the window. The setting sun bathed the terrace and the first row of vines in a soft, dancing light. For a long while, she could only hear Christian's lonely sobs and Grégoire's vain murmurs of appeasement. It was hard for herself to comprehend this sudden turn of destiny. And worse: if Julia hadn't died, they would have probably never found out about her real identity. While it was gratifying to learn that Judith had survived Auschwitz, Julia's death closed this circle in a cruel way.

'Tell us what happened, Papa,' said Grégoire after a while. 'Please.'

Béatrice turned back around and saw Grégoire hand his father a handkerchief. Christian took it, blew his nose and tucked it into his jacket. Then he looked at his son through tired, swollen eyes.

'Judith . . .' He sighed, fixing his gaze back on the fireplace. 'It's a very long story. I would have given my life for her . . . everything.' He exhaled sharply and rested his forehead on his hand. Again, he said nothing for a long while, the memories seemingly too painful to speak out loud. Eventually he raised his head. 'I've tried for sixty years to forget her. But I couldn't. Her face. Her smile. Her voice. It's all so alive within me, as though I had seen her only yesterday.' He pursed his lips. 'She was my one true love. I never loved anyone like her.'

Grégoire laid his hand on his father's arm.

'And now I find out she was alive the whole time.' He shook his head. 'That all of this time was in vain.' The tears overwhelmed him again.

Béatrice sat on a small chair next to the window, deeply moved.

Christian sniffled and wiped his eyes. 'We met at the Sorbonne,' he said eventually. 'In 1940, shortly after the Germans had seized Paris.' His voice was hollow. He cleared his throat, reached for one of the wine glasses which stood untouched on the table and drank. The wine seemed to reinvigorate him. He took another sip and straightened his shoulders. 'The swastikas were hanging everywhere,' he continued. 'The Wehrmacht marched through the streets, certain of their victory, occupying apartments, cafes and restaurants. The Hôtel de Crillon became their headquarters. For our family back then, life went on as normal. My father was a respected bank director and continued with his business as if nothing had happened. We got everything we needed on the black market and my parents even hosted champagne receptions for the Nazi bigshots. Only much later did I understand how closely my father collaborated with the Germans.' He scratched his ear. 'And I – I was in love. Head over heels in love. With the beautiful, intelligent Judith, who worked in the reading room of the university library.'

Béatrice sat motionless at the window, listening, enthralled.

'But Judith was a Jew, and for her everything changed. As the raids became more frequent and the Nazis began to deport French women and children too, I hid her where I thought her presence would be least suspected.' He took the bottle out of the cooler and poured himself more wine. 'In the tiny attic room in our building, on the sixth floor. Judith and I were planning to flee together, but it was only towards the end of 1943 that I finally obtained a counterfeit *carte d'identité* for her.' Christian paused and lowered his gaze. He swallowed heavily.

'What happened then?' asked Grégoire, who had sat down in the armchair next to him.

Lost in thought, Christian rotated the wine glass in his hand. 'The thing I feared the most.' He drew his breath sharply and put the glass back on the table. 'On the day of our planned escape, I went up to the attic at midday and told her that I was going to pick up the papers, that we would leave immediately afterwards. When I returned, Judith had vanished. Without leaving a note. Without taking anything with her. Her diary was still open on the table. It looked as though she had only left the room briefly. But it was like the earth had swallowed her. I almost lost my mind. I didn't know where to look for her. I ran to see my driver, who was supposed to prepare the car for our escape. But he had no idea where she was either. I roamed the streets for hours, crying. Without being able to think a single clear thought. The next day I got a high fever. For weeks I went up to the attic every day, to see whether Judith might perhaps have come back. I would sit up there in that tiny chamber, rummaging around in her things, crying and knowing that something inside me had died.'

He looked exhausted, resigned. 'In her purse, there was a note with the address of her father, who lived in Romania. She had almost never spoken of him. I had no idea whether she was even in contact with him. In my despair, I wrote the letter. The letter you just showed me.' He looked over at Béatrice. 'I didn't know what else to do. I had the letter smuggled out of France with a friend, otherwise it would have fallen into the hands of the Germans. The post was subjected to strict censorship. It's really a miracle that it arrived in Romania. I never received an answer, of course.' Christian clasped his hands and lay them on his lap. 'It was only much later that I found out my father had taken her and turned her over to the police. The bastard!'

'How did you find out?' asked Grégoire, gesturing to Béatrice to sit down next to him, which she did at once.

Christian laughed bitterly. 'My father eventually admitted it. I'll never forget that moment. It was a Sunday in June of 1944. My parents were eating lunch, and I was late to arrive. As soon as I stepped into the room, my father put down his spoon and took out his gold pocket watch. "You're five minutes too late, son," he announced, holding the watch up towards me. "I'm guessing you were upstairs on the sixth floor again, grieving for your Jewish whore." For a moment, I couldn't breathe. He knew about Judith and the attic!'

Béatrice listened, her eyes glued to his lips. Her hand searched for Grégoire's and gripped it tightly.

'Father clapped his pocket watch shut again, grinning maliciously, and put it back in his waistcoat pocket,' Christian continued. 'Then he just carried on eating his soup. Filled with an awful foreboding, I went over to the table, summoned all my courage and asked him where she was. "Where she belongs," he replied in an icy voice, without even looking at me. "In a camp in the German Reich, where they know how to get rid of human garbage." He sprinkled a pinch of salt into his soup. "You'll never see her again. I promise you that." Christian stared at the half-full wine bottle on the table. 'I collapsed right at

Father's feet and threw up. He kept eating calmly and
didn't say a word. Even today, I can still picture his polished
black shoes in front of me and hear the tinkle of his spoon
while I was lying there, howling, drowning in the pain of
my loss. Mother ran to the telephone and called our family
physician. He came and injected me with a sedative.'
Christian leaned back. His eyes were shimmering, his
pupils dilated. He looked as if reliving this last conversation with his father had sapped him of the little energy
he still had left. 'Back then I swore that I would never
speak another word with my father,' he said then. 'And I
never broke that vow. After the war I ended all contact
with my family, left Paris and moved to Bordeaux.'

'How did your mother deal with that?' asked Béatrice,
moving her chair even closer to Grégoire's.

'My mother . . .' Christian let out a derisive hiss. 'She
was far too weak to stand up to my father. He had the
money and the control, and she could buy anything her
heart desired. She always stood by him. Either through
loyalty or fear. I felt sorry for her.'

'And he never tried to reconcile with you?'

Christian raised his eyebrows. 'No, he never did. He
always believed he was in the right. My mother died early.
Even at her funeral, he didn't approach me. But when he
eventually passed away himself, he left his entire fortune
to me. Perhaps it was intended as a small, posthumous
attempt to make amends or something. Or, more likely,
there was no one else. The old furniture and the paintings
over there in the drawing room, he left those to me too.
I could never bring myself to sell them. My mother had
chosen them and was very attached to all that stuff. But

his money, I didn't want to touch that. As a bank director, my father froze Jewish accounts and plunged families into ruin. I gave my entire inheritance to various Holocaust foundations, for research projects and memorials. Château Bouclier is my own doing. It took years of painstaking work to build it. The wine hasn't made us rich, but we've never lacked for anything.'

'Did you ever try to find Judith?' asked Béatrice.

Christian nodded emphatically. 'Of course. I tried everything. Immediately after the liberation I went almost daily to the Hotel Lutétia, which after the end of the war was the venue where returning concentration camp survivors were registered and looked after. I walked around with a photo of Judith, asking after her and trying to recognize her amongst those emaciated, traumatized faces. I sat on one of the leather armchairs in the lobby and watched for her for hours. But . . .' He paused. His eyes became moist again, his lips trembled. 'Judith didn't come. Eventually, I was advised to give up the search.' He sighed deeply and rubbed his nose. 'If only I hadn't. Then I would have found her. And my life would have had meaning again.'

Pain twisted Béatrice's belly. And Grégoire had spent months around Julia, without having the slightest idea who she was. What a horrible irony of fate!

Ewa appeared with a steaming bowl. 'May I serve now?' she asked.

'Yes, of course.' Christian had clearly regained his composure. He nodded and bent down, reaching for his walking stick that was still lying on the floor. 'The young people are sure to be hungry. Let's eat before it goes cold.'

Grégoire stretched out his hand towards his father and helped him up. Leaning on his arm, Christian limped across the finely woven rug to the dining table and took a seat at its head, from where he had a view across the terrace. Béatrice followed them, dazed. Christian unfolded his serviette and spread it across his lap. Ewa poured him some red wine from the carafe. Béatrice and Grégoire sat down across from him and watched as Ewa filled their glasses too.

Grégoire leaned forward and sniffed at the large, hot terrine. He ran his tongue across his lips with pleasure. 'Ewa, that smells delicious. Let's dig in.'

He plunged the ladle into the aromatic beef stew and spooned a large portion onto Béatrice's plate. Ewa went back into the kitchen. A few moments later she reappeared with a bowl of rice and silently passed it around.

Grégoire held up his glass. 'To truth. And against forgetting,' he said ceremoniously, smiling at Béatrice and taking a sip.

Christian didn't respond to the toast, but he looked more relaxed now.

After Christian's revelations, food was the last thing on Béatrice's mind, but she didn't want to insult her hosts and Ewa. So she picked up her fork and tried the meat. It was exquisite and melted on her tongue like butter. For a short while they ate in silence, the only sound the clatter of their cutlery against the plates.

When Béatrice looked up again she noticed that Christian didn't seem to have much appetite either. He seemed lost in thought, pushing the rice from one side of his plate to the other. He raised the fork to his mouth only now and then, chewing slowly.

'Grégoire,' he said suddenly. 'It is still hard to comprehend that you worked with Judith. Did you tell her anything about you and your family? I mean, surely she must have pricked her ears up at your surname.'

Grégoire put down his knife and fork and dabbed his mouth with the serviette. 'She only knew me as Grégoire Bernard. I had applied for the scholarship under my legal name.'

Christian looked disappointed. He picked up a box of matches from the table, opened it and closed it again. 'Tell me about her,' he said. 'What was she like?'

'She was . . .' Grégoire furrowed his brow. 'She was different in every way. Extraordinary.' He studied his father's sad face in the flickering light of the candles. 'Always elegant. Smart. Eager to help. And humble. But firm and exacting too. She wouldn't tolerate carelessness. The visitors loved her, and she was highly regarded by all our colleagues. She had such a peaceful way about her. Of course, word got around about her traumatic past. We all knew that she was an Auschwitz survivor, but she never wanted to talk about it herself. The museum is always looking for survivors to tell visitors their stories. There are two older gentlemen who do that twice a month. Two Polish men who emigrated to the USA after the war. Judith firmly refused. We, of course, respected that, even though we would have liked to find out more about her.'

'I met her twice,' Béatrice interjected. 'I would never have thought that she was French. She spoke English without the slightest accent. And she had these sparkling blue eyes. Almost like . . . like aquamarines.'

A corner of Christian's mouth lifted into a pained smile.

'Yes,' he said, more to himself than to Béatrice, 'aquama-rines . . .'

'Why did you never tell me about Judith?' asked Grégoire, taking another spoonful of rice.

Christian's smile faded; his upper body slackened slightly. 'It wouldn't have been fair to your mother.'

'What do you mean?' asked Grégoire.

Christian stared at his plate. 'Okay,' he sighed. 'I've told you the first part of the story. Now you should know the rest too. After Judith disappeared, I became a shadow of myself. Outwardly I was alive, functioning, working. But inside . . .' – he tapped his bony hand against his heart – 'everything was dead. The images tormented me. Not just the memories of Judith, and how she waited for me every day, imprisoned in that attic room. But also the images of Auschwitz, fed by my terrible fears of what they had done to her there. Bit by bit, more came to light about the abominable reality of the concentration camps. Reports from survivors. Numbers. Photos. It was hard to process all of that with the knowledge that the Nazis had brutally killed my Judith in one of their death factories.' He paused, drank a sip of wine and leaned back. His face was suddenly sallow, his eyes stared dully ahead. 'Then came the self-accusations. I felt responsible for her death and kept replaying the same recriminations: if only I hadn't hidden her in our building, then my father wouldn't have found her. If only I had convinced her to flee with me sooner, I would have been able to save her. If my contacts in the underground had worked faster, we would have left earlier. I began to drink heavily, suffered from insomnia, and fell into depression. The guilt was about to destroy me. When

I was in my early forties, I finally saw a therapist. It was the first time I opened up to someone about my inner battles. The psychologist worked hard to convince me that I wasn't responsible for Judith's death. He told me I had to free myself, once and for all, from this burden and build a new life. In my head I knew he was right. But my heart wasn't free. And then . . . then I met your mother. She was a great deal younger than me and had only experienced the war as a small child in the countryside. Full of life, beautiful. She loved me. I longed to fall in love again. Start a family. We got married, and a short while after, in 1962, you were born.'

Christian took Grégoire's hand and squeezed it. 'When I saw you for the first time, my emotions came back. The love I felt for you was a miracle. Your birth freed me of my destructive forces. I stopped drinking overnight so I could be there for you. Experience how you, such a tiny thing, would grow into a person. I would sit by your bed often, to watch you sleeping or to be ready to comfort you when you cried.' He smiled nostalgically. Then he turned serious again. 'When you were born, your mother became less important to me. At first, I didn't realize it. Our lives were so busy. The wine trade was improving, we expanded our production and won awards. But your mother wasn't happy. I never gave her what she needed most: sincere, deep love. My heart belonged to Judith – and you. I became more and more impatient with her, we argued constantly, and I started to drink again. For a while she tried to get pregnant again, hoping that another child might save our marriage. And she did. But unfortunately she lost the baby after just a few weeks into the pregnancy. From then on, we lived separate lives. I paid no attention to her and what she felt. Work kept me constantly on the road, and I had affairs with other women. It was over.' He crumpled up his serviette and threw it next to his plate, his meal half eaten. 'We separated in the early 1970s. She moved to Paris and you went with her. A few years later, she met Henri. I hope she's still happy with him.'

Béatrice glanced discreetly over at Grégoire, who sat rigidly, his face expressionless.

'You're right,' he whispered. 'It wouldn't have been fair to tell us that.'

Béatrice wished she could wrap her arms around Grégoire and say something to comfort him. But in his father's presence she felt shy.

'And I didn't even need to,' Christian replied. 'She knew it. It was the right thing for us to separate.' He stood up and limped over to an antique console which stood alongside the door to the kitchen. He pulled out a drawer, rummaged around in it and produced a book. With a tender gesture he stroked across it. Then he came back to the table, his steps faltering, and sat down. He laid the book next to Grégoire's plate. 'Here,' he said. 'Judith's diary. The only thing I have of hers.'

Béatrice stared at the thick, leather-bound volume, which was tied with a brown cord.

Christian turned his head to the door and called for Ewa. The housekeeper immediately hurried into the room and cleared away the crockery.

'Perhaps it's for the best that I never saw her again,' said Christian, as though talking to himself, letting his gaze wander over the terrace. 'I wouldn't have been able to bear the fact that she had found another man.' He paused, then turned back to Grégoire and Béatrice. 'Enough for today.' He stood up. 'I'm going to turn in now.'

Grégoire remained sitting and nodded silently.

30

Judith

Aboard the Sea Breeze, *August 1948*

The ship's horn blared as the engines began to roar and the steamer glided into motion. I stood at the stern of the huge passenger ship, alone, lost amongst hundreds of passengers, and stared back at the harbour. First the people became smaller, then the ships. Soon the houses and the hills which lined the harbour shrunk too. Eventually, I could only make out a few tiny black flecks on the horizon.

I silently said my goodbyes to Europe, to its ruins, its atrocities and its poverty. I swore to myself that I would never set foot on this continent again, not for as long as I lived.

My hands clutched the railing, the sun burned down on my head. I was wearing the old-fashioned blue dress with the ripped seam which I had received several months before in a clothing handout from the American Jewish Joint Distribution Committee. Who had it belonged to before? I wondered. The fabric fluttered around my knees, and the salty air blew my hair into my face.

Finally I was on my way to America, a faraway, unfamiliar land where I would get the chance to reinvent myself. In less than two weeks' time I would reach New York. A city of extraordinary scale filled with great things to be discovered. No raided houses where Jewish people I knew had once lived; no street cafes where Christian and I had sat holding hands, our heads full of dreams. And no window from which my mother had jumped.

Maybe America would also set me free from the nightmares that constantly dragged me back into the misery of the camp. I didn't want to be surrounded any more by those ghostly figures that used to be humans, all of us waiting for death.

Before my descent into hell, I had been a French citizen with a home and an address. Now, having emerged from the ashes of the corpses of Auschwitz, I was a *displaced person*, a DP, as the occupied forces called us survivors.

On the day of my liberation, I had believed that the horror was finally over. How wrong I had been! I was moved to another camp, except it was no longer called a concentration camp, but instead a DP camp. Once again, I was imprisoned and lived behind barbed-wire fences, side by side with those who had previously been my guards and tormentors. I was close to surrender and ending my own life. But I had survived Auschwitz, I told myself again and again. I wouldn't give in now either.

Eventually our living conditions improved. We were moved to different camps and received help from America, help that we needed so desperately.

Even back then it was clear to me that I couldn't return to France. The French were responsible for the death of my mother; the French had handed me over to the Nazis. Never again would a French word cross my lips. That, too, I swore to myself.

Europe had been turned to rubble and was a graveyard to me. There was no going back. Not to Christian either. Not because I had ever doubted him or his love for me. I hadn't believed his hateful father for a second. Christian would never have betrayed me. But I knew I wouldn't be able to find my way back to him. Too much had happened to separate us. I no longer bore any resemblance to the young, naive girl from the library. The woman I had become couldn't marry a man whose father had sided with the Nazis and contributed to annihilating my people – no matter how strained Christian's relationship was with this monster. I would always love Christian. But loving him, for me, now meant letting him go. I had to break with the past so I could live again.

In America there was a place for me. Of this I was sure. I imagined the art and culture in New York, the expansive prairies in the west, the majestic canyons, and the endless flow of water of the Niagara Falls. America was rich, modern and full of possibilities. A land without kings or despots, where democracy ruled and hard work was rewarded with success and prosperity.

I had already been promised a position as a maid in a small hotel in Manhattan. In the evenings, I planned to learn English, and on the weekends, I would explore the city. I would become a proper American – chew gum, smoke Lucky Strikes and drink instant coffee.

Suddenly I realized I was smiling. The first smile in a long time. I made my way past the people and their suitcases, hearing them speak in many different foreign languages and laugh. They were DPs too, just like me, anxious to start a new life somewhere in that gigantic foreign land.

I strode across the freshly scrubbed wooden planks to the bow of the ship and looked out across the ocean, to the horizon where my new home would soon appear. The gulls screeched above me, the wind tore at my dress. I had faith again.

Judith Goldemberg no longer existed. But I was alive. I couldn't ask for more.

31

Béatrice

Château Bouclier, Pomerol, 2006

'I always thought I knew him, this eccentric loner.' Grégoire lay on the bed, his shirt unbuttoned, his hands clasped beneath his neck. 'I used to sympathize with my mother, believing that no woman would be able to tolerate a man like him long term. And then you come along, pull an old photo out of your bag, and my father bares his soul to us.'

Béatrice stood in a nightshirt, leaning against the window, and looked over at Grégoire. It was late. Just before midnight. Despite her long journey and the emotionally draining day, she was wide awake. Now that Christian's tragic story lay in front of her like an open book, it was impossible to even consider sleeping. She kept imagining the young couple in occupied Paris, picturing Judith in the narrow attic and Christian roaming the streets in despair after she had disappeared. Tomorrow she would call Jacobina and tell her everything. And, as soon as she was back in Washington, Béatrice would try to get in touch with Julia's two children. What a wonderful new opportunity, to connect Jacobina with this part of her family and, through them, posthumously with her half-sister Judith. All those years, Jacobina had had family in Washington, D.C. without knowing it. What a joy it would be to bring them all together.

'He kept the story to himself for sixty years,' Grégoire continued, sitting up. 'Sixty years! How must it feel to pretend that everything is okay to your wife and son every day when you are consumed with grief?' He got up and paced back and forth on the creaking parquet floor.

'What else could he have done?' asked Béatrice.

'He should never have married my mother in the first place.'

'You are being too harsh,' she replied, approaching him. 'It was wartime, the world had turned upside down. His father had betrayed him. And then he fled to Bordeaux to escape his past and suppressed everything. Years later, your mother saved him and brought him back to life.'

'She loved him. And he only used her,' retorted Grégoire sharply, stumbling over his shoes, which lay by the bed. Cursing loudly, he kicked them.

Béatrice touched his shoulder. 'I'm sure that he himself believed for a long while that he could start a new life with your mother. And that he really tried hard to make it work.'

Grégoire pulled her close and embraced her. 'I know,' he murmured. 'It's just . . . It's all such a shock.'

Béatrice pressed her head against his bare chest and felt his heartbeat against her ear. She closed her eyes. For a long while they stayed like that.

'Could you imagine . . .' asked Grégoire, breaking the silence. 'Could you imagine living here with me?'

She pulled back and blinked. 'Here with the two of you?'

'Not with my father, of course. He's been wanting to move to Bordeaux for a while now. We have a small apartment there. All the walking and stair climbing here is too much for him.'

At the thought of building a life together with Grégoire, Béatrice was overcome with joy and happiness. Then she thought about her job and her forehead creased. 'And my career?'

'As the PR manager of Château Bouclier, there's more than enough work for you,' said Grégoire with conviction. 'You aren't that happy at the World Bank anyway, right? I urgently need someone to help me create a new marketing and outreach strategy. Someone I can trust. And in a month's time I'll be organizing several exclusive wine tastings in Asia to bring in new customers. Hong Kong. Tokyo. Shanghai. We'd go together . . . and make our wine famous.'

It all sounded so simple. So tempting.

Béatrice nodded. The word *we*, which he used so naturally, still felt unfamiliar and new to her. But she could see it, that new, wonderful future with Grégoire that beckoned. Back home in France. And even though things looked much better now for her at the bank, she wouldn't have any regrets leaving it for a fulfilled life with her love.

She looked at him, wanting to imprint this special moment in her memory for ever: his cosy room with the crumpled bedsheets. The warm light of his eyes. His expectant gaze.

Everything around them came to a stop.

'Yes . . .' she said. 'I'd like to live with you.'

They smiled at one another. It was an intimate, loving smile between two people who were bound by something so deep that it couldn't be explained with words.

Taking his hand in hers, Béatrice picked up Judith's diary and they sat down on the bed. Together they read:

I was standing on one of the middle rungs of the rickety library ladder when I discovered the note. It was written on unusually thick, sky-blue paper, folded multiple times . . .

Acknowledgements

My deepest gratitude and appreciation goes to five special people who helped me make this book come alive:

Pascal, my wonderful, extraordinary husband – always patient, always loving. Your support means everything to me. I can't imagine my life without you.

Jacklyn Saferstein-Hansen, my thoughtful literary agent at Renaissance Literary & Talent. You really made me understand the emotional depths of my characters. So glad we found each other.

Gillian Green, Publishing Director at Pan Macmillan, whose comments and queries completely changed and improved my novel. Such an honour to be working with you, Gillian.

Jacobina Löwensohn – without you there wouldn't be a book. Thank you for entrusting me with the historic documents you compiled over the many years during your search for Melanie Levensohn.

Vanessa Gutenkunst, my literary agent at Copywrite in Germany and my first reader. It all began with you, Vanessa, and I'll always be grateful for the time we had together.